CHAMPAGNE WRATH

ORLOV BRATVA
BOOK 2

NICOLE FOX

Copyright © 2023 by Nicole Fox

All rights reserved.

No part of this book may be reproduced in any form or by any electronic or mechanical means, including information storage and retrieval systems, without written permission from the author, except for the use of brief quotations in a book review.

❦ Created with Vellum

MAILING LIST

Sign up to my mailing list!
New subscribers receive a FREE steamy bad boy romance novel.

Click the link below to join.
https://sendfox.com/nicolefox

ALSO BY NICOLE FOX

Uvarov Bratva
Sapphire Scars
Sapphire Tears

Vlasov Bratva
Arrogant Monster
Arrogant Mistake

Zhukova Bratva
Tarnished Tyrant
Tarnished Queen

Stepanov Bratva
Satin Sinner
Satin Princess

Makarova Bratva
Shattered Altar
Shattered Cradle

Solovev Bratva
Ravaged Crown
Ravaged Throne

Vorobev Bratva
Velvet Devil
Velvet Angel

Romanoff Bratva

Immaculate Deception

Immaculate Corruption

Kovalyov Bratva

Gilded Cage

Gilded Tears

Jaded Soul

Jaded Devil

Ripped Veil

Ripped Lace

Mazzeo Mafia Duet

Liar's Lullaby (Book 1)

Sinner's Lullaby (Book 2)

Bratva Crime Syndicate

Can be read in any order!

Lies He Told Me

Scars He Gave Me

Sins He Taught Me

Belluci Mafia Trilogy

Corrupted Angel (Book 1)

Corrupted Queen (Book 2)

Corrupted Empire (Book 3)

De Maggio Mafia Duet

Devil in a Suit (Book 1)

Devil at the Altar (Book 2)

Kornilov Bratva Duet

Married to the Don (Book 1)

Til Death Do Us Part (Book 2)

Heirs to the Bratva Empire

Can be read in any order!

Kostya

Maksim

Andrei

Princes of Ravenlake Academy (Bully Romance)

Can be read as standalones!

Cruel Prep

Cruel Academy

Cruel Elite

Tsezar Bratva

Nightfall (Book 1)

Daybreak (Book 2)

Russian Crime Brotherhood

Can be read in any order!

Owned by the Mob Boss

Unprotected with the Mob Boss

Knocked Up by the Mob Boss

Sold to the Mob Boss

Stolen by the Mob Boss

Trapped with the Mob Boss

Volkov Bratva

Broken Vows (Book 1)

Broken Hope (Book 2)

Broken Sins *(standalone)*

Other Standalones

Vin: A Mafia Romance

Box Sets

Bratva Mob Bosses (Russian Crime Brotherhood Books 1-6)

Tsezar Bratva (Tsezar Bratva Duet Books 1-2)

Heirs to the Bratva Empire

The Mafia Dons Collection

The Don's Corruption

CHAMPAGNE WRATH
ORLOV BRATVA DUET BOOK 2

**I thought he was my savior.
But what if he's really my downfall?**

At first, Misha Orlov was the boss who got me pregnant.

But he has become so much more than just that.

He's my husband and the father of my babies (yes, as in plural).

He's my pakhan.

He's my last hope.

Because of all the people in this messed-up world, he's the only one I can trust to save me.

As bad men loom and my babies prepare to arrive, we're both faced with a choice.

Can we let go of the pasts that shaped us?

Or will our scars become our undoing?

CHAMPAGNE WRATH is the second and final book of the Orlov Bratva duet. The story begins in Book 1, CHAMPAGNE VENOM.

1

MISHA

The driveway is a crater. Smoke hangs in the air, a deadly haze. The car—what's left of it, anyway—litters the grass and the cracking concrete.

I scan the scene for Paige. For any sign of her, any piece of her. Even as my mind begs me not to.

I've seen too many people I love die already. I don't want to see another.

But I can't stop looking.

"What happens when we die?" I asked my brother once. When I was a kid, I thought he knew everything. That thought never really went away.

"We're buried and our bodies decompose," he told me bluntly.

"What about the rest of us? We have to go somewhere."

Maksim smiled. *"I believe every person gets to decide what happens to them after they die. Take me, for example. I'm going to become a comet and shoot from universe to universe."*

I glance up at the sky. It's a persistent, eye-watering blue despite the wreckage in front of me. Is Paige up there now? Is Maksim?

"No," I say aloud. "No fucking way."

People are milling around in the entryway and the kitchen. My men, alerted by the chaos, are now standing useless on the periphery.

Because there was nothing they could do. She's gone.

"Konstantin!"

If she's gone, I don't want to hear it from some soldier. I don't even look at them, worried I'll see the answer in their faces.

"He's in the atrium," someone says to me.

I shift in that direction, preparing myself for the worst. I heard the explosion on the phone, but it was still bigger than I thought. If Paige was in the drive like Rose said on the phone, she was definitely within the blast radius.

Bile rises in my throat. My palms are sweating and my knees are shaking. I've never felt so sick in my entire life. The only rival is the moment I watched the light fade from my brother's eyes.

This can't be happening again.

Paige.

Our unborn children.

My future.

All gone in an instant, a breath. They aren't comets, no matter what Maksim said. They can't be. A comet is a physical thing. An object that exists in the world. Wherever people go when they die, it's beyond anything even I can manipulate.

That's what makes it so terrible.

Then I hear it.

Sobbing.

I slide around the corner into the atrium and freeze.

Paige is sitting on the sofa. She's coated in ash and dust, and more of the same stuff hangs in a dense cloud around her, like she was a mistake in a drawing that someone tried to smudge away.

But they failed.

They fucking failed.

"Paige." I collapse to my knees in front of her.

It takes a moment for her to look up at me. When she does, her eyes are glassy with tears. But she still reaches for me.

I grab her hands and kiss her scraped knuckles. "Tell me you're okay." Before she can answer, I look over my shoulder and yell at anyone and everyone who might be listening. "Get Dr. Mathers down here immediately!"

"She's already on her way," Konstantin assures me.

I'll thank my cousin for that later. Right now, Paige is all that matters.

"Paige, look at me. Are you okay?"

"R-R-Rose." Her voice is cracked and dry. "S-she... she—"

I squeeze her hands. "I know."

"I-I was looking right at her. One second, she was there and then…" She flinches away from the memory.

"Someone tampered with your car." I deliver the words calmly, but that calm is harder to hold onto with every scrape and bruise I find on her body.

And that someone will pay for this.

"She landed on her back," Konstantin explains as he comes running back up to us. "Paige, I mean. I saw it. The explosion threw her backward, but she landed on her back. The babies should be okay."

I stand up, but Paige grips my hands with all the remaining strength in her body. "Don't leave me."

"I'm not going anywhere," I swear to her. "Don't worry."

She nods, but doesn't loosen her grip. Every footfall in the hallway, every hushed voice—it all makes her flinch. It's like she's expecting the next explosion at any moment.

I glance at Konstantin. We both understand without words that Paige is in shock.

"Where the fuck is Dr. Mathers?" I growl just as the door opens.

"I'm here!" Simone calls out, rushing into the room with her black bag in tow. Her eyes widen as she takes in Paige, but she maintains her unflappable bedside manner. "Let's give you a quick look over, alright, sweetheart?"

I shift out of the way, but Paige refuses to let go of my hand. I lean in close, voice low. "Dr. Mathers is going to need to examine you. You and the babies."

Paige looks at me, but her eyes are focused on something far beyond the reaches of this room. "R-Rose…"

"Paige, we have to get you checked out," Simone insists.

"She has a child," Paige chokes out. "A girl. Molly. Her daughter's name is Molly."

Simone moves to my side and puts her hand on Paige's arm. "Paige, you've been through something traumatic. I'm so sorry for that. But all I can do right now is make sure you are okay. Can you be strong? For your babies?"

Paige doesn't answer. Instead, she looks to me. "Are you going to stay?"

There's an uncertainty in the question. An indication that she's not sure she can trust me to stay with her.

"Of course I will," I murmur.

But even as I say it, something inside me dies.

2

MISHA

"I've treated her wounds." Simone removes her gloves one finger at a time. "The worst of them are cleaned and bandaged, but she'll still need a wash. She's covered in dirt."

"I can do that."

Simone nods. "Don't submerge her. Just wet some towels and run them over her body. I've prescribed her a painkiller and a sleeping pill if she needs it. She needs to rest."

"The babies?" I ask.

"They're fine." *For now.* She doesn't say that last part, but I hear it lurking behind her words. "Her blood pressure is higher than I'd like it to be. She needs a stress-free environment. Suffice it to say that what she's been through today is… not that."

No fucking kidding, I think to myself.

"I'll be back tomorrow to check on her." Before she leaves, she looks back. "You need to be her rock, Misha. She's going to need you to get her through this."

The bed is empty when I walk into Paige's room. Instead, she's standing with her back to me, gazing into the fireplace.

"Paige." She flinches when I say her name. "I'm moving you upstairs."

She gives me a half-hearted nod and takes a step towards me. Before her foot can even hit the floor, I bend and scoop her into my arms.

She doesn't struggle or protest, which is as good as stabbing me right in the goddamn heart. Her head just falls against my shoulder and she lets out a weary sigh. Her eyes are red but dry. Her tears have finally dried up.

For now.

Rada is standing in the hallway when I leave the atrium. Her eyes are fixed on Paige. "I can get her cleaned up, sir," she offers.

"No. I'll do it." I leave her behind and carry Paige up the stairs.

I don't make a conscious decision to take her into my bedroom. It just feels natural to take her to the space that was meant to be ours.

I kick the door closed and carry her into the bathroom. It's cool in here. White. Dim and safe and quiet. I strip her down slowly, taking care not to snag her clothes on her fresh bandages.

She watches me work silently. I have no idea what she's thinking, what storm is brewing behind those limpid eyes.

I only have the bandwidth to deal with the storm brewing inside me.

You were wrong about me, Maksim. I'm not brave. I'm not strong enough to jump into this fire. I'm not strong enough to overcome this kind of fear.

Her body is one giant purple bruise beneath her joggers. I grit my teeth in an effort to keep the rage inside. I'm worried they might shatter from the pressure.

The only thing that keeps me from erupting is the same thing that's done it since Maksim died.

Revenge.

Petyr Ivanov doesn't understand the hell he's just unleashed on himself. I'm not just going to destroy him; I'm going to destroy every single man and woman who has ever aligned themselves with him. The fucking doctor who delivered him into this world from his mother's womb will feel my wrath. They are all guilty by association. I will annihilate the Ivanov Bratva until there is nothing left. I will—

"Misha."

Paige's voice pulls me back from the black hole of rage I'm sinking into. I raise my gaze and catch her eyes.

"I'm okay," she says softly. "Take a deep breath. I'm okay."

How did she even see my pain through her own? How did she know what I needed?

She places her hand on the side of my face. Her breath washes over my face, a reminder that she's alive. Every one of her exhales breathes new life into me.

I want more of it. More of her.

My survival instinct takes over. I lean forward and press my lips to hers. She is soft and alive. And *fragile*, I realize a moment too late.

The kiss is brief, ending when I pull back. But for a brief kiss, it somehow stays with me, as heavy and overwhelming as full-body contact.

Every time I see another bruise or cut marring her body, I'm reminded of the fact that she almost died. And that if she had, it would have been my fault.

Just like with Maksim.

I promised to keep her safe, and I failed.

Just like with Maksim.

"Stop thinking, Misha." She pulls me out of my black hole for the second time in as many minutes. "Just stay here with me."

I try. I pull off her sports bra and then her underwear. Her beautiful, pregnant body stretches out in front of me.

Newly scarred. Covered in the proof of my failure.

3

PAIGE

She spotted me from the end of the driveway. She waved, a smile on her face.

In the last seconds of her life, Rose was thinking about the stupid file she needed to give me.

I don't even have to guess what she would have been thinking about if she knew she only had seconds to live.

Her daughter.

One moment, she was there. The next, there were only pieces of her.

Humans are so fragile. So easy to kill.

I can't stop thinking about how temporary life is.

And how much of it we waste.

∼

I wake up gripping my pillow tightly. I've sobbed into it so hard it's soaked through.

His arm wrap around me gently—at first. But his hold tightens the more I cry.

Misha's body is pressed against my back, spooning me tightly like he's trying to take some of my pain with his touch. Amazingly, it does work. A little, at least.

"Don't let me go, Misha. Don't let me go."

He doesn't say a word. Maybe he recognizes there's nothing he can say. He just holds me and waits for me to stop crying. When I finally do, he soothes me back to sleep.

Where the nightmares wait.

∼

The next time my eyes open, I'm shaking with guilty sobs yet again. And again, he's still there, ready to shield me with his body, ready to give me some of his strength.

The sobs are softer now. The images in my head are just as visceral as they were before, but I'm already learning to live with them.

Humans may be fragile, but we're also adaptable.

I roll over so I can see Misha. His face is half-covered in shadow, and what I can see of his silver eyes looks otherworldly in the pale light coming through the window.

"I'm not letting you get any sleep, am I?"

"I can't sleep anyway."

There's a sliver of space between us now, but I can still feel the heat of his body warming mine. I slide a little closer to him and wedge my feet under his legs. His hand comes to rest against my hip.

"The first time this happened, I was alone," I hear myself whisper.

"Clara." Misha needs no explanation.

"I spent weeks in my bed with the curtains drawn. I slept constantly. But only because I never got any rest."

"I know what you mean."

"Maksim," I say softly.

I'm not sure why it's important that we say their names now. Maybe because in some inexplicable way, they're all linked now. Clara. Maksim. Rose.

They all died with so much life left to live.

"I wasn't very nice to Rose at the beginning," I admit. Because why not? I have so much guilt built up inside me; inviting in more won't make any difference. "I was threatened by her. Because… because I thought you hired her as a replacement for me."

His silver eyes are hooded, but I don't miss the shadow that passes over them.

I push myself up onto my elbow. "Misha? What aren't you telling me?"

His forehead wrinkles.

"Was I right to assume that?" My heart rate is rising rapidly. "Was she meant to be a threat to me?"

"No." There's a heaviness to the one-word response that I don't understand.

"Then what—"

"She was meant to look like you, Paige. That was the whole point. The resemblance wasn't a coincidence." I frown and he blows out a breath. "Petyr had already made too many attempts on your life. I wanted insurance. Rose was exactly that."

I feel a wave of nausea wash over me. "You're… you're saying she was… you meant for her to—"

"She was hired to be your assistant, but she was also hired as your body double. She knew the risks involved with the job. I made sure to spell them out for her explicitly."

"You're… you're really not kidding."

My veins run with ice. Air squeezes in and out of my throat, which is tightening every second with panic and nausea.

Misha squeezes my hip. "Breathe, Paige," he tells me in the same tone I used with him earlier. "Breathe."

The tightness in my chest eases and I inhale. "Why would she even agree to a job like that?"

"Because she wanted to provide for her family. She wanted to make sure her daughter never lacked for anything."

"She was willing to risk her life for it?" I shake my head. I'll never understand this. He could explain it a million different times in a million different words and I will never, ever understand.

"We can't always question other people's decisions. Sometimes, we just have to accept them."

"You'll still pay her, won't you? Her daughter?"

"Of course. The agreed-upon money has already been transferred into Rose's account. I'll set up a trust fund for her daughter that will mature when the child comes of age. She will be taken care of."

I close my eyes for a moment and count heartbeats. My pendant is resting snugly inside my palm, but this is the first time that it hasn't felt like enough.

I want to hold Misha more than it.

"Do you believe in an afterlife?" I ask abruptly.

There's a long silence before Misha speaks, so softly that I almost miss it. "I believe in shooting stars."

I tilt my head, inviting him to continue.

"I'm not sure what I believe in," he corrects.

I want to press him to explain himself, but there's something in his eyes that stops me. We can get attached to our pain. It's personal and intimate. I don't want to press.

"I like the idea of an afterlife," I whisper when he continues to stonewall. "I want to believe it. I suppose because believing in it means I'll get to see Clara again one day."

"Maybe you will." He's saying it for my benefit. I know he doesn't have that same hope.

"Maybe you'll see Maksim again one day."

He shakes his head. "No, I don't think so. He'll be hard to track down. He's going to be traveling through the universes."

I frown, and then start to put the puzzle pieces together in my head. "Is Maksim a shooting star then?"

He actually chuckles a little under his breath with the barest hint of self-consciousness. The sound, so human and raw and real, goes a long way in helping to heal my bruised heart.

"I didn't think you heard that."

I prop my chin in my hand. "Clara would probably be a shooting star, too. She had that kind of spirit. She was a wanderer."

"That's fitting for the afterlife. No more schedules, no more places to be. Wanderers are happy there, I'm sure."

"I hope that's true. I'd hate to think that even in death she's wandering around, aimless and unhappy."

"Was it that bad?" he asks softly.

I've talked about Clara before, but somehow, this feels different. She spent so much time putting on a front, showing people what they wanted to see. I've rarely betrayed her by revealing the truth beneath it all.

"Sometimes, yes." I pick at the mattress, twisting the sheet between my fingers nervously. "Sometimes, I could actually see the light in her eyes dim. She always put on a brave face for my benefit, but I knew her well enough that I could see the truth. She wanted to do so much with her life. We had a plan. We were going to graduate and hitchhike out of Corden Park. We'd get odd jobs along the way and save enough money to move to New York."

"New York was the dream?"

"The dream was just getting out of Corden Park. It didn't really matter where we went after that."

I feel a trace of that old sadness again. I thought I threw it off, left that weight behind, but maybe we never really rid ourselves of our past. Maybe we just fool ourselves into thinking it doesn't feel so heavy for a while.

Right now, though, I just want to move closer to him. There's only a sliver of space between us, but it feels like a canyon.

Wanting him feels wrong. I feel horrible about Rose. Even more so for the little girl she's left behind. But the thing about watching someone lose something is that it makes you feel grateful for what you have. It's selfish, but undeniable.

When I lost Clara, I had nothing to be grateful for. But now, I have Misha. I have our babies.

I have, for the first time in a long time…

Hope.

4

MISHA

I remember calling Maksim a few months into his marriage, righteously pissed off. *"Where the hell have you been, man?"* I demanded. *"You have a fucking Bratva to run."* I heard a giggle in the background. *"For God's sake, are you with Cyrille?"*

"No, nuh-uh. definitely not her. Just some loose-moraled floozie I picked up off the side of the road."

I heard Cyrille mutter an almost inaudible *"asshole."* Maksim cried out, feigning pain. *"Ouch, that hurt. The wife didn't like that joke."*

"The wife needs to learn to share. I haven't seen you in weeks."

"Aw, do you miss me, little brother?"

Yes, I should've said.

"Fuck you," I snapped instead. *"I just need to discuss shit with you. You know... Bratva business."*

"Bratva business can wait. Love is in the air, little brother. Can you feel it?"

"*No*," I retorted flatly. "*I can't.*"

"*And therein lies the problem. I'm going insane for this woman, and it's fucking awesome. Highly recommended. Go find one and try it for yourself.*"

He hung up before I could tell him that he sounded pussy-whipped. I fumed about the whole conversation for days after. But Maksim's self-constructed love cocoon lasted longer than my anger. By the time he re-emerged, I'd already forgiven his absence.

And now—almost a whole decade later—I finally understand it. I understand the instinct to build the cocoon, somewhere safe and comfortable, a private place just for Paige and me.

That's what it feels like in this bed, with her body twined through mine like a knot that'll never come undone. I don't ever want to leave this space.

It's not just the physical experience, the excitement of having her body so close to mine, the knowledge that I can touch her wherever I want.

It's the mental, emotional comfort of feeling truly content.

A hole in my soul that is no longer screaming.

Paige's eyes are still swollen from all the crying she did yesterday afternoon and throughout the night, but she's no less beautiful because of it. She reaches out and slides her finger up and down my arm.

I close my eyes, reveling in the feel of it. I desperately want to kiss her and let my hands explore her body. I want to make her feel something other than regret or loss or sadness. But she's too bruised and tired and vulnerable right now.

"I can't stop thinking about it," she whispers. "Can you hold me?"

I pull her against my chest and wrap my arms around her. She looks up at me for a moment and then she smiles.

"You're so damn beautiful," she whispers. "Has anyone ever told you that?"

"No one who mattered," I rumble back.

She gives me a tired smile and closes her eyes. Her burgeoning belly is pressed against my torso. The gentle swell reminds me of everything I stood to lose today.

And it hits me—I was more terrified of losing Paige than I was of losing the babies.

The realization sinks in like cyanide. It twists at my stomach painfully and reminds me of all the reasons I swore off romantic love.

This is the third attempt on Paige's life. That I know of. Petyr is bound to try more. What if he succeeds the next time around?

I didn't think my brother was capable of dying before I saw that bullet sink into his chest. All it takes is one failure. A split-second wrong decision. A false instinct.

I look down and see that Paige's eyes are shut tight. Her breathing has turned slow and even. Her body has relaxed.

But mine hasn't.

Suddenly, in the shadows of our little cocoon, I can see my mistakes clearly. I broke my own damn rules, and it has landed me here. I made myself weak. I made myself vulnerable. And now, I've put a giant target on her back.

Of all my mistakes, what if loving her is the worst?

5

PAIGE

It feels strange to wake up without him next to me. His arms were starting to feel like an extension of my body. Now that they're gone, it's like I'm missing a part of myself.

"Mrs. Paige?" I sit up and realize Rada is hovering at the foot of my bed. "Are you okay?"

"Fine. Just a little lightheaded."

She rushes over to me. "Let me help you to the bathroom."

I hold up a hand to slow her down. "Where's Misha?" I look around the room, hoping that he'll walk out of the bathroom or the closet, gather me up, and pull me back into a dreamless sleep.

But I know that if Misha was here, Rada wouldn't be.

"He's downstairs in his office, Mrs. Paige. With Mr. Konstantin."

I nod. "I can get myself to the bathroom alone. Thank you."

Rada doesn't look sure, but she releases my arm. "I'll get breakfast set up for you by the window."

"There's no need, Rada. I can go downstairs to eat."

She glances at me nervously and shuffles from one foot to the other.

"Is that a problem, Rada?"

"Mr. Orlov told me specifically to bring breakfast up here for you."

I suppress a sigh. "Well, I'm saying it's no longer necessary. I feel strong enough to come downstairs. I think I'm capable of deciding that for myself."

Rada nods quickly and slips out of the room without further argument. I feel guilty when she's gone. I was harsh with her, but it's only because the person I'm actually annoyed with isn't here. It crosses my mind that if I'd woken up next to Misha, I wouldn't have minded having breakfast in the room.

At a few points over the last couple days, I thought I'd be content to stay in this room forever so long as he was with me.

The way he took care of me, trailing warm washcloths over my bare skin, cuddling me to his strong chest like I was a fragile creature in need of shelter… I could tell that the accident scared Misha as much as it had terrified me. But we were gentle with one another, pulling ourselves and each other back from the brink of despair with a silent touch or a single word.

After all that, I didn't expect to wake up to an empty bed.

I get dressed carefully, easing my bruised body into soft, loose clothes. Then I make my way gingerly downstairs to the kitchen.

There are pancakes on the table in the breakfast nook alongside a pitcher of fresh orange juice that glows in a beam of morning sun. I'm pouring myself a glass when Misha enters the kitchen. He looks distracted. When he sees me, his frown tightens. "What are you doing down here? You should be resting."

"I didn't feel like staying in my room. Besides, I'm sitting down, which is restful, and I've spent the last two days lying down, which is more of the same. You should know—you were with me." I didn't plan to say anything else to him, but the words slip out anyway: "Until you weren't."

He grimaces, but then exhales all the tension away. "I'll have Simone come check on you in the evening."

"She was here yesterday."

"And she'll be here today," he growls. "Tomorrow, too. As well as the day after. She'll be here every fucking day and every fucking night until those bruises have healed and I'm confident that you and our babies are out of harm's way. Is that going to be a problem, *moya zhena?*"

It's pathetic how much I love his protectiveness. How much I cling to it like a lifeline, hoping that maybe it'll translate to love.

The feeling I have that something is off persists, though, niggling at the back of my mind. I get the sense that he doesn't want to stick around. Like he's waiting for an excuse to leave me.

"Have you spoken to Rose's family?" I ask finally.

"The funeral is being held tomorrow. I'll tell them you send your condolences."

"You don't have to send them my condolences; I'll take them myself."

His eyes narrow. "That's not happening." I open my mouth to protest, but he holds up a hand and cuts me off. "You need to rest, Paige. And with Petyr making attempts on your life at every turn, I don't think it's wise for you to be moving around out in the open."

I'm starting to get suspicious that the real Misha is somewhere else and the thing I'm talking to is just a robot programmed to repeat *You need to rest, Paige,* over and over again until I jump off a cliff.

"They detonated that bomb the moment the car pulled into the driveway, Misha. Petyr didn't just want to kill me; he wanted to send you a message. He also believes that message has been delivered. He thinks I'm dead. So he's not going to be looking for me." I can see that he's less than pleased with my logic. It gives me a perverse sense of satisfaction to win one over on him. "I may have fallen pretty hard, Misha, but I'm still in full control of all my faculties. I'm going with you tomorrow."

He takes a step towards me, his eyes catching mine in a death grip that sucks the air straight from my lungs. "No, you're really fucking not."

"You can protect me without suffocating me. I'm your wife, not your prisoner."

"If being my prisoner is what it's going to take to keep you alive, then I'm fine with that."

Adrenaline buzzes under my skin. But it's not just anger that's adding fuel to this fire; there's a persistent throbbing between my legs that's goading me into this fight.

"I'll be with you. What's the problem?" I demand.

"The problem is I'm not interested in being caught out in public with a liability chained to my hip." He spits out the words like he's disgusted with me.

I take a step back, shaken by the venom in his tone. What the hell could have happened in the last twelve hours that could have brought about this one-eighty change?

"What's wrong with you?" I ask, incredulous. "Why are you being like this?"

"This is who I am."

"No it's not!" I'm livid at him for changing the rules on me again. For pulling this bait-and-switch, this Jekyll-and-Hyde act, *again*. "You were by my side for two entire days and nights. We slept next to each other, shared secrets in the dark. You held me through my nightmares and my tears. The man who did that is *not* the same one standing in front of me now."

I can see it again: the storm raging under that calm silver gaze. His jaw is set.

There's no going back now.

I inch closer to him. Unlikely as it is, I still want to reclaim the closeness we had. "Misha, you told me—you promised me—that you'd stay with me."

He flinches and then turns away from me. A cold shoulder has never felt so frigid. "I shouldn't have made a promise I didn't intend to keep."

6

MISHA

When I walk into Orion, the atmosphere is tense.

No one speaks to me as I move quickly through the lobby and up to my office. I'm not surprised, considering the war raging inside of my chest. The violent struggle between doing what I want and doing what needs to be done.

I feel like a powder keg ready to explode. A feeling not helped by my wife, who seems deadset on doing stupid shit like attending a public funeral when she's supposed to be dead.

My quiet walk through the building ends abruptly when I step into my office and am assaulted by a strong floral fragrance.

"You came in today." Konstantin is frozen in the middle of my office, a vase of white lilies in his hands. "I thought I had time to get rid of all the flowers."

Bouquets and house plants perch on every conceivable surface. Three identical arrangements of white roses and pink carnations sit on my desk, and another next to the door. Peace lilies and bristling ferns line a path to my desk chair. One arrangement of purple and blue flowers has tipped sideways, leaving topsoil sinking into the fibers of my carpet.

"Looks like the news is out," I drawl. "The don has lost his wife."

"I can have the place back to normal in half an hour," my cousin promises me. "I already told your assistant to forward future deliveries to my office. Or directly to the dumpster."

I wave him away. "Don't bother. Leave them where they are. We need to keep up appearances. If the world believes Paige is dead, then Petyr will, too."

Konstantin sets down the vase he's holding into the only open space on top of my bar cart. "I've put the word out there that we had a small, private ceremony for Paige. You're a private man, so no one is questioning it."

"Good."

"That being said, I made a judgment call and told Cyrille, Nikita, and Aunt Nessa the truth. They were in hysterics. The news spread faster than I expected."

I feel a twist of guilt that I wasn't the one to make that call. "Did you make sure they understood—"

"Of course." Konstantin nods. "They'll lean into the story. No one wants anything to happen to Paige."

"Good. And Rowan?"

Konstantin cringes. "She was here yesterday when the news broke. She had a bad reaction. She fainted in the break room."

I raise my eyebrows. "And…?"

He draws in a shuddering breath. "And… as far as she's concerned, Paige is dead."

"Let's keep it that way."

"Fuck, that's cold. I mean, you're right, but fuck." He shakes his head as if to steady himself. "What about Paige? Don't you think she might call or text Rowan?"

"I anticipated that. Which is why I've confiscated her cell phone and all the lines in the house have been blocked. Only Noel has an open line to outside the mansion, but Paige doesn't know that."

He whistles. "She's going to be *piiissed*."

Beyond pissed. She was mad I wanted to serve her breakfast in bed, so I'm sure she'll go apoplectic when she realizes I've severed all means of communication.

I check the condolence cards attached to the floral arrangements as I pass. One is from Klim Kulikov, the eldest member of my inner council, a man who served Maksim and my father before him.

Konstantin notices me inspecting the arrangements. "After what happened to Paige the last time someone sent flowers, I checked everything for chamomile or anything else that could be dangerous. They're all clear. Not so much as an aphid in the lot of them."

"It's a note from Klim." I pluck the card from the plastic holder and hold it out to him.

Konstantin takes it and reads the card out loud. "'Sow this tragedy and reap it into his downfall.' Jesus. That's some condolence note. That man is Bratva to the core."

I take it back and slip it into my pocket. Something about the sentiment matches my mood perfectly.

A knock at the door draws our attention. We turn as one to see a courier holding a jaw-droppingly huge bouquet of red roses and orange zinnias. It stands out against all the other somber arrangements made up of mostly whites and soft pastels.

"Set it down and walk away," Konstantin advises the pasty teen delivery boy. He does as he's told and scurries off.

I have a nasty gnawing sensation in my gut as I approach. I know before I even read it what I'm going to find. Sure enough, when I withdraw the card, I see the name written there clear as day.

Petyr Ivanov.

So sorry for your loss, my brother. To lose a wife so soon after the marriage must sting. At least you have my corporation to keep you warm at night. Don't get used to it, though—I will take it back soon enough.

I rip up the note the moment I'm done reading.

"Misha?"

"Get rid of it."

Konstantin realizes what's going on. "Is it from—?"

"Yes."

"Fuck. What did he say?"

"He knows he's lost and his company is mine now. The attempt on Paige's life was revenge. And he won't stop there."

"Look on the bright side; he thinks Paige is dead."

"For now," I snarl. "It's only a matter of time before he learns that she is very much alive."

"Well, then we need to finish him before he finds out."

Konstantin is calm, but I see the determination propping him up. We've been playing this game with Petyr for so long. I know without asking that Konstantin is thinking the exact same thing as I am.

We're almost at the end of this.

Soon, Petyr Ivanov will be dead.

7

PAIGE

I hear a shuffling from just beyond my door.

It can't be Rada, because she doesn't usually appear until at least eight in the morning. She doesn't like to bother me if I'm sleeping. But there has been a phantom leaving me breakfast at the door for the last few mornings. A phantom who manages to slip away before I can even get out of bed.

But not this time.

I yank the door open, barely managing to keep a screamed *"Gotcha!"* inside my head. As I do, I come face to face with a broad, familiar chest.

Misha is just straightening upright after placing the breakfast tray on the floor. His silver eyes are misty with preoccupation, but their focus sharpens as they land on me. He looks annoyed to have been caught.

"What are you doing up so early? It's barely six o'clock."

"You've been avoiding me like the plague," I accuse.

"I've just been busy. I still am. I have to go to the office."

"In sweatpants?" *Gray sweatpants, nonetheless. The male equivalent of lingerie.* "At…" I check the clock on the wall. "5:43 in the morning?"

"Yes," he drawls, deadpan. "In sweatpants, at 5:43 in the morning."

I had a whole speech planned. A list of things I was going to say to him the next time we were in the same room. Each point was painstakingly thought-out, meticulously detailed, devastatingly phrased.

And yet now that the moment has arrived, I'm drawing a blank. Somehow, looking at his intoxicating eyes, the sexy roll-out-of-bed hair, and his stoic features sharpened to right angles, I can't seem to remember any of them.

"You are so damn frustrating," I snap. "Do you realize that?"

He sighs. "It's early, Paige. You really should be in bed sleeping."

"Why?" I protest. "Because then you can leave this tray at my door like the half-assed, half-hearted apology it is and disappear?"

His jaw tightens and I know immediately we're not going to be having anything resembling a civil conversation today. It's doing that ticking thing, where that one muscle under the surface twitches like it's alive. Mine is probably doing the exact same. "I bring you breakfast each morning because you and the babies need to be healthy and strong. It is not an apology. I have nothing to apologize for."

"Are you—You're kidding. You have to be. Surely, for the love of God, you are kidding."

He turns away. "I don't have time for this."

"Oh no, you don't." Leaving the door to my room open and stepping over the tray of food, I follow him down the spacious hall until I can grab his brawny forearm and force him back around. "We are *not* done here."

He pulls out of my grasp and resumes his trek down the hall. Gritting my teeth, I follow him all the way down to his office, which is still serving as his bedroom now that I'm back in the master. The pull-out couch is a mess of sheets and pillows, stained with sweat. The sweat of someone who spent their night tossing in frustration or outracing nightmares. Maybe a little of both.

Serves him right.

Although it also makes something in my chest flutter uneasily.

I lean against the doorframe. "How was the funeral?"

He drops down on the end of the bed and rubs at his eyes with the heels of his hands. "It was a funeral. There were flowers and sad people. Your condolences were conveyed with a giant arrangement of flowers to Rose's family and an even bigger check." He's doing his best to stay calm, but his voice rises the longer he talks until it dies suddenly.

"A check, how nice. Impersonal and cold. I wouldn't expect anything different from you," I bite out. "I wanted to look her parents in the eyes and tell them how sorry I am. I wanted to see her daughter—"

"To what end?"

That gives me pause. "Excuse me?"

"Even if you had gone, what purpose would it have served? It wouldn't have made Rose any less dead."

My mouth flops open and closes a few times. It's not very graceful, but I'm literally speechless. "How can you be so… so heartless?"

"Because that's the only way to survive this world," he snarls, though it doesn't have his normal dose of venom. "That bleeding heart of yours isn't going to beat for much longer if you let it break for every sob story you trip over."

I shake my head and shuffle my feet. There's too much going on in my head to formulate a response. Misha is impossible to argue with. He lives in another world. Another universe.

Another bedroom.

"Not avoiding me, my ass," I hiss. "Look at this room. You're sleeping in here!"

He frowns at the abrupt subject change and looks around the room. "I work late."

"Bullshit. We both know that if you want to do something, Misha, you do it. If you wanted to sleep next to me, you'd be sleeping next to me. Call this what it is: cowardice."

"Last time I checked, *Paige,* you're the one who wanted separate lives. You willingly moved into the bedroom downstairs."

"And you moved me back into our bedroom after the explosion," I remind him.

"That was to take care of you and the babies. To make sure you recovered. It was easier to do when you were in my space. But now, you seem to be fully recovered."

Before the bomb blast, I thought he was interested in reconciliation. It felt like he was asking me for another chance.

But now...

"You want me to move back downstairs?" I ask softly.

He stands and turns away from me. "I'm fine sleeping in my office. You can stay where you are. I don't care where I sleep."

"As long as it's not with me."

He glances at me out of the corner of his eyes. "Is there a reason you followed me in here?"

The truth vibrates through my chest like the ringing of a gong. But I dampen it. "My phone is missing, and I can't find a landline with a dial tone."

"Hm. Strange."

His nonchalance solidifies my suspicions. "Don't bullshit me, Misha. That's not an accident. You're trying to cut me off from the outside world!"

He leans against the edge of his desk and fixes me with tired eyes. I can tell from the circles underneath them that he hasn't slept properly in days.

I hate how, despite my anger, I still feel for him. I still feel the need to be there for him, to comfort him, support him—to just fucking *touch* him, for God's sake.

"The outside world is dangerous for you right now. This won't be forever."

"How long? Can you give me a timeline?" When he says nothing, I nod. "Yeah. I didn't think so."

"It's for your—"

"Protection," I snap. "I know. I've heard this all before."

"Then I don't understand why I'm being forced to repeat myself."

"Because I'm not just gonna lie down and accept every stupid rule you throw at me, Misha!"

I march closer to him, trapping him between his desk and my body. His eyes flare, rich with that uninhibited wildness that makes my knees weak.

"Do you want to hear my theory?" I ask. "I think you *like* when I fight you. Everyone else is scared of you, but I press back. And you like it. It turns you on. Doesn't it, baby?"

He scowls down at me, but doesn't make a move.

I followed him down here looking for a fight. But now, I just want him to spread me across his desk and fuck me until we forget what we were fighting about.

He opens his mouth, and in my head, I'm urging him on. *Go on then. If you're not being a coward, then don't be a coward. If you love me, if you care about me, if you ever cared about me...*

Then kiss me.

"Go back to your room, Paige."

I stiffen. "I'm your wife, not your soldier. Or do I need to remind you of the difference?"

"You're not getting out of this house any time soon." His eyes dip down to my cleavage and back up. It's just a twitch, just a flash, but it's enough to make my heart race. "Petyr thinks you're dead, and we're going to keep it that way as long as we can."

"Fine. Then at least give me my phone back."

"No."

I curl my fingers around the neckline of his t-shirt. "I'm only going to call your mother, Niki, and Cyrille. No one else."

"Bullshit," he says, leaning in as though he can't resist it. "You're going to call Rowan."

"How do you know?"

"Because of the crease in your brow here." He presses his finger to my forehead, smoothing away the crease in question. "I know you, Paige. You want to assure your friend that you're okay."

"She deserves to know! She won't tell anyone. I promise."

"You can't make that promise. And even if Rowan swears on her mother's grave, I'm not about to take her word for it. Not with your life on the line."

"But—"

"No buts," he growls. "We're done here."

Then he pushes me off him and walks around his desk.

"You can't control everything, Misha! I get it, okay? You lost Maksim, so now, you think that if you follow your rules and control everything and everyone around you, you can prevent the same thing from happening again. But life doesn't work that way."

He whips around, jaw set. "How the *fuck* would you know? You've never been responsible for anything or anyone in your entire life."

"I was responsible for Clara!"

"Yeah. And she's fucking *dead*."

I stop short. Just like that, the fight drains out of me. I have nothing to say back. No defense, no excuse, no explanation.

Because he's right.

He's right.

It was my job to take care of her, just like she took care of me all those years. And I watched her walk into the lion's den and did nothing.

His eyes are trained on me, waiting for a reaction.

Instead of giving him one, I turn and walk away.

8

MISHA

Through my office window, I see Cyrille and Niki walking towards the greenhouse. I haven't spotted Paige yet. I know she's with them, and that ought to be enough to reassure me. But I can't seem to turn away without first catching a glimpse of her.

"Misha?" Konstantin asks.

I'm about to respond when I spot her.

Her dark hair spills over the delicate arch of her spine. She's wearing a white, strapless dress that fits tight around her chest and flows over the rest of her body. She's also wearing a sun hat and carrying something under her arm.

She places a hand on her hat and turns her face up abruptly as though she can sense me staring. But then I realize she's not looking at me at all.

Ilya hops up to her, bouncing with the endless energy of youth. They link hands and follow Niki and Cyrille to the greenhouse. There's such an ease about their relationship. It makes a spot in my chest tighten uncomfortably.

Ilya is nine. He stopped wanting to hold anyone's hand years ago. And yet here he comes, racing up to her and twining his fingers through hers like it's the most natural thing in the world. Like he's always done it.

Like she's always been here.

I wait until Paige and Ilya disappear into the greenhouse before I turn back to Konstantin. He is staring at me with a mixture of amusement and frustration.

"What?" I snap.

"What?" His voice is mocking. "You know damn well *what*. Brother, you need to talk to her."

"I already have. I said everything I needed to."

And then some.

I can still see the way she paled when I lobbed those vile words at her. I knew she felt guilty about Clara, and I used it against her anyway.

It worked exactly as I intended.

Violently.

Still, I haven't taken it back. Because taking it back would require being in the same space with her, and I can't bring myself to do that. I just fucking can't. Being around her is too hard right now.

"The two of you care about each other," Konstantin insists. "You—"

"She's better off not caring about me at all," I growl. "It's a waste of fucking time."

My cousin raises his eyebrows. "Are you saying I'm wasting my time? Because, shocker of shockers, I care about you, too."

"If the shoe fits."

"You're not usually the type to throw your own pity party," Konstantin observes. "What happened?"

"Maksim happened. And then Paige happened. It's not a pity party; it's reality."

"It's the reality *you're* creating. The rest of us—"

"We don't have time for this," I interrupt. "We need to figure out a plan of action going forward and I think I've landed on a solution."

Konstantin is torn about letting me change the subject, but he must realize that he'd be fighting a losing battle because all he does is sigh deeply.

"What's the solution?" he grumbles.

I raise my eyebrows. Waiting. He'll get in three, two, one...

Konstantin's face slowly twists into horror. "No..." he whispers. "No. Misha, no."

"Yes," I say firmly. "Petyr is vulnerable right now. Not only have I taken over his company, but he thinks he's just killed my wife. He's going to be expecting me to come at him hard to finish the job."

"Which is why he's gone underground. You don't need to do this!"

"Exactly. I'm guessing he's not going to resurface for a while. Not until he has a plan of action to strike back at me. Which means I need to beat him to the punch."

"Brother, this is the Babai we're talking about. *The Babai.* The name alone should make your skin crawl. Those fuckers are deadly."

I lean forward, elbows on my desk. "Precisely. So why not turn their brand of poison on Petyr? They'll take out everyone he associates with. Complete annihilation, erase him from the earth. Everyone who's ever shaken his hand will die right along with him."

"You're placing too much faith in their 'code,' man. The Babai have been known to change allegiances on a whim. They're aliens. Unpredictable. 'Wild card' doesn't even begin to cover it, Misha—you're flipping the whole damn chessboard over!"

I wave him away. "It's a risk I'm willing to take. I'll certainly be paying them enough. Petyr doesn't have the funds to counter my offer."

"The Babai aren't always an investment, Misha. They're a death sentence."

"Who do you think you're talking to?" I demand as I jerk to my feet, voice crackling with authority. "I'm not some random civilian off the street. I'm the pakhan of the Orlov Bratva. I am Misha fucking Orlov, and I will not be denied."

Konstantin drags a hand through his hair. "They could decide to go to our enemies in search of a better offer."

"Then I'll make them one they can't refuse."

He takes a deep breath to steady himself. "Fucking hell. You're serious about this?" He mutters another curse.

"I want this over, Konstantin. I'm not about to sit around and twiddle my thumbs while we wait for Petyr to gather strength and resurface. That could take years. This has to end sooner than that. The Babai is the means to that end."

My cousin drops his head into his hands for a long, quiet moment. "Fine," he breathes at last without looking up. "I'll make inquiries. Get a location on them."

"Thank you, brother."

"Don't thank me." He leans back in his chair, shaking his head. "I'm not sure I'm doing you any favors."

"It'll all work out."

"And if it doesn't?"

"Then I'll make sure the Babai die before I do."

9

PAIGE

The greenhouse is my favorite room in the house. I like being surrounded by flowers and trees—blooming, living things. I like it even more when I'm surrounded by family.

Cyrille and Ilya are pressing petals between the pages of an old encyclopedia. They're doing it on the table where, not so long ago, I signed my name on my marriage license.

It feels like yesterday and a lifetime ago. How much has changed since then...

Nessa sits down on the sofa next to me, her ankles crossed delicately. "I bought you something."

I blink from my thoughts. "For me?"

In answer, she pushes a tissue paper-wrapped bundle into my hands. I peel the paper back carefully and reveal a gorgeous, blush-colored scarf. "Oh, Nessa... It's beautiful."

"It's a pashmina shawl," she explains. I smile blankly, and she chuckles. "It's cashmere. Very nice cashmere. It'll keep you warm, and it has the added benefit of looking absolutely stunning."

I run my fingers over the soft fabric, marveling at how luxurious it is. Like petting a cloud. "Thank you so much, Nessa. But really, you shouldn't have. You've gotten me so many gifts already."

"You deserve them." Her expression darkens. "After everything you've been through."

I blush and my gaze falls down. "Don't worry about me; it was just a few bruises and scratches. Dr. Mathers said the babies are fine, too."

"Oh, I know." Nessa takes the pashmina and folds it carefully so she can drape it across my lap. "I wasn't talking about the explosion. I was talking about my son."

Nessa has always been honest with me, but we've never discussed Misha quite so candidly. I smooth my hands along the shawl, trying to decide what to say. "What do you mean?"

"A mother always knows when her child is going through a hard time," she says cryptically.

I snort. "My mother didn't know anything. She would've stepped over my cold, dead body to get to her cigarettes."

Nessa gives me a sad smile. "Not everyone was meant to be a parent, Paige. But you are."

I can't help but laugh again, though it's not a particularly happy sound. "I'm glad you think that, because lately, I'm not so sure. I always thought I'd have a child one day, especially when I was with Anthony. But then the doctor said we couldn't have children, and… And I figured it wasn't in the cards for me. Which is why it was easy to think of motherhood as this idyllic, magical time that would never be mine."

"It is," Nessa insists. "It is idyllic. But it can also be difficult and exhausting and painful. Motherhood is very human in that way. It's everything all at once."

"That's what I'm worried about."

"It's not for the weak of heart, that's for certain." She gives me a reassuring smile. "But you, Paige, are certainly not weak of heart. You love fiercely. You take care of people."

Misha's accusation echoes in my mind. I've worked hard to forget it, but I can't.

She's fucking dead.

"I'm not so sure you're right about that. The only person I was responsible for in my entire life… I lost." Tears clog my throat, making my voice shaky.

"Oh, darling," Nessa pats my leg. "All we can ever do in this world is try."

I look down at my small stomach. "But these babies—"

"Those babies are going to arrive innocent and sweet and pink-faced. You'll be responsible for clothing them, feeding them, and raising them, yes. But they'll grow up and form their own opinions. They'll make their own decisions. How can you be responsible for that?" She lets out a sigh that sounds surprisingly weary for someone who's normally so upbeat. "I raised three children, Paige. I lost one to death and another to the Bratva. And Nikita is… well, you know her. She's wonderful, but she's her own person. Truth be told, I'm not sure I ever had control over her. All we can do as mothers is our best."

Her words are comforting and kind and wise.

Deep down, I don't believe I deserve them.

"I wish I had a mother like you growing up," I mumble. "I would have turned out so much better. Half my life was spent wishing my parents would just show up. I didn't even care if they were drunk or high. I just wanted them *there*."

"There you go," Nessa says pointedly. "You've stumbled across the bottom line of parenting: just show up."

"It sounds easy when you say it like that."

She winks. "You got my son to fall in love with you. If you can do that, you can do anything."

10

MISHA

I arrive home, deflated and exhausted.

Konstantin's inquiries into the Babai have all come up blank. That means another day of searching. Another day further from my goal.

Another day that Petyr Ivanov still draws undeserved breath.

The sun is low in the sky, golden rays casting the garden in comfortable light. I follow the sound of laughter around the house to the pool deck.

There, I see Nikita and Ilya splashing around in the water—but I'm preoccupied by the long pair of legs sunning poolside.

Ignoring my better judgment, I keep walking until I spy the rest of Paige stretched out in a lounge chair. She's bathed in warm light, her eyes closed, wearing a knitted string bikini that reveals tan bits of skin between the weave. The cups of her top can barely contain her growing breasts.

What really steals my attention, though, is the swell of her stomach. It's still a small bump, but this is the first time she's looked undeniably pregnant.

Seeing her that way, breathtakingly beautiful, swollen with my children inside her… It unearths this primal possessiveness inside me. I want to scoop her in my arms and carry her to our room. I want to mark her as mine.

I want to destroy her like she's destroyed me.

In the best way possible.

"Hello there," Nikita greets, alerting everyone to my presence. "If you're done ogling Paige, why don't you come and join us?"

I throw her a dirty look, but she just gives me a smile and a wink. I don't risk a second glance at Paige. We've barely said two words to each other since the day I told her that she was responsible for Clara's death. I don't blame her. I wouldn't blame her if she slipped a knife between my ribs, either.

"No. I've got work to do."

"Aw, c'mon, Uncle Misha!" Ilya whines. "Stay! Just for a little while?"

The kid turns the full force of his dark brown eyes on me. *Why the fuck does he have to look so much like his father?*

In the face of that, I don't stand a chance.

I sigh. "Okay. Fine. For a bit."

I go up to my room just long enough to change into a pair of swimming trunks. When I get back down, Nikita has claimed a chair next to Paige. I can feel their eyes on me as I dive into the pool.

The second I surface, a volleyball bounces off my shoulder.

"One point for me!" Ilya cheers.

I give him my best game face. "And it's your last point, you little punk."

We start batting the ball back and forth, cackling every time the other fumbles it. After a few minutes, I'm not just going through the motions—I'm actually playing the game.

And I'm enjoying it.

I almost forget that Paige is sitting a few feet away in a string bikini. Almost.

Ilya launches the ball at me again, but I'm distracted by my wife and I miss it. It bounces out of the pool, onto the deck, and rolls down the grassy hill.

"Yes!" Ilya crows, punching his fist in the air. "I did it. I beat you!"

"Calm down, you little beast. The game's not over yet. Go get the ball."

He jumps out of the pool, dripping wet and heads off in search of the ball.

"Oh, let him win once, won't you?" Niki calls from the sidelines. "It'll do wonders for his self-esteem."

"If he wins, he will earn it." I try not to let my gaze linger too long on Paige in my peripheral vision. She's got a book over her chest, but I'd bet my little finger she's not actually reading. She seems overly interested in our exchange.

"Maksim let you win a thousand times over before you ever even sniffed deserving it."

I freeze. Like Niki unclogged a drain, my head is suddenly full of memories I never asked for.

Maksim smiling mysteriously as I threw down a triumphant hand of cards.

Maksim shrugging as I shot down the last of the glass bottle targets we hung from the willow in the backyard.

Maksim clapping me on the back. Maksim grinning. Maksim proud.

A second later, my opponent re-enters the ring, splashing me in the process, and thumps the ball into the side of my head. Just like that, the memories vanish.

But the feeling they brought with them remains.

We continue with our clumsy game of volleyball sans net. Halfway through the match, I start watching Ilya. Really *watching* him. The kid's giving it his absolute all. He's hustling after every ball and hitting with all of his strength.

So I lunge for the next ball and, just before I reach it, I pull back, ever so slightly, to let it drop into the water instead.

Ilya hoots with victory, both hands thrust in the air. His eyes are full-moon bright, and the grin spreading from ear to ear is happier than anything I've seen on any member of the Orlov clan in a long, long time.

More points follow. I win some; he wins most. As the sun sets, Ilya takes home his first ever game against me amidst raucous applause from the audience.

"I did it!" he screams so loud that I'm sure the neighbors can hear. "I actually beat him! Aunt Niki, Aunt Paige, did you see?"

"We saw!" Paige is standing up now, clapping hard. "That was amazing. You were amazing!"

Niki ushers him out of the pool and towards the house. "Come on, champ. Let's get you dried off. Your mom wants us back home in an hour."

As they disappear into the house, I turn my attention fully to Paige for the first time since I arrived. She is gathering her book and her towel, although she doesn't seem in a hurry to wrap herself with it. She glances at me out of the corner of her eye in a way that tells me she's still very aware of my presence.

When she bends to pick up her sunglasses, I feel a rush of blood south. I appreciate the mirrored surface of the water for keeping my lower half out of her sight.

She tucks her things under her arm and perches her sunglasses on her forehead. I expect her to walk back into the house without saying anything, but she looks back at me.

"That was nice of you," she says. "Letting Ilya win."

I keep my face expressionless. "I didn't. He won on his own."

She arches a skeptical eyebrow. "That's the story you're sticking to?"

"Yes."

She almost smiles. "Good."

11

PAIGE

"Paige?"

I can tell by Cyrille's tone that she's been trying to get my attention for quite a while now. I don't blame her—we made plans to hang out and I've been drifting off in La La Land from the moment she arrived.

"Sorry, Cy," I say, turning to her apologetically. "I was just—"

"Daydreaming," she finishes with a shrewd smile. "About anyone in particular?"

I bite my lip. Cyrille drops the new dress she was showing me and jumps onto the bed next to me. "Okay, spill. What's going on with you?"

I take a deep breath, wondering whether I should be telling anyone this. "I've been... thinking lately."

She waves me on. "Yes?"

"Misha and I..."

"I knew it!" She grabs my hand. "I knew it. Something's brewing between the two of you, right?"

"I wish it was as simple as that," I admit. "I've just been doing some soul-searching the past few days. Being locked up doesn't give me much else to do. Misha and I—we're married."

Cyrille frowns. "I'm not sure that counts as a revelation, sweetheart."

I throw her a scowl. "We're married, we're having these babies together, and divorce is not really an option. Not as far as the Orlov family rulebook is concerned. So I guess I was thinking, considering all the above… Why shouldn't we make an attempt at a real marriage? The kind that includes sex and friendship. Maybe more."

"More. 'More' as in, a certain four-letter word that starts with L?" I nod shyly, and Cyrille beams at me. "I suppose the fact that you're already in love with him helped you come to this conclusion, huh?"

I blush even as I'm shaking my head. "Misha told me in no uncertain terms that love is not something he is interested in. I thought I could convince him, but every time I feel like we're moving in the right direction, he does or says something that pushes us back ten steps."

"But…?" she prods, sensing the flipside of that coin before I even say it.

"But I suppose I want to beat him at his own game," I admit. "I want to force him to see what we really have—what we could have—if he would just stop being so damn stubborn. I want him to admit that he has feelings for me. I want him to want me."

Cyrille looks like a proud older sister. "I think that's a great plan."

Her confidence bolsters mine. "I know I might fail, but I have to try. Not just for my sake, but for my children's. He has the potential to be an amazing father, Cyrille. I watched him play with Ilya yesterday in the pool and I saw…"

"You saw your future," she says gently.

I nod. "I know I sound so naïve."

"No," she says, squeezing my hand. "You don't. You sound hopeful."

"That's the problem: he knows that. And he's really, really good at hitting me where it hurts." I take a deep breath and fall back against my bed. "I have a feeling I'm going to regret this."

Cyrille collapses onto the bed next to me. "I felt that way so many times after I agreed to marry Maksim. Felt it a few times even after I married him, actually."

"When did that stop?"

"When we both got out of our own way," she says. "And each other's."

"So you're telling me I'm fighting an uphill battle?"

"Maybe. But hard won battles lead to the sweetest victories."

12

MISHA

Malen'kaya Rossya. Little Russia.

My home away from home.

Konstantin sits beside me in the passenger seat with a sour scowl on his face. "Come on, cousin," I goad him. "Think of this as an adventure."

He tosses me a sidelong glare that does little to hide his obvious misgivings about today's little road trip into this corner of the city. "You need to update your definition. This isn't an adventure; it's dangerous."

"You like danger."

"I do like danger. I also like math. And I know that two of us versus three of them is not great odds if they decide they don't like your attitude."

"One against three," I clarify. "You're not coming in with me."

Konstantin whips around to face me, eyes wide. "The fuck I'm not! I'm not letting you go in there to face the Babai alone."

"I thought you didn't want to go?" I tease.

"I want to keep you alive more than I want to avoid the Babai," he snaps. "Though it's getting pretty close. Regardless —I'm coming with you."

"You're staying in the car. And that's a fucking order, Konstantin."

His jaw drops. I rarely use the don card on him out of respect for our familial bonds, but there are some days when it's a necessity.

"It took eleven nights and three dead bodies before I managed to get their location and their names," he grumbles, as if I needed the reminder. "No, not their names—because they don't have fucking names anymore. Just titles."

I roll my eyes. "I'm sure they're extremely intimidating. Let me guess, Tweedledee, Tweedledoo, and Tweedledumbass? No, wait—Eenie, Miney, and Moe. Or—"

"The Bear. The Tiger. The Wolf," Konstantin intones ominously.

I resist the urge to laugh in his face, because he's actually sweating now. He runs his palms up and down the legs of his pants in a nervous tic.

"Catchy."

"Don't make light," Konstantin spits. "This is no laughing matter. These are men who are capable of doing unspeakable things."

"So am I."

Konstantin falls silent as we turn down a deserted road. Derelict buildings rise up on either side like rotten teeth. "I forgot how depressing this place is." He leans forward to look through the windshield, his lip curled.

I park along the cracked curb in front of The Alley Cat. The greased-over windows and fading neon lights are appropriately grim.

"What am I supposed to do?" Konstantin demands as I kill the engine. "Just sit here and wait for you like a trained poodle?"

"Exactly."

He grits his teeth. "Misha."

"I just gave you an order, Konstantin."

He falls silent, his body tense. I clap him on the shoulder and get out of the car.

Three older babushkas are standing out front of a salon on the opposite side of the street. None of them bother to hide that they're gawking. Even when I make eye contact, they don't stop.

I forget all about the women when I step into The Alley Cat. The musty room is shrouded in shadows. The walls are a burgundy red, faded to black in sporadic places after years of cigarette smoke. It's no wonder that most of the tables in here remain empty.

"Charming," I mutter. I walk over to the bar to deliver the line Konstantin was instructed to use.

The bartender has the sallow skin and yellow-tinted teeth of a lifelong smoker. In Russian, I tell him *"Ishchu okhotnika."*

I'm looking for a hunter.

The bartender drags his bloodshot eyes up to mine as if the effort required pains him. He takes me in for a long moment and then jerks his head towards a curtained door in the corner.

Unknowable sticky substances pull at my shoes as I cross the creaky floor. The curtain is the same red as the walls, but it's moth-eaten. When I pull it back, a cloud of dust rises into the air.

The back room is much smaller than the main bar, but just as dingy. A single light hangs over a grimy, circular table. The kind of place where evil men play high-stakes card games for prizes that would turn your stomach.

It's not that far off, I decide. The stakes are indeed high.

I'll need to watch my back. At least until an arrangement has been struck.

If there's one thing the Babai have, it's a reputation. Once they've struck a deal with someone, they must honor it. If they don't, the remaining Babai are honor-bound to kill the brother who breaks the pact.

The four chairs around the table are empty. It would seem I'm the only person in the room. But I can sense eyes on me from the shadows.

If this is a waiting game, I'm prepared to play. I sit down at the table and relax. Showing fear is a good way to get yourself killed.

After a few very long minutes, the shadows in the far corners of the room begin to move.

The first man to step forward from behind a wooden room divider is built like a wrestler. He's a few inches shorter than I am, but he makes up ground in the thick muscle of his neck, arms, and chest. He's wearing a thick beard and a nasty scowl.

The moment he sits down, the second Babai appears. This one is tall and lean, built like a gazelle, all wiry sinew and stretched skin. Unlike the first Babai, he bears a semi-smile as he approaches the table. I'm surprised by how young he looks—mid-thirties at the latest. Young to have such a reputation. He slides gracefully into his seat, his blue eyes fixed on me, unblinking.

The last Babai joins us at the table a few breaths later. He's more grizzled, more scarred, more intense than the others. I can sense his aura radiating dangerously, as if the shadows he emerged from have stuck with him, cloaking his shoulders and face.

The room charges up with the static that precedes a thunderstorm. The lights feel dimmer. Every creak louder than the last. Only our breathing breaks up the silence.

The legend of the Babai has boiled for hundreds of years in the underworld. It immigrated here right along with the Russians. It's the stuff of stories to scare children and fools. But as I sit here, at a round table with these three nameless ghouls, I realize that even I bought into the myth. I let legend cloud my common sense.

Because the three men that sit before me are not phantoms or ghosts or demons. They're men.

And men are something I can deal with.

"I am The Bear," the eldest Babai says, breaking the prickly quiet. He points towards the thickly muscled wrestler to his left. "This is The Tiger." Lastly, he points to the skinny one. "This is The Wolf."

I nod to each of them in turn. "Thank you for agreeing to this meeting."

"You have a job for us?" The Bear rumbles.

The Tiger looks bored. His eyes glaze over and he crosses his arms over his chest, causing the sleeves of his shirt to pucker. If he strains any harder, the fabric will just give up.

"I do," I say. "If you are willing to accept it."

The Bear glances towards his brothers. I notice that he makes eye contact with The Wolf, but not The Tiger. "First, you must answer three questions. One-word answers only. One word is all we require. Then we will decide if we want to accept your proposition."

My pulse quickens, but I remain still. "Ask me anything."

"The first question," The Bear rasps. "Why are you here?"

My answer is immediate: "Revenge."

"For whom are you here?" The Tiger growls.

"Family."

"Now, the third question," The Wolf intones with a sinister twinkle in his eye. "What will you do after the job is done?"

Celebrate? It's one word, but not exactly true. I rummage around for an answer—the truth, really. But I draw a complete blank.

"The clock is ticking," The Wolf warns. "You must answer before we stand. What will you do after the job is done?"

With a deep breath, I clear my mind and say the first thing that pops into my head: "Mourn."

Apparently, my answer is as surprising to them as it is to me. The Bear and The Wolf exchange an intrigued glance. The Tiger smolders like dying embers. The silence in the room grows heavy with expectation.

But of what?

Finally, The Bear nods. "Very well. We accept your offer. Tell us who must die."

13

MISHA

We're almost at the mansion and Konstantin hasn't stopped asking me questions since I returned to the car. "I've never heard of the three questions thing before. And you said you had to give them one-word answers? That's some medieval shit. Cryptic. Very biblical. What did they look like?"

"They looked like men." I turn into the driveway of the mansion and park. "Men who bleed and get sick and make mistakes. They're human, Konstantin. No matter what the legends say, they're just men."

He opens his mouth to say something as we get out, but we're interrupted by the sharp click-clack of heels on tile. My mother rounds the corner like a sudden storm. I imagine thunder and lightning and brimstone and sulfur all trailing behind her.

"Misha, I've spoken to your chef about dinner tonight. It's going to be a family affair." She turns to my cousin. "That means you, too, Konstantin."

I frown. "He and I have—"

"I don't care what you have," she snaps. "Work, play, a dentist appointment—all of it can wait. You can spare an hour to sit with your family and break bread."

Before I can argue further, she turns and stomps off back the way she came. I glance towards Konstantin, who has a shit-eating grin smeared across his face. "How does your mother factor into your 'no one is invincible' theory?" he cackles.

"Make yourself scarce until dinner," I warn in a grim mutter.

Konstantin slinks away, far too pleased with this turn of events. Sighing, I follow my mother to the atrium, where she's set up camp. She has an overflowing writing desk and a steaming mug of tea.

I check to make sure we're the only two people in the room. "Where's Paige?"

"Upstairs," she says. "Resting. She's gone through a lot."

"I'm aware of what she's gone through, Mother."

"Are you?" she asks accusingly, scribbling with greater intensity as she refuses to look up from her papers. "Because sometimes, it seems like you're as oblivious and insensitive as your father."

"I'm not oblivious to anything." I speak with excessive calm to hide my irritation. I know her feelings about my father. I don't welcome the comparison.

"What about your wife? That woman is pregnant with your babies. You realize that, don't you?"

"I'm not so busy that that's escaped my notice." I sigh. "Are you getting all your frustrations out before dinner? Or do you plan to keep up this attack through the entrees? I'm sure that'll make for lively entertainment for the whole family."

At that, she sets her pen down and looks up at me at last. "Your father kept a separate bedroom," she says softly. "He only visited me when his mistresses were busy. When there was no one else."

"Mother—"

"Did you know that there was a point in the beginning of our marriage when I actually thought I loved him?"

I blink, momentarily stunned. "I can't imagine that."

"Of course not. By the time you children were born, any remnant of that love had long since curdled. Our marriage was loveless and hopeless. But before I realized he would never change, I had hope."

"Paige and I are not—"

"Paige is not like me," she continues as if I'd never spoken. "She will not stay just because you refuse to divorce her. She will not sacrifice her pride or self-respect for the sake of your rules. She'll take those children and leave—and by God, Misha, I will not allow you to alienate that girl. I will not let you break her heart." She's standing now, all fire and brimstone, with one manicured nail thrust in my face. For a small woman, she's fierce.

"She's not going to leave, Mother."

"I know that." She jerks her chin upwards and sets her jaw firmly. "Because I will be moving in tomorrow to ensure it. I've already had the maids prepare my room."

"Excuse me?"

She nods, daring me to defy her. "If you refuse to take care of your wife, then I will. I'll stay for as long as she needs me to."

"She doesn't need you." More importantly, I don't need my mother living in my house. There's a reason I bought her a house in another neighborhood with an entire city between us. "She has me."

My mother just scowls. "I think we both know that's not true."

14

PAIGE

There's a strange energy at dinner.

Everyone is together and talking and being polite. Bowls of food pass from hand to hand, wine flows, and Ilya fills each pocket of silence with a steady stream of chatter.

Still, I feel the thorns poking at the underbelly of every interaction. Not painful—not yet, at least—but certainly irritating.

Misha is sitting directly opposite me, the long expanse of the table separating us like a lacquered ocean. It's apparently customary for the hosts to sit like this, but I can't help but wonder if it's actually because he wants to be as far from me as possible.

This dinner is the first time I've seen him in a few days. Even now, he barely looks at me. When he does, it's fleeting. His eyes are glazed over, unseeing.

I wonder if his dampened mood has anything to do with his mother moving in with us. I'll admit, I'm excited about it.

If for no other reason than to have someone around who actually wants to talk to me.

"How are things going with the takeover?" Niki asks abruptly.

Konstantin was in the middle of explaining how he supposedly shot a bullet directly into the barrel of another man's gun once, but he looks up with a start at Niki's interruption.

"That is not dinner-appropriate conversation, Nikita," Nessa warns.

"I'm bored. I thought I'd take a stab at turning the superficial chit-chat into something more interesting." Niki turns to Misha. "Well?"

He sighs and sips his wine. "It's going according to plan. I've officially taken control of Petyr's holdings in Ivanov Industries."

Nikita inhales sharply. "You're serious?" She hurls her cloth napkin down the length of the table at him. "Why didn't you tell any of us? That's huge!"

"I didn't tell you anything because it's not over yet," he explains. "Petyr needs to be fully dealt with before I'm willing to celebrate anything."

Nikita and Nessa exchange a glance. Cyrille stares straight down at her plate like it's the most interesting thing on the table.

"Don't you think you've exacted enough revenge?" Nessa suggests. "Perhaps now is the time to take a step back and focus on your family."

Misha puts his fork down and slides his plate away from him. "I *am* focusing on my family. This is how I'm doing it."

His mother sighs. "It's like you didn't learn anything from your brother."

The atmosphere in the dining room turns icy. There's no ignoring the thorns anymore. They're here and they're sharp and they're breaking skin.

Cyrille pats Ilya's back tenderly. "Honey, why don't you go grab your backpack? We'll be leaving soon."

"But I wanted another bread roll!"

Cyrille snatches one from the basket and shoves it into her son's hands. "Here you are. Now, go."

Pouting, Ilya slumps off to retrieve his backpack. As soon as he's gone, Cyrille reaches for the wine she's been sipping on all night and tosses it back in one gulp. Then she claps her hands on the table. "Well, this has been great. But we really should get going."

"We haven't had dessert yet," Nikita butts in. "And Misha hasn't finished telling us what his next magic act will be."

"And I'm not about to," Misha says harshly. "My plan is not for you to know."

"Maksim was never so fucking rigid," Nikita snaps.

"No? Well, I'm not fucking Maksim!" Misha slams his fist on the table and looks at every person at the table in turn. Everyone—except for me. "Excuse me. I need some fresh air. I'm sure you can show yourselves out."

Without waiting for a response, he exits through the sliding glass doors and stalks off into the night.

The room is silent and still in his absence. Then Nikita stands up and shoves her chair in. "I guess we're not having dessert then."

The group files out silently. I take up the rear, escorting everyone to the door.

The first person to break the quiet is Ilya. "Goodnight, Aunt Paige," he offers in a timid mumble.

I pull him in for a tight hug, ruffling his hair. "Goodnight, Ilya."

He hops down the steps after Nikita, but Cyrille stops in the doorway. "Are you okay?" I ask her as she lingers, twisting uncomfortably in place.

She nods. "Yeah, I'm fine. It was just… surprisingly emotional for me to sit at that table today. Not so long ago, Maksim and I were in your places."

I knew something was bothering her tonight, but I didn't even think of that.

"Oh, Cyrille. I'm so—"

"Don't apologize," she says quickly. "I didn't tell you that to make you feel guilty. You have nothing to feel guilty about. It's just…"

"You miss him," I fill in softly. "I know. For what it's worth, I think Misha was feeling a lot of the same things you were feeling tonight."

"I noticed that, too." She looks back into the house, her gaze straying to the same place my heart is tugging me. "What are you going to do?"

I take a deep breath. "I'm going to go after him."

15

PAIGE

Misha may be a big man, but he's surprisingly stealthy when he wants to be. I wander the dark paths of the back lawn and gardens for fifteen minutes before I find him sitting behind the greenhouse.

He's in a rock garden that edges a burbling stream. It winds around the greenhouse and through the flower beds before it pools out into the fishpond.

I move as silently as I can, creeping up from behind him. I don't want to scare him, but I'm not ready for the dismissal I know is coming.

"You should be in bed."

Dammit. So much for my ninja aspirations.

I sigh and relax as I approach him. "I'm not tired."

He turns to look at me sidelong. "You seemed tired at dinner."

"Is that a chivalrous way of saying I look like shit?" I stop in front of him. "Need I remind you I'm five months' pregnant with twins?"

His mouth twitches, but it's a far cry away from being a smile. "You look beautiful. You always do. I meant it in the most literal sense."

I'm not sure what to say to that. I wasn't fishing for a compliment. Even if I was, I wouldn't have expected him to offer one.

"Dinner was tense," I say, changing the topic.

He grimaces and leans forward, elbows on his knees. "You can thank my mother for that."

"Don't blame Nessa. She just wants her family back."

"Her family is not coming back. Not the way she knew it, anyway."

"Maybe if you stopped fighting it so hard—"

Misha turns his silver eyes on me, and I lose my train of thought. Even with half his face covered in shadow, those eyes shine as brightly as the stars hanging above us.

"I'm fighting against Petyr Ivanov," Misha says coldly. "He's the only person I'm at war with."

Ya coulda fooled me, I want to say.

But I saw the way he reacted when his mom pushed. It's the reason we're having this conversation in the backyard instead of at the table.

Misha isn't ready.

"Can I tell you something?" I ask anxiously.

He casts a wary glance in my direction. "If you must."

"Before the explosion happened, it felt like maybe you'd changed your mind. About me, I mean. It felt like you wanted... more. More out of our marriage."

He doesn't say anything. Not even a glimmer of acknowledgement on his face. So I bite the bullet and just keep going.

"I'll admit, at that point, I was still reeling from the fight we had in the hospital. I was hurt and angry and I was trying to protect myself. So I was resisting your attempts to make amends. But I want you to know... I'm over it. I forgive you."

I study him for some kind of reaction, but there's nothing. He looks at me with vacant eyes, and *fuck*, I can't stand that. I'm tired of feeling alone in my own house, in my own life.

I want him here with me.

"Are you hearing me, Misha? I forgive you. I want to move on. I want us to make things work between us for the sake of the family. And for the sake of our children."

He lets me stew in the silence for so long that every second that passes without a word from him is physically painful.

"You're really not going to say anything?" I ask at last.

"There's nothing to say." He works his jaw one way and then the other. "This arrangement is all I can offer you, Paige."

Once again, hope shatters at my feet. I should let it lie there —and yet here I am once again, gathering the pieces, my hands sliced and bleeding from the jagged edges.

"So... am I right in assuming the explosion changed something for you?"

"I lost focus," he says quietly. "Nothing can get in the way of my plan to get revenge on Petyr for all that he has cost this family."

He looks away, but I reach out and stroke my hand along his jaw. He tenses under my touch, but he turns back to me. His eyes bore into mine, unending depths of emotion there for me to explore.

If only I had all the time it would take to do that. Centuries. Lifetimes.

"This is all new for me," he says at last.

"What is?"

He shakes his head. "It doesn't matter."

"It matters to me. Just tell the truth, Misha. That explosion changed your mind because it scared you. Petyr got close to you, your house. You made one slip and almost paid for it. But—"

"He got too close to *you*," he says suddenly.

The words bump me off-balance. But I try to recover as quickly as I can so we don't lose this momentum. "And that scared you, didn't it?"

"Paige..."

I grab his hand and hold on tight. "Look at me, Misha. You can tell me the truth. You can tell me you were scared you were going to lose—"

"I was scared I was going to lose the babies," he growls.

But I know that catch, that wobble in his voice. There's more here than he's willing to say.

"And that's all it was?" I press. "You were only worried about the babies?"

He sighs. "You know the answer."

"I don't," I lie. "Tell me."

"Fine!" He jerks his hand out of my hold, his steady calm cracking under the pressure. "You want me to say it? Fine! Yes, I was beyond fucking terrified when I heard that explosion go off. I could barely see straight. It's a wonder I managed to get myself down to you in one piece. But—*fuck*—but…" A shadow passes over his face as he forces his eyes to level at mine. "But letting myself care about you was a mistake. Nearly losing you blinded me to everything else. I can't afford to let that happen again."

What he's saying, what he's admitting to me… It should be a special moment. *He cares about me.* I want to wave that fact in the air and celebrate. I want to scream it from the damn rooftops, actually.

But there's nothing celebratory about the look on his face. The fear. The fury. Two things that he just can't get over, no matter how hard he tries.

"Misha, love doesn't have to be a weakness. It can make you stronger."

"We're staying married, Paige," he says firmly. "We're having those babies. But we're going to do what you originally wanted. We're going to live our separate lives, you in your wing of the house and me in mine."

My heart sinks at the determination on his face. "I don't want that anymore. That doesn't make any sense, Misha. We can have more."

"It doesn't have to make sense," he says softly. "It is what it is."

16

MISHA

The council meeting lasts all of fifteen minutes before I cut it short and send everyone home.

The senior members don't seem pleased as they say their terse goodbyes and file out of the conference room. Only Konstantin stays behind, swiveling his chair back and forth with an air of relief.

"That was quick," he observes.

"Felt like a fucking lifetime."

When Maksim was don, I skipped these meetings as often as I could. Sitting in a chair, making a presentation, talking facts and fucking figures... It was never my strong suit.

I preferred simple things. Violence. Fire. Pain.

Things I knew well.

Things that don't talk back.

"Did you notice the faces?" Konstantin asks. "Klim, Vasily, Danil… All those fuckers looked like they swallowed a raw egg on their way in."

"I noticed." I sit down in my chair and recline back. "They're not happy with how I'm handling things. Obviously."

So many of the older Bratva members are too conservative. They want me to handle things the old way. But the old way got my brother killed. If they don't understand that, then there is no amount of time in the world that will change their minds.. I'll just have to show them.

"We have the Ivanovs by the fucking balls," Konstantin says. "No one has heard or seen from Petyr in weeks. He's running scared."

"He's lying in wait. There's a difference."

Konstantin snorts and waves the idea away. "No don worth his salt 'lies in wait.' If that rat bastard had a card to play, he would be playing it right now."

I shake my head. "He threatened retaliation."

"In a fucking *note*, Misha. Words on a piece of paper, like he's a middle schooler asking you to 'check the Yes box if you're still mad at me.' Nothing but a desperate taunt from a desperate man."

I want to believe my cousin, but I know better. "Petyr Ivanov is shrewd. He's not one to make a hollow taunt. He was goading me, trying to provoke some kind of reaction. He has disappeared because he's planning something."

"Which has given you plenty of time to get the Babai on your side. He's got nowhere left to hide."

I nod, but I'm restless. I won't feel confident again until Petyr is in the ground. "I'm not willing to put all my faith in the Babai."

I pull out a thin file and pass it to Konstantin. I didn't even consider presenting this off-the-cuff idea in the meeting, but I have a feeling my cousin will be more amenable to it.

"Well, fuck," Konstantin breathes after a minute of perusing. "You want to smoke him out. Literally, by the looks of it." He flips the page and glances at the aerial photo of the plot of land where the Ivanov mansion has stood since my grandfather was don. "*Quite* literally."

He drops the file back on the desk and folds his hands together in his lap. "So I've been thinking…"

"I thought I warned you about that."

He scowls at me but continues anyway. "I've been thinking about the third question. The one The Wolf asked you. *What will you do when it's over?* And… and I guess it made me wonder what life will look like once there is no Petyr Ivanov. No Ivanov Bratva, period. I mean, shit, Misha: what the hell will we do with ourselves?"

"This is the Bratva, Konstantin. There will always be another enemy around the corner."

He doesn't look mollified. "Sure, but Petyr has always been the biggest bad in the business, you know? He's your archnemesis. Enemies we can handle; enemies are easy. But Petyr has fundamentally reshaped our lives. He's the reason Maksim isn't here. Once he's gone… I mean, do you think we'll finally be able to move on?"

Move on? I feel my chest knot up painfully. There's muted hope in Konstantin's voice when he speaks about our possible future. Light at the end of the tunnel, when you see it through his eyes.

But I can't seem to find the brightness. Moving on? The thought just leaves me feeling empty. What is left when revenge is gone? What will get me out of bed in the morning?

"Time will tell," I mutter evasively.

"I think I'm gonna travel a little once we've fed Petyr to the Babai," he muses, going starry-eyed at the prospect. "I'll hit Asia. Japan. Maybe head north from there and stop by the motherland. Could be fun."

"You have a life here," I remind him. "And a job."

Konstantin laughs. "You say that like they're separate things. Let's face it, Misha: our jobs *are* our lives. Have been since Maksim died."

I flinch a little at how casually he throws those words around these days. Almost like it doesn't hurt him anymore to say them out loud. When did we get past the point of speaking about Maksim's death in uneasy, harrowed whispers?

"Of course," he adds, "you'll have a wife and two kids to go back home to at the end of the day."

I glare at him. "No, I won't. I'll have my children. But Paige and I are an arrangement. Nothing more. She'll understand that."

"Do you really believe that?" he asks. "Or is that just what you're hoping for?"

Hope. There's that word again.

No one hopes for a hurricane, but when one is headed your way, you might as well be honest about it. That is why I'm honest with myself about my future with Paige. It will only ever lead to destruction. The sooner it hits, the sooner I can rebuild.

"It has to," I snarl. "I'll make sure it does."

Konstantin doesn't match my energy. He just smirks and shrugs, breezy as ever. "You have a natural talent for being an asshole, but I'm not sure even you can change that girl's mind."

"Agree to disagree."

He snorts derisively. "Paige has worn her dead best friend's necklace for almost two decades without ever taking it off. She put up with her scumbag ex despite everything he did to her. The woman is loyal and fueled by the blindest faith known to man. She ain't breakin', my man."

I stroke the edge of my desk. "Oh ye of little faith."

Konstantin smiles and leans forward. "Misha, you're my cousin, my don, and my best friend. I've known you my entire life, and I've loved and respected you for the entirety of it. But if it comes down to betting on you or Paige... brother, I'm betting the house on her."

17

PAIGE

"Never, never, never," I chant, holding my closet door closed. "Step away from the door. Leave right now. I'm never coming out."

"Please, Paige. It can't be that bad." Cyrille pushes weakly on the other side of the door.

I glance back at the full-length mirror behind me and then away again, horrified. I was excited about the lingerie when Cyrille first pulled it out of the bag. But now...

"There's no way I can wear this. I look like a pregnant stripper. I look like a Winnie the Pooh sex doll. I look like Shrek ate Shrek."

I hear a tiny snort of laughter from the bedroom.

"You wouldn't be laughing if you could see me!"

Cyrille laughs again. "I'm not laughing! Just come out and let me see. You can't hide in there forever. The cookies are out here, remember?"

I groan. Cyrille has a hook-up downtown for the best white chocolate macadamia nut cookies I've ever tasted. And the witch refuses to tell me where she buys them.

"Slide them under the door!"

"Not a chance," she cackles, still far too amused by this situation. "Come out and show me and you get a cookie."

"I'm not a dog," I grumble. That being said, I am absolutely conditioned to obey.

Grimacing, I slowly crack the closet open.

Cyrille backs away from the doors, motioning me out with both hands like the guys at the airport runway with the glowsticks. The bag of cookies sits behind her on the bed, and I briefly consider whether I can tackle her, grab the cookies, and get back to the closet before she sees anything.

But there's no way.

"Come on," she urges. "Open the door all the way, baby. Let's see the damage."

I open the doors wide and wrap my arms around my unfamiliarly full middle.

Cyrille's eyes go wide. "Oh my God."

"I know! I look—"

"Hot!" Cyrille grabs a cookie from the bag behind her and shoves it into my hand. Then she yanks my arms down and spins around, doing a full inspection of the itty bitty lingerie. "Absolutely, ridiculously, stupidly, almost offensively hot. Like, I'm mad about how hot you look."

I glance down at the black silk set, trying to understand what Cyrille is seeing that I'm not. The top is lace. Right now, my bra is visible through the material, but once I took it off... well, *I* would be visible. The lace cuts in a V down my midsection, transitioning to silk that floats around the top of my thighs.

A few months ago, I would have loved this. But now, the lace pulls strangely over my round belly. No matter which way I turn or how hard I suck in, there's an obvious bulge. It's so large that the hem barely covers the matching lace panties.

I take a bite of a cookie and shake my head. "You're just saying that."

"I'm not." She crosses her fingers over her heart like she does with Ilya. "Seriously, Paige—you look smoking hot. I knew this would look amazing on you."

"But… I look pregnant."

She raises her brows, looking at me like I'm dumb. "You *are* pregnant."

"Yes, but I don't need to announce that fact to the world tummy-first."

"Why?" Cyrille argues. "Because pregnant women aren't sexy? That's bullshit. Real men love a pregnant woman. Especially one who's carrying their child. Child*ren*, in your case. It hits some real primal, protective instincts."

"But—"

"You're keeping it," she announces with finality. "More importantly, you're wearing it. Your ass looks great, too."

I shift uncomfortably on my feet. "I'm not used to thongs."

"Well, get used to them. You asked for sexy and that's what I brought you."

"What are the other options?" I start to move past her towards the bag she brought, but Cyrille blocks me.

"We've gone through all of them."

"Already? That was it?" Everything I've put on today made me feel like a blimp with legs.

She smiles. "You know what the most attractive quality in a woman is, Paige?"

"If you say 'confidence,' I'm gonna barf."

Cyrille laughs. "It's true. *Confidence.* You need to find your inner lioness and embrace her. This was your idea, remember?"

I grab my robe and slip it on. "I remember. I just can't remember why I thought it was a good one."

"You're trying to seduce your husband. Lingerie is catnip for men."

I sigh. "If it was just about seducing him, this would be easier. I'm trying to make him fall in love with me. What's the outfit for that?"

She dismisses me with a wave of her hand. "Easy. He's already halfway there. Probably more."

"Everyone seems so sure of that."

"Because we've all got eyes. We can see the chemistry between the two of you from a mile away," she says. "I know I'm starting to sound like a broken record, but it really does remind me of the early days with me and Maksim."

Her smile shifts, taking on a sad tilt. I walk to the bed and she drops down next to me. We sit in silence for a minute, trying to sort through the emotional wreckage in our heads.

"You talk about him more lately," I say finally.

She nods. "The more I do, the less painful it becomes. I think it helps Ilya, too. He likes talking about his dad."

I want to believe she's right, but I don't know that I can. If I talked about Clara more, would it stop hurting so much that she's not here?

"I remember exactly where I was when I found out he was gone," Cyrille reminisces in a shy whisper. "I was in our bedroom, folding sheets. One of the maids ran in and told me that Nessa was in the sitting room. I figured it was something about a charity event. So I finished putting the bedsheets away before I went downstairs…" She takes a deep breath before she continues. Like telling this story requires a recharge. "Nessa was on her knees on the carpet. Nikita was hugging her from behind. And Konstantin just stood there, ashen-faced."

"Misha wasn't there?"

"No. Konstantin is the one who broke the news to us," she admits. "For a second, I thought he was there to tell us that *Misha* was gone." Her eyes are watery. She speaks between shuddering breaths. "In fact, I hoped that's what he was going to say. I feel horrible about it now. I know that's an awful thing to have hoped for, but—"

I grab her hand and stop her talking. "No, it's not horrible. It's human. We bargain with fate, even if it's not our bargain to strike."

"I love Misha," she says. "He's like a brother to me. But—"

"Maksim was your husband and the father of your child." I squeeze her hand. "You don't have to explain yourself to me, Cyrille. I get it. It's okay."

She gives me a shaky smile. "Do you remember where you were when you got the news?"

"What news?"

Her gaze flickers down to my pendant. Just like that, the weight of this conversation swallows me up. I want to hide in the darkness, avoid pushing through the pain.

But I've done that for so long—decades now; where did the time go?—and it hasn't helped.

Maybe it's time to try something new.

"Clara was with Moses that day," I whisper. "Her boyfriend. She never usually told me when she was hanging out with him because she knew I didn't like him."

"Why not?"

"He was a bad guy, and he ran with a lot of other bad guys, too. And he was older, and controlling, and… well, she never told me he hit her, but I could swear I saw the potential for that in him. You know how some people just have violence right on the surface? He was like that. Brittle. Like he'd snap at any moment."

"Did you ever tell her that?"

"I begged her to go slow at first. Then I warned her to be careful. Eventually, I pleaded with her to leave him." I shrug. "She ignored me."

It's funny how vibrant the memories are now that I'm unpacking them. Locking them away has kept them in perfect condition. They haven't been softened and faded by retelling.

I glance towards Cyrille, wishing that I could turn back time for the both of us. "I was sitting at the window of my trailer when I saw the police coming. I don't know how, but I just knew they were there because of Clara. I ran outside and watched them knock on the door of her trailer. I dropped to my knees."

"It was Moses?" Cyrille asks.

"Yes," I say. "But not in the way I thought."

18

MISHA

For over one hundred years, the Ivanov mansion has stood like a cancer on the earth.

For over one hundred years, it has loomed and brooded.

It won't last the rest of the night.

After we set it alight, Konstantin and I watch the flames blaze from a distance for almost three hours before the firefighters manage to put it out. The fire ravages the old mansion, turning its bones into ashes.

Just like I knew it would.

"Well, looks like the fun is over." Konstantin tosses his empty beer bottle into the back of the truck and stretches. "What time is it?"

"Almost three in the morning."

He whistles. "That explains why I can barely keep my eyes open. Time for me to hit the hay."

It's strange—I don't feel in the least bit tired. But I get to my feet anyway and climb in the passenger seat of Konstantin's truck. We don't talk on the way home until he drops me off in front of the mansion.

"You sure you can make it back to your apartment?" I ask.

"Are you worried about me, Misha?"

I roll my eyes. "You look like shit, and I don't want to have to find your replacement if you drive off the road."

He blows me a kiss. "I'll be fine. Love you, too." He's laughing as he pulls away.

The house is dark when I get inside, but I see the warm glow of a fire flickering in the sitting room. It's so late that my first thought is that Petyr has already retaliated.

As I get closer, I realize it's the fireplace still burning, and two bodies are laid out on the couch. Paige and Cyrille are bundled under fleece blankets. A trail of cookie crumbs winds across the table in front of Paige. More of her cravings, I'm sure. She's insatiable lately.

I walk over to the fireplace and put out the last of the flames. When I turn back around, Cyrille is blinking awake and sitting up.

"M… Misha?"

"I didn't mean to wake you."

"I'm a light sleeper." She rubs her eyes and checks the time on her phone. "Shit. I didn't mean to crash here."

"There are plenty of guest rooms you can claim for the night."

"I wouldn't have fallen asleep at all if you'd have had the decency to show up at an appropriate hour."

Her venom catches me off-guard. "Excuse me?"

Standing, she grabs my arm, making sure to dig her nails in hard, and pulls me out of the sitting room "I didn't want to leave Paige until you got home. Which, of course, you never did."

"There are two dozen armed men patrolling the perimeter of the grounds, Cyrille. You don't need to sit with her until—"

"She was waiting for *you*, Misha," she snaps. "Even after the way you've treated her, she was still waiting up for you."

Maybe Konstantin was right. Maybe Paige's hope will be harder to squash than I thought.

"Well, she shouldn't have."

Cyrille shakes her head. "You're a complete and utter fool. You know that, right?"

"It's better this way, Cyrille. I need to be alone. It's the only way this will work."

She rolls her eyes, exasperated. "You realize that if you insist on being alone, you're forcing Paige to be alone, too? Do you really think she's going to be satisfied with that in the long run? Do you think that's fair?"

"She agreed to it."

"You took advantage of a vulnerable woman," she hisses. "The way that all men do. You found a woman who had no family, no support, and no financial freedom, then you offered her all three. Of course she was going to accept your offer! Even if it meant that love wasn't part of the bargain. Just because she agreed to it doesn't mean she should have."

"Whose side are you on?" I growl.

She sighs and puts her hand on my arm. "Believe it or not, I'm on your side, Misha. Which is exactly why I'm speaking up. Now, I'm going to crash in one of your bedrooms." At the base of the staircase, she turns back to me. "Take care of her. Or else you'll have Nessa, Niki, and me to answer to."

With that, she turns and leaves. I watch until she disappears up the stairs. Then, shaking my head, I return to the sitting room.

Paige is still sleeping. Her hair is a mess of curls around her head. I can't help but smile when her lips part on an exhale, her lashes fluttering in a dream.

She's wearing one of her favorite silk robes. It's one of my favorites, too. It floats over her curves and makes me want to do deplorable things to her body.

Which is exactly why I make sure the damn thing is properly secured before I lift her into my arms and carry her up to our bedroom. I place her on the bed and make sure she's comfortable before stepping away.

The plan is to retreat immediately. Go back to my office, strip down to my boxers, and find a few hours of sleep before the sun comes up again.

Instead, I find myself slipping onto the bed beside her.

I lie down on top of the covers as I gently brush the hair from her face. She looks so peaceful like this.

After a few minutes, I worry the heat of my gaze alone might be enough to wake her. Those plump lips of hers were designed to be kissed. A siren call to a man like me with crumbling willpower.

I force my eyes from her face and glance down at her rounding belly. It's still small, but large enough to serve as a reminder.

I'm going to be a father soon.

A mix of panic, excitement, and fear twine inside of me.

Is this normal? I want to ask Maksim how he felt when Cyrille was pregnant. I reach over and trace gentle circles on her belly.

"I want to give you the best home, the best life," I whisper to my future children. "But I'm not sure I'm capable of being a good father. The only thing I did right is choose the best mother for both of you. She has everything I lack. And already, I know she's going to love you the way that every child deserves to be loved." I sigh and correct myself. "The way every *person* deserves to be loved. She deserves that, too. A full life with a husband who can step up for her. Someone to be the protector she never had. To be the kind of husband that she always wanted. But I don't have it in me to love her that way. Because if I lose her…"

I close my eyes for a moment and let my hand rest a little heavier on her skin.

I so desperately want to sink into the bed next to her, to spoon her the way I did in the days after the explosion. It had been the perfect excuse to hold her.

Now, that excuse is gone.

Now, touching her requires an admission I'm not prepared to make. A truth I'm hoping to bury.

"The two of you are our gift to each other," I whisper into the darkness. "I'm hoping that will be enough."

19

PAIGE

I'm certain my racing heart will give me away. But Misha's voice carries on, soft and insistent, as he whispers promises to our unborn children.

He doesn't know I'm awake. It's the only reason he's revealing so much.

He has spent so long hiding behind responsibility, behind the Orlov rulebook that he wears like a coat of armor. But all the armor in the world can't protect him from the truth beating in his own chest.

Or from the life in my womb.

"I'm hoping it will be enough," he whispers, his fingers pressing against my belly.

It won't be enough, I want to scream back at him. *They need more. I need more.*

I need you.

But I don't say any of that. His hand slips away and I feel the mattress shift under his weight. He's leaving, and he's taking my aching heart with him.

I'm trying to battle through my own fear and nerves, so I crack open one eye—and watch him walk into our bathroom instead.

The moment the door shuts, I jump out of bed, feeling wide awake. Adrenaline and excitement course through my body like drugs.

His words have filled me with the kind of reckless hope I haven't dared to let myself have. The kind of hope that makes me want to do crazy things.

Like quickly slip into the silk lingerie I swore I'd never wear.

The water is still running in the bathroom, so I take a moment to look at myself in the mirror. I try to see myself the way I want Misha to. The way Cyrille promised me he would. But all the adrenaline in the world can't quite overcome my nerves.

Then I hear the water stop.

No time for being self-conscious now.

I rush back to bed and lie with my legs stretched out, trying to find a position that's sexy without being obvious. As if I just yawned awake and slipped out of my robe.

Turns out that's not so easy to do when you're five months' pregnant with twins.

I give up and stand just as the bathroom door opens.

Misha stops short when he sees me standing there. But surprise shifts to something much more heated when his eyes snake over the rest of me.

"You should be sleeping," he says at last, his voice thick.

"Couldn't sleep. I was a little hot in the robe."

His eyes flicker down to my breasts, but he doesn't let them linger. "That doesn't look very comfortable."

"It is, actually." I spin around so that he can see my thong. "It's so comfortable. Almost like I'm not wearing anything at all."

His mouth tightens. "Almost."

I've never seen him look quite so uncomfortable. It's a delicious tension. "What do you think of it?"

"It's... nice."

"Nice?" I raise my eyebrows.

"Paige," he says on a taut exhale, "it's the middle of the night. You should be sleeping."

"I spend most of my days resting. Right now, I have a lot of... *energy* I need to work out."

I smooth my hands down my thighs, and he watches the movement with a singular kind of focus. "Then maybe I'll leave you to work it out yourself."

He's going to leave me alone with this lingerie on. I know Misha is more than capable of that kind of torture. Which is why I kick things up a notch.

"Or you could stay." I pinch the sleeve of his shirt between my fingertips, toying with the fabric. We both watch my fingers work. "You could help, even."

"What are you doing, Paige?" He sounds out of breath, but we haven't moved.

I slide my hand over his chest and undo his first button. I curl my fingers through the dark chest hair curled there. "You did tell me that you would meet any needs I had. That you would do 'anything to make me comfortable.' Weren't those your exact words?"

He frowns, his heart thudding against his ribs. I undo the next button and the third before Misha can speak through his clenched jaw. "That's not a good idea."

I act innocent. "Why not? You're my husband. It's just sex. Are you worried I'll get pregnant or something?"

"I'm—"

"You've made it very clear that you can't love me." I slide my hand under his shirt, caressing the warm skin of his chest. My entire body is buzzing from the contact. I feel high. "But that doesn't mean you can't make love to me, does it?"

His eyes dilate at the prospect. He's right there for the taking. *We* are right there for the taking.

I just have to be persistent. I can convince him. I know it.

"Or maybe you're not willing to do that because you already have feelings for me." I shrug like I don't care either way. Like it isn't the most important thing in the world to me.

"You're mistaken," Misha says in a gravelly rasp. "But you still need to recover. You almost died a few days ago, Paige."

"Mhmm," I purr. "That's exactly right. I *almost* did. But I didn't. I'm right here and very much alive." I press my body to his, closing the distance between us. "Want me to prove to you how alive I am?"

A groan rumbles through his chest, desperate and wanting.

He's so close. *So close.*

I touch his bottom lip with my fingers. Then I trail my touch down his shoulder to his elbow and grab one of his hands. I place his palm on my hip. "Come on, husband," I coo. "Make me yours."

"Jesus." He rips himself away from me and crosses the room.

Instead of feeling discouraged, triumph pounds through my body. I'm getting to him. I'm actually getting under his skin.

"Is it the lingerie? Do you not like it?" When he doesn't answer, I slide one of the straps down my arm. "If you don't like it, I can take it off."

I'm in the process of pulling off the other strap when he encircles my hand with his own. "Don't touch a fucking thing." He's so close I can smell his woodsy cologne and the raw, manly musk of him. His breath comes in harsh spurts. "I'm not sleeping with you tonight, Paige."

He can't even look at me. His eyes are pinned on the wall just over my shoulder, his hand still locked over mine.

So close. The tension is unbearable. My heart is in my throat. Every cell burns.

"Fine." I shake his hand off and walk to the bed. "If you won't help me, then I'll just have to get myself off."

I pull my thong down and sling it at him. It hits him square in the chest before he catches it, crushing the delicate material in his fist. "What are you doing?" he murmurs.

"You're a smart boy." I lie back on the bed and spread my legs. "Figure it out."

Then I slip my hand between my legs and touch myself. I'm beyond frustrated with him, but I'm still wet. Dripping.

Misha leans forward for a second, tongue visible past his parted lips. We're there. We're right there. *Come on,* I plead silently. *Don't be so stubborn. Don't be a fool. The future is lying on the bed with her legs parted. All you have to do is—*

Just like that, the door clicks closed.

He is gone.

I flop back on the bed, pull a pillow over my face, and scream. It feels good, so I do it again, and that one feels good, too, so I go for a third time.

But then my throat is raw and I'm still aching with need.

Energy buzzes under my skin. I need release. I need to see this through.

Then I remember the tablet. The stupid tablet Rada gave me to do puzzles and play games. It doesn't have internet access, but what it does have is a camera.

I cast aside my frustration and start rooting around in my writing desk until I find it. When I do, I position the clumsy thing on the dresser across from the foot of the bed and toy with it until the angle is right. Then, once it's recording, I spread out on the bed, arch my back, and touch myself as if Misha is watching.

And I put on a *show*.

I moan in all the right places. I coax myself to the leg-shaking edge and then back off, torturing myself and Misha alike with my orgasm.

Finally, I can't hold back. I look into the camera as I mount the peak and pleasure pulses through me. Then the words dissolve into breathless moans.

"Just a sneak peek at what you could have had," I whisper when I regain my sense of self, rolling against the palm of my hand.

What we *could've had.*

Then I turn the video off.

20

MISHA

"It's been a week. A whole fucking week." I stare daggers at Konstantin as though he's the one responsible. "I thought the Babai were supposed to be good."

Konstantin frowns. "Maybe Petyr's too good at hiding."

"Not a chance. No one is that good. Or that stupid. We burned down his house and the bastard still refused to show face." I shake my head. "No, my instincts were right—he's planning something. I should have stormed in and strangled him myself."

"And gotten yourself killed? Genius plan."

"That would be preferable to the alternative," I snarl.

Konstantin doesn't beat around the bush. He knows what I mean. "You're worried about Paige."

Yes. Of course I am.

"Of course I'm not," I scoff aloud. "I don't have any reason to be. As far as Petyr is concerned, she's dead."

He purses his lips. "In our world, there's always a reason to be concerned about the people in your life. Petyr could somehow know she's still alive."

"Are you suggesting we have a mole?" I ask.

Holding up his hands, he says, "I'm not accusing anyone of anything definitively. But you know as well as I do that nothing stays secret for long."

Nothing about this conversation is making me feel any better. The only thing that might make me feel better is seeing Paige.

Preferably in the same outfit she wore last night.

My cock still aches from the sight of her. Pregnant and beautiful and *willing*. So fucking willing.

Which is the entire problem.

"Listen, I know you're not going to like this suggestion," Konstantin begins, interrupting my dirty thoughts, "but we do still have a card up our sleeves."

I catch the look on his face and don't even have to ask. "Fuck no."

"Come on, Misha. I've been tracking the man for weeks now. He has stuck to his end of the bargain."

"He's a rat."

"Rats can be useful," Konstantin argues. "They can get into places no one else can."

"He's a last resort. And we're not there yet."

"Fine. Your call. I just wanna say that I think…"

Konstantin is still talking as my phone vibrates. I glance down and see a video message from an unknown number. The only people who have this number are people I've handed it to personally.

My intuition buzzes. It's Petyr. It has to be. This is the opening ceremony to whatever shit he has planned next.

Tension ripples through me as I open the message and press play. The video is dark at first. Shadows against blacker shadows.

But as the seconds tick past and my eyes adjust, I start to see things I recognize.

A curve. A familiar curve. Bared, with just a trace of black lace stroking over the hip.

The shadow takes shape and color. It's my wife. Paige turns back to the camera and lowers herself to the mattress. Her legs spread slowly, and I've never been so riveted in my life. The silk lingerie rides up her thighs, revealing exactly what she's wearing underneath.

Which is… nothing.

I can see the matching thong on the floor. She threw it at me, right before I walked away from her. From *this*.

Regret and desire chase each other for top billing as my wife palms her own breasts, arching into her own touch. When she uses her fingers to spread her pussy wide, I almost drop my phone.

"… Misha? You okay, bro?"

Konstantin is talking to me, but I can't find the words to respond. All I can do is stare open-mouthed at the hypnotic video.

Paige circles her hand over her sex. A low moan escapes her parted lips. It's loud enough that Konstantin jerks back.

That pulls me out of my trance.

I hit pause fast. "Get out."

Konstantin stares at me for a second. Then his face splits in a shit-eating grin. "Oh, damn. *Damn.* And here I was thinking that you were going through a rough patch with Paige. I shoulda known better."

"Get out," I hiss again.

He chuckles. "Sure thing, dude. I'm gone."

Right before he leaves, he grabs the box of tissues on the far edge of my desk and throws it at me. "Just in case."

I swat the box out of midair. It hits the ground with a soft thump as the door clicks closed. As soon as he's gone, I hit play again.

Paige's lips pucker in a whimper as she works her fingers between her folds. She touches herself in a way that tells me she's used to handling things on her own. That annoys me almost as much as it turns me on.

A woman like her shouldn't have to get herself off at all.

I should be doing it for her.

She writhes on the bed and her shoulder straps slide down her arms. With a quick jerk, she pulls the fabric down over her breasts, and it's my turn to moan.

Her breasts are swollen and huge, begging to be sucked. I unzip my pants and pull my cock out.

Suddenly, I don't care that I'm in the office. I don't care that I haven't heard from the Babai. I don't care that Petyr has managed to disappear into the shadows.

None of it matters right now.

I stroke my cock as she touches herself. Her moans fill my office, vibrating through my body like music meant for my ears alone.

She moves as though she's completely unaware of the camera. Then, just when I least expect it, she glances right into the lens.

She winks.

Then she comes.

And so do I.

It only occurs to me when I can finally breathe again that my wife knows exactly what she's doing.

For the first time, this is a war I might lose.

21

PAIGE

It's been almost an hour since I used Rada's phone to send my little home movie to Misha.

I felt a surge of confidence as I watched the message load and deliver. When I saw he opened it, I couldn't even hold onto the phone.

But every passing minute where Misha doesn't respond sees my anxiety double.

I've gone for a jog around the property and then spent an hour in the pool doing lap after lap after endless, exhausting lap. None of it has helped soothe the restlessness in my bones.

Rada can sense my nerves. She's been checking in on me every fifteen minutes like clockwork. She appears in the doorway to the patio now, perfectly on time. "Mrs. Paige, can I get you anything?"

I stand up, shaking off the last of the pool water and squeezing it out of my hair. "No, thank you. I'm actually headed upstairs now to change."

She nods and turns to leave. I want to let her go without being pathetic. I don't want to ask again. But I can't stop myself.

"Um, Rada? Has Mr. Orlov… Has he messaged back?"

She shakes her head, looking apologetic. "No, ma'am. Nothing."

She has no idea what I sent to him. I deleted the video from her phone after sending it. I also assured her that Misha would know who sent it to him and she wouldn't be in trouble, but I can see she's still terrified.

"If he asks you anything about it, just tell him I hijacked your phone, okay? Say I made you do it. He'll believe you."

She swallows and nods. "I will."

I thank her again and head upstairs to my room. Maybe a cold shower is what I need.

I'm about to slip out of my white bikini when I hear thundering footsteps just outside my room. My heart soars at the thought of Misha. But it's the middle of the day. He wouldn't leave the office before lunch to come home and—

"Paige!" Misha's voice roars down the hallway.

Whoops. Maybe he will.

My bedroom door bursts open, and I wipe the emotion from my face. When I step out of the walk-in closet in nothing but my bikini, I look as pure as the driven snow.

"Aren't you supposed to be at the office?" I ask innocently.

His eyes are angry slits. His jaw is flexing. Every muscle in his body radiates tension, and I love knowing I'm the one who put it there.

"What the hell do you think you're doing?"

I tug playfully on the strap of my bikini. "I was considering taking a shower. Maybe a bath, actually. Care to join?"

My hand trails slowly over my chest. Misha watches it the entire way, his anger never abating. "What were you thinking?" he growls at me. "You sent that from the maid's phone!"

"You confiscated mine. I didn't have a choice."

"There's always a choice."

I nod. "You know what? You're right. I gave you one last night. You chose wrong. Never too late to fix your mistakes, though."

His lips part slightly and his tongue flickers out. He's panting, though I'm not sure he even realizes it. His whole body vibrates with anger, with frustration, with lust. At least I hope it's with lust. Although the Lord knows I've got enough of that for the both of us. I feel like I'm about to combust.

"That's not going to happen." I can't tell if he's talking to me or himself.

I sigh. "Disappointing. Looks like I'll have to get myself off again. Want me to send you that video, too?"

"Paige—"

"Or we can just cut out the middleman and you can watch me right now." I drag my finger down his chest, my gaze following the path down to the obvious bulge between his legs. "What do you say?"

His chest rises and falls once, twice. Then he hooks his finger around the tiny string holding my swimsuit together and rips it. The material flutters to the floor; my breasts spill loose. His breathing hitches with desire.

But still, he refuses to touch me.

"Get on the bed and spread those legs for me like a good little *kiska*."

I don't think I've ever felt this turned on in my life. I do as he says and lie back on the bed, keeping my eyes on him the entire time.

But I don't wait for further instruction. I suck on my fingers and then roll them over my nipples before sliding my palm down my torso.

Misha pulls up a chair and sits in front of me. He watches my every move with an almost clinical gaze. I don't even think he's blinking.

"Touch that tight little slit for me, princess."

His voice is guttural, primal. My swimsuit bottoms are soaked with my desire. I push them aside. The first wisp of cool air on my pussy makes me suck in a breath. I gasp again when my fingertip dances along my lip.

"Good. Go deeper. I want to see how you like it."

I run my fingers over my clit and gasp. But I want *more*. As satisfying as this feels right now, it's not nearly as satisfying as feeling him inside me would be.

"I want to see your cock."

"No," he says with finality. "Only good girls get my cock. You are anything but good. Now, lick your nipples for me."

With one hand still in my pussy, I lean forward and suck my nipple into my mouth. I flick my tongue across my nipple a few times until my neck complains. Then I let my hand take over and slump back on the pillow. I look at him—never anywhere else—through the curtain of my eyelashes, the same way I looked into the camera lens last night.

"Misha..." I whimper.

"Keep going," he commands. "Don't stop."

I don't want to get off this way again. I want more. I want him.

"I want you. Please..."

"Don't beg," he snarls. "Begging won't help. I told you already—bad girls get nothing."

"I'll be good then. I swear I'll be good."

"You haven't been so far," he says. "You don't listen."

I bite back a moan. "Then punish me. Help me be better. Teach me what you want."

He growls a low, dangerous sound. Then he stands up.

Finally. Thank God.

"Take your pants off." I'm breathless now, desperate for him.

He smirks, cold and unyielding. "You're not getting cock tonight, *kiska*."

He roughly grabs my legs and yanks me to the end of the bed. He rips my bikini bottoms off in the same possessive way he disposed of my top. Then he drops to his knees.

I don't even have time to ask before his face disappears between my thighs.

"Oh, God!"

He starts to lick my aching pussy, and just like that, fireworks explode. The music swells. Whatever sensation I was feeling moments ago has nothing on what Misha is capable of giving to me.

I am writhing like a woman possessed. I can't catch my breath and my body ripples with wave after wave of pleasure. It's so much. Too much. I'm—

"Fuck!"

Immediately, the pleasure stops.

"I thought I'd made myself clear the first time we met," he growls. Between my legs, I can see his silver eyes shining and his lips wet with my juices. "No swearing. You do that again, and I'm going to fill that filthy mouth of yours."

I lick my lips. "Do you promise?"

One corner of his lips turns up in a vicious little smirk. "Oh, you definitely need a firm hand. Such a bad girl. You need to be punished some more."

Then he dips down again. His tongue slides over my slit before disappearing into it. I have to shove my hand in my mouth to keep from screaming.

He adds two fingers, hooked inside me and searching, searching, searching, until *bam,* they find the spot that sends me over the edge. I'm bucking and crying out as the orgasm consumes me, with half-screamed *Pleases* tumbling uselessly from my lips.

But Misha doesn't stop, no matter how nicely I ask.

He keeps eating me out until, minutes later, I'm coming on his face again. This one is softer than the first, crackling as much in my fingers and toes as in the core of me. When it subsides, all the strength goes out of my muscles.

Then Misha stands up and wipes my orgasm off his face with the back of his hand.

I'm splayed out in front of him, unable to move, barely able to breathe. And still… I want more.

"Come here," I beg him. "Let me take care of you now."

His eyes trail over me hungrily, but he shakes his head. "No." He looks me over one final time and then turns for the door. "It's late, *moya zhena*. Get some sleep."

22

MISHA

The next day, my entryway is lined with boxes. I curse under my breath.

I forgot my mother was moving in today.

The plan is to head straight for my office and stay there until I have to leave again tomorrow morning. I don't want to run into my mom or the temptress I married. But when I walk into my home office, I find it's already been infiltrated.

"A little late to just be getting home, isn't it, dear?" my mother asks.

I hide my surprise at finding her here. It would only encourage her. "It's nine o'clock."

"Your wife ate dinner at seven. I could tell she missed you."

Like I need a fucking reminder.

Paige has been in my head all day. No matter what I did, I couldn't get her out of there.

The dirty video of her that is now seared into my phone's memory didn't help. Neither did the fresh image of her ripe and writhing body on my mouth last night. That one will be emblazoned in my mind for all eternity. They'll dig up my skeleton in a thousand years and find traces of it still marked on the inside of my skull.

It's the memory I'm going to replay in my head on my deathbed. Sure fire way to die happy, no matter the circumstances.

"Is there a reason you're here harassing me, Mother?"

"I want to take Paige out tomorrow."

"No."

Her forehead creases in disappointment. "She's been cooped up in this house for weeks. She's going stir-crazy."

"That might have something to do with your presence here."

She gives me a ladylike scowl. "I think you're projecting. Your wife actually likes having me around. That makes one of us."

I can't exactly deny it. Paige does have a ridiculous amount of affection for all my family members. I didn't think it was a big problem until I realized the feeling was mutual. Now, everyone is on my dick about how I treat her.

"I'm happy you two have found each other then. You'll find lots of fun activities to do—within the confines of the property."

"We'll be discreet."

"I'm not taking any chances," I snarl. "The world thinks Paige is dead right now. Which means Petyr thinks Paige is dead. I want to keep it that way."

Nessa sighs. "It's not realistic to keep this going for much longer, Misha."

She's not wrong. I thought I'd have caught Petyr by now. But the motherfucker's ongoing absence is stalling my plans more than I care for.

"She'll just have to be patient a little while longer. You all will."

My mother doesn't look happy, but for a change, she doesn't push it. She gives me a curt nod and slinks out of the office, leaving me alone with my thoughts.

Honestly, I'd prefer her company over my own.

I'm desperate to go upstairs and take a shower in my own bathroom, to wash off the stink of today. But I don't want to risk running into Paige.

The woman has decided to play dirty. It came way too close to working last night. Almost twenty-four hours later and I still can't stop thinking about her.

"A Paige moratorium it is," I mutter, stepping into the bathroom adjoining my office.

It's spacious, but not nearly as luxurious as the one upstairs. And not nearly as filled with one specific naked woman as I'd like it to be.

I crank the shower faucet on as cold as it will allow and force myself underneath the flow. I'm washing the soap from my tense body when I hear the door open. I see a flash of dark hair through the steamed glass. It's enough to make my cock jump in misplaced hope.

Then Paige slides the glass door open, nervous green eyes taking me in. *All of me.*

"What are you doing here?" I rasp.

"I need to talk to you. I figured I'd catch you before you ran away again."

Ah. So my avoidance technique hasn't gone unnoticed. The sexy white dress she's wearing tells me she's not about to let me get away with it.

The top three buttons of the simple cotton dress are undone, and it doesn't exactly take Sherlock fucking Holmes to see that she isn't wearing a bra. Her skin is smooth and flawless, way more tempting than it has any right to be.

"This is not a good time, Paige."

"I think this is the best time actually." She looks supremely unconcerned as she steps into the shower doorway, blocking my path out. "I have your undivided attention."

"If this is about leaving the house tomorrow with my mother, I already told her the answer is no."

I don't care if she strips down and gives me a lap dance, I'm not budging on that.

Of course, at the thought of her doing that, my cock springs to life. It likes the idea a little too much, but it's the wrong place and wrong time for that. Paige can see exactly what she does to me.

"So you're going to keep me trapped here for… God knows how long?" she snaps.

"This is about your safety," I retort. "And the safety of our children."

She moves closer. The spray from the shower is dotting the material of her dress. The moment she steps fully into the shower, it'll turn transparent.

I really need to stop imagining how it'll look if and when she does.

"I could wear a disguise," she suggests. "A wig, big sunglasses, the whole nine yards. Would you like that?"

I cringe at the very thought. "No."

She raises her eyebrows. "No?"

"What I mean is I'm not willing to take the risk," I say firmly, although that's extremely not what I meant. "Until I've got Petyr locked down, you're safest inside these walls."

She presses her lips together, thinking. Plotting. Scheming. "How about a compromise?"

"I don't do compromises."

"Tell me something I don't know." She rolls her eyes. "But hear me out: I'll stay inside like a good little girl… if you give me back my phone."

"Paige—"

"Why not? The only person I actually talk to outside this house is Rowan."

"Which means she's going to be your first call the moment you get your phone back."

Champagne Wrath

"What if I promise not to contact her?" she asks. I hesitate, and Paige sees her opening. She steps right into the shower with me. "Are you saying you don't trust me, Misha?"

I ignore that. "You're getting wet."

"I'm already wet," she purrs suggestively.

I sigh, and Paige glances down. Her eyes widen at my erection before she looks back up to my face. "Why are you fighting me so hard? It's clear we want the same thing."

I shake my head. "I very much doubt that."

She sighs in frustration. "I'm not an idiot, Misha. I can recognize an excuse from a mile away. I've heard more than enough of them my entire life. So tell me what you're really scared of." Before I can stop her, she wraps her hand around my cock. "Are you worried I might force you to *feel* something?"

I swallow down a groan as she strokes her fingertips gently down my throbbing length.

"You don't want to hurt me," she continues. "You want me to recover. Fair enough. So just stand still. Let me take what I want."

Then she drops to her knees right in the middle of my shower and slips my cock into her mouth.

The moment her full lips engulf me, I know there's no way I'm stopping this. I'm not sure it's even physically possible to pry myself loose from her.

So I do the only thing I can do: I lean against the wet bathroom tile for support as she sucks me deep. Instinctively, my hips start to move to the rhythm.

No. I cannot fuck her face. Because that will make me want to—

I stand as still as I can, but she grips my hips and sucks me faster, harder. Her head is bobbing up and down my cock, and I can feel the orgasm building fast.

"*Blyat'*," I moan and pound my fist against the wall. I'm surprised the tiles don't shatter.

At the sound of my growled curse, Paige unlocks a new level of intensity. She swallows me down even deeper, and there isn't time to warn her before I come right into her throat.

She takes it in.

Every.

Last.

Drop.

I empty my fucking soul into her. When I'm finally finished, she pulls away, gasping greedily for air. Her dress is plastered to her body and her hair is soaked. She looks up at me, her lips swollen and eyes watering.

It's the sexiest thing I've ever seen.

She doesn't seem to be in a hurry to get off her knees, so I grab her and pull her up to her feet.

"What are you trying to do?" I demand. "Destroy me?"

"I'm not trying to destroy you." Her fingers tenderly stroke my cheek. "I'm trying to save you."

"I don't need saving, Paige."

She takes me off-guard by leaning in and kissing me on the cheek. It lasts longer than it ought to. Long enough that I feel that innocent kiss spread through my body like an elixir.

Then she leaves, trailing water as she goes. Her dress clings to her hips like a second skin.

When I manage to get out of the shower on wobbly legs, my cock is already eager for round two.

Paige, more than any enemy I've ever faced, is forcing me to reckon with the one truth I've tried hardest to avoid since becoming don.

I'm only human.

23

PAIGE

"He's never going to come home again." I bury my face into the couch cushion to hide my embarrassment.

Cyrille chuckles. "Don't be a drama queen. He'll come home."

"Every time he does, I jump his bones. I'm like a sex-craved predator."

I've already given Cyrille the PG version of me walking in on Misha in the shower last night. It seemed like such a good idea at the time. Now, I'm worried I might have played my last card. Where do I go from here?

"He's your husband! It's not like you're some perv in a trench coat, approaching him in a dark alley," she says. "He could say no if that's what he chose."

I shrug. "Yeah. I know. And I know he wants me, too. I could… I could tell."

"The erection was a little bit of a giveaway, was it?" I throw a pillow at her, and she laughs. "Sorry. Misha is stubborn. You just need to wear him down."

"I'm trying! Every time I think I'm making progress, he walks away. The man has superhuman willpower."

"No one has superhuman anything. Especially not Misha. He used to go through like five bags of Doritos whenever we had movie nights."

I can't help giggling. "I'm not sure what to unpack first: the fact that Misha likes Doritos or the fact that you used to have movie nights."

"All the time. Back when life was... normal." Her smile falters, and I take her hand. "It's so weird. There are days when I get through a full hour without thinking about it. I laugh and smile. Then I turn a corner and see a painting Maksim bought or a snack he loved and it brings it all back." Then her smile brightens back up. "Doritos, though—those were all Misha. Everyone knew better than to get between that man and his chips. You'd lose a finger."

I nod. "I used to walk a half a mile out of my way just so I could avoid seeing Clara's parents' trailer. I still hate that shade of green. You never stop missing them, but I suppose you just get used to not having them around. Which, to be fair, sometimes feels preferable to having someone around and *still* missing them."

Cyrille rests her head sympathetically on my shoulder. "Hey now! It's too early to give up."

"I know, I know, you're right. He actually gave me my phone back last night. So that's a win."

"He did not!"

I nod. "He didn't make the delivery himself, obviously. He had Rada hand it over. Such menial tasks are beneath Don Orlov's station."

She grins and nudges me with an elbow. "All hail the Golden One. Still, it's a big gesture, especially given how controlling Misha can be. It shows he wants to make you happy. You just—"

I gasp mid-sentence, jerking upright as a shooting pain sears through my side. "Ow."

"What was that?" Cyrille asks. "Are you okay?"

I take a deep breath. "Um, I'm not sure. I just felt—oh God, shit...!"

Tears of pain prick at the corners of my eyes as I lean forward, trying to find a comfortable position. Everything hurts, like there's a hot sun burning me from the inside out.

"Paige? Paige, honey, talk to me!"

"Something really hurts," I manage to choke out. "C-can you call Dr. Mathers?"

Cyrille rushes out of the room, and I try to stay calm. But I replay everything I've done in the last twenty-four hours. Did I run too hard? Maybe the swimming was too much exertion.

Are my babies okay?

Are my babies okay?

I'm close to a full-on meltdown when Cyrille rushes back into the room. "Stay put and try to breathe, hon. Simone is on her way."

I hold my stomach as though I have the power to heal whatever is happening right now. "That hurts so bad, Cy. It almost feels like I'm going into labor. But that's not possible. Right?"

Cyrille frowns. "It could just be false labor. Hurts like a bitch, but it's normal. Let's just stay calm until Simone gets here, okay?"

I wince in pain and nod. Words are beyond me as the next wave of pain crashes down hard.

"Don't worry," Cyrille says, grabbing my hand. "I'm right here."

I give her a shaky smile. I am glad that she's with me. I couldn't be more grateful for her support. But there are moments when you just need your husband.

This is one of them.

∼

"Are you sure?" I ask for the tenth time. I'm still clutching my pendant like prayer beads. I haven't let go of it since Dr. Mathers arrived.

Dr. Mathers nods. "I'm positive. Braxton Hicks is perfectly normal. It's just your body preparing itself for the birth."

"But I'm still months away from having these babies."

"True, but stress can sometimes aggravate your body. You've been through a lot recently."

I breathe slowly. "You can say that again."

Before I can ask Dr. Mathers my follow-up questions, the door bursts open and the monster himself storms in. He's dressed for the office in dark slacks and an ivory-colored button down, but the tornado in his eyes looks ready for war.

"Where is she?" he barks, spinning around the room.

I raise my hand. "Right here."

As soon as he spots me, he races over. "What happened? Cyrille told me you were having pain."

I shoot a glare at that traitor, Cyrille, who winks in return. "I was, but I'm fine now."

"What do you mean?" Before I can answer him, he turns to Dr. Mathers. "What was it?"

"Braxton Hicks contractions. Completely standard. Painful but harmless. Both Paige and the babies are doing fine. Everyone's healthy."

"You're sure of that?" Misha asks. "Absolutely certain?"

"She needs a stress-free environment," Dr. Mathers says. "But yes, she's fine. So fine, in fact, that I'm going to pack up and head off."

Misha's jaw ticks with the tension rippling through him. He walks Dr. Mathers to the door, murmuring to her under his breath all the while. Cyrille gives me a reassuring smile before she departs, too.

Once we're alone, Misha stays close to the door. He doesn't turn to me right away, and I wonder if he's going to make a run for it.

"Planning your escape route?" I ask bluntly.

He sighs and turns to me. "Are you okay?"

"I'd be better if I knew you weren't going to run for the hills the moment I say I'm fine."

"I'd be better if I knew you and my children weren't going to —That you're fine." He drags a hand through his hair, and I can see how scared he really is.

"You heard the doctor. I'm fine. So are the babies."

Nothing I say seems to be connecting, though. He looks at me, but there's a thread of uncertainty that I can't quite understand.

"Misha," I say softly, "talk to me. What's going on with you?"

He gestures to the bed. "Come on. Let's get you back to bed. You want anything to eat? Drink?"

I feel my hopes dwindle. "I have a maid and a chef, Misha. You know that."

I ignore the bed and go for the window seat instead. I curl my legs underneath me and stare unseeingly out the window. I expect him to slip out of the room and leave me to brood, but then I feel him standing behind me.

I turn around, eyebrow raised, waiting for whatever is coming next.

"You can ask me for something right now, and I won't deny you." His face is neutral, but his eyes burn. After the last few days, I know what he thinks I'm going to ask for.

"Anything?"

"Within reason," he adds on quickly.

"Okay. I'll keep it simple then." I lift my chin and face him head-on. "I want you to take me out on a date."

He blinks. "A date?"

I nod. "We don't even have to leave the house. But you have to make it feel like a real date."

He considers it for a moment and then exhales slowly. "I'll pick you up tomorrow at eight."

I'm happy, but he seems distracted by something on the table in front of me. I glance over and see that he's looking at my phone.

"I haven't texted Rowan," I tell him before he can ask. "I promise."

"You don't have to promise. I know."

I frown. "Have you had my phone tapped or something?"

He almost smiles before he kills it at the last second. "No. I just decided to trust you."

24

MISHA

"Hey, I picked those paint samples you asked for," Nikita practically yells, waving the options in my face.

I glance up at the staircase with a wince. "Fucking hell, will you lower your voice?"

She shrugs, unapologetic. "Paige is still in bed. She doesn't eat breakfast until at least nine o'clock. That's when her nausea subsides. As her husband, you should know that."

As Paige's husband, there are lots of things I should know that I don't. Nikita doesn't need to be rubbing that in my face, though.

"Unless you're not sleeping in the same room as her...?" she continues. "Are you still sleeping in your office?"

"I have a lot of work to do."

She rolls her eyes. "You're pathetic."

"Why are you here?" I try to coax her towards the front door, but she dodges me and scampers further within.

"Because you asked me to do you a favor, remember?"

"Only because I thought you'd be less annoying about it than Mother or Cyrille. Turns out I was wrong."

She doesn't seem in the least bit offended by that. "Personally, I like the green. But the—"

I pluck the samples out of her hand and flip through them one by one. When I look up, I realize that Niki is smiling at me.

"What?"

She shakes her head. "Nothing. It's just that you can still surprise me sometimes."

I roll my eyes at her. "Spare me. I've got shit to do."

"Any of that 'shit' involve preparing for the big date tonight?"

"She told you?" I groan.

Nikita looks far too smug about it for my liking. "Obviously. We're besties now."

"There was a time when you weren't sure of Paige. Remember that? Wasn't it nice?"

Nikita shrugs it off. "I was just protective of you. I wasn't sure of Paige's intentions. But I've since come to realize that Paige is far too good for you. Now, *you're* the one I'm not sure about."

"Thanks for the vote of confidence."

"Please—you don't need anyone else to boost your ego. What you need is someone to keep you humble," she says, dancing towards the staircase.

"What is with you today?" I ask. "You seem to be in a suspiciously good mood."

She laughs. "Turns out having a whole mansion to myself feels pretty good. With Mom living here now, I'm the woman of the house. It's a nice change of pace."

"You know that Mother is not living here permanently right? This is temporary. Just until the babies are born."

"Yeah, you wish," she snorts. "Once those babies are born, you'll *never* get rid of her."

"Don't joke about that."

Niki just laughs. "I know Mom will move back eventually. By the time that happens, maybe I won't be living there anymore."

She lifts her chin, annoyed that I didn't even think of that possibility. Truthfully, I didn't.

"How long have you been thinking about leaving?" I ask her quietly.

"Long enough," she says. "I'm twenty-seven, Misha. It's time. I need to figure out my own path. You and Maksim knew what you were gonna be from day one. But me? All anyone expected from me was to marry well. I want more for myself."

"Good. You should."

She leans in, her voice low. "FYI, most women want more for themselves than a powerful husband."

It's not hard to guess who she's talking about or what she's trying to get me to understand. I wave her away. "Make sure Paige doesn't see you with those samples."

"Aye, aye, captain." She gives me a dramatic salute and disappears down the hallway.

~

It strikes me as I mount the stairs that I haven't been on very many dates in my life.

There were always women, of course. But they came and went like ships in the night. I met them in clubs, parties, on yachts and private planes. They were always well-spoken and well-dressed, each one vying to make an impression.

But in the end, I barely paid attention to what they said. I was only ever interested in getting them in my bed. And the moment the fucking was over, I lost interest in them completely.

Which is why I always assumed the same thing would happen with Paige, too. That the interest would wither and wane. I'm still floored that it hadn't. That it *still* hasn't…

I put on the three-piece suit that I picked specifically for this occasion. It might be overkill, but fuck it, Paige wanted a date. She is going to get a *date*.

Once I've spritzed myself with cologne and aftershave, I grab the single long-stemmed rose that I'd had Mario bring in from the garden and take the stairs to pick my wife up for our date.

Outside of her door, I straighten my jacket and then knock twice.

Seconds pass with no answer, so I try again.

"Misha?" she calls from within. "The door is open. You can come in. I'm almost ready."

I hesitate, unsure if I want to wait and come back or what. But then the door opens.

And my God, she is a fucking vision.

Paige is standing in the center of the room in a stunning silver dress, one high-heeled shoe in her hand and the other on the carpet next to her bare feet. Her hair tumbles gracefully down her back in a mocha waterfall. Her skin glows, her lips beckon. Every curve is a fucking poem.

She looks down at the shoe in her hand. "I was having trouble deciding which shoes to wear. Is it eight o'clock already?"

"Don't worry. I'm sure they'll hold the table for us."

She giggles, then bites her lip and waves me into the room. But I stop on the threshold. The last thing I need is for my willpower to buckle before we can make it to dinner. The more distance between us, the safer we are.

She must sense that hesitation, because her smile fades. She sits down on the end of the bed and starts to fasten one shoe in place. But the buckle is stiff and her nails are giving her trouble. I watch her fumble with the straps for a moment before I can't take it anymore.

Striding forward, I kneel at her feet and snatch the shoe from her hands. I place her palms flat on the bed at her sides, lingering there just for a moment so she understands that she is not to move them until I give her permission.

Then, holding my breath deep in my chest, I pull the shoe back on her foot. Her calf is smooth and supple beneath my fingertips, and so, so warm. Her fragrance makes my head swim. I latch one shoe, then take the other from the floor behind me and do the same.

When I'm done, I let my hands fall to my lap. Only then do I breathe at last.

This was stupid. Keeping my distance was the better idea.

I back away as she swallows and stands. "Okay," she announces a moment later. "Now, I'm ready."

∽

I try and fail to get my head out of the gutter as we make our way down the stairs. But all I can think about is Paige. Paige's ankle in my hands. Paige's perfume in my nose. Paige's lips on my—

No.

She turns for the front foyer, but I stop her and point in the direction of the French doors at the rear. Her doubt turns to delight as we take the garden path towards the greenhouse.

When she sees it, she stops cold. "Oh my God!"

I had half the staff toiling on our little date night venue all day today. Mario and Danica spent most of the afternoon stringing fairy lights through the greenhouse rafters. The whole thing glows like it has a night sky of its own trapped beneath its glass roof, shining out to match the one above. Green and gold as far as the eye can see, bejeweled for us and us alone.

Paige clutches the single rose to her chest. "It's magical."

"We aren't even inside yet." I take her hand and lead her into the greenhouse.

A table and two chairs have been arranged under a canopy of lush greenery. Candlelight flickers off the glass panes.

"I can't believe you did all this," Paige breathes.

"When I do something, I don't do it halfway."

I pull a chair out for her and sit across from her. Our knees brush under the table, and she gives me a shy smile.

When she notices the menu on the edge of the table, she picks it up with trembling fingers. I watch, knowing what she's reading as her eyes flick down the page and her lips slowly part.

Caviar and lobster.

Fragrant greens with black truffle.

Lemony, butter-rich risotto and pan-seared scallops still dripping ocean water.

When she finally looks up at me, I realize that her eyes are watery.

"I... I just... I didn't expect all this, Misha. No one's ever made this kind of effort for me. Whether I asked for it or not."

How could anyone not make an effort for this woman? She's fucking flawless.

Sitting in the presence of her grace and beauty, I realize something: treating her right doesn't feel like it takes any effort at all.

25

PAIGE

Misha in a suit is a sight to behold.

When I made my demand for a date, I expected him to drag his feet through every aspect of it. I expected a generic dinner, maybe a movie if I really pushed my luck. But a three-piece suit, personalized five-course meal, and hundreds upon hundreds of fairy lights threaded through the rafters overhead? It's beyond my wildest imagination.

And the craziest thing of all is, I think Misha might actually be enjoying himself.

I lean back in my chair and sip my sparkling grape juice. My stomach is painfully full with five courses of deliciousness, but my taste buds are still buzzing pleasantly. "This may be the best date I've ever been on."

"Good. I've never done this before, so I'm glad it worked out."

"You've never planned a date like this before?"

He shakes his head. "I've never been on any kind of a date before."

I nearly drop my glass. "That's… that's not possible."

"I'm not really the dating type."

"Oh." I nod in slow understanding. "You didn't date, but you still…"

"I wasn't celibate, if that's what your eyebrows are insinuating."

Obviously, a man like Misha isn't a virgin. Still, a twinge of jealousy twists in my stomach. "So what did you do after the night was over? Kick them out of your bed?"

"They knew what they were getting into before they climbed into my bed in the first place," he says unremorsefully. "I didn't lie to any of those women. I wanted sex; I had no use for conversation. That didn't stop a lot of them from trying to change my mind."

I can't help but wonder if he's referring to our situation. Misha laid out clearly what our relationship would be: a business deal, nothing more. Now, here I am trying to change his mind.

Guess I'm just like the rest.

"They thought they could convince you that they were the exception?"

"They thought that if they could coax me into a conversation that I'd let them spend the night. And if they spent the night, maybe I'd ask them on another date. That second date might turn into a third and, eventually, I'd be so in love that I'd want to keep them around forever."

"It never worked?"

A second ago, I was jealous of these unknown women. Now, I'm suddenly rooting for one of them to have left a mark on Misha. If even one woman made a lasting impression, maybe I have a chance.

"No. I know what I want. I've always been up front about that."

Never mind. Whatever hope I was trying to drum up washes away in the face of Misha's cold reality.

"That's true," I say softly. "Like when you told me that you could be a husband to me in name only. Yet I still convinced myself that maybe, just maybe, I could convince you to fall in love with me."

I didn't intend to say all that out loud. But there it is. I'm just like all the other women who have come before me.

He sighs. "Paige…"

"It was nice of you to do all this." I fold my napkin and place it on the table. "You've been a true gentleman."

"Did you have a good time?"

"Yes." I bob my head back and forth, trying and failing to keep the truth inside. "And no."

He frowns. "Explain."

I don't want to get into this, but I'm powerless against his command. Even after everything, I want to give Misha whatever he wants.

"Tonight has been perfect. All of it. The food, the lights, the setting…"

"But?" he prods.

"But… you were forced into it." I sigh. "It's hard to enjoy when I know you're only here because I made you."

"I wasn't forced into anything, Paige."

I shake my head. "There's no need to pretend, Misha. You're right: you never lied to me. You told me exactly what you were willing and able to give me. I was the one who chose not to believe you. I convinced myself that if we had one more conversation or one more night together, if we slept together and it was more than just sex, maybe then I could convince you to take a real chance on this marriage."

I'm a head-to-toe blush, but I press on. I might as well lay it all out there now.

"I was so mad at you before the explosion. I convinced myself that loving you was not worth it. Then I almost died, and I guess it… it made me want to embrace life. It made me want to live to the fullest, the way I promised Clara I always would." I smile sadly. "The explosion meant something different for you, though. It made you realize how much you stood to lose if you let yourself care."

He's unnervingly silent as he stares at me, his expression reserved and unreadable.

"It's funny, really. The timing. We never seem to be on the same page, do we? We keep zigging when the other one zags." Misha still hasn't moved, so I drain the last of my sparkling juice. "Dinner was wonderful, but I don't think we should repeat it. No matter how strongly I feel, I can't make you feel something you don't. It will only hurt both of us more if I keep trying."

I stand up and smooth down the silver material of my dress. It's clingy and uncomfortable, but I knew Misha would like it.

I made myself uncomfortable for him without even considering what I wanted.

I'll have to unlearn that.

I stop at the edge of the table. "Can I ask you for just one more favor before I go?" He still hasn't said a word, so I continue on. "I haven't contacted Rowan yet, but I want to. She's my friend, Misha. Konstantin told me that she's called in sick every day since the news broke that I was dead. I can't let her continue to think that. Not when I know what it feels like to get that kind of call."

His eyes focus on me. It feels like I might turn to ash in the intensity of his gaze.

"You can tell her."

I sigh. "Thank you." I start to turn and then stop. "By the way, you look really handsome tonight."

Then I walk out of the greenhouse on my own.

26

MISHA

Paige cut across the lawn towards the south garden twenty minutes ago.

And I've spent every single one of those minutes trying to convince myself not to follow her.

I've been hoping she would give up on me. I wanted her to accept the reality of our lives and move on from this naïve dream that we can ride off into the sunset together.

So if I've finally gotten what I wanted, why does this feel so much like losing?

Eventually, I leave the greenhouse. Even as I swear I'm not looking for her, I scan the grounds for any sign of her.

Is she back in the house now, barricaded in her room, cursing the day she met me?

Then I hear a sniffle.

I turn towards a corner of the garden I've avoided for so long now. Since the day after Maksim's funeral.

Paige is sitting on the white bench I had installed in his memory, gazing up at the stars through a thickly woven canopy of ivy vines. She's so intent that she doesn't notice me until I'm standing next to her.

She jumps when she sees me. "I didn't even hear you." She tries to discreetly wipe her eyes, but they are swollen and puffy. She has been crying. "I thought you'd be back in your office by now."

I sit down next to her. "Do you come to this part of the garden often?"

"In the evenings, sometimes. It's such a beautiful little spot."

"This was Maksim's favorite spot." Paige looks over at me, and I continue. "This was his house before I inherited it." I twist at the wedding band on my finger. "There are days when it feels like I see him everywhere."

She nods in understanding. "That's one of the reasons I left Corden Park as fast as I did. I saw Clara everywhere. It got to be too much." She runs her hands over the white paint of the bench. "It's a nice tribute, though."

"He commissioned it himself before he died," I admit. "It arrived a few days after the funeral. I tried to send it back, but they told me they wouldn't accept it. Then I thought about smashing it to pieces and burning what was left. In the end, I didn't; I put it here. It felt right. Out of sight, so I wouldn't have to see it every day. But not gone. Never gone."

Her breath, low and raspy, is all I hear. "I think you owe it to him to try and forgive yourself, Misha."

"What would I be without my guilt?" I ask, only half-teasing.

"What's left without it?" she fires back.

I think of the Babai and their questions. I give her the same one-word response I gave them. "Revenge."

She wrinkles up her nose. "I'm not sure revenge really makes a difference, Misha. In fact, I know it doesn't. Because there was a time when I thought revenge was what I needed to sleep better at night."

"Who did you want revenge on?"

"Moses," she sighs. "I blamed him for Clara's death. I was sure he was the one responsible for it. I wanted him to pay." She glances down at her lap, then back up to me. "I went to see him a few days after Clara's funeral. Asked him to tell me what happened. He spun me some wild, stupid story that I refused to believe. I cursed at him, told him to go to hell, and left. But not before I planted a whole bunch of drugs in his apartment."

I look at her with new eyes. "You did not."

"I did. And the moment I left, I called the cops and left an anonymous tip." She stops for a moment. "I wouldn't blame you for judging me. It was awful what I did."

"What you did was fucking justice. He ended up where he belonged for what he did."

She shakes her head, getting emotional. "That's the thing, Misha… He didn't kill her."

I frown. "What makes you say that?"

"When I went to see him, he told me that if he had wanted to kill her, he would have done it when she asked him to."

The puzzle pieces of their friendship start coming together slowly in my head. Clara was Paige's family. Her closest friend and confidant. But she was not a happy kid. She was deeply troubled, deeply depressed.

Suicidal.

"He claimed that she stole his knife. He said it wasn't a murder. It was… It was…" She wipes away her tears. "I think I believed him that day. Deep down. I just wasn't willing to admit it to myself yet. Either way, his weapon was the one she used to kill herself. I felt it was still his fault." She shakes her head. "They charged him with possession and dealing, all of it. He went to jail for a long time. As far as I know, he's still there. But I can't bring myself to check."

"Don't tell me you feel bad about what you did."

"It doesn't matter what I feel about him," she says, meeting my eyes. "Getting revenge didn't make me feel any better about Clara. She was still gone; I was still alone. You think you're going to take care of Petyr and then you'll be free to live your life. If you're not living it now, then getting revenge is not going to change anything. That's all I'm trying to say."

Her words hang in the air between us. Insects sing into the night. The wind swirls between the trees.

It really is a beautiful spot.

"Maybe I… I stopped living after Maksim died."

"That's only because you think it should have been you," she offers gently.

I shiver. This woman *gets* me. It's terrifying.

"You're the first girl I've ever wanted to take on a second date," I hear myself say.

She shakes her head. "You don't have to tell me things like that just to make me feel better."

"I'm being serious."

"No, you're not. And it's fine," she says. "I won't send you any more videos. I won't barge into your shower. I won't dress up in stupid lingerie and embarrass myself for the sake of your attention. I'm done with that."

She was right about the two of us having bad timing. When one of us is hot, the other is cold. Without fail.

"That's the thing, Paige. I thought I'd be happy to hear you say that. But I'm not."

She stares at me, eyebrows knit together. She's dubious, and she has every reason to be.

I stand up and offer her my hand. "Come with me."

"Where?"

I smile. "You'll see."

She eyes me suspiciously, but after a second, she slips her fingers into my hand and lets me pull her to her feet.

I have no clue what I'm feeling or what I'm doing. But I do know that we can't continue on like this. Forever fighting, living in an endless push and pull, a tug of war that's wearing us both down to the bone.

So I'm going to make a decision.

I just have to hope I'm not a fool for daring to believe I can have it all.

27

PAIGE

The house is eerily silent. I assume Misha is taking me back to my room, but he passes right by it. Instead, he stops at the room next to mine.

He gestures to the ornate brass doorknob. "Go on."

"Nothing is going to jump out at me, right?"

He smiles. "Trust me."

And, because he asks, I do. I swallow my nerves and turn the knob.

The space is large and it takes me a second to get my bearings. To understand what I'm looking at. Then the details click together one at a time, a beautiful puzzle.

The massive bay window with the plush window seat. A rocking chair. Two side by side cribs in the middle of the room.

"A nursery."

I walk to the plush rocking horse in the corner like I'm meandering through a dream. That's what this place is. *A dream.*

"It's not finished, obviously," Misha explains. "I wanted you to be able to have a say in the decor, too."

The white armoire on the back wall is mostly empty, but there are sets of swaddle cloths and baby blankets folded on the top shelf. On the bottom one, I see colored, patterned squares arranged in a neat row.

"Wallpaper?"

"I had Niki pick them up. You can choose whichever one you want."

"Has she been helping you out with this?"

"Unfortunately." He sighs. "But as much as she irritates me, she is good at this kind of stuff. If we want any help, she'd love to volunteer."

Emotion burns in my throat. I turn to him, eyes brimming. "This is… Misha, this is amazing. Everything in here is so beautiful. I can't believe it. My babies are going to live here. In a few months."

"Feels surreal, doesn't it?"

"Completely," I agree.

Somehow, we've drifted together. He's only a few feet away now. Close enough that I can feel the heat building between us. The same heat that's been burning there from the start.

"Thank you for giving me a say."

He nods. "Of course. You're their mother."

"Sure, but I thought that counted for less in your world." He frowns, and I feel like a bitch. "Sorry," I add quickly. "That was unnecessary. Here you are, doing something nice for me and—"

"You don't have to apologize, Paige. That's exactly how I made you feel in the beginning. I'm the one who should be apologizing."

I stare at him in surprise.

"It seems I have a lot to apologize for," he continues.

The vulnerability in his voice has that pesky hope standing back up, ready to try again. It's been battered and bloodied, but it hasn't been killed.

Not yet.

I tilt my head to look at him from a new angle. "Why did you bring me here, Misha?"

He cracks his knuckles frustratedly. "As you can probably tell, I'm not good at talking about how I feel. Or admitting when I'm wrong. I figured maybe this gesture would say all the things that I can't bring myself to."

"Like?"

His silver eyes meet mine. "Like that I was wrong, Paige. I thought that a loveless marriage would spare us both heartache. But in the end, it's been the cause of it."

I'm barely breathing. "What are you trying to say, Misha?"

He edges forward and takes my hand. He holds it in both of his, running a finger up and down my palm. I get chills from head to toe. "I didn't think things would get this complicated."

"You didn't think you'd develop feelings for me, you mean?"

He smiles. "See? That's what attracted me to you in the first place. You call it like you see it. You're not trying to be anything you're not."

"That's not entirely true. I want to be the kind of wife you need me to be, Misha," I whisper. "And I try at that every day."

"You don't have to try. You deserve so much better than you've gotten out of the world. You deserve better than Anthony. And you deserve better than me."

My eyes go wide as he tightens his grip on my hand and pulls me flush against his body. "Misha, what are you saying?"

"I'm sorry I made you feel like you were not worthy of me, *kiska*. I'm sorry I forced you into a loveless marriage. But I'm most sorry for making you think that I didn't care. Because the truth is, I love you, Paige Orlov." He brings my hands to his lips, pressing a kiss to my knuckle. "I'm sorry I took so long to say it."

28

MISHA

There's no going back now.

Paige stares up at me, caught between disbelief and hope. "Misha…"

"I know I've said a lot of stupid shit in the last few weeks," I say. "But starting now, I'm going to be honest."

"I'm not sure what's happening right now. If you're messing with me, it's cruel."

"I'm not messing with you, Paige."

She shakes her head. "But what's changed? You've been pushing me away since the explosion. So why this? Why now? *What changed?*"

"Everything and nothing," I explain. "I just realized that fighting my feelings for you would be infinitely harder than getting over my fear of losing you."

"And that's why you were keeping me at arm's length all this time? You were afraid to lose me?"

I nod. "It wasn't because I didn't want you, Paige. I've always wanted you."

"Even though we don't make any sense?"

I raise my eyebrows. "You don't think we make sense?"

"Come on, Misha. Look at the other women in your life. They're all educated and cultured and glamorous. I'm the ugly duckling in a pond full of swans."

"You are not ugly," I growl.

"You know what I mean."

"Actually, I don't. I don't know where you get the impression that you're inferior. It's easy to be cultured and glamorous when you have a headstart in life. What's more impressive is to achieve those things when you have to work at it all by yourself."

She's breathing heavily. I can see in her eyes that she doesn't fully believe me yet.

But she will.

I'll show her until there's no denying the truth of it.

"I said some really awful things to you in the hospital room that day—"

She holds up a hand to stop me. "Don't."

"No," I insist. "You need to hear this. I didn't say any of those things because I believed them. I just wanted to hurt you. I wanted to hurt you the way I thought you had hurt me."

"You really believed I was conspiring with Anthony to bring you down?"

"At the time, yes."

"You should have known better."

"I should have," I agree. "But the thing is, I couldn't trust my instincts around you because my feelings were getting in the way of every decision I made. I assumed you had hoodwinked me. I couldn't see it because I was so—"

I stop short, still held back by the power of those words. Saying it once doesn't make it easier to say again.

"You were in love with me," she says softly, putting her palm against my beating heart.

"Yes."

She places her forehead against my chest and stays there for the longest time. Finally, she lifts her head and looks into my eyes. "How do I know you're not going to freak out on me again?"

"I can't promise you that I won't," I admit. "This is the first time I've ever felt this way about a woman. I'm pretty sure it will be my last, too. So you'll have to forgive me while I work out the kinks."

She smiles, but it's reserved. She wants to dive in head-first, but she's cautious.

"I know this will be trial and error for a while, Misha," she says. "But we can't escape the fact that we have two children on the way. Whatever our issues are, we can't let it affect them. I want them to grow up in a healthy environment. I want them to be happy and safe and loved. I want them to have what I never did."

"I know. I want that, too."

"Well, it's up to us then. We're the grown-ups."

I take both her hands and kiss her knuckles one by one. "You're going to be a fantastic mother."

She shakes her head self-consciously. "I have no idea what kind of mother I'll be. It's not like I have a blueprint to follow."

"You don't need one. Some things are instinct, Paige. You let your heart lead you. That's what counts."

She nods, but I can see how nervous she is. How much the pressure of motherhood weighs on her. I lean in to kiss her cheek, but she turns her face and I catch her lips instead.

We hold that chaste, soft kiss between us, letting it change the fabric of our relationship. It's not about power or control. It's not about anger or submission.

This kiss is the start of something new.

29

PAIGE

He takes his time undressing me. Like each layer of clothing removed is a chance to memorize my body in a fresh light. He roams over my body slowly, taking it all in. His eyes never waver and his pace never quickens.

The only thing he doesn't take off is my pendant. He strokes his hand down the chain, rubbing the worn metal of the charm with his thumb before he moves to my panties.

"Should we be doing this in the nursery?" I ask with a teasing smirk as he pushes me backwards on the window seat.

"It's not a nursery yet." His lips whisper over my skin. "That won't happen until the babies come. And we have a lot of time before that happens. Time we should spend wisely."

The bay windows don't have curtains. If anyone were to look up right now, they'd see the man and woman of the house going at it like horny rabbits. But I'm not concerned with that right now, and apparently, neither is Misha.

He steps back and pulls his shirt over his head, and just like that, all my arguments die on my lips.

I marvel at the way his muscles ripple in the moonlight. The way his body flexes with every movement. All the while, he's watching me with the same intensity, growing more lustful with each passing second. We're both burning up from within.

When he is naked, I wrap my hand around his dog tag and use it to pull him towards me.

His weight presses between my thighs for a second, but then he pulls back. "I don't want to hurt you."

"You're not hurting me," I insist. "Trust me. Come here."

His eyes flicker down to my belly. My bump is more and more noticeable every day, but still small. Barely an intrusion.

Right now, I'm so wet that nothing could get in the way.

"Misha, I want you."

Desire pools in his silver eyes. Watching him get turned on is more than enough to do the same for me.

"I want you, too."

I know he does. I can feel his cock between my thighs. But he doesn't sink into me like I want him to.

I grab his hips and try to pull him closer. "You're killing me…"

He chuckles and runs his hand from my breasts down to my stomach. "Your body has been through a lot lately, Paige. I don't want to—"

"You're picking *now* to start overthinking? Just fuck me, Misha."

His eyebrows rise. But he still stands resolutely still.

"Oh, I forgot." I run my nails down his chest and over those granite abs. "You don't like when I use that word, do you?"

Something sparks in his eyes. One finger twitches against my thigh.

"Well, then I guess you have to punish me." I thrust my hips towards his erection.

Suddenly, he grabs both my hands and pins them to my sides. I gasp, pure excitement pooling between my legs. He just stares down at me, his silver eyes even more striking in the moonlight.

"No. No punishment today," he says softly. "I have something else in mind."

Then he rolls me to the side and settles in behind me.

His hands come around to palm my breasts. He teases my nipples, turning this into the most erotic spooning I've ever experienced. With a deep breath, he enters me slowly from behind.

He's moving so gently and deliberately, exhibiting a kind of restraint I don't possess. I try to arch back to take more of him in, but Misha keeps a firm hold on my hip.

"Relax," he whispers in my ear. "Let me take care of you."

I reach back and wrap my hand around his neck. I hold onto him as he rocks his body into mine.

It's slow and sensual, and my body is thrumming with warmth and need. Still, I'm not prepared for the way my body responds when he strokes my clit.

I moan and roll my hips against his hand, grinding myself into his hand and back onto his cock. Even Misha can't seem to bite back his emotions.

"Good girl," he growls. "Like that."

My hips buck harder and faster, keeping feverish pace with his fingers. He doesn't let up until my body is so sensitive that I can feel every single movement of his hands on my skin, every wisp of breath. His fingertips explore me, dipping and tracing circles around my most sensitive areas. I gasp, my breathing becoming shallower with each touch.

He teases me, alternating between fast and slow strokes, never letting me get too comfortable. I moan and start to quiver and tremble as I get closer to the edge.

He knows just when to increase the pressure and when to back off, pushing me to the brink of pleasure before cruelly wrenching the temptation of it away again. He nibbles on my ear and laughs and kisses and promises me he won't ever let me go.

Finally, when he says that, I let out a long moan as I come, my body trembling as I ride out wave after wave of pleasure. He doesn't stop until every bit of energy is drained from my body. I collapse against him, my head buried in his chest.

Only then does he start to take care of himself. His gentle thrusts come faster and faster. His breath warms the back of my neck. If I wasn't already so spent, the sound of him falling apart could make me come again.

"Fuck... Paige..." My name stays imprinted on his lips as he spills inside of me.

The orgasm wracks his body. I clutch his hands against my belly and wait until his breathing has settled. Until both of us can talk without gasping.

Then I roll onto my side so I'm facing him. "That was... different. Good different."

He kisses my nose. "Seems appropriate."

"Yes." A lot of things are different now, apparently. "Can I tell you something?"

"Anything."

"Sometimes, I forget I'm pregnant." He arches his eyebrows, and I continue. "I guess I still don't quite believe that I'm pregnant at all. I mean, it was never supposed to happen for me."

"Maybe it just wasn't supposed to happen with Anthony." His hand curls possessively around my hip. I like that, even now, he doesn't want to let go of me.

"Did you always want kids?" I ask.

"Not at all. I never thought I'd have them," he admits. "There wasn't any pressure to have kids until Maksim died. Even then, we still had Ilya."

"So it was always for the Bratva? You didn't want them just for you?"

He shakes his head. "I didn't think I'd make a very good father."

"Why?"

He frowns. "I don't know. Just a feeling. The things I'm good at don't translate to kids."

I prop myself up on my elbow and look down at him. "Tell me five things you like about yourself."

He arches one brow. "Excuse me?"

"I'm serious. Five things you like about yourself."

"I'm not sure I have five to tell."

Blind, stupid man. I could list a thousand. "Fine. Name three."

"Is talking after sex important to you? Or can I—"

He pretends to get up, and I swat his arm. I bury my nose in the crook of his neck and breath in that heady, masculine scent of him.

"You're wonderful, Misha Orlov. You may not be able to name five things you like about yourself. But I could keep going forever."

He looks down at me. His eyes are bright and warm, but this conversation has entered a territory of vulnerability that he's not quite ready for.

Finally, he wraps an arm around me and pulls me close. "You're full of shit, *kiska*. Now, shut up and let me hold you."

We burst out laughing while he does exactly that. I cling on to him and let everything else go for now.

The list can wait. You can't win every battle at once.

30

PAIGE

I wake up in the middle of the night with Misha's body curled around me.

I'm not surprised to find him in bed with me. After everything we've talked about, I know he'll stay.

Maybe that new certainty is why I can focus on the other thing that's bothering me: the fact that my only friend outside of the immediate Orlov family still believes I'm dead.

I slide myself out of Misha's arms. He stirs, but doesn't wake up. I grab his discarded shirt and pull it on. Then I find my phone and pad out onto the balcony.

It's cool outside, but I'm flushed with anxiety as I dial Rowan's number. When she finally answers, her voice is groggy with sleep. "Hello?"

I can tell she didn't even check who was calling before answering. She sounds blissfully ignorant of what's about to hit her.

"Rowan?" I say as gently as I can.

The initial silence is loaded. I imagine her pulling the phone away, checking the number like it can't be real, and then lifting it to her ear again.

Still, she doesn't say anything.

"Rowan, it's me. It's Paige."

This wasn't the right way to do this. I should have prepared her. Springing this on her with a phone call in the middle of the freaking night was not the right move.

So in the name of damage control, I speed through my explanation before she can freak out and hang up on me.

"Rowan, it's me. I know what you've heard. But it's not true. I'm alive. The bombing was all just a ruse. I mean... not a ruse, exactly. There was a bomb that was meant for me and —" I stop talking when I realize I'm getting no response from the other side. "Rowan? Are you still there?"

I can hear the whistling of her breath.

"I'm so sorry I called like this. It was colossally stupid and selfish. I'm so sorry," I say again.

"Paige?" she finally whispers.

"Yes."

"It's... it's really you?"

"It's really me."

"You didn't die?"

"No. Petyr's attack was real, but someone else was in my car." A lump rises to my throat at the thought of Rose. "I know this is a lot."

"But... I spoke to Konstantin..."

"Misha thought it was best to let Petyr think that I was really dead. Which meant everyone needed to believe it. I was in bad shape for a while after the explosion. I wanted to tell you sooner, but—"

"Misha wouldn't let you."

"Not at the time, no."

She's still wary. "So he knows you're calling me now?"

"I told him we could trust you. And he trusts me, so…"

She lets out a long, tortured breath. "Dear God, Paige."

"I know. *I know.* I'm sorry."

"Stop apologizing." There's a bite in her voice now that the shock is waning.

"Are you okay?"

"I… I gotta tell you, it's really unnerving to get a call in the middle of the night from a friend you thought was dead."

I can only imagine how I would have felt if I'd gotten a call from Clara out of the blue. "I know. My timing is terrible."

"Your timing is the least of it," Rowan says. "In my head, you've literally risen from the dead."

"Are you mad?"

There's a long silence from the other end of the line. Then I hear her breathe out slowly. "I'm just… shaken. I really thought you were gone, Paige. I was grieving like you were."

"I know."

"And the thing is… we haven't been friends for that long," she says. "But you are the first person I've connected with in a long time. Losing you hurt a lot. More than I thought it would."

A tear slips down my cheek. "I'm sorry."

She sighs again. "They don't prepare you for this in school."

I bark out a strange, strangled laugh. "No. No, they do not. Or if they do, I missed that day in class." I twist my hair around my fingers. "Can you just… tell me how you've been? Tell me what you've been doing. And I mean all of it. The mundane stuff. The stuff you think is too boring to share. I heard they closed the coffee shop for renovations. Did they fix the copier at the office? Seen any good movies lately?"

There's another tense silence, and I wonder if maybe there's no coming back from this. Maybe some pains are too much to recover from.

But then Rowan exhales and I hear a little more life return to her voice. "Who takes six months to renovate a goddamn coffee shop? I've been *dying* without my pastry fix—not in a sort-of-literal way like you, you bitch—but I'm an absolute fiend to everyone in the office; they all think I'm nuts…"

I laugh and we settle in and it feels… normal.

My husband back in my bed.

My friend back in my life.

Maybe the future I hoped for isn't out of reach after all.

31

MISHA

Two weeks of waking up next to Paige, and the euphoria hasn't faded.

The pleasure at seeing her sleep creased face. The reassuring warmth of her body next to mine.

You'll get it one day, Maksim told me not long before he died. *When you wake up next to a woman and realize that your sole purpose in life is to make her happy and keep her safe. That the quiet moments are the ones you're living for.*

He was right, of course. It just took me a little while to catch up to his way of thinking.

Paige stirs next to me. I'm startled out of my thoughts. I thought she was asleep, but her eyes are wide open and clear.

"How long have you been up?" I ask.

"An hour or so," she says. "But you were sleeping so peacefully. I couldn't wake you."

I lean down and kiss her cheek. "Is there a reason you seem wired this morning?"

She smiles conspiratorially and reaches into her nightstand. "I have something for you." she says, pulling open the drawer and taking out a little black box. She jumps back into bed, her legs tucked underneath her, and hands it to me. "Go on. Open it."

"Are you proposing to me? Because we've been there and done that. Twice, actually."

"Just open it, smart ass," she says impatiently.

I open the lid and see a sleek, silver dog tag sitting on a velvet cushion. It matches Maksim's, except this engraving reads, "*Kiska.*" There's a small infinity symbol etched underneath it.

"You had this done for me?"

She smiles and nods. "You don't have to wear it all the time. Or at all, really. There's no pressure. I just thought you could wear it sometimes. Mix it up a little, you know?"

I lift it out of the box and loop it around my head. It sits a little higher than Maksim's. Closer to my heart.

"Thank you."

"You're welcome." She looks so pleased to see me wearing it. When I pull her onto my lap, she yelps. "Don't! I'll squash you."

"Please," I growl. "You're light as a feather. It's those babies that weigh a ton."

She pushes me back onto the bed playfully and kisses my neck. I can almost hear my brother's voice in my ear.

The quiet moments are the ones you live for.

That motherfucker was always right.

32

PAIGE

"Talk to him," Nikita says adamantly. "This imprisonment has gone on too long. It's been a month!"

"This is the first entire day you've spent with me in the house. Imagine how I feel!" I say. "I've explored every nook and cranny of this place. There's nothing more to see. I'm going insane. Cabin fever times, like, a billion."

Niki chews on a carrot stick from the snack tray we're sharing and flops back on the sofa. Cyrille pats her leg. "Misha can be reasonable. I'm sure he'll be okay with breaking your little lockdown."

Niki and I both look at Cyrille like she's grown a second head. She sighs. "Oh, okay, fine, so he's not always reasonable. Never really is, actually. But I bet you can persuade him. I mean, he gave you back your phone, didn't he?"

"Yeah, with conditions. I can't call anyone outside of the immediate family."

"He let you call Rowan," Cyrille counters.

"Yeah, that's pretty significant," Niki concedes. "I never thought he would allow that. Stickler for the rules, that one."

I take a deep breath. "I definitely want some more freedom. I've been stuck in this house for far too long. I just… I don't want to rock the boat."

The happy, sexy boat where I wake up to my husband every day. Where he goes to work wearing my nickname on a chain under his shirt, tucked close to his heart.

It's a good boat to be on.

Nikita and Cyrille exchange a glance, and I get defensive. "We've just gotten to a great place. I don't want to ruin it all by fighting."

"That kinda depends on him, doesn't it?" Niki asks.

"Listen to me, Paige," Cyrille says. "You are a Bratva wife now. That is not the submissive role you think it is. You have to go toe to toe with him if you want him to treat you like an equal. Maksim was the best husband there was, but even he needed to be reminded that he didn't call all the shots in our relationship."

Nikita nods in agreement. "You gotta fight for what you want, Paige. Don't make the mistake of trying to please him all the time. Trust me—that gets old fast."

I sigh. "I know. I know you guys are right."

"Then stop avoiding the conversation," Cyrille concludes. "He's admitted that he loves you. Use it."

I laugh nervously. "He may love me. That doesn't mean he's going to handle me pushing back any better than he used to."

Cyrille shrugs. "Hey, fighting isn't all bad. It can lead to some really great sex. The best sex, actually…"

"Ew!" Niki scrunches up her nose with distaste. "I think I'm done with this conversation now. I really need to get some new friends."

"Hey!" I lightly slap her arm.

"I just mean that my only two friends can't be my brothers' wives," she explains. "It's not like we can really talk sex lives now, can we? Because I definitely do not want to know what goes on between—"

"What don't you want to know?" Misha asks as he walks in.

Niki's eyes widen in panic. "About giving birth. I'd rather not know the gory details of dilating and—y'know. The biology of it all."

"Pity. I was going to send you the birth video," Misha teases.

She flips him off and then gives me a hug. "I'll call you tomorrow, okay, P?"

"Does that mean you aren't coming by tomorrow?" I know I sound pathetic, but I'm so lonely I'm past caring.

Cyrille bites her lower lip. "Sorry, love. I've got an event I need to plan."

"Yeah, and I'm looking at houses across town," Niki adds.

Misha crosses his arms and turns to his sister. "You're really striking out on your own?"

"It's time, o brother of mine. And no, I will not be convinced otherwise. I even spoke to Mom about it. She's cool."

"Or so she would have you believe," Misha rumbles.

"Mom is not gonna miss me. She's perfectly happy living in this house with her precious baby boy and her new favorite daughter."

"Her stay here is temporary," he growls. But none of us are fooled—Mama Orlov is here as long as she damn well pleases.

Niki laughs as she leaves. Cyrille waves and follows her, shaking her head and still chuckling.

Misha eases the moment they're gone. He drops a kiss on my cheek and joins me on the floor. He plucks a grape from the snack tray, pops it in his mouth, and asks as he chews, "How was your day?"

"I can't stay in this house any longer!" I blurt out.

Misha pauses his chewing and swallows with effort. "And here I thought things were going so well between us."

"Ha. Ha. Ha. You know what I mean."

It's nice that I know Misha really does know what I mean. The last few weeks have changed everything. No more pretending. No more playacting.

He and I are together. A real couple. Which is why he knows what I mean.

And why I know he isn't happy about it.

"And I thought you understood—"

"I've been cooped up in here for over a month, Misha," I interrupt, softening my tone. "We are no closer to knowing when Petyr is going to emerge. I can't be expected to stay holed up behind these walls forever, can I?"

Champagne Wrath

His eyes are steely. Any hope I had withers in the face of that icy determination.

"Petyr has made several attempts on your life, Paige. Lest you forget."

He sounds so weary that I have half a mind to cave. Then I remember Cyrille's words. Misha is never going to respect me if I keep buckling under the pressure of those silver eyes. He may not know it just yet, but he doesn't want a doormat for a wife.

"Don't talk to me like I'm clueless," I snap. "I've been the one under attack. I'm aware of what Petyr has been doing. That doesn't mean I'm prepared to hide away forever. I'm not scared of him."

"This won't last forever, Paige. Just until—"

"Until the next threat comes along?" I ask. "Or the one after that? Or the one after that? I want to live my life *now*. I want to be able to grab brunch with Nessa or get coffee with Rowan. I want to go house hunting with Niki. I should be able to help Cyrille organize her charity events. Your mother has bought all of the baby clothes so far. I want to be able to pick them out myself."

He doesn't respond, and I sense an opening. I lay my hand on his arm and draw closer. "It's a miracle I'm even pregnant in the first place. It's unlikely to ever happen again. I don't want to miss out, Misha."

"And I don't want you to risk the babies that science says shouldn't have been conceived at all."

"I'm not suggesting I take risks. I'm suggesting I live my life *and* send a giant 'fuck you' to Petyr at the same time."

"Well, you can't have both," he snarls, his frustration rising to the surface. "Either live your life—or send a fuck you to Petyr and die in the process."

I almost forgot how hot he is when he's angry. His eyes glow and his jaw twitches, clenching into granite that I want to soften with my mouth. It's this weird push and pull of desire and anger working hand in hand, making my center throb and my pulse quicken.

Cyrille might be onto something with her little theory on sex and fighting.

"And if Petyr never surfaces?" I say. "I'm just supposed to live inside these walls forever, pretending I'm dead? Like Rapunzel?"

"If the crown fits," he growls.

I narrow my eyes. "I never pegged you for the type of man to frighten so easily."

"And I never pegged you for the type of woman to behave so recklessly."

"Apparently, you're rubbing off on me."

"Maybe I should rub some sense *into* you, too," he growls.

I lift my chin, meeting his eyes. We're a breath apart, practically on top of each other.

Somehow—and for the life of me, I don't know how—we end up tearing each other's clothes off.

I rip his shirt open, a few buttons skittering across the floor. He does the same, rending my blouse down the sleeve so my breasts fall out.

A part of my brain registers that we're very exposed in the sitting room. The French doors are thrown open and I can hear the faint churn of the lawnmower as Mario tends to the grass. Light filters in through the open windows. The smell of lunch rolls in from the kitchen.

But it doesn't stop Misha from lifting me on top of the grand piano and pushing my skirt up.

He doesn't even bother taking my panties off; he just pushes them to the side and shoves his tongue into my pussy.

I cry out as I curl my fingers through his hair and hold him there, wringing every second of pleasure out of his mouth until I come on his face.

My moans are still echoing through the room when he stands up and pushes inside me with one strong thrust. Our bodies slap together, and I have to cling to him to stay upright. He is never this rough with me anymore. Not since I started showing.

"Fuck me, Misha," I pant.

He growls and thrusts into me. He has one hand wrapped around my neck and the other hand on my breast, his grip iron like cuffs. My bones shake with every primal slam of his hips, but it fills something in me that only he can touch. The sighs that come out of my lips are for his ears and his ears only. I love coming apart for him like this. I love him coming apart like this for me.

Finally, he groans out his release, spilling into me before going still.

He lays his forehead on my shoulder. "Fucking hell, Paige."

I stroke the hair at the back of his neck, relishing this moment. But the longer we sit, the more reality creeps back in.

Then I look over and see Mario through the large picture window.

Which means he can definitely see us, too.

"Shit!" I push Misha off me and try to adjust my clothes so I look presentable again. "Do you think there's a chance that nobody heard us?"

Misha just smirks. "No chance whatsoever."

"Oh, God." I fall onto the sofa and cover my face with my hands. When I peek through my fingers, I see him watching me, an amused smile playing on his lips. "You know," I venture, "if you let me out of the tower, we can have this same kind of fun in the office when we're supposed to be working."

The steel in those silver eyes begin to melt. He drops his chin to his chest. "Fuck."

That's how I know I've won this one.

33

MISHA

Even as we drive to Orion together, I'm not sure exactly how my wife managed to talk me into this.

But here we are.

Paige is wearing a red power suit that screams "boss bitch." Her words, not mine. The material hugs the soft swell of my children inside of her.

I have never been prouder.

Or more on edge.

"Stop looking so worried." Paige puts her hand on my knee. "Everything will be fine."

"He's going to know before the sun goes down that you're alive."

"Which means he's going to know that he can't touch either of us," she says smugly. "He's going to know he can't mess with you."

"Or he's going to try harder."

"I know you, Misha. I may be out of the house, but let's be honest—I'm being monitored. Every step I take is going to be recorded in some security guard's notes."

I smirk, because she's not wrong. "I think this is what we call a compromise."

She sighs, but she doesn't argue. I have a feeling I might get some pushback when she sees just how many safety measures I've taken in preparation for her assimilation back into everyday life. But I'm not going to budge on any of them. Not even the promise of her sweet pussy can convince me otherwise.

(Though I'm willing to let her try.)

When the car stops, she doesn't wait for me to walk around to her door before she climbs out. She doesn't even wait for me to escort her up the front steps and through the lobby. Paige keeps a half step ahead of me, her head held high, her shoulders held back.

One thing is for sure—the woman knows how to make an entrance.

We drop quite a few jaws as we head to the elevators, offering no explanations and not talking to a single soul. Neither of us speaks until we're behind the closed doors of Paige's office.

"Wow," she squeals. "That was awesome!"

I want to temper her enthusiasm. But I can't help smiling at the same time. She looks like a child on Christmas morning.

"Did you see their faces?" she continues. "And that's just our employees. Think of Petyr's face when he realizes that I'm still alive!"

That gives me mixed emotions. I love the idea of pulling one over on the motherfucker who killed my brother. But I don't relish what he'll do when he finds out.

She stops suddenly and pirouettes on the spot, surveying her office room with new eyes. "Is that a new desk?"

"Brand new. Japanese. Handmade."

She frowns. "What was wrong with the old one?"

"Nothing. But this one has a few extra features that might come in handy if you're ever in trouble."

She looks dubious. "Exactly what kind of 'features,' Misha?"

I show her the panic button just underneath the lip of the desk. "One touch and it will trigger a silent alarm and a video feed." I turn and point at two other corners of the room. "There's another there, another there, and a fourth in the bathroom."

"Don't you think that's a little overkill?"

"No, I don't." I take her hand and lead her over to the massive painting hanging on the wall. It's a frontward-facing view of a running stallion.

"Does the stallion come to life, rip out of the canvas, and come to my defense?" she asks, deadpan.

I glare at her until she starts giggling. Then I grip the right-hand edge of the canvas and pull it forward on hidden hinges, revealing the steel door behind it.

"Oh my God," Paige breathes. "Misha! Is that a secret passageway?"

"Unfortunately, no. The building doesn't allow for secret passageways. But it is a panic room. There's another button on the inside that you can press for help."

I click the canvas shut and she stares at me with disbelief. "Honey…"

"Don't 'honey' me," I growl. "This was all necessary. You want your freedom? This is the cost. I'm not taking a chance with your life or our children's lives."

She gives me a soft smile and steps into the circle of my arms. She rests her head against my chest and hugs me until I hug her back.

When she pulls back, her expression is tender. "Thank you for looking after me. For looking after us."

"It's my job."

"Still, I feel like you need to be thanked. Properly."

I frown. "What do you—"

"You locked the door behind you, right?" She slides her fingers over the buttons of her red coat, popping them one by one.

I raise my eyebrows. "Are we christening your new office?"

"I don't see why not," she says. "We've christened almost every room in the house. It's about time we found some new territory to defile."

She pulls off the coat and lets it fall to the ground. She's wearing a white silk blouse underneath that just manages to hide her growing stomach. She doesn't seem as conscious of her new curves these days. Probably because she's learned that seeing her blossom with my babies only turns me on that much more.

She steps out of her pants and reveals her pink lace lingerie underneath. She still has her heels on.

"Fucking hell, *kiska*, you look unbelievable."

"Why don't you sit, husband?" she suggests. "I don't mind you borrowing my chair for the next hour."

"Hour?" I ask. "Someone is feeling ambitious."

"If I wasn't ambitious, I wouldn't be here at all," she says, placing her hands on my chest and pushing me down into her swivel chair.

She runs her hands over my hair and down the back of my neck. I stare up at her in awe, mesmerized by this creature. It still strikes me as a miracle that we ever crossed paths. That one sip of champagne soldered our lives together forever.

Then she straddles me, pushing her nearly naked breasts into my face, and all thoughts like that vanish on the spot.

She rocks her hips back, torturing me with the friction, and presses her lips to mine. She kisses me long and deep and slow.

"I've never been comfortable in lingerie," she admits when we come up for air. "Not until I met you." She nips and licks down my neck. "Now, it's all I want to wear."

"Prove it."

She looks confused for a moment. "Prove it?"

"I want a photoshoot. Picture of you in all the lingerie I've bought you. A private album just for me. Something I can look back on and remember exactly how I felt."

She looks amused by the idea. "And how do you feel?"

I look her in the eye and say the only word that feels right: "Alive."

34

MISHA

"You were in Paige's office for a suspiciously long time." Konstantin is lounging on my sofa, a computer open in his lap and that undying twinkle in his eye.

I drop my jacket on the back of my hair and fall into my chair. "I had to bring her up to speed with the company accounts."

Usually, I'd try to come up with a more convincing lie, but I'm completely spent. My wife has a libido that's dwarfing mine.

Konstantin snorts so loudly that he actually chokes a little. "I passed by Paige's office earlier," he says. "I wasn't aware that 'catching up on company accounts' involved such heavy breathing and squeaking chairs."

"You listened at the door?"

"I wasn't trying to. But it was pretty obvious what was going on in there." He gives me a mischievous grin. "Look at you, living the high life."

"Shut up."

Konstantin just laughs again. "I can't quite believe it. First, Maksim; now, you. Who knew the Orlov men were such romantics at heart?"

Crossing my legs requires a little more effort than usual. My legs feel like jelly, a direct result of fucking Paige against her desk for almost fifteen minutes straight before we came the second time.

I wave him away, switching into business mode. "Enough of that. Let's talk moves."

"Changing the topic. How predictable."

"We're at work, Konstantin."

"Sure, but I want to be at work the way *you're* at work. Because apparently, your way involves hot midday sex."

"She's my wife. It's different."

"Meaning what? I have to marry a girl before I fuck her on my office desk? If so, you won't have to worry about ever overhearing my sex noises. I'm not the marrying kind."

"Famous last words."

Konstantin laughs once more, though this one comes tinged with bitterness. "Yeah, yeah, I know. But I'm not like you or Maksim. I'm a lowly bastard, remember? What sexy little vixen would want to marry an off-brand Orlov like me?"

That catches me by surprise. We don't usually talk about Konstantin's parentage. In fact, we never do.

"You are my cousin," I say. "Legitimate or not, you're family. That's all there is to it. You have the respect of every man in this Bratva."

"Because I'm your right-hand; not because I carry the name. A name that's not even technically mine."

"You—"

Konstantin smiles placidly as he interrupts me. "You're right. We should discuss moves."

I'm not sure what triggered that conversation. It strikes me that while I've been sorting through the swamp in my head, Konstantin has been going through his own shit.

When was the last time I asked him how he was doing? He always seems so relaxed, so carefree, so calm. A clown, through and through.

But there's a reason clowns wear tears painted on their faces.

"Konst—"

"The Babai," he says, putting an abrupt end to his brief moment of vulnerability. "No word from them yet?"

I sigh. I won't press him if he isn't ready for it. "Only a brief message I received late last night. They asked for more time."

"Does that worry you?"

I shrug. "I paid their price because they're supposed to be the best. Results—that's what the Babai are known for. And yet here they are, requesting another week."

"It's not much in the grand scheme of things," he offers.

"It's far too much when you consider that Petyr Ivanov should already be six feet under."

"There's something else…"

I glance at my cousin distractedly. "What is it?"

"There's been some... chatter within the ranks," he says diplomatically. "The council is grumpy."

"Fuck me," I mutter. "Not this shit again."

Having the lesser ranks grumbling is one thing. But the council is made up of senior Vors that influence everyone else. The fact that they're uneasy is not good.

"What's the pulse?"

"Discontent," Konstantin summarizes. "They feel like too much attention is being put in the wrong places. But mostly, I think they just don't like being left out of the loop. Maybe it's time to organize another council meeting. You can fill them in and calm their nerves. Hold their hands like the little boys they sometimes are."

"It's not my responsibility to babysit them," I growl. "I've got enough shit on my plate. I'll organize a council meeting when *I* need to talk, not when *they* need to."

"So..."

"So let the chatter continue. I need to focus on keeping Paige safe." She is the only thing that matters. "Speaking of, I wanted to ask if I could borrow your apartment in the city for the night."

He does a double-take. "Can I ask why you need a measly little four-bedroom penthouse in the city, when you have a big-ass mansion in the hills?"

"I thought I'd surprise Paige with a change of scenery," I explain. "But I also want to keep Petyr guessing. I'm certain he has eyes on us. I don't want our moves to be predictable."

"Got it. Well, it would be my pleasure. Consider my bachelor pad your honeymoon nest for the night. If you need any little blue pills, they're in the medicine cabinet. So is the lube. And in the chest underneath the bed, there's a—"

I hold up a hand before he can start describing what kind of sick paraphernalia he keeps on hand. "Say no more, for the love of God. Thank you."

Konstantin smiles and leans back in his seat. His blue eyes catch the light and for a moment, he looks a lot like Maksim.

"What are you doing tonight?" I ask suddenly. Once upon a time, we used to ravage nightclubs from the time the sun set until it rose again. I can't remember the last time we did that.

"I find ways to keep myself occupied," Konstantin says vaguely. I get the feeling that there's more to his life than he's letting on. But I'm not about to pry, even if I want to help. "Life's changed a lot since you found your woman. I've adapted."

I cringe. Without even realizing it, I've left Konstantin behind.

"Don't," Konstantin snaps out of nowhere, glaring at me harshly. "Don't fucking feel bad, for God's sake. I'm a big boy; I can take care of myself. I may be alone, but I'm not lonely."

He seems to mean it.

But it makes me worry all the same.

35

PAIGE

Rowan's arms are a vise grip around my body. It's been like this for minutes, and I'm not about to tell her to let go.

"I'm sorry," I say for the billionth time.

When Rowan releases me, her eyes are wet. I feel close to tears myself. "You have to stop apologizing. You did what you had to do. Or Misha did. Either way, there was a reason."

"You're mad at me, though, aren't you?"

"No," she says a little too quickly. Then she sighs. "I was just so heartbroken when I heard, Paige. Getting the call from you was a shock. It made me feel like all that emotional trauma I went through was kinda a 'gotcha' moment. Which I know it wasn't! But that's how it felt."

I don't try to justify myself or give her more excuses. I've done all that already. So I just nod and accept her feelings as they are. "It must have been horrible."

"The thing is..." She shakes her head. "No, never mind."

"No, tell me." I lead her to the chaise in the corner by my office window and pull her to the seat. "Please."

She gives me a self-conscious smile and runs her fingers through her long blonde hair. It looks inches longer since I last saw her. Maybe I've been away longer than I thought.

"I've never really told you about my parents, have I?"

I shake my head.

She nods. "I think it's because, if I don't talk about them, I can pretend like I had a nice, normal family. The kind of dad who volunteered to be the softball coach. The kind of mom who baked cookies for the bake sale and picked me up on time every single day."

I put my hand on hers. "I wouldn't know how to relate to a person who had parents like that."

Rowan laughs. "Here's to the resilient kids of shit parents."

Both of us descend into laughter. When we recover, the atmosphere has changed distinctly. It's calmer now, ready for conversation and healing.

"My father was abusive," she says without mincing her words. "Emotionally and physically. I used to hide under the staircase and watch while he hit my mother. If I interrupted, he'd hit me, too."

My mouth drops open. "Oh my God, Rowan."

She shakes off my horror as though she's embarrassed by it. "The thing is, I was about six when my mother died. It was just my father and I after that. It was… well, it was what you would expect."

She doesn't go into details, and I can't bring myself to ask.

"About a year before you and I met, I got a call from this girl. She said her name was Grace and she claimed that she was my half-sister. Apparently, my mother… She didn't die. She left."

I stare at Rowan in shock. "No…"

She nods sadly. "I confronted my dad about it shortly after I got that call. He told me that, when she left, he decided she was dead to him, so he just told me as much. I didn't think there was anything worse than losing a parent so early. Turns out, it's preferable to discovering that your mother abandoned you without thinking twice about it."

"Oh, hon, you don't know that."

"Don't I?" Rowan challenges.

I check myself. This is not the time to try to justify Rowan's mother's choices. "Have… have you spoken to your mother?"

"Fuck no!" she says. "I hung up on Grace, too. She called a few more times, but I didn't pick up. I think she's got the message now. She hasn't tried to contact me in months."

Rowan exhales slowly, and I get the impression that maybe a small part of her is disappointed that she hasn't gotten a call recently. "I guess learning that you weren't really dead brought it all back."

"Shit, I can imagine," I gasp. "I—"

"Don't apologize again," she says firmly. "I mean it."

My jaw snaps shut. "Right, I won't. So, um… your hair looks nice."

Rowan laughs. "Thank you. You look good, too. Especially for someone who has risen from the grave."

"It's been a trying few months being trapped in the mansion. First world problems, I know, but—"

"Hey, I get it. Even a castle can be a prison when you know you can't leave," Rowan says. "How did you manage to get out?"

"I pleaded with my husband."

"Pleaded, huh? Is that all you did?" she asks suggestively.

I smile. "Things have been going well between us."

"I can tell."

"Really?"

She bats a hand at me. "Please, I've always been able to sniff out a good relationship in my friends. Ironic, really, considering I can't seem to do it for myself."

"It'll happen for you, Rowan."

She shakes her head emphatically. "Oh no. I've taken myself off the market. Some women are just meant to be single."

"That's fine if that's what they want," I say. "Is that what *you* want?"

She hesitates. "I don't trust myself anymore, Paige. I choose all the wrong men. I choose men like my father. If that's my only option, I'd rather be alone."

I take her hand and give it a comforting squeeze. "Maybe I should choose a man for you then?"

Rowan looks intrigued by that notion for a moment before the fear settles back into her expression. "I appreciate the offer. But I'm happy on my own."

I squint at the forced smile on her face. She's trying very hard to be convincing, but she's not really selling it the way she thinks she is.

"I'll keep my eye out for you all the same," I say. "Who knows? Maybe one day you'll be ready to shed the trauma and embrace your life."

"Have you embraced yours?" she asks.

"It's a process. But I'm trying. Even if it's never going to be perfect, I'm still trying."

"Forget perfect, Paige," Rowan says with a sigh. "I'll settle for peace."

36

MISHA

Konstantin strolls into my office and drops the keys to his penthouse on my desk. "Are you taking off soon?"

I can tell from the look on his face that something is not right, but he's trying to play it off like it's no big deal. "What's going on?"

"Nothing is—"

"Bullshit, Konstantin. Tell me."

He sighs. "I didn't wanna ruin your big night. But three of our men have gone missing."

My fist tightens around my pen. "Since when?"

"They were supposed to report to me at noon. None of them checked in. That's literally never happened before." He chews on his thumbnail. "They're low-level guys. Runners and intermediaries, mostly. But still—they're usually dependable. Now, I can't get in touch with any of them."

"Petyr is having a temper tantrum," I growl.

"You really think this is retaliation?" Konstantin ponders. "It's only been, like, eight hours since Paige made her appearance."

"Which is clearly enough time for news to travel. Son of a *bitch*." I slam my fist on my desk. "Why the fuck have the Babai not been able to locate the *mudak*?"

Konstantin whips around and closes my office door. "Shh! Don't say that so loud."

"What," I drawl, "you think the Babai can hear us?"

He glances around like they really might. "Just saying, I don't want to risk it."

"You need to get over this, Konstantin. There's healthy fear and then there's… whatever the hell this is."

"When it comes to the Babai, any fear is healthy fear." He drops into a seat and leans closer to say in an anxious whisper, "My mother used to tell me stories about them, okay? I took them to heart."

I can't believe that we're talking about Konstantin's past twice in one day. I wonder what his mother told him. I never really knew her. Whatever hazy memory I have of her is born out of old photographs.

"But look, don't worry, alright? I've got this handled," Konstantin assures me. "Everything is ready at my place. Security has been briefed. You and the missus are good to go."

I ponder the situation for a moment. But I chose Konstantin's place for a reason. Petyr won't be looking for me there. For tonight at least, everything will be fine. We can close ranks and seal up the castle in the morning. Paige won't like it, but that's a problem for a future Misha.

We walk out of my office together. "Do me one favor?" Konstantin asks before we part ways. "Don't do anything too nasty on my furniture. I have to live in that space."

I smirk. "No promises."

"Oh God," he groans. "That was not convincing."

Laughing, I head down the hall towards Paige's office. She's in there with Rowan, still going over reports she missed from the last month, one line at a time. Rowan looks ready to drop dead, but Paige is a Terminator with unlimited battery.

In the bedroom, I adore how thorough my wife is.

Right now, though, I'm ready to leave.

I knock on the door. Paige looks up, a distracted smile on her face. "Hi. We're just finishing up." She marks something with a blue ballpoint pen and hands it to Rowan. "There you go. Thanks, Ro."

"Of course. See you tomorrow?" Rowan asks, stacking up her belongings with a weary exhale.

"Yes, ma'am. Have a good night."

As Rowan heads for the door, she gives me a tentative smile. It's gone the moment she looks away.

I cross my arms and lean against the doorjamb, watching as my wife rearranges her desk. "She doesn't like me."

Paige looks up at me in alarm. "Not true at all. She doesn't know you."

"She has worked for this company long enough to know something. And what she knows, she doesn't like," I say. "Not that I'm very concerned with her opinions. I just don't want her opinion of me rubbing off on you."

Paige smiles as she straightens up her files and deposits them into her desk drawer. Then she rounds the desk and wraps her arms around my neck. "You are super cute. Have I told you that lately?"

I twist my mouth into thought as my hands find her hips. "I've gotten handsome. Sexy. Powerful. Charismatic. But no, never 'cute.'"

She chuckles. "Well, that is exactly what you are right now."

I growl in mock distaste. She laughs some more and presses her lips against my cheek. "Don't take it personally; it's not about you at all. Rowan and 'men' have a history. And considering she knows you're dangerous, it doesn't really calm her nerves to know that I'm fully committed to you. I think she's just waiting for the other shoe to drop."

Those words sound ominous.

Mostly because I'm waiting for the exact same thing.

"Your protection is my top priority."

"I know that. Which is why I showed her all the new safety features in this office. Somehow, that backfired. Big time, actually."

"The security system made her feel less secure?"

"It just seemed to signal to her that I was in imminent danger." She bites her lip. "I told you it was overkill."

"Nothing is overkill when it comes to keeping you safe."

"See? That is why I know she'll come to love you like I do." I give her a look, and she giggles. "Well, not *exactly* like I do."

I grab her by the waist and steer her towards the door. "I don't care about what your friend thinks about me, Paige. I only care what you think of me."

She smiles and rests her head back against my chest. "Then you're in luck. Because I think the world of you." I kiss the top of her head, and she sighs. "Today was so good, Misha. It was so great to be in actual clothes. To see people, talk business, do work. I needed this."

When we reach the garage, I help her into my Bentley. But even as I close her door, my eyes are roving. As I walk around to the driver's seat, I'm scanning every corner, every nook, every cranny, every shadow. Nothing seems amiss, but I know enough not to believe in calmness on the surface.

Someone is watching us, even if I can't see them.

"How was your day?" Paige asks as I drive deeper into the city.

"Fine."

"That's it?" she asks. "You have nothing more to share with me?"

"Not really."

She frowns. "Okay. We'll have to work on that."

I turn the corner and she seems to realize that we're driving in the wrong direction. "Are we going somewhere?"

I'm busy trying to determine if the red sedan behind us is tailing us or just happens to be traveling in the same direction. "Yes, we are."

"Dinner at a fancy restaurant?"

"Dinner, yes. Restaurant, no. But we'll have an amazing view."

"Am I supposed to guess?"

I drive straight at the intersection and watch as the red sedan takes a left. My grip on the steering wheel eases slightly. *We're fine. Everything is going to be fine.*

"Too late for guesses. We're here." I drive up to the endless, black-glassed skyscraper that houses Konstantin's den of sin.

Paige looks out the window in confusion. She turns to me with a raised eyebrow. "You are full of surprises, Misha Orlov."

I smile. "Just trying to keep you interested."

"Don't worry about that. I'm in no danger of losing interest." She laughs, and despite everything that's going on right now, that laugh—it's like honey to my soul.

37

PAIGE

I turn in another circle and nod. "Alright, final analysis: I'm impressed."

"By what, exactly?" Misha scoffs. "The complete lack of personality in this penthouse?"

"Look at those paintings!" I point to the collection Konstantin has hanging in the hallway that leads to the master bedroom. "They're gorgeous."

"He used to paint a lot as a kid," Misha explains.

"Used to? He doesn't anymore?"

"No, my father put a stop to that. I believe his exact words were, 'Men don't paint.'"

"Wow. He sounds like a gem."

He chuckles darkly. "He was Bratva."

"*You're* Bratva," I retort. "Would you tell our hypothetical son not to paint if he was passionate about painting?"

"Depends." He shrugs.

"Misha!"

He sighs. "No, no, of course I wouldn't."

"Good. I was gearing up for a fight."

He wraps his arms around me from behind and plants a kiss on my cheek. "I don't mind. I enjoy fighting with you."

"Is that why you do it so often?" I tease. He forces me down the passageway, and into the master bedroom. "Are we even allowed to be in here?"

"Why not?"

"It's the master bedroom. Konstantin's space. It's private."

"What's his is ours. Konstantin is an open book."

"I don't know about that. Konstantin seems a lot more complicated than he lets on." I turn around so that I can catch Misha's expression. He's looking thoughtfully out of the massive windows that overlook the city.

"You may be right about that."

Before I can ask a follow-up question, he spins me around and hoists me up into his arms. I yelp. "We are not having sex in here!"

"I didn't intend to," he says as he carries me back out of the room and into the kitchen. "I just wanted to give you the tour. And God forbid I make you do it on your dainty little princess feet."

I slap him on the shoulder and laugh. "I'll shove a dainty little princess foot up your ass if you keep talking down to me, Mr. Orlov."

He chuckles, but the moment we enter the open plan kitchen, my attention diverts. I'm hit with the smell of Chinese takeout. It's still in the paper containers, but the scent is overpowering. Not to mention mouthwatering. My lunch today was more about talking than eating.

"Oh, wow, that smells good."

"Brought in from the best place in the city." Misha sets me down on one of the swivel chairs that line the center island and points me in the direction of the food. "Hungry?"

I stroke a hand down his muscled arm. "I am now."

"I was talking about the food."

I giggle, realizing we're flirting. It feels so natural, but it's a new thing for us. I'm constantly surprised by it. I'm still getting used to this new dynamic, this one where things can just be *okay*. No buts. No catches. Nothing but love.

"Not that I don't love the spontaneity," I tell him, "but can I ask why we're having dinner at Konstantin's instead of our own home?"

"Because you needed a change of scenery."

I eye him for a moment. "You wanted to give me what I asked for, but you don't want me traipsing all over the city."

He smiles guiltily. "It's true what they say: smart women are sexy."

I place my hand on his. "I appreciate the effort, but we can't kick Konstantin out of his home every time we want a date night."

"Please," Misha scoffs, rolling his eyes. "Look at this place. It's not a home."

I have to agree with him there. As tasteful and beautiful as this penthouse is, it's definitely not homey. It looks like a model apartment..

"I can't imagine living here," I muse out loud.

"Well, then I'm glad I moved out when I did."

My mouth falls open. "*You* lived here?"

"Not here, exactly. Across the hall. I put it on the market when I moved into the mansion. I lived here for a few years before that."

I look around the space with new eyes. "Did it look like this?"

"Pretty much. It was just a place to sleep. I wasn't interested in making it feel like mine."

"What about when you... entertained?"

"I took business partners to clubs or restaurants. But if you mean women—"

"Obviously, I did, yes. That's what we in the business call a 'leading question.'" I circle a hand in the air to direct him to spit out the truth. "Now, out with it."

He laughs. "I was a monk. Never even looked at a woman until I met you." He gives me a lopsided smile that makes my heart melt and my center throb. Honestly, I feel sorry for all the women that have come before me.

None of them stood a chance.

"Fine. Keep your secrets." I lift a bite of food to my mouth, then stop and put it back down. "Can I ask you kind of a weird question?"

He sets down his chopsticks. "Oh, boy. Let's hear it."

"Do you think you'll miss it?"

"Miss what?"

"You know, like... going out on the town? Dirty dancing with hot strangers, flirting and drinking, sleeping with a different girl every night..."

"First of all," he says, holding up a finger, "I never 'dirty danced' with anyone."

"Misha, I'm serious."

He takes my right hand and brings it to his lips. "No, my love, I don't miss it. Nor will I ever."

"How can you be so sure?" I know that my insecurities are on full display, but sometimes, that's just how life goes. These days, I have too many feelings to keep them all to myself.

"Because even when I was out 'on the town,' as you put it, it was all empty."

"You're making it all sound so terrible, and yet I'm still burning up with jealousy."

"I'm the one who should be jealous," he says, squeezing my thigh beneath the counter. "I wasted my life on meaningless sex. You married your ex. Which tells me that, at least at one point in your life, you were in love with him."

"Yes, I thought I loved him," I agree. "But meeting you has forced me to question that."

He arches a brow, disbelief in the quirk of his mouth. "Oh?"

"I'm not trying to spare your feelings; I'm being honest. What I feel for you is so much... *bigger*. It feels so much more intense, more all-consuming. I can't stop thinking about you. I can't stop fantasizing about you. Whenever we fight, it feels like I'm carrying around this giant weight. I can't wait to make up. It never felt that way with Anthony."

"What did it feel like with him?"

I think about that for a moment. "Calm. Unruffled. And for a girl who spent her entire childhood and adolescence without either one of those things, I guess I clung to that when I found it. I called it love, and whenever I started to maybe question my feelings for Anthony, he'd do something sweet that would force me to reconsider. Even when his parents disapproved of our marriage, he married me anyway. But Anthony was just the calm before the storm. It was never going to last."

"Am I the storm?" Misha asks with amusement.

I lean in and press my lips to his. "You are everything."

38

MISHA

After an hour of working out, I've worked up a good sweat. I feel good. Strong. In control.

A sensation that's all too fleeting these days.

Petyr is still a phantom, the Babai are thus far next to useless, and my three enforcers are nowhere to be found.

Konstantin has launched a full-scale search for the missing men, but it's hard to do that effectively when we're still keeping the news from the council. I haven't decided if it's a generational thing or not, but the older council members tend to lead with brawn, rather than brain. Once they find out, it will be all-out war. Whereas I'd rather know what exactly we're up against.

I'm finishing up a set of curls when I hear a timid knock at the door. I drop my weights on the matted floor and wipe the sweat from my brow. "Enter."

Rada slinks in, her hands knotted in front of her. "I'm sorry to disturb you, sir, but a package has arrived at the gate. It's a big one. Addressed to Mrs. Paige."

I frown. "Who is it from?"

"There's no note, sir. Mr. Konstantin asked for your presence before they open it."

That can't be good. "Thank you." She turns to leave but I catch her. "Rada?"

"Yes, sir?"

"Don't mention this to my wife."

Her brow pulls in concern, but she nods. "Yes, sir."

I go downstairs, but the entryway is empty. The porch is empty, too. Then I look down the drive and see Konstantin standing inside the security shack with a handful of my guards gathered around him.

My suspicions swirl violently as I walk down there without even bothering to put a shirt on. "Konstantin?"

My cousin waves me over, his voice low. "Get in here. The package arrived about ten minutes ago. It's sealed ten ways to Tuesday. We've almost got it open."

"Rada said it was addressed to Paige."

Konstantin nods. "It was in a crate when it arrived. Carried in by a delivery driver." He snorts, hardly able to believe it himself. "He was in a brown uniform and everything. It was legit."

"But you're worried." He better be. This is suspicious as fuck, and I pay my cousin to pay attention.

"Absolutely. The thing had like ten layers of wrapping. By the time we got down to the last one, I started to smell something."

He gestures me into the security room, and I know exactly what he means. The smell is rancid. And familiar.

There is nothing so singular as the smell of rotting flesh.

"Open it," I order.

Konstantin pushes a guard out of the way and breaks the last seal himself. The box opens and the smell that was faint before becomes suddenly overwhelming. It's a foul, cloying mist in the air. My lungs are coated in it.

"Fuck," I hear someone mutter, just before two of my guards run out of the station to throw up in the bushes outside.

I press a forearm over my nose and lean forward to see exactly the kind of thing I expected: three severed heads sitting on a bloodstained cushion like artifacts in a history museum.

Konstantin pulls the collar of his shirt over his nose. But even with half his face covered, I can see the sickly gray pallor of his skin. "That's quite the statement."

"It'll be answered in kind." The threat is growled, vibrating through every bone in my body. "Start picking off his men one by one. Drop them off at his personal properties, his remaining businesses, his mistresses' houses. Make it fucking rain blood. Don't let up until we flush him out."

I step out of the security shack and take a deep breath of fresh air. My fists are knotted tight at my sides and my pulse is a pounding drumbeat at my temples.

Konstantin follows me out. "And if he still doesn't show?"

"He'll show. No one can stay hidden forever."

"Did you tell Paige about the delivery?"

"No." I turn to him to fix him with a harsh stare. "And she's not going to find out, either. Addressing the package to her was a cheap attempt at riling me up." I grimace. "Have the men bury the heads. Make sure we can trust them all to keep this thing quiet."

"That's going to be hard to do." Konstantin glances back at the guards warily.

"She only needs to stay in the dark for a short time. Until I figure out our next move."

"The Babai—"

"The Babai have been silent for far too long. Your mother's bedtime ghost stories notwithstanding, it's starting to make me question going to them in the first place." I shake my head in disgust. "I'm going to go shower. The smell of blood always takes forever to rinse off. Let me know when the corpses are disposed of."

I take the back stairs to my office. Paige is in the nursery with my mother, and I don't want to risk running into her before I've washed the stink off my body.

When I walk into my office, the window next to my desk has been pushed open. Last time I tried to wedge it open, the hinges were so rusted they wouldn't budge.

I scan the room, but nothing else is out of place. There's no other sign of anyone having been here.

Then I turn to my desk and see the note.

It's sitting in the center of my chair, out of sight from the doorway, but obvious once I come around the desk. Written in cursive with thick black ink. The paper itself is thick and pristinely white.

It will take time. Have patience. The Babai never fail.

"Fucking hell," I breathe.

How the fuck did they get in here undetected?

I spend the next hour checking my security feed again and again. All I find is a minute and eleven seconds of static and dead air. When the feed comes back on again, the window is open and the note is where I found it.

"Fuck," I mutter again.

Konstantin may be right about his old wives' tales.

39

MISHA

Days pass without any more packages. I'm returning from work, head lost in thought, but as I pass through the gates, I notice a flashy black convertible purring out front of the mansion.

Konstantin notices it, too. He leans forward and whistles. "There are only three cars like that in the world. And one of them belongs to—"

"Klim," we say together.

Konstantin smirks and drops back into the passenger seat. "The old man is paying you a house call. Must be important."

I park behind Klim's showboat and get out, then take the stairs three at a time until I burst into the foyer.

Noel is pacing the floor. He droops with relief when he sees me. "He's in the formal sitting room, sir. With the lady of the house."

I brush past him and straight to the sitting room to find Klim reclining in my favorite chair, a glass of wine in one hand

and his full attention fixated on my wife.

Paige is sitting prim and proper on the sofa, her hands folded in her lap. While the floral dress she's wearing can hide her burgeoning stomach, nothing can hide the swell of her breasts.

Klim may be pushing seventy, but he isn't blind. His eyes flit down to her chest every few seconds. When he sees me, he raises his wine. "Misha, there you are."

"You should have told me you were dropping by." I step behind Paige and put my hand on her shoulder.

"It was a last-minute whim. And a good one, too. I got to have some one-on-one time with your lovely wife. She's delightful, Misha. Your father would have loved her."

"My father wouldn't have cared who I married as long as she was fertile." My voice comes out desert-dry.

Klim smiles, all boundless joy and charm. It's a great cover. The man is anything but joyful.

Paige reads the room well and stands up. "I'll give you two some privacy. It was lovely getting to know you, Mr. Kulikov."

She walks around the sofa and lays a hand on my arm. I pull her in for a quick kiss on the cheek before I let her go. When she's gone, I take her spot on the couch.

"She really is lovely, Misha," Klim says, sounding surprised. "Where did you find her?"

"If I told you, I'd have to kill you."

He laughs without making a sound and takes another drink of wine. I wait for him to bring up the reason he's decided to drop in on me unannounced.

If he was anyone else, I would have brought it up myself. But Klim has established himself as more than just a senior Vor and a council member over the decades. I once called him "Uncle." Until I was old enough to realize he was more like a wolf in sheep's clothing.

He's on my side—for now. But men in my position know that even your own dogs can rip your throat out at a moment's notice.

Lips pursed, Klim places his glass on the side table and turns to me. "I remember every phase of your life, Misha. I remember when you were running around in diapers. I remember when you were your brother's shadow. You kept that up until he died. Where Maksim went, there went Misha."

I try not to flinch.

"Now, look at you. Don in your own right, a beautiful wife on your arm, and a child on the way."

Children, actually. But I don't bother correcting him.

The only thing I'm concerned with is discovering why he came in the first place. Klim has been notoriously reclusive the last few years. Looking at him now, I can see why.

Cancer has aged him. He looks ten years older, at least. His skin is sallow and wrinkled, his eyes bulging out of his shrinking head. All his old charisma is still there, but it comes with the sensation of fading batteries. A toy doing the same old song and dance as the movements slow and the recording degrades.

"Your father would be proud," he concludes.

"My father is dead. Pride is the least of his concerns now."

Klim is unmoved by my little outburst. "He was proud of you, too."

"He was proud of himself and little else. Enough games, Klim. Why don't you tell me why you're really here?"

He gives me a cold smile. "Straight to business. Very well. There is displeasure in the ranks. Much of the council feels you are handling the Ivanov insurrection all wrong."

"Ah. And they sent you as their spokesperson?"

His smile tightens. "You are the don, but we are the power that sits behind you, Misha. We have the right to question your decisions when they fly in the face of reason."

"No," I say curtly. "You have the right to ask for clarification. Anything more than that amounts to treason. And you know as well as I do how we handle traitors in the Bratva."

Klim sits up a little straighter, his eyes floating over to the half-full wine glass for a moment before they land back on me.

"Very well," he says. "Then I will ask for clarification. What is your plan?"

"It's unfolding as we speak. We have Petyr in a stranglehold, which is why he's missing. He's trying to hit me from the shadows, but I plan on weeding him out soon."

His papery lips press together in distaste. "Vague."

"Some plans depend on secrecy. Even from those closest to me."

He leans forward, a small movement that seems to require a lot of strength. "Forgive me if I sound like I am questioning you, but the council feels your strategy is too… cerebral. You're trying to outsmart the man rather than make a show of strength."

"There are many ways to skin a cat, Klim. Or, for that matter, to skin an Ivanov."

He grimaces distastefully. "We have one tool in our world: power."

"Power doesn't have to be so dumbly obvious."

"Of course it does," he snaps. "That's the whole fucking point."

Klim is losing his cool, but I keep mine. The last thing I need is him returning to the council with claims that I'm erratic.

"Petyr knows me, Klim. Loathe as I am to admit, he knows me. He went underground because he anticipated a show of strength. He expected me to come at him hard. If I were to take your suggestion, I would be playing right into his hands."

"Does it matter? You're on top. You can strike him from there. It's a good position to be in!"

"It would have been a good move, in my father's time." I make sure to choose my words carefully. "But that time is gone. It's my time now."

Klim stiffens. That's the thing about powerful men: their egos are as big as they are sensitive. He doesn't like feeling redundant.

"Well, you are the don."

I reach over and hand him his wine glass, pushing it gently but firmly into his hand. "My priority is this Bratva, Klim. I will do whatever it takes to make sure it's protected."

"And what about that pretty little wife of yours?" he asks. "It's quite a talent to rise from the dead. But I'm not sure she'll be able to pull it off a second time."

"She's protected."

"She's a liability," Klim spits. "She's a pretty thing, but you should know better. Maksim made the same mistake—falling for the woman he married. A wife exists to make more dons; nothing more is required of her."

I have to press my hand into the sofa to prevent Klim from seeing the fist I've made. Today's not the day to alienate an old ally, redundant or not.

I rise to my feet, signaling that this little visit is at an end. "I will let you know when there's something to know. Feel free to take your wine with you."

He sighs and struggles to his feet. I offer him my hand, but he flicks it away. By the time he's making his way towards the door, his neck is red and he's out of breath.

"I hope you know what you're doing." Klim studies me closely. "You know, you look a lot like him."

"Maksim?" I guess.

He shakes his head. "No. Your father."

I manage to hold my tongue as I walk him to the door. The silence is cool but cordial. I can feel the ghost of my father between us now, reminding me of what the Orlov Bratva used to be.

I'm not concerned with what the Bratva once was, though.

I'm only concerned with what it could be.

40

PAIGE

Misha is sitting in front of me, his long legs stretched out in front of him off the end of the bed. My fingers knead and work at the knots in his shoulders, but it's been twenty minutes and he's still tense.

"My fingers are going to fall off if I keep this up." I slump against the pillows and pull him back against my chest. He is warm and heavy against me as I run my fingers through his hair. "You seem distracted today. Is everything okay?"

"Everything is—" He sighs and lets the almost-lie of a sentence die. "I received something. But it's taken care of now."

"What kind of 'something'?"

"A threat from Petyr."

My heart jolts in my chest, but I try to remain outwardly calm. If Misha isn't worried, I don't want to be worried. "Is that why Klim came to visit yesterday? Was he checking in on the threat?"

"No."

He's holding out on me, I know it. He just doesn't want to stress me out.

I lean forward and press my lips to his neck. He arches into me, softening in my arms. "Klim seems... interesting."

"I don't want to talk about Klim while you're kissing me like that," he growls.

I smile and look into his eyes. "Then I'll stop. Tell me about him."

Misha sighs. "Klim should have retired years ago. The man doesn't want to admit he's past his prime."

"He seemed fond of you." Klim spoke briefly about Misha as a little boy. He seemed almost like a grandfather-type figure.

Then I kept catching him staring at my breasts, and I realized he might not be quite that wholesome.

"Trust me; it's not fondness. It's a perverse sense of nostalgia. I remind him of a time in his life when he was still useful."

"I'm sensing some hostility there?" I guess, smoothing my hands over the rippling muscles of his chest. He feels like a washboard under my fingers.

"I don't take kindly to being told how to run my Bratva. Or my life."

"Did he say something about me?" I surmise.

"No, not really."

I roll my eyes. "Which means he definitely did. It doesn't matter what he said, Misha. Don't let him get inside your head."

Misha pushes off me and twists around so that we're facing each other. "He isn't inside my head. But that doesn't mean he doesn't have a point."

"A point about what?"

He grabs my hands, squeezing them between his large fingers. "You're vulnerable right now. Petyr knows you're alive. He also knows that you're my Achilles heel. He's going to try to hit me where it hurts."

"You've taken every precaution to protect me, Misha," I remind him. "I'm safe. This mansion is a fortress."

"Even a fortress can be breached," he mutters.

He mumbles something else, and I think I catch the words "The Wolf," but I'm pretty sure I've misheard. I don't know how a wolf would get mixed up in this business.

"Petyr is not going to get close enough to me to do me any harm. I have tons of people watching me at any given moment. There are guards and cameras, extra layers of protection ready to step up as soon as one fails. I'm safe."

He meets my gaze, and I can see an idea forming there. He doesn't seem to be in a hurry to share it with me, though. Instead, he presses a distracted kiss to my forehead and gets off the bed.

"Where are you going?" I ask.

"I have some things to sort out. You should get some rest."

I rise to my knees, barely resisting the urge to lunge after him and grab his shirt. "It's almost nine o'clock. You're really going back down to the office?"

"I won't be long," he assures me. "An hour at the most."

I sigh, recognizing the look on his face. There's no way I'm going to be able to convince him to stay. So I decide to let this battle go.

My phone buzzes somewhere under the blankets, and I start searching for it. It's probably Rowan or Cyrille calling to chit-chat.

Misha pulls on a shirt, and I point a warning finger at him. "If you're not back in my arms in an hour, I'm coming down to get you."

He leans over the bed and kisses me on the lips. "Deal."

I continue fumbling around for my phone, but I don't find it until it has already stopped ringing and Misha is long gone.

The missed call is from an unknown number. It's been so long since I've had a call from anyone beyond the immediate family. They were the only ones who knew I was alive for a long stretch. I guess I shouldn't be surprised that other people are reaching out now that I've resurrected myself.

It's late and I'm thinking about ignoring the call altogether when it starts vibrating again.

"Shit," I mutter, acting on instinct and answering the call before I can chicken out. "Hello?"

"Hi. Is this Faye… the accountant?"

I frown. *Faye the accountant?* Who the hell is—

Then I recognize the voice. *Her voice.*

"Jillian?" I ask.

"You're that accountant woman, right? The one who works for my daughter?"

I hear a man in the background shout, "*Our* daughter!"

When was the last time I heard my father's voice? He sounds so much older. His voice is like a flat tire flapping on gravel. I hear decades of cigarettes and bourbon soaked into the fabric of each word.

"No, this isn't Faye," I say automatically.

"Huh? Then how'd you know my name?" Jillian demands. "Who the fuck're—"

"Faye doesn't exist, Mama," I snap. "It's me. Paige."

A pause. A long, pregnant pause. Then: "… P-Paige?"

More scrambling on the other line. Dad's breathing comes through the line clearly. "Fucking hell. Is that my Paige girl?"

I would roll my eyes if they weren't brimming with tears. I don't know why I'm so emotional. They don't deserve my sadness. "You have literally never called me that in your life."

"Oh, for fuck's sake," my mother interjects. "Bawling like a baby because you didn't get a nickname? Grow up."

I exhale. There isn't enough time in the world to outline all the things I didn't get from them. I don't even want to try. "I just want to know why you called me in the first place."

"Well… we just wanted to know how you were doing," Garrett says.

"We haven't seen or spoken to you in years," Jillian adds in this false, high-pitched, wheedling, *you-owe-me* voice that sets my teeth on edge. "And then you call us with a fake name—"

"I called you to give you money," I interrupt. "I called you to make sure you were both doing okay."

"You pretended to be someone else!"

"I thought it would be easier!" I snap back. "I mean, come on, Mama. It's not like you were happy to hear from me again."

"Whoa, honey," Garrett chimes in. He's never called me "honey" before. "That's heavy shit you're saying. It's totally wrong."

"Unfair!" Jillian crows. "Totally unfair. We did the best we could."

"*That* was your best?" I scoff. "I'd hate to see your worst."

"It was that Cori kid; she was the one who poisoned you against us," Jillian says. "Before her, you were a quiet little girl who minded her own business."

"Her name was *Clara*," I grit out. "She was my best friend. My family. What kind of mother doesn't know her daughter's closest friend's name?"

"Don't be so snotty," Garrett says sourly. "You had your own thing going on, and we had ours. It was nice, actually. You were so independent."

"I had to be. It's not like I had parents who could take care of me!"

"It's not easy being a parent, you know," Jillian whines, sniffing into the phone. Crocodile tears if I've ever heard them. "You'll know that soon enough."

"What do you mean?"

"We know you're having a kid."

Goosebumps erupt over my skin. "Who told you?"

She doesn't answer my question, though. "We didn't realize how well our little girl was doing for herself."

"You must have gotten an idea from the checks I send you every month. Is that what this call is about? You want more money, don't you?"

"Don't say it like that, Paige," Garrett hisses. "We looked after you all those years. I mean, it's the circle of life, right? We took care of you, and now, you take care of us."

I knew this would happen the moment I set up a separate account for them. Still, nothing could have prepared me for the acidic taste in my mouth. The twist of my stomach at their shamelessness.

Or the plunge of self-shaming guilt when I realize I'm still going to give them what they're asking for.

"How much do you want?"

"We are thinking about upgrading to a better trailer. Something with a little leg room, you know?" Dad laughs.

Mama has gone silent. I want to believe it's because she feels guilty for asking in the first place, but I know it's just because she thinks Garrett is more capable of extorting me.

The fact of the matter is that he doesn't even have to try. I'd pay them a million dollars to end this call.

"I'll transfer more money to you in a few days."

"And it gets pretty cold here during winter. Getting a half-decent heater is expensive, though…"

I should cut them off and hang up. But I've never been as good at casual cruelty as the two of them are.

"Is that all?" I ask.

I wait for something. A tiny little gesture of affection, a word of gratitude, maybe even regret. But the silence on the other end of the line just reminds me of why I left in the first place.

There's nothing for me in Corden Park.

Without Clara, there never was.

"Okay then. That's what I thought. Goodbye."

I hang up, fling my phone onto the bed and wrap my arms around my body. I may not know what kind of parent I'll be, but I sure as hell know what kind of parent I won't be.

I have Jillian and Garrett to thank for that.

41

PAIGE

After the call, I go to the nursery to distract myself for a while. I'm seated on the floor, looking at paint colors and wallpaper samples, when Nessa bursts through the door, bags hanging from her arm.

"I come bearing baby gifts!" She pulls out a set of matching onesies and drapes them over the edge of the crib. "Look at these little outer space outfits. Aren't they the cutest?"

"They're precious! Hopefully, they'll have time to wear them. We have so many clothes already."

"Babies go through outfits like crazy. All of the spitting up and drooling and diaper explosions. Trust me, you're going to need all of these. The moment you two tell me what the genders are, I'm going to go wild. The only reason I've been as reined in as I have been is because it's hard to find gender-neutral baby clothes."

I watch as she takes her new purchases and stacks them in the overflowing closet. These two babies aren't even born yet and they have a wardrobe ten times the size of any I ever had.

Almost as if she can read my mind, Nessa winces. "You must think I'm being very excessive. Wasteful, even."

"Oh, no!" I rush to reassure her. "Of course not, Nessa."

She runs her hand along the tags hanging off all of the new clothes. Then she drops herself down in the window seat. "Sometimes, I think the same thing myself."

I join Nessa, folding my legs underneath me. "I don't think you're wasteful. Really. This is just different from what I'm used to. There's nothing wrong with that."

She waves me away. "I know I have a tendency to go overboard. I suppose it's the way I self-soothe."

She looks down into her lap, and for a moment, I see what she must have been like as a young woman. Isolated and afraid, uncertain the way everyone is in their early twenties, embarking into a new marriage without any clue what her future would hold.

"I didn't have much of a marriage, as you know. I suppose I found comfort in caring for my children. Then, when they stopped needing me, I threw myself into charities and shopping. Every time I felt sad, I went out and bought myself a new dress. Eventually, I had the wall knocked down between two guest bedrooms and I turned that into my new closet." She gives me a guilty smile. "I know this must not seem like a very real problem to you."

"Unhappiness is unhappiness. It doesn't really matter if you live in a castle or a hole in the ground."

"That's kind of you to say." She sighs. "It's not the life I imagined for myself, but I wouldn't change any of it now. He gave me my children."

"I've never asked how you met Misha's father."

"The marriage was arranged between my father and Maksim." She sees my frown and hurries to explain. "My husband's name was Maksim, too; we named our firstborn after him. It was my idea, actually. Stupid. I thought that would make him love me."

I can't blame Nessa for having the kind of hope I've harbored for so long. Especially when it worked out for me. Misha and I are happy together now. My heart breaks that Nessa never got to experience that.

Nessa's gaze is distant, hazy with memory. "It all happened so fast. I was nineteen when my father told me that I would be marrying Maksim Orlov. A few months later, I had my first baby. I thought it would bring us closer together, but my husband moved Maksi into his own nursery with a live-in nanny. Then he moved me into a separate wing of the house with my own staff."

I shift in place uncomfortably, remembering the time Misha suggested the same thing for us. It feels like a different life now. A different man.

"It took me a while to realize that he had moved me out to make room for his mistress. I still remember her. She was a willowy blonde with the bluest eyes I'd ever seen. She used to lounge by the pool in the evening and wait for him to come home."

"Oh God. I can't even imagine what that must have been like."

"It felt like a nightmare. But by the time I realized that my husband's mistress was living in the same house as me, I was already pregnant with Misha."

I cringe. Her pain is so tangible, so real, even all these years later. I feel it like it's my own. "You don't have to share all this with me if you don't want to," I tell her gently.

"It's actually nice to say it all out loud," she confesses. "I think I've kept it in too long. But if you don't want to hear all of this, I don't have to share."

I look at Nessa and see the vulnerability there, but also the trust. Right now, we're not mother-in-law and daughter-in-law. We're just two women who have both been through a hell of a lot.

"I'm always here if you need to talk."

She smiles. "And I'm always here if *you* need to talk. I know I'm an irritant to my children sometimes."

"They don't know how lucky they are," I say softly.

"No one appreciates a parent quite as much as the child who's never had one." She looks up at me with a sympathetic smile. "I'm glad to have you as a daughter now. I'm even more glad that my son has chosen to accept you as a wife."

"I'm glad, too," I admit. "Surprised at all of it—like you said, it happened so fast—but glad."

Nessa laughs gracefully. "My son was raised by a father who taught him that women were nothing more than objects to be used and discarded. A wife was required to bear legitimate heirs, manage the household, and give the appearance of respectability. But other than that, she served no purpose. But my husband didn't take into account one very crucial possibility." She leans closer with a conspiratorial twinkle in her eye. "Maksim assumed that our sons would turn out just like him. But the truth is, their deepest natures ended up being more like mine. My children are capable of great love, Paige. Which is why they try so hard to fight it."

I nod, remembering how hard Misha fought me.

"But the thing is, when you meet the right person... you can't stop love. No matter how hard you try."

42

MISHA

I find my mother and Paige in the nursery. Mother gives me a strange glance and disappears without a word. Paige looks at me and for a moment, I see something swim in her eyes. Some fleeting pain, some hushed melancholy. Then it's gone, and she smiles.

"Everything okay?" she asks as she stands up.

I hold out my hand to her. "C'mon. We've got plans."

~

Paige walks into the Swan Suite with wide eyes. "This hotel is amazing. But we live literally ten minutes away, Misha. Is this really necessary?"

"Of course not. No one *needs* a heated mattress pad, a television that rises out of the floor, or a jacuzzi tub big enough for an elephant. But we can, so why shouldn't we?"

"Because it's a waste of money?"

I raise my eyebrows. "I didn't realize we were strapped for cash."

She rolls her eyes. "You know what I mean."

"No, I don't," I retort. "I work hard and so do you. Plus, you're the one who wants to get out of the house more. This is how I'm helping you do that." I pull her against my chest and press my nose to her hair. "If it will make your bleeding heart feel better, we can make a large cash donation to a charity of your choice when we're back home."

"You're joking, but I'm gonna hold you to it."

"I have no doubt." I breathe in deep. "You smell amazing."

She smiles as a blush warms her cheeks.

I stroke my thumb across her chin. "I like that I can still make you blush."

"I'm pretty sure you'll be able to make me blush twenty years from now."

"I guess we'll have to wait and see." I gently kiss the backs of her fingers, and just like that, she swoons in my arms.

I've realized slowly over the last couple of weeks that these small gestures mean so much more to her than the grand ones. Take her to an expensive five-star hotel across town, and she's politely ambivalent. Kiss her hand, and she turns to putty in my arms.

"Are you in the mood for something different tonight?" I ask.

She gives me a suspicious look. "Are we talking sex stuff? Because I'm not sure how adventurous I can be in my current state. These babies are playing bongos on my rib cage."

I laugh. "That wasn't exactly what I had in mind, now. But now that you mention it, that dress is doing things for me…"

She slaps me in the arm. "Keep it in your pants, Mr. Orlov. But aside from whatever depraved things you seem to be picturing, I'm up for whatever. We did just get here, though?"

"And we'll be back later tonight," I say as I take her hand and lead her out of the suite. "But right now, we have to get to the Fox Acres Warehouse."

"What's there?"

I smile cryptically. "You'll see."

∼

My refusal to give her so much as a single hint does not deter Paige from spending the entire drive guessing what we might be doing tonight.

"Oh, *I* know," she says for the fifth time. "You've set up an open-air movie for us to watch! Popcorn and everything."

"Nope."

"Dammit." She frowns. "I'm officially running out of guesses."

"You're way off. It's not nearly as romantic as you're imagining." I park just outside the warehouse, grab the duffel bag I stashed in the trunk, and walk around to the passenger side door to open it for Paige.

She slips out of the car, looking around in confusion. I take her hand and we walk into the warehouse together. It's a cavernous space made even larger by the lack of anything at all inside.

Except for the targets set up at the far end of the room.

Paige hasn't even noticed them yet. "You didn't bring me here to kill me, did you? 'Cause that would definitely not be romantic."

I pull her to my side and kiss her temple. "Not today." I point to the mannequins standing at the opposite end of the room, red and white bullseyes taped to their chests.

"Oh, God!" she gasps. "I thought they were real people for a second. Are those… targets?"

"That's precisely what they are." I open up the duffel bag and pull out two guns.

"Misha! What's going on?" she yelps as I check the magazines and clear the chambers.

"The other day, you said something when we were talking. You said that I didn't have to worry about you because there were so many people protecting you," I remind her. "That struck a nerve—because people can fail. Systems fail. If they do…" I take her hand and press one of the guns into her palm. "I want you to learn how to protect yourself."

Her eyes bug out with realization. "You're going to teach me to shoot?" She looks down at the gun in her hand. "It's heavy."

"You just have to get used to the feel of it in your hand. Once you do, it'll start to feel like an extension of yourself."

She wrinkles her nose. "I'm not sure I want that."

"Either way, you might be thankful for this knowledge one day in the future."

Her warm, green eyes find mine. "Things with Petyr are heating up, aren't they?" she asks in a quiet, somber voice. "That's why you've been so worried lately."

I want to protect Paige from the gruesome details. I don't want to worry her.

But part of protecting her is making sure she's prepared.

"Yes, they are. I will do whatever it takes to protect you, Paige. I'll wade through hellfire to keep you safe. But if I can't be there, I want you to be able to protect yourself."

She stares at me for a long moment. I have no idea what the hell she's thinking.

Then she reaches out and squeezes my hand. "You were wrong," she says. "This might be the most romantic thing you've ever done."

43

PAIGE

The date started out fun. Full-on rom-com style, with Misha wrapping his arms around me, swaddling me in his warmth and his smell while he whispered instructions in my ear. He was so tender, so attentive. When my ear protection slipped just barely out of place, he firmly put it back where it belonged and told me I was worth protecting, every part of me.

"Even your selective hearing," he teased.

My first few shots went wildly off-target, of course, even with him there to steady my hands and show me the ropes. I offered up silent apologies to the warehouse rafters that'll forever be scarred by my shit aim.

But then an hour passed, and another, and by the end of it, I was hitting four or five out of every ten with reasonable confidence.

The first time I went ten for ten, I whipped off my goggles and headphones and whirled around to look at him. I wanted to see him beaming with pride. I was so, so sure that's exactly what he'd be doing. That he'd sweep me up in his embrace and kiss that soft spot below my ear that functions like a *TURN PAIGE ON* button.

But he didn't do any of that.

He looked at me with that cold, gray, glacial distance I hate so much and said, "Good."

That's it. Just, "Good." No "I'm so proud of you, *kiska*." No sweet nothings.

Good. The word has never felt so frigid or meaningless.

Now, we're stepping back into the hotel suite, and I can feel the distance between us like I'm standing on the edge of a huge, dark canyon filled with shadows at the bottom. He's taking off his shirt in the bedroom when he speaks for the first time in twenty minutes.

"We're hosting a dinner next week."

"A dinner?" I ask, trying to get him to make eye contact with me. He refuses.

"We need to address your resurrection, and we need to introduce you to the Bratva from a position of power. It's a good time to announce your pregnancy, too. Strategically, the timing is right."

I frown. "Okay. Strategic dinner. Got it."

"This is important, Paige," he tells me, as though I've just told him that I'm not willing to host it. "It won't be just the family—it'll include council members, senior Vors, and long-time business partners. We need to establish ourselves as the ones in charge."

He sits in the middle of the sofa in just his undershirt, with his arms and legs spread in a limp, exhausted kind of way. His eyes are trained on the open doors of the balcony, but the light in them is bleak.

Nervously, I slip off my dress, revealing the jade green lingerie I have on underneath. It was supposed to be a surprise. The grand reveal of the night, so I could repay him in part for the things both big and little he does just to make me smile.

The set came with a garter belt, but it wouldn't fit over my baby bump. But the lace bra and matching panties—what little there is of them—still fit fine.

I kick my dress to the side and wait for Misha to pounce. But he doesn't even seem to notice. His gaze stays locked on the double doors to the balcony and the cityscape spread out below us.

"I had no idea I'd be competing with architecture," I blurt. "Maybe I should have worn a skyline under my dress."

He smiles at the joke, but it's thin. "You're beautiful, Paige."

Actions speak louder than words, I think. Usually, Misha shows me exactly how beautiful he thinks I am.

What's stopping him now?

I move in front of him and slide gently between his legs. I press my hands to the back of the couch on either side of his head, displaying all of my cleavage. "Would you like to tell me what is going on with you?"

"Nothing is going on."

"Ah, see? There's the trouble." I slide onto his lap, straddling his thighs. "Usually, you'd say something like, 'I'm about to fuck you until you convert to the religion of me; that's what's going on.' But you aren't even interested in my lingerie."

In response, Misha grabs my ass and rocks me over his crotch. Heat swirls low in my belly when I feel his excitement. "You're hard."

"I'm always hard for you," he growls, though it sounds sort of pained, in a way I can't quite explain.

I swallow down my nerves. "Okay, then what's with the hesitation now? Ever since I started hitting shots at the range, you've been... distant."

His hands stroke gently over my hips and my thighs, slowly massaging away my worries. He's quiet for a long time before he finally speaks. "It was a strange experience, watching you with that gun. Stranger than I expected."

"You didn't like it?" I ask. "It was your idea."

He nods. "I know. I know it was. And for the first ten minutes, it was sexy. You looked so powerful."

"But?" I prod.

"But then... reality sank in."

I stroke his dark hair away from his forehead. "What reality is that?"

At long last, he makes eye contact with me. The gray in his eyes is gone, replaced by sadness that makes my heart wrench. "You're a target, Paige. And you're a target because of me."

"So it's a pity party. That's why you're pouting."

"I'm not pouting."

"Please, this is a total pout fest you've got going on here." I trail my fingers over his face. "You're just lucky you look so good doing it."

His brows are knotted together. "This is serious, Paige."

I move my hips against his erection and I can see the lust pool in those silver eyes of his. "I'm being deadly serious right now. I want you, Misha."

"You aren't prepared." The stubborn set to his jaw tells me he isn't talking about sex.

"You just taught me how to fire a gun, remember? I'd say I'm prepared for anything."

His voice rips out of him in an unexpected snarl. "That statement alone proves how unprepared you are!"

I push his shirt up and bend down to kiss his abs as I ease him back into his seat. "I can take care of myself, Misha. And if you'd let me, I'd love to take care of you, too."

His body is responding to me the way it always does, but he's still tense above the shoulders. "I wouldn't be so cocky if I were you."

I smirk at the unintentional double entendre. "Believe me, I'd love to be cocky right about now."

He huffs in frustration. "You're still a beginner. It shows."

"Then teach me," I say slowly, really wrapping my lips around each word. "Practice makes perfect. That's why I always keep working at my skills. I practice and practice and practice…"

Champagne Wrath

As I speak, I unbutton his pants and free his hard cock. I take him in my palm, stroking him gently. It draws a strangled growl from his throat.

"But I can do new things, too," I tell him. "*Hard* things. Like this dinner we're going to throw."

He blinks, surprised at the change in direction. For a second there, he was lost in the rhythm of my touch.

"What about the dinner?" His voice is breathless.

"I'm going to be the best hostess there ever was."

"You've never done anything like this before," he reminds me.

I circle my hand around the base of him, pulling and massaging as I consider my game plan. "I'm going to pick the perfect dress, plan the perfect meal, choose the finest wines."

"It takes more than that to impress these people."

"I know." I let go of him and sit up. "I'm not naive, Misha; I know what the men must think of me. One look and they can tell I haven't been bred for this sort of life. This dinner is not just about power, is it? It's about me proving myself to the rest of them. Same as those board members. They want to rip me apart, and it's my job not to let them."

Now, he does look impressed.

Misha grabs my ass and stands up, taking me with him. He carries me to the long table just behind the sofa and lays me down on the marble top.

He hovers over me, his eyes black with desire. "You need to prove yourself to them because they don't know you as well as I do. They don't know they're the ones who ought to be afraid." He kisses over my ribs and nips at the lacy edge of my bra. "This color of green suits you."

"Really? Because I'm beginning to second guess it. I think you should rip it off of me."

He doesn't crack a smile. The desire in his eyes fades, and he looks at me with almost professional scrutiny. "They're going to tear apart every single thing you do. Every single thing you say."

I'm thrumming with frustrated desire. "I can handle it, Misha. Just—"

He rips my panties off, and the words stick in my throat. When he slips his fingers between my thighs, my thoughts are gone, too.

"Perfect," he sighs, working his fingers in and out of me. "They're going to expect you to be perfect."

"No one is perfect." I'm trembling all over. I have no idea why we're even having this conversation right now.

I'm trying super hard to care about anyone else on the face of the earth, but right now, there is only Misha and me. I can feel his cock against my thigh. His fingers pushing into me, stroking places I didn't even know existed.

"Misha, I can't—" I swallow down a moan and shift my hips, trying and failing to squirm away from the sensation building between my legs. "I need—"

"You're walking into a world you don't know. You can't slip. You can't falter."

I know he's right. But when he's inside of me like this, it's easy to forget that I'm an outsider. Being married to Misha is not enough; his men have to accept me, too.

His cock strokes my entrance, and I arch off the table. "F-f-fuck." My thighs quiver as I try to draw him in closer. "For the love of God, Misha. If you don't make me come right now, I'm going to die."

"Well, we can't have that, can we?" he growls.

Then he thrusts inside of me.

I'm filled to the brim with him, physically, emotionally, mentally. Misha is everywhere. All consuming. I cry out and cling to him as the beginnings of an orgasm tremble through me.

I want Misha. All of him. All the time.

But I want to be the perfect Bratva wife, too. For no other reason than to make my husband proud.

44

PAIGE

We've been at this for hours. But as my mother-in-law keeps reminding me, I can't afford to make a mistake. I need to be perfect.

Nessa claps her hands each time I get a name right. But before the praise can sink in, she's already holding up another photograph. "Who is this man?"

I study the color photo. I've seen it already, I know that. Like most of her other flashcards, this one looks like a mug shot. The man's graying hair is mussed, his skin ghostly pale. His canines are more like fangs.

"Kol something?" I guess.

Nessa arches a brow. "Try again. He'd never forget that insult."

"Shit." I study the picture again and a flicker of some memory from earlier arises. "Kolzak? Kolzak Gusev?"

Nessa beams. "Correct!"

I give myself an internal pat on the back just before Nessa presents me with another photograph. This time, it is of a beautiful woman with long, dark hair. She's wearing an alarmingly small bikini on a breathtakingly gorgeous beach.

"I haven't seen this one before, right? I'd remember her."

"Now that you know Kolzak, I figured I'd introduce you to his wife, Isidora."

My mouth falls open. "That's his *wife*? I would have guessed daughter."

"There is a thirty-three age difference between them," Nessa informs me. "And Kolzak watches her like a hawk. When he's not around, she's got her own personal watchdog in the form of this man."

Nessa reveals another photo of a short, balding man with a thickly muscled neck. His mouth is twisted into a cruel sneer.

"The rumor is that Kolzak had Manuel castrated years ago to make sure he would never be able to touch any of his women."

I stare at Nessa in shock. "Is that true?"

She shrugs. "It doesn't really matter what's true or not, Paige. What matters is what people believe."

"I feel like you're trying to tell me something here."

She smiles. "You're a sweet girl—kind-hearted, honest, sweet. All wonderful qualities. Qualities that I deeply appreciate in the woman my son chose. But I'm not sure they'll endear you to the guests you're going to be hosting next week. You need to be—"

"I need to be a Bratva wife," I echo in a monotone for the hundredth time since this study session began.

She nods. "Exactly. Misha will have your back, but it can't look like he's coming to your defense all the time. It will make you look weak."

I was confident with Misha the other night, assuring him I'd be the perfect hostess. But now that I'm back in my normal clothes and faced with the reality of the situation, nerves are starting to win out.

I didn't expect there would be so much to learn. It feels like I'm about to step into a minefield without a map.

"How did you manage when you first married Maksim?" I ask.

"Trial and error," she says simply. "My first dinner was a disaster. I picked the wrong food and chose the wrong wine. It could have all been okay, but the other wives descended on me with their judgment and critiques, and I burst into tears and ran out of the room."

"Oh no!"

"I was already pregnant at the time, so Maksim made excuses for me and blamed my outburst on hormones. But once the guests were gone, he stomped up to my bedroom and threw a fit. He broke a mirror, threw things, ripped the dress I was wearing to tatters. I swear the only reason he didn't hit me is because I was pregnant."

"Oh, Nessa. I'm so sorry."

"It's nothing for you to worry about." She gives me a reassuring pat. "Misha is a different man than his father was."

"He is," I say adamantly. "That's exactly why I want him to be proud of me."

She smiles. "He will be proud of you no matter what. He loves you."

"Yes, but his men need to love me, too. It's important to Misha. That makes it important to me. I just…" I break off, caught up by my own vulnerability.

"Tell me, darling."

"I don't want him to regret choosing me," I admit in a whisper. "I don't want him to ever think that he might have been better off if he'd picked a different woman to be his wife. Someone who knows more about his world and how to exist here."

Nessa shakes her head. "That won't happen. You can do this, Paige."

"How can you be so sure?"

"Because you've got fight in you," she says. "I know that because you managed to wear down my stubborn son. He had himself convinced he was going to be a bachelor for life. And now, look at him! He's become the man I always knew he could be."

The lump in my throat swells. It's threatening to send me into complete hysterics. I can't even blame my hormones; I would be fighting the exact same emotions even if I wasn't pregnant.

I wait until the lump has softened before I give her a shaky smile. "I've never known what it feels like to have a real family. But now, thanks to you, I do."

"If you ever need advice or help or anything at all, you can always come to me, Paige. I'm as good as your mother now."

Well, that'll do it. There's no squashing down the emotion now. I swipe at my eyes. "You're going to make me cry."

Nessa laughs and puts her hand on my knee. "If you need to cry, my shoulder is right here."

Okay, *that'll* do it.

Tears roll down my cheeks and she holds me while I cry. Happy tears, emotional tears, regretful tears, resentful tears, all the tears. But for the first time in my twenty-eight years, I feel like I have a mother who will hold me through all of it.

45

PAIGE

I walk out of the closet and twirl for Cyrille. "What do you think of this one?"

I've tried on so many dresses that they are starting to blur together. Truth be told, I'm not even totally confident that I haven't tested this one out already.

Cyrille looks up from her book and offers a thin, tired smile. "Pretty."

I turn to the full-length mirror and catch a glimpse of Ilya spread out on the carpet behind me. He's working on a model warship and hasn't offered his opinion on a dress in over half an hour. He gave up after dress two, poor kid.

The dress is white and floaty, but the bodice is clingy. It makes my bump look huge. I feel like a yeti.

"I have to look perfect for this dinner, Cyrille. I need to look like I belong by his side."

Cyrille nods and squints, studying me. "Okay. Okay... I think I know what dress you need to wear for this dinner."

She disappears into the closet, and I wait while she rustles around, sliding hangers and tossing a pile of discarded dresses through the doorway and onto the carpet. Finally, she reappears holding a shimmering gown with a tight corset top and a sculptured balloon skirt.

"That's for me?" I clarify.

"Who else would it be for?"

"Oh, I don't know, maybe someone who isn't pregnant with twins!" I lay a hand on her shoulder. "Cy, I love you, but there's no way I can wear that."

She brushes off my hand and moves around, holding the dress in front of me in the mirror. "Look. It's a short corset that ends right above your stomach. And the skirt is big enough to hide your bump. You can totally pull this off! Especially since you haven't gained weight anywhere else. Have I mentioned how annoying that is, by the way? How much I hate you for it?"

I take the dress and give it a once-over. "I don't know…"

"Just try it on and see," Cyrille encourages. "It can't hurt."

There's no reason not to at this point. I've tried on every other dress I own; this is kind of my last resort.

I walk the dress back into the closet and admire the shimmering fabric. The color shifts from jade green to gold and ends in burgundy around the hem. It reminds me of a mermaid tail.

I step into the dress, expecting it to make me look as large as I feel. But somehow, the voluminous skirt doesn't make me look bloated; it makes me look powerful. It's eye-catching in all the right ways.

"Well? How's it going in there?" Cyrille asks impatiently.

"Get in here."

The doors slide open and Cyrille takes one look at me and claps her hands together. "What did I tell you?"

"It's amazing," I admit. "You were right." I twist around and show her the zipper. "I couldn't quite get this all the way up, though."

Cyrille rubs her hands together, determination in her eyes. "Lemme at her."

She pulls a few times, but the zipper doesn't budge past my low back.

"Okay, so it's a little small," she concedes. "But no worries—my seamstress can let it out a few inches and we're good to go. I'll take it with me today and have it back to you on the day of the dinner."

"Are you sure? I could always wear something else instead…" I look hopelessly at the multi-colored carnage of my closet.

"What were you planning to wear?" she challenges. "Because it wasn't anything I saw today. It was all awful."

"Hey! You said they were all nice!"

"Only because I didn't think you had any other options," she laughs. I swat at her arm, and she dodges me.

We laugh, and I reach for her again—this time, to pull her in for a hug. "You're the best, you know."

She pats my back. "That's what sisters are for."

Grateful tears well in my eyes, but I blink them away. I look back in the mirror, admiring the silhouette.

"You look great. And better yet, this dress is perfect for hiding a weapon."

I arch a brow. "A weapon?"

"I was nervous about my first dinner as a Bratva wife, too," she confesses. "My solution was to strap a knife to my thigh."

I stare at her reflection, wide-eyed. "You went *armed*?"

"I know it sounds ridiculous, but it helped me. All the men carry weapons, so why not me?" she explains. "I didn't want to be left out. I never had to use it, but the point is that I knew it was there. That made all the difference."

"Did you know how to use it?" I ask.

"Aim the pointy end at the other guy and swing. How hard could it really be?"

I spin around. "You can't be serious."

She giggles. "No, I'm not. Maksim would never have allowed me to shoot guns or learn to use any kind of weapon. He was okay with me learning self-defense, but that was about it."

"Okay, so how did you learn?"

"I went to Konstantin."

"Behind Maksim's back?" I yelp.

She shrugs. "Konstantin is wicked with a knife. He'd definitely help you out if you asked."

Misha would probably help me if I asked. But teaching me how to shoot threw him for a loop. I don't want to upset him again for nothing. So if Konstantin is game…

Suddenly, the list of things I need to do before the dinner feels impossibly long. I drop down onto the bench and shake my head. "Food, music, outfits, weapons training... Party-planning isn't what it used to be."

"You know what they say in the Bratva, right?"

I shake my head. "No."

She smiles. "It isn't a party until someone starts bleeding."

I hope to God she's only joking. But I'm too afraid to ask.

46

PAIGE

Konstantin blinks at me, utterly blank-faced. It's like I just spoke a foreign language.

"Hello?" I ask, waving a hand in front of his eyes. "Earth to Konstantin. Can you hear me?"

He shakes his head. "Hit me with that again. I think I was hallucinating."

I roll my eyes and repeat myself slowly. "Can you teach me how to fight?"

"Wow. I take it back: I wasn't hallucinating."

"Don't be so dramatic. I just want to be able to take care of myself. I heard from a little bird that you're great with a knife, so maybe that would be a good place to start."

His chest puffs up with pride. "Remind me to thank Cyrille for the compliment." Then he deflates. "But no, I can't do that."

"What?" I gasp. "But you taught Cyrille!"

"Cyrille wasn't pregnant at the time. And I knew Maksim wouldn't string me up by my balls. I'm not so sure about Misha…"

"Misha took me shooting. He wants me to learn this stuff," I argue. "And as for the pregnancy, just… just pretend that I'm not pregnant."

He glances down at my stomach quite pointedly. "I'm not sure my imagination is that powerful."

"I'm wearing stretchy fabric today. I look way bigger than I am. And self-defense is necessary whether I'm pregnant or not. I need to be able to protect myself."

Konstantin rubs a hand across the back of his neck and sighs. "If Misha is teaching you to shoot, then that should be enough."

"Misha's lessons have been great, but they're not good for him. He has to look at me as a vulnerable target in order to train me, and then he starts worrying. He doesn't need the stress. And frankly, neither do I. Especially with this dinner approaching."

"That's actually a great point. You have a dinner to plan. Maybe you should focus on that."

"I am! That's why I want to train. I want to be armed. Just in case."

Konstantin sighs. "How serious are you about this?"

"I'm prepared to follow you around all day and buzz in your ear like a mosquito until you give in."

He grimaces like he's in physical pain. "How both my cousins managed to find women so similar to each other, I'll never know. Guess the Orlov boys have a type."

"You're an Orlov boy, too," I point out. "I'm just giving you a taste of what the future has in store."

"I'm not an Orlov," he says, a hint of bitterness in his voice. Before I can ask what he's talking about, he gestures for me to follow him. "If you're going to be a brat about it, then come on. First lesson starts now."

I clap my hands and celebrate. "How exciting."

He rolls his eyes, but he's smiling as we head to the second floor gym.

The room is large with floor-to-ceiling windows on one side and floor-to-ceiling mirrors on the other. The natural light helps to create a welcoming space even as the intimidating machines in a straight line across the room warn me to stay far, far away.

"Do I need to, like, stretch or something?" I ask.

I know how to stretch. I stretch before every run. I can do that. But the torture-like weight machine closest to me? I can't do that. Not yet.

Konstantin shrugs. "Sure. You can stretch if you want."

I loosen up for the next ten minutes before I finally join Konstantin on the mat for our first lesson. He takes a moment to look me up and down. His gaze is critical, and I feel oddly self-conscious.

"Okay." He moves forward and grabs my right arm. He lifts my hand into the air between us. "First of all, when it comes to a street fight, you want to avoid using your fist."

"Really?"

"For you, yes. You've got a bunch of fragile bones there that can break easily, especially if you don't know how to throw a proper punch."

"So what am I left with?"

"The rest of your body. Elbows, knees. All the pointy stuff. A good elbow to the stomach or a knee to the groin will go a long way in protecting you."

I bend my arms and legs lightly, feeling my joints as they hum with anxiety. "Got it."

"Okay, so I'm going to come up behind you. I want you to think about the best way to throw me off."

Konstantin moves up behind me, his arms wrapping around my shoulders. And I drive an elbow back into his stomach with all of my strength.

"Ow!" he grunts, stumbling back. "Maybe operate at half-power for right now, yeah?"

I blush. "Sorry."

He waves me off, and we go a couple of rounds. I pick it up quickly. The moves come naturally, and after a while, it becomes instinct. The anxiety doesn't completely go away, but it does recede a bit.

"Excellent," Konstantin says, peppering me with encouragement every now and again. "You're learning fast. Next thing to work on is your legs. Those are powerful muscles, and a good kick can be better than a punch."

I give him an example of my roundhouse kick and he backs away, looking alarmed. "Jesus."

"What? I learned that in a movie."

"Makes sense." He stifles a laugh. "Your form is all wrong. Movie kicks are all about style, not substance. You need to learn to do it properly. When you do, you create distance between yourself and your attacker."

Konstantin walks me through the proper form, and I practice until I'm sweating.

Then he moves onto the next thing.

Despite his earlier protestations, he doesn't seem to acknowledge I'm pregnant at all. He doesn't hold back or check in to see if I'm tired. He treats me like an equal.

It's… nice.

By the time we're done, I'm soaked in sweat. Even Konstantin is a little damp.

"Wow," I pant, hands on my knees. "That was a great lesson."

We both drop down on the mat, breathing hard.

"That's because I'm a great teacher," Konstantin says. He tosses me a cold bottle of water from the mini-fridge in the corner.

I take a long drink and swipe my forearm across my mouth. "I still want to learn how to handle a knife, though."

He shakes his head. "Stubborn."

"I have to be, to deal with your cousin."

He chuckles. "Fair point. Luckily for you, I anticipated that."

Then he reaches around behind him and reveals a small, sleek dagger. It's sheathed in black leather, but when I pull it out of the holster, it gleams wickedly.

"It's so beautiful," I murmur. "So tiny, too."

"Just what every man likes to hear about his weapon."

I snort with laughter. Then something subtle catches my eye. "The hilt is engraved."

He nods. "It belonged to someone I used to know."

He doesn't tell me who, and I reluctantly decide not to ask. If he wanted to tell me, he would have. Instead, I sheath the knife and place it on the mat between us.

"Can I ask you a question, Konstantin?"

He nods and takes a long drink.

"Why did you say you weren't an Orlov earlier?"

I watch him pause mid-gulp, surprised by the question. Then he does his best to relax back into a reclined position. "Because I'm not."

"It's not your last name?"

"It is, but it's a technicality," he explains. "My mother was an Orlov. She was the elder Maksim's younger sister. She gave me her name instead of my father's. They weren't married, and she was the first Orlov to have a child out of wedlock in… well, probably ever."

"That's not so unusual anymore, though. Tons of people have babies before they get married."

"What's unusual is that they never *got* married. If there is a pregnancy in this family, a marriage quickly follows," he says. "My mother not only had the gall to stay unmarried; she also chose to keep me."

"Well, she sounds like a badass. I like her already."

He smiles sadly. "Yeah, I suppose she was."

"Where is she now?"

"Fuck if I know," he says. "That was another thing she did that Orlov mothers never do: she left me."

I feel horrible for asking, but Konstantin doesn't seem too bothered. "I'm sorry."

"Don't be. I figured it out. Aunt Nessa has always been like a mother to me. And my uncle may have been an asshole, but he kept me around. I'm grateful for that."

"What about your father?" I ask before I can stop myself.

"I never knew him," he admits. "My mother never told a soul who he was. I'm not sure if she was ashamed or if she wanted to protect him. Either way, no one even knows his name. Which means I know nothing about the man."

I wonder if Konstantin tried to search for his father and his mother. If he ever wanted to see where they were or try to reconnect. Or if he simply turned his back on his past and made his own way into the future.

"Getting to know your parents isn't all it's cracked up to be," I tell him. "Most of the time, I wish I didn't know mine."

He smiles, realizing what I'm trying to do. "I don't want a relationship with my father, Paige. Don't worry about that. I'm not sad. I just want to know where I come from."

"So you really have no idea where your mother disappeared to?"

"None at all," he says. "She was a smart woman. She wanted to disappear and she did it well. Not even my uncle could track her down. Trust me—he tried."

I'm guessing he wasn't the only one.

"Thanks for sharing all that with me, Konstantin. And thanks for helping me out. I know I kind of forced you into it."

He shrugs. "It's no big deal. You're family."

47

MISHA

Paige walks out of the closet, and suddenly, I'm no longer breathing.

She twirls, her gown shimmering in the light. "Well?" She holds out her arms. "What do you think?"

I struggle for words. "You look like... like... Fucking hell, *kiska*, you look incredible."

She blushes adorably. "I wanted to make an impression."

"You'll do that and more. The men will be drooling and their women will be green with envy."

"I hope not." She frowns. "I want them to like me."

I reach out and tip her chin up. "That is not the goal here. It doesn't matter if they like you," I explain. "We need them to *fear* you."

"Oh, yeah?" she says, a playful light flashing through her eyes. She plants two hands on my chest and slowly walks me back to the bed. I let her do it, grinning as we match step for step backwards until the mattress hits me in the backs of my knees and I sink onto it. "Well, I can't speak for them quite yet, but I'd say *you* should fear me."

"Is that so?" My grin twitches like it's electrified.

"Very much so." She straddles me, one knee planted on either side of my hips. Her scent is tantalizing up close like this. The heat between her thighs makes me groan when it brushes over my hardening dick. "You should be very, very afraid of me."

"Give me one good reason," I tease.

She leans down close, her hair a perfumed curtain, her breath a breeze lighting up every single one of my nerve endings. Her lips stroke against my ear and she whispers, "How 'bout this?"

Then, to my surprise, she jerks upright, flips up the hem of her dress, and withdraws a glistening knife from a leather holster strapped to her upper thigh. Quick as a flash, she presses the tip of the blade gently against my chest.

"Dead," she pronounces solemnly. "And your gravestone will read, *Should've been more afraid of his wife.*"

The only thing dead is my mood, though.

"Paige," I growl in a stern voice. "Why the hell are you wearing a knife?"

"It's my good luck charm for tonight. What do you think?"

"I think it's unnecessary, unsafe and extremely, *extremely*... sexy." I sigh. As much as I hate saying it, I have a raging erection that won't be denied. "Go on—let me see it again."

She happily raises her skirt to reveal the black strap hugging her thigh. "Fucking Christ," I mutter. "You're going to be the death of me."

She tilts my face up so I'm looking at her. "I wanted to feel like a badass tonight. And I was inspired."

"By whom?"

"Your mother and Cyrille," she says. "I want to stand next to you and feel like I belong there."

"You belong there because I say you do," I say fiercely.

"That's not enough, Misha," she replies in a quiet murmur. "These men and their wives, they need to respect me. You said that yourself. They need to know that I'm not just some ditzy, white trash fool you picked up off the street and scrubbed up. I want to show them that I have something to offer." Her voice drops one register lower. "This is going to be my world from now on. My children are going to be part of it. Which means I need to know how it works."

A strange sensation spreads across my chest. It takes me a moment to identify properly. Then it hits me.

Pride.

This is what it feels like to truly want someone to succeed.

I slip my hands up her legs, feeling my way over the knife strapped to her leg. "Who gave you the knife?"

"If I tell you, you can't get mad. They need full immunity from punishment."

I scowl. "I'm not making promises."

"Then I'm not telling."

"I'll find out eventually."

"Maybe. But not from me."

Annoyed as I am, I can't deny that I respect her for it. "You are more Bratva than I care to admit," I sigh. She laughs and leans forward to kiss my forehead. "Fine. Whoever gave you the knife is off-limits."

She gives me a triumphant smile. "Konstantin."

"*Mudak.* I should have known."

She laughs. "Don't worry. He taught me how to use it."

I frown. "You could have come to me for that. I would've made the time for you."

Her smile grows soft. She sits herself down on my lap. "I know. That's not the point. I didn't want you worrying. You got really stressed out during our last lesson. And before you deny it," she adds as I open my mouth to do exactly that, "don't bother. I'm learning how to read you, so I know I'm right. Does that freak you out?"

"A little."

She presses her forehead against mine. "Don't worry about that, either. It's a good thing."

I nod, but I can't convince myself she's right. As our connection grows stronger, our dependency grows right along with it. My entire life has been about how to be self-sufficient, and I have the scars to prove it. It feels like a death wish to throw away three decades of hard-won lessons.

Paige frowns. "You look worried still. I think I'm making it worse."

I slide her off my lap gently and get to my feet. "We have a big night ahead of us," I say, deflecting. "In less than half an hour, the guests will start arriving."

She takes a deep breath and straightens out her dress. "You don't think this is all too much, do you?"

"Fuck no. You look like a dream."

"Such a poet." She winks at me and heads to her vanity.

I watch and contemplate as she touches up her lipstick and adds a few sprays of perfume to her neck and wrists. I give myself a quiet moment to admire her.

The woman is fucking beautiful. And she's all mine.

Which is why I don't relish throwing her to the wolves tonight.

Not that she's unprepared. She has a knife strapped to her thigh, after all. That thigh…

"You know, it's bad form to wear another man's weapon on your body."

"Is that another Orlov family rule?" She rolls her eyes. "Well, too bad. I like the knife and I'm wearing it."

"There are consequences for that kind of behavior, woman."

Her eyes glow with desire. "Maybe I'm okay with those consequences."

I smirk. "You've been warned."

48

PAIGE

I take Cyrille's offered hand and squeeze it like I'm sinking and she's my life preserver. "I'm so nervous."

"Breathe," she advises me.

"Easy for you to say. You look like an Oscar statue, all sleek and golden. I look like a blimp. Who convinced me this dress was a good idea?"

Cyrille slaps my hand lightly. "Shut your mouth! You look amazing. Now, you just need to back up that look with attitude."

I thought I looked amazing an hour ago, when Misha was breathing horny sweet nothings in my ear. But now, I've circled the event space half a dozen times and caught flaws in my table settings on every single pass. I don't have any confidence left.

"Is there any way you could take over hosting duties for tonight?" I beg, only half-joking.

"Absolutely not. You've got this."

Her confidence in me is reassuring and terrifying in equal measure. I try to let it strengthen me, but I can't help but think it just gives me even further to fall.

I take comfort in the fact that the mansion looks beautiful. The staff has gone above and beyond to make sure this night will be a success. They all know what a big deal it is.

The dining room is teeming with people. I haven't officially met any of them, but I know all of them by name. Nessa's flashcards were a godsend, and I only hope I'll remember everything under the immense pressure I'm feeling.

"Paige!"

I turn towards the voice to find Klim has spotted me in the crowd. I've only met the man once, when he visited the house, but he's still a friendly face—friendly-ish, at least—so I gravitate to him.

"Klim, thank you for coming."

He pulls me in, and I air kiss both cheeks, just like Cyrille taught me.

His eyes slide down my body. It's not salacious, though. More like he's trying to size me up. Like he knows what's strapped to my leg, actually.

"I wouldn't miss your big debut for the world, my dear."

"What do you think? Will I impress?"

"The night's still young, but you certainly look the part."

I grin and blush at the same time. "Are you here alone?"

"My mistress is at the bar." I'm glad he's not concentrating on me as he says it because my double take would have been obvious. Klim points out a woman in the crowd. "Strike that —there she is. Natasha, come here."

The woman who sidles up to Klim's side is in her late thirties or early forties, Russian, blond. She's gorgeous and dripping with diamonds, and her boobs have enough plastic to keep Lego in business for centuries.

"You must be the woman of the hour," she says. "I'm Natasha."

I offer her my hand. "Paige Orlov."

"There's been a lot of chatter about you, Paige. I'm glad to finally get the chance to meet you myself."

"I hope I don't disappoint."

"Well, you can't please everyone." Her eyes snake over my body, and I wonder if I've just been insulted. Before I can come to any conclusion, she turns to Klim. "I've changed my mind. I'd rather have wine than champagne. Excuse me."

She heads off without acknowledging me. It's my first brush with icy judgment from someone skilled at wielding it. "Well, she seems charming."

Klim smiles. "I find myself partial to women with insufferable attitudes. The rule is that she can be as much of a bitch as she wants with everyone but me."

"How lucky for the rest of us."

The old man barks with laughter. "I like you, Paige. And I don't say that often."

I lift my glass to him as I back away with a wink. "Enjoy your evening, Klim."

I continue to move around the room, taking in the pulse of the crowd. I am clearly, as Natasha put it, the woman of the hour. Everyone is interested in me, either coming up to introduce themselves or watching like hawks from the edges of the room.

But the only faces I'm interested in are the familiar ones.

I make sure to circle back around to Niki, Cyrille, or Nessa every fifteen minutes or so for a little boost of confidence before I throw myself back into the fray.

Misha is making the rounds like I am, but I stay clear of him. I don't want it to look like I need him to feel secure about my position in this house.

I'm at the bar for a refill on my sparkling grape juice when two women appear on either side of me. It feels like an ambush, but I try to keep my cool.

The older woman smiles. "Hello, Paige."

Shit. What was her name again? Raisa? Roksana? She wasn't in my flashcards, but I met her half an hour ago with her husband. I should've been paying closer attention.

"I don't think you've been introduced to Isidora yet," she says.

I turn to the stunning blonde in the red dress. This woman I do recognize. She's the trophy wife who is thirty-three years younger than her husband.

"Isidora Gusev." I smile warmly. "Nice to meet you."

Her expression is pleasant, but she doesn't smile. "What an amazing dress. I actually saw it on the runway in Paris earlier this year. Or was it Milan? To be honest, some years, they all blend together when you're going from show to show."

"That's fun."

Her brows pinch together. "I had a front row seat. It was an honor."

It's painfully transparent that she's trying to flaunt her status. Like a cat lying on its back, revealing its claws, she wants me to see how important she is and how scared of her I ought to be.

I nod and take a sip of my beverage. If I wasn't pregnant, I'd be two glasses deep into something that would make me forget I ever cared about impressing these people.

"Have you been to any shows recently?" she presses.

"Never, actually."

She raises her eyebrows and glances at the older woman whose name I still don't remember. "That's unforgivable. I'll have to bring you with me sometime."

I may not know this world well, but I know female cattiness when I see it. That's not unique to the Bratva. *I can get you into exclusive shows. I can show you the ropes.*

I have no desire to learn Isidora's ropes.

"Your kindness would be wasted on me," I tell her with a smile. "I have no eye for fashion. The only reason I show up to work in anything remotely appropriate is because Misha does the shopping for me."

She blinks at me as if I'm speaking another language. "Your husband buys your clothes?"

"He's got a knack for it. I've always had more of a head for numbers and business."

"A head for business?" Isidora raises one thin eyebrow. "That's a new one."

"Women in business is hardly a new concept."

"Yes, but you are first and foremost a Bratva wife," she says.

"I am first and foremost my own person," I correct. "I like the work I do."

Isidora studies me for a moment and then nods, some realization washing over her. "I'm sure it's also a good way to keep an eye on your man. Especially a man like Misha. They do tend to wander if you aren't careful, don't they?"

I give her a cold smile. "My husband is a handsome man, but I don't work at Orion to police him. I happen to trust him."

Both women laugh until they realize that I'm not laughing with them.

I give them both a curt smile. "I trust Misha, but I also trust that I am more than enough woman for my man. He doesn't need anyone else."

As I turn away from their shocked expressions and mingle back into the crowd, I know I may not have won their respect just yet. Not fully, at least.

But I gained something else.

Confidence.

49

MISHA

I'm leaning against the wall between the sitting room and the kitchen, watching my wife work a group of senior Vors on the patio, when Nikita comes to stand next to me.

"She's doing well," my sister observes.

The men laugh at something Paige has said. It's not polite, pandering laughter, either. She's genuinely said something funny.

"I never had any doubt."

Nikita snorts. "Liar."

She doesn't need to know how nervous I was for Paige coming into tonight. I hid it well enough from Paige and that is all that matters.

"She's definitely holding her own, with the old perverts and the bitchy wives alike."

"Not all of the perverts are old. Not all of the bitches are wives."

Niki sniffs pointedly. "Please—if you think I'm going to talk to the mistresses, you've got another thing coming."

"Your loyalty is admirable," I say. "But if you remember correctly, Mother spoke to everyone at her parties. Mistresses included. Sometimes, most of all."

Niki glances over at our mother. She's locked in intense conversation with another wife. "That's because she's a better woman than I am."

I lean in, voice low. "Aleksandr Golubev is looking in this direction."

"Then go talk to him if you want to. What do I care?"

"He's not looking at me."

She rolls her eyes and does her best to look disinterested, but her cheeks redden.

"He's not a bad choice, Niki. He's wealthy, accomplished, speaks four languages. As far as I've heard, he has no mistresses."

"That's because he doesn't have a wife," she snaps. "You can't have a mistress without a wife. Once he is married, the mistress will sure as shit follow."

"I've spoken to Aleksandr enough times to know that he's a decent man," I tell her.

She turns her dark gaze on me. "Are you trying to get rid of me, brother?"

"I just want to see you happy, *mladshaya sestra*."

That catches her off-guard. She looks away quickly, trying to blink the tears back before they fall. She clears her throat and grabs a glass of champagne from the tray of one of the passing waiters before taking down half of it in a single gulp. "A man can't make me happy, Misha."

"A woman then?"

She gives me a half-hearted smile. "When I figure it out, I'll let you know." She takes a sip of her champagne, and looks around the room. "Cyrille has disappeared again."

My sister-in-law has made herself scarce tonight. Usually, Nessa is the one who is gun-shy about these kinds of parties while Cyrille works the crowd, but it seems the roles have reversed for this one.

"She used to like this kind of thing."

"Yeah—when she was the one hosting," she reminds me. "She's no longer the lady of the house. There are a fair few people here who've probably enjoyed reminding her. Especially *that* bitch."

I look towards the platinum blonde woman my sister is gesturing to. "Yustina Smirnova? She used to be Cyrille's little shadow."

"Yes, because Yustina Smirnova is an unrepentant fucking ladder climber. And at the time, Cyrille was the woman in power. She…"

Niki trails off when we notice Yustina corner Paige by the champagne fountain. Without saying a word, we move closer so that we can hear their conversation.

"… a wonderful night, Paige," Yustina is saying, flicking her hair over her shoulder. "You've outdone yourself."

"That's easy to do, considering this is my first party. The bar couldn't be lower."

Yustina laughs uproariously. "Of course. You're just such a natural that it all feels effortless."

Pleasant as her words are, there's an edge of malice in her voice. I'm guessing seeing my beautiful, young wife take on the Bratva pack and succeed is killing Yustina on the inside. Jealousy is a cancer, and Yustina is as sick as they come.

"I was surprised to see Cyrille here, though."

Paige's polite smile sharpens. "What do you mean?"

"She is a part of the old order, isn't she, darling?" Yustina explains. "There's no place for history when you're trying to build the future."

I don't even realize that I've started to step forward until Niki's hand clasps down on my arm. "Don't. Give her a chance to handle this on her own."

Paige tilts her head to the side, her eyes narrowed to slits. "The future I have in mind includes Cyrille and Ilya."

Yustina curls her lower lip in surprise. "But Ilya is the son of the late don, is he not…?"

"Ilya and Cyrille are *family*," my wife hisses. "They will always have a place in this house."

Yustina seems to realize she's made a mistake. She smiles and inches backward. "I was only trying to offer you my advice, Paige. I have been in this world much longer than you have. You need to make sure Cyrille understands that you're in charge now. Her son won't be inheriting the Bratva; yours will."

"When I want your advice, I'll ask for it," Paige snaps. "Until then, I'll thank you for sticking to what you know. Judging from your appearance, that seems to be botched plastic surgery and low self-esteem."

Niki gasps and claps a hand over her mouth to stifle a stunned giggle. "Whoa! Did she really just say that? That was fucking brutal!"

I watch as Paige stares the woman down for another seconds before Yustina turns and glides away, cheeks blazing with shame.

"Yes," I murmur as pride sears through me. "Yes, she did."

50

PAIGE

I might've just committed a terrible mistake.

Yustina Smirnova is the wife of a senior Vor. I remember her picture from Nessa's flashcards.

"Be careful of this one," Nessa warned.

Then I met her, and I wasn't careful at all. I just made an enemy.

I don't regret it, though. I only regret that it had to happen, that Yustina gave me no other choice. Because no one is going to say a bad word about Cyrille or anyone else in my family. Ever.

I march away from Yustina and straight into the drawing room across the hall. I click the door shut behind and take a deep, shuddering breath. It's been a difficult evening and it isn't close to being over.

Turning to the console table next to the door, I grip the edges with trembling fingers and stare at my reflection in the mirror hanging above.

I try to see myself the way they all do. Do I come across like the ditzy young bimbo who doesn't have a clue what she's doing? Or do I come across as someone strong and in charge? Someone who knows her own mind and refuses to apologize for it?

I felt confident going into this dinner, but these women drinking my drinks and eating my hors d'oeuvres live and breathe this life. They know the rules. They know how to present the right front and manipulate people to their whim.

Now that I've spent an evening amongst them, I'm not sure I'll ever measure up.

The door opens, and I jolt away from the mirror. But the thudding in my chest settles when I see Misha enter. He closes the door and looks over at me, his expression unreadable.

"Did I fuck up?" I ask bluntly. "I know she's important. Or her husband is important, which makes her important, I guess."

"Her husband has served under four different dons," he tells me. "My grandfather, my father, my brother, and now, me."

My palms are starting to sweat. "I know I was rude, but she was being a bitch about Cyrille."

"I heard."

I came into this night wanting to make Misha proud. That is still true, but I won't do it at the expense of the other people I care about.

I square my shoulders. "I'm not going to apologize to her. I understand that she and her husband are important, but she insulted my sister-in-law. I won't stand for that. No matter what you have to say about it."

He stands less than a foot away from me now. "Nothing I say will make you apologize to her?"

I grit my teeth and dig my heels in. "No. She deserved to be called out. The only thing I would take back is the plastic surgery comment. She was enough of a bitch that I didn't need to bring her looks into the equation."

He glowers at me for a moment… and then he bursts out laughing.

I stare at him in shock. "You're… you're laughing."

"Because you're funny, *moya zhena*. And Yustina deserved it. Even the crack you made about the work she's had done."

Tension flows out of me, replaced by relief. "I thought you'd be furious."

He shakes his head. "I'm *proud*, Paige. You held your own. You looked like a true Bratva wife. It took everything I had in me not to stand and clap."

I smile shyly. "She's probably not too happy with me."

"No, probably not. But you are my wife, and she has to swallow her pride or risk being on the outs with you. No smart woman would take that risk."

"I'm not about to blacklist her or anything like that," I say. "I just want her to know that she can't go around talking about Cyrille in that way."

His eyes soften as he steps closer and takes my hand. "You're too good for this world, my love."

My heart does a little backflip. "I want to fit in. It's too early for me to make enemies."

"Having enemies is what makes you Bratva." He pulls my hand to his lips and kisses each finger. "You look very sexy in this dress, by the way."

"Deadly, too. Don't forget I'm armed and dangerous tonight."

"How could I forget?" He runs his fingers up my thigh. Then he grabs my waist and pulls me flush against his body. "You should be wearing *my* knife, though. Not another man's."

"Then you should have offered me *your* knife," I counter.

"Are you going to give me a tongue lashing now, too?"

"I'll leave the tongue lashings to you," I purr suggestively. "They're one of your many talents."

"You're asking for trouble."

I bat my eyelashes. "Maybe trouble is what I want."

The heat between us is an inferno. It's burning up all of my worries and anxiety. Every single scrap of my inhibitions.

When Misha spins me around so I'm facing my own reflection in the mirror, I don't even startle. I plant my hands on the wall obediently, ready and willing.

He raises my dress, revealing the black thong I'm wearing. "Fuck," he says, hissing between his clenched teeth.

He snaps the thin string with one sharp tug before he kisses his way between my legs. When his tongue slides down my slit, I can barely remember that we have a room full of important guests just across the hall. Anyone could walk in at any moment, but I don't have the strength to make Misha stop.

His tongue works inside of me as his hand wraps around my hip to circle my clit. I lose all semblance of self-consciousness, sticking my ass out to let him eat me out from behind.

"Misha," I gasp.

I grip the sides of the table and try to keep my screams from being heard over the music and chatter from the other room.

I'm dripping with desire when Misha rises to stand behind me. His eyes meet mine in the mirror, and I don't look away as he lines his cock up with my pussy. His eyes are feral. There is only raw lust and possession.

In one thrust, Misha seats himself inside of me.

"Misha!" I grip the table harder to stay upright as he slides out and drives into me again.

Each time he does, his name falls from my lips. I'm sure someone can hear us, but I can't keep it in. I give myself over to him.

"Say my name, baby," he growls. His thrusts become more fierce, more demanding.

Until I can't hold back.

"I'm coming, Misha," I cry. "I'm coming."

His fingers coax my clit, milking the orgasm from my body until I'm limp. Misha wraps his arms around me to keep me upright and pulses into me. I feel him twitch with release, and I lean into him, reveling in the feel of him everywhere.

"You're going to break me one day," I whisper.

He smiles at our reflection. "Nothing can break you, Paige Orlov."

I turn my head to the side and catch his cheek with my lips. All I want to do right now is go up to our room together and spend the night under the sheets.

"We have to go back." He sounds as regretful as I feel.

"Duty calls," I say. "But first, pass me a tissue."

He smirks and pushes the tissue box away. "No, I think I prefer for you to walk around with my seed inside you."

"It will drip out!" I exclaim.

"Let it," he insists. "They'll smell me on you."

"Misha!"

He refuses to hand me the tissues. Instead, he helps settle my dress back into place. "There. You're perfect."

I shift uncomfortably. "You're really gonna make me go out there like this?"

He gives me a wink. "That's your punishment for wearing another man's weapon."

I fail to hide my smile as I shake my head at him. "You're evil."

"Aren't you glad I'm on your side?"

"Are you?" I ask, our hands finding each other instinctively.

"Always," he whispers. "Always."

51

MISHA

All eyes are on my wife and I as we walk through the crowd hand in hand.

I expected to be trailing behind Paige at every turn, reminding everyone that she is mine and deserves respect. But Paige demanded that respect from them herself.

I'm not the protector guarding a helpless fawn; I'm the back-up muscle only if she decides she needs it. Thus far tonight, Paige has certainly proved that she doesn't. She can hold her own among these people.

They fear her like they ought to.

I grab a glass of champagne from the bar and turn, raising my glass. The moment I do, the room goes silent.

"I thank you all for being here tonight," I say, addressing my guests. "You are here because you are valued members of the Orlov Bratva. Because you are family. Which is why it gives me great pleasure to announce that this family is growing."

Paige squeezes my hand.

I smile down at her and then back at the assembled guests. "My beautiful wife and I are delighted to announce that we're expecting."

There's a moment of stunned silence, then a burst of applause and cheers that rise from the crowd.

"At the end of this year, we will be welcoming not one, but two children."

A gasp. More applause follows, louder and more boisterous.

"Let us toast," I say. "To the future of the Orlov Bratva."

We toast as one, and the atmosphere in the room brightens. This is big news. News that has the power to roust Petyr from his hiding place.

As if reading my mind, Paige whispers to me, "Petyr will find out about this."

I smirk. "I'm counting on it."

Klim is the first to approach. He saunters up to us with a thin smile on his face, though any warmth in it is reserved solely for Paige. "Who knew you were hiding two bundles of joy underneath that dress?"

"I'm very resourceful."

"I'm starting to realize that," he says before turning to me for a handshake. "This is big news, Misha." He leans in, voice low. "This will crush that little fucker."

Paige pats my chest and slips away from me. "If you two will excuse me, I'll go make some rounds."

"I must say, I underestimated her," Klim remarks, watching her work her way across the room. Everyone is offering Paige congratulations, and she looks radiant. "She has settled into the role quickly. I see how fond your family is of her. What a treasure that must be."

"Things are falling into place. Now, all we need to do is finish things with Petyr."

"Do you have a plan?"

"Always."

Klim nods. "Then I will trust that. I will advise the men to do the same. Enjoy your evening, *pakhan*."

As Klim is walking away, I notice Konstantin by the door. He tips his head, gesturing me forward.

I cross the room to meet him. "What is it?"

"The Babai," he hisses. "They're *here*."

"Here?" I repeat. "As in, on my property?"

"Yes. I have no goddamn clue how they got in," he growls.

I never did tell him about their first breach, when they slipped into my office unseen to leave a note on my desk. I didn't want to contribute to the sick sense of foreboding he carries with me where the Babai are concerned.

"I'll speak to them."

He shakes his head. "Let me come with you this time."

"No. Just go back to the party and play host until I return."

Konstantin looks skeptical, but he obeys, albeit not without a few muttered curses under his breath.

I walk outside, searching the driveway for a car or a silhouette. There is nothing at first. Then, as I turn, a large shadow separates itself from the cluster of darkness in the western corner of the facade.

It's The Wolf. He's wearing a long overcoat and a shrewd expression. Behind him, I spy two more silhouettes. They all step forward in unison, unsettling in their inhumanity.

"I wasn't expecting the three of you tonight," I say. "In fact, I wasn't expecting you at all."

The Wolf just blinks and smiles at me. His eyes are alien in a way I can't explain. Flat like a fish's, but huge and intelligent.

"We came to pay our respects to the pakhan," The Wolf intones.

"That'll do for tonight. But what is your excuse for the last time you made your way onto my property?"

"That was to give you a little bit of reassurance. This job has proved trickier than we expected," The Bear says from behind The Wolf's shoulder. "We will need more time."

I raise my eyebrows. "I was told the Babai never needed such petty things."

The Wolf smiles. "You shouldn't believe all that the legends hold. Even if your men do."

I don't miss the unsubtle reference to Konstantin's fears. I know its only purpose is to shake me up, but knowing that doesn't stop it from working.

That being said, I doubt I'm the only one displeased right now. The imperceptible frown tinging the corner of The Wolf's mouth says that the Babai aren't happy at how things have gone.

That makes four of us.

"I want results," I say at last. "No matter the cost."

"We will give you what we promised. Our deal will be honored. You have nothing to fear."

I want to believe in them. In the legends, in the stories that Konstantin holds so dear. But as the Babai themselves just informed me, they are only human.

And humans make mistakes.

52

PAIGE

During my congratulations tour, Nikita slides in next to me. "You look like you could use some backup," she whispers, slipping her arm around mine.

I hold her tightly. "Thank you."

I'm even more grateful for her presence when Isidora Gusev makes her way back over to us. Her eyebrow arches in a way that suggests she isn't so easily impressed.

"He must be thrilled with you," she remarks when she's in range. "Two heirs in one go? It's every man's dream. If they're boys, you'll be set for life. His heir and a spare."

I glance at Niki just in time to see her eyes roll. Suppressing a smile, I turn to Isidora. "I'm not giving him heirs; I'm giving him children."

"What's the difference?"

"The difference is that I'm interested in creating a family, not a legacy."

She scoffs. "You might have stumbled into the wrong marriage then."

Nikita inhales to respond, but I hurry before she can. "If there's one thing I know about the Orlovs, it's that family comes first."

"The Bratva and the family are inextricably linked. Your sons will inherit their father's crown. Unless…" She looks to Nikita. "Unless of course you're planning on allowing Maksim and Cyrille's son to take over after Misha?"

Nikita's jaw twitches. I have no idea if she's offended by that question or not. I have no idea if I should be, either.

"I haven't thought about it," I admit.

Her smile widens. "It didn't sound like Misha is willing to pass over his own children in favor of his brother's. But maybe you can convince him, if that's what you want."

Nikita takes a step forward. "Are things so boring in your house that you've decided to create drama in ours, Isidora?"

Isidora looks only mildly embarrassed. "I'm just curious."

"It's not your place to be curious about matters that don't concern you," my sister-in-law says fiercely.

Isidora pats Niki's shoulder, an obviously condescending gesture. "Nikita, I think it's time to find you a man. You're so sensitive. You need someone to take care of, to give you perspective."

"When I want a man, I'll find one myself," Nikita snaps. "Until then, I'm happy to be single and in control of my own life. I'd hate to have to spend every day with my own personal watchdog shadowing my every move."

Sure enough, Manuel, the castrated bodyguard Nessa described to me, is lurking a few yards away. At the mention of her jailer, Isidora's face falls. And in that moment, I catch a glimpse of just how unhappy she seems. How miserable and cruel. How she's so sick of tearing herself apart that she has to do the same to other people, just to get by.

Isidora turns her scowl from Nikita to me. If looks could kill, we'd both be struck dead. "Excuse me, ladies. I haven't said hello to Morgen Antonov yet."

With that, she stomps away, tossing her blonde hair over her shoulder.

I whistle softly. "I feel drained after watching that."

"That's what's known as a beatdown," Niki proclaims. "I hope you were taking notes."

"I was too scared of you to take notes."

She smirks. "It was my privilege to put her in her place. Isidora is a condescending bitch who thinks she's better than everyone else."

"That's a mask," I say, clutching my pendant instinctively. "She's miserable and lonely. She's trying to hide it behind her pretty clothes and her expensive jewelry. In another world, the two of you might have been friends."

"Sure, if she wasn't such a colossal fucking bitch."

"Did she strike a nerve, Niki?" I ask gently.

Nikita's closed expression tells me that my assumption is definitely on the nose. "No, of course not. Why should I care about being married? I have no interest in being trapped that way. No offense."

"None taken."

Nikita sighs. "I forgot how much I hate these parties. Where is Misha? He's supposed to be talking to these people so I don't have to."

I've been wondering the same thing. The room feels so much lonelier without him. The fact that I have his handiwork drying on the insides of my legs is keeping him on the forefront of my mind as well.

"I think I saw him leave with Konstantin a little while ago."

But when I scan the room and see Konstantin standing with a few of the council Vors by the grand piano, I don't see any sign of Misha. Instead of interrupting Konstantin's conversation, I decide to slip out myself and track down my husband.

"I'll be back in a bit, Niki. Going on a scavenger hunt."

She waves me on, having spotted an opening in the line at the bar.

I try our bedroom first and then his office. When I find that they're both empty, I poke my head outside. Maybe he was in need of some fresh air as much as I am.

As soon as I step down off the porch, I hear hushed voices. It takes me a second to pick Misha out of the darkness.

He's standing with his back to me in front of three other men, all dressed in black. I can tell immediately they aren't our guests. They have the creeping aura of men who don't really belong anywhere. Except for prison, maybe. Or a locked box at the bottom of the ocean.

"Misha?"

The tallest of the creepy trio turns to me. "You must be Paige." His voice is slick like pond scum.

My skin crawls at the sight and sound of him, but I don't want to look weak now. I pull my shoulders back. "I am. And you are?"

He smiles blankly. "A friend of the family."

Misha turns to me with cold eyes. "I'm finishing up here. Wait for me inside."

I shouldn't have come out here. Misha's expression is setting off every alarm bell I have.

"Of course. I'll see you soon."

I slink back into the house, but I can't bring myself to rejoin the party. Not when I know my husband is out there with three men who unsettle me so viscerally.

I'm still pacing the foyer when Misha comes back inside. "Oh, thank God," I breathe.

His face is twisted into a deep frown. "What the hell were you doing? You shouldn't have come out there."

"You'd been gone for a while and I wanted to know why. Who were those men?"

"Colleagues," he says.

To the untrained eye, the answer was fast and confident. To my eye, he's full of shit.

I cross my arms. "I know when you're lying to me, Misha."

"No, you don't."

"Yes, I do. We share a bed; we share our lives. I know you better than you think."

He's studying me, and I know exactly what he's thinking: that letting down all of those walls means more than a happy relationship and amazing sex.

The call is coming from inside the house, Misha Orlov.

"Are you going to keep lying to me or are you going to come clean?"

He walks past me. "I am going to go back to the party we're hosting."

"No, you're not," I snap, blocking his path to the sitting room. "I want to know who they are."

"Some things aren't for you to know. Some things are for me to handle on my own."

"I thought this whole night was to show everyone that we are partners. That we work together. I'm not just your trophy wife!"

It's been a while since we fought. I naively thought that we'd put this part of our relationship behind us. I should've known better—with Misha and me, I'm not sure we'll ever be done fighting.

He rolls his eyes. "You're being ridiculous."

"I'm not! I'm your colleague more than those creeps. I deserve to be treated with that kind of respect."

He grimaces. Standing up to Yustina was hot, he said, but I get the sense he doesn't find this version of my fire quite as appealing.

"For fuck's sake, Paige, we don't have time for this right now. We're trying to convince a room full of people that we're a solid foundation for the Bratva to rest upon."

"How can we build a future for the Bratva when you refuse to build a future with me?" I demand.

I'm grateful for the laughter, conversation, and music flowing out of the party. It's a nice sound buffer for our fight.

He grabs my arm and twists me into his body. "I made you my wife. I chose you. I love you. My cum is drying on your thighs *right fucking now*, and you think I'm not prepared to build a future with you?"

I'll admit, his words and his intensity are both turning me on. I have to try really, really hard to block out my throbbing core and focus on my point.

"Building a future together depends on more than just sleeping together and fighting each other, Misha," I tell him. "You have to open up to me. You have to share things with me and be vulnerable."

He glares at me, his expression unchanging. I can practically see my words bouncing off the walls he has erected around his heart.

"Those men out there are dangerous, aren't they?" I press, hoping that if I stumble on some version of the truth, he'll realize he doesn't have to hide anything from me. "If they are, Misha—if you're employing them because you think that's the best way to keep me safe, to keep our family safe—then don't. We don't need them; we only need you."

But there's ice in his silver eyes and nothing I'm saying is thawing them out.

Finally, he shakes his arm out of my grip and walks past me. "We have a party to host."

He leaves me standing there in the foyer, alone.

53

MISHA

"What happened tonight?"

I lift a hand as the last guest pulls down the driveway and disappears through the gates. "Not now, Mother."

"You and Maksim were always so much alike," she remarks. "But there are moments when you remind me so much of your father."

"Then you should know by now that your disappointment isn't going to change me. It never changed him."

It's a cruel thing to say, but she doesn't even look mad. She just looks tired. "When are you going to understand that I'm on your side, son? All I want—all I've ever wanted—is your happiness. I just happen to know that no matter how important the Bratva is to you, it will never bring you true happiness."

I grab hold of my dog tag and shove it in her face. "You know what this says better than anyone else. *Vse dlya sem'i.* Everything for the family."

"I do," she says, stoic as ever. "I know why your father wore it, and I know why your brother did. It was for very different reasons than the one that's kept it around your neck."

Paige is standing down in the grass with Nikita. She saw everyone to their cars and thanked them each for coming. It had nothing to do with being a good hostess, though—she just didn't want to be near me.

"You need to stop punishing yourself for Maksim's death, Misha. It wasn't your fault."

"You weren't there," I tell her harshly. "You don't know if it was my fault or not."

"I wasn't. But Konstantin was there. He told us all what happened. No one blames you."

"Cyrille—"

"Do you really think that Cyrille would blame you for Maksim's death?" she scoffs. "Just because you were foolish for a split second doesn't mean you could have anticipated what was about to happen. You were young and confident. You thought you were invincible. You made an error in judgment, and your brother was exposed for a moment. Petyr took his shot."

"Mother—"

"It's what happened," she continues over my growl. "It's time to accept it. So that you can move forward. So that *all of us* can move forward."

She waits for me to say something, but I don't. I'm not sure if it's disappointment on her face or fatigue, but whatever the case, she blows out a breath and pats me on the arm. "If you'll excuse me, I'm tired. Make sure that Paige is comfortable. She deserves your thanks for tonight. She did you proud."

Paige did so many things right tonight.

But the one thing she did wrong is the only thing I can think about.

I hated the way the Babai looked at her. The way The Wolf looked at her… Like he wanted to devour Paige whole.

I wait by the door as Paige walks up the steps towards me. She does a good job avoiding my eyes. I can tell from the way her shoulders tense that she's not done fighting tonight.

But I am.

I walk inside before she reaches me and turn left at the staircase. I'm hoping that Paige is pissed off enough that she'll go upstairs without addressing it, but no such luck.

"Where are you going?" she calls up to me.

"I have some work to finish up in the office."

"Bullshit," she snaps. "You just want to avoid talking to me."

"If only it were that easy," I say before I can stop myself.

It's not in my nature to back down from a fight. And the more she pushes this, the more I want to rise to the challenge.

"I'm not letting you push me away," she insists. "I deserve to know what's going on with Petyr just as much as the rest of your Vors do."

"What makes you think I've told them anything?"

"Because they're *men*," she hisses furiously. Her eyes are bright with anger. Her hair is coming loose from the braided bun at the back of her head.

"As if anything in this world is so simple."

She doesn't back down. "I saw the way those people treated Cyrille tonight. They respected her once, but now that she isn't married to the right man, she's worthless to them. I'm not going to live that way. Especially not with my own husband. Either I'm worthy of your trust and respect or I'm not. It really is that simple."

I sigh and pinch the bridge of my nose. "You don't need to know who those men are, Paige. It doesn't matter."

"Maybe I should ask Konstantin?" she suggests. "He gave me his weapon. Maybe he'll give me an answer, too."

"Don't you fucking dare."

"Oh, I'm going to dare!" She leans forward, eyes narrowed and jaw clenched. "I'm going to dare every chance I get. Because apparently, that's the only way you're going to listen to me." Her fingers tremble from the heat of her emotion.

"You're working yourself up," I tell her, in the calm voice that I know riles her up even more. "Go get some sleep."

"I don't want to sleep."

"That might be the case, but you need to sleep regardless. For the babies."

"Right, because when it comes to taking a step back, that's *my* responsibility, not yours."

"You're the one carrying them," I point out. "If you want to be mad at something, be mad at biology for that."

"You're being a chauvinistic asshole!"

"And you're sticking your nose where it doesn't belong like a stubborn little nag."

She gasps, her eyes going wide with shock. For a moment, the twitching in her hand seems almost purposeful. Like she wants nothing more than to use my cousin's knife on me.

"Go to bed," I tell her before this escalates any further.

Then I turn and retreat to my office.

For one night, that will keep me safe. The door will lock; the walls will stand between us. But who the fuck knows what the morning will bring?

If only it were that easy to keep my distance.

54

PAIGE

I'm still standing at the foot of the staircase where Misha left me when Noel turns the corner. "Mrs. Paige." He lowers his head in a subtle bow. "I was just about to lock up for the night. Is there anything else you need?"

I turn to him, trying to swallow down the whirlwind of memories that are assaulting me as I stand there. Trying to bat away old demons that won't quit.

But I'm losing the fight—badly.

"It's late, Noel. You should be done working by now."

"I'm not done until the house is sleeping."

He watches me with observant eyes, seeking out whatever I might need. But what I need, he can't give me. So for now, I just need to be alone.

"Thank you for all you do, Noel. I really appreciate it. I know you don't get told that often enough."

He flushes with pleasure. I get the feeling that he doesn't get very many pats on the back. "It is my pleasure, ma'am. Always happy to be of service. Can I help you up to bed?"

"No." I turn towards Misha's office. "Not just yet. Go ahead and lock up, Noel. Goodnight."

As I go, my thoughts are a pounding drumbeat of one word, again and again. Nag. Nag. *Nag.*

That word—I loathe it. I have a long and complicated history with it. I linger on the stairs, remembering how I felt the first time Clara had hurled it at me.

"You're such a fucking nag," she snapped. *"No, I didn't hurt myself on purpose. I slipped and fell. That's why I have the scar."*

"What did you cut yourself on?" I pressed.

"You don't believe me?"

"I didn't say that. I asked what you cut yourself on."

Clara laughed cruelly. *"You're going all red and blotchy. What's the problem, Paige? It's not a big deal. It's nothing but a little scar."*

All those years ago, I let her shut me up like that. Now, I wish I'd kept asking. Kept nagging.

Because one little scar turned into more, and more, and more.

Until she drew a cut that she wouldn't ever come back from.

My heart is thundering, but I ignore my nerves and bust into his office just in time to see Misha pull out the sofa bed. Shirtless. I force my gaze from his abs to his eyes.

"You've got another thing coming if you think that hiding in here is going to solve anything."

He sighs without looking at me. "I'm not hiding, Paige. It's been a long night."

"Then you should go to our actual bedroom and go to sleep."

"I'm avoiding a fight."

"You can face those shadowy men in the yard, but you're too afraid to face your wife when she's angry?"

"I didn't want to spoil the victory of your first dinner party. You did amazing tonight. You deserve to feel good about that."

I nod angrily. "I agree. I do deserve to feel good about that. Except that all I'm feeling is hurt and pissed off that my husband called me a 'stubborn nag' and walked away."

He raises his eyebrows. "What do you—"

"See the thing is, Misha," I say, powering through the half-formed speech I drafted in my head while stomping over here, "it's not nagging when you care about the person. It's not nagging when you love the person. Clara used that word to shut me up, and I refuse to let you do the same thing."

"Paige—"

"Any time I tried to get past her walls, any time I feared she was going to do something dangerous or unsafe, I'd question her. All she had to do was throw that word at me, and I'd shut right up. I'd step aside and let her make mistakes I could have prevented because I didn't want to be perceived a certain way. And now, well… Fuck that," I continue. "The day she died, I knew deep down that something was wrong. I asked her not to go see Moses. I told her I thought he was trouble. She turned around and said, *'Stop with the nagging and get off my back.'* That's what she said to me, and I let it work. Then she walked out of my life and she never came back. So I'm not about to let you hurt me in order to get me to back down. I'm your wife, Misha. You gave me a ring and said I could never take it off. So I won't. But guess what? If I can't take it off… neither can you."

He holds my gaze for a long moment.

Then he walks around the sofa bed and grabs my hips.

"That was quite the speech."

I frown. "Don't distract me."

"How am I distracting you?" he asks. "I'm just standing here, talking to you."

"Stop looking at me with those eyes."

"They're the only eyes I've got."

"Well, they should be illegal," I snap. "It's not fair. I came in here to shout at you."

"And you have accomplished what you set out to do. Very effectively, I must say. I was wrong. You were right."

My anger drifts away in the silver pools of his eyes. I try to remind myself that he hasn't exactly copped to anything. He hasn't even apologized. Just because he's calm and hot and shirtless and touching me does not mean anything is resolved.

"I'm sorry I called you a nag."

Okay, so we have an apology now.

"Thank you. But I need an explanation, too."

He shakes his head. "No one except Konstantin knows who those men are."

I hold up my ring finger again. "Unless you want to take this ring and put it on Konstantin, I suggest you fill me in."

One corner of his mouth twitches up. "I'd have to get it resized. Konstantin has sausage fingers."

I shake my head and sigh. "You're doing it again."

"Doing what?"

"Charming me. Trying to make me forget the reason I stormed in here in the first place."

He shrugs. "You're a smart woman. I'm not sure I could make you forget anything." He sits on the edge of the sofa bed and pulls me, still standing, between his legs.

"Misha…"

His hands slide under my dress until they find the knife strapped to my thigh. "Were you planning on using this tonight?"

"I thought about using it on you when you were being an asshole earlier."

He smiles that sexy, lopsided smile of his. "It's a shame you didn't. I would have liked to have seen that."

"I'm better than you think I am. Don't underestimate me."

He shakes his head firmly. "I would never make that mistake." He removes the knife and unbuckles the leather strap from my thigh. "Leather suits you."

"I know what you're trying to do." I announce it as if revealing the truth might be able to stop the throbbing between my legs.

"What am I trying to do?" He slides my wet panties off my legs and drops them to the ground.

"Who were those men, Misha?" He slips two fingers inside me, and my pussy swallows them up. I lose my train of thought for a moment. "Fuck."

"You were right about them," he says, his fingers pulsing deeper. "They are dangerous."

I place my hands on his shoulders for balance. "Th-then why… Why were they here?"

"I hired them to corner Petyr. But he's proved to be far more elusive than I anticipated."

My breath is catching. All the questions that I might've had with a clear head completely slip from my grasp. "Oh, God," I moan as he teases me more and more with his fingers.

"You want to keep talking?" he asks. "Or do you want me to make you come?"

"Does it have to be one or the other?"

He doesn't make me choose, though.

He just chooses for me.

In one quick motion, I'm flat on my back, Misha's broad body between my legs. His lips find my neck and his fingers keep exploring my pussy. I try to remember the reason I came in here in the first place.

When his tongue swirls over my clit, I give up completely.

Questions can wait until morning.

55

MISHA

I make her finish first. I can't help myself—every moan that crosses her lips makes me want to draw a hundred, a thousand, a million more.

She's still trembling from release when I peel her out of her dress. Paige is always gorgeous, but the way she is growing and softening in pregnancy drives me mad. The gentle swell of her stomach reminds me how intimately the two of us are tied together now.

A few months ago, that might have terrified me.

Now, I want to revel in it.

I crawl over her, keeping my weight on my arms, and drive into her wetness. She claws at my shoulder blades and drags her hands down my biceps, but I hold back. I fuck her slowly, working her into a tangle of lust and desire.

I suck on her nipples and I kiss her neck. I lick my way down to her belly button. I tease her until she's breathless, until she's moaning my name amidst a string of unintelligible words.

Pleasure tightens like a fist in my stomach, but I hold off. I wait until she's ready.

"Misha," she cries, grinding her hips into mine. "I'm coming."

Her body tightens around mine, and I pull out, climb on top of her, and release.

My cum pours onto her breasts. I paint her beautiful chest, then massage my signature into her skin as she moans and whimpers her way back to limp silence.

"Fuck," I growl.

She's lying prone on the bed, eyes closed, chest heaving. The sight alone has me half ready for round two. But I ease off of her and wipe myself clean.

Paige sits up and reaches for a tissue. "What?" she asks when she notices me looking at her. "Am I not allowed to wipe your cum off me at all?"

I smirk. "I'll allow it this time."

She smiles and towels off her chest and legs. Then she curls up in the top sheet.

"What are you doing?"

She holds it tight under her chin. "I'm covering up."

"I can turn up the heat if you're cold."

"No, I'm not cold. I just… I'm feeling a little vulnerable right now."

"Why?"

She throws me a skeptical look. "It's no secret my body's changing. I'm getting bigger."

I grab her arm and pull her against me. "In the sexiest way possible."

She is still trying to pull the sheet over herself. I growl and kick the blankets away.

"Misha!" she protests, trying to grab at the sheet.

"I'm serious, *moya zhena*. You're perfect. Your body has never looked sexier. Why do you think I can't keep my hands off of you?

Her forehead furrows. "So... you still find me attractive?"

"Did you just miss the last half hour?" I ask, gesturing to our naked bodies and the mangled bedding. "Even when I'm pissed at you, I'm so fucking turned on by you that I can't stay away."

"That's right," she says like it just occurred to her. "I was mad at you when I walked in here."

I sigh. My mother's words from earlier are still echoing in my head. "I'm not used to having a partner, Paige. It's not natural for me to share certain things with you. I also don't want to stress you out."

"You know what stressed me out? Walking out there and seeing you surrounded by three scary-looking monsters."

"I know; I just didn't want you anywhere near them. They're bad men, the Babai. Dangerous men."

"The Babai?" she repeats, testing the unfamiliar word on her tongue.

I nod. "They're mercenaries, of a sort. Guns for hire, the most powerful guns you can get, and dangerous in the wrong hands—but they follow a code. There are rules they must abide by."

"Is that why you went to them? Because of their code?"

"I like people who stick to their word."

She considers that for a moment. "What I'm hearing is that you hired assassins. Assassins who know where we live and can get onto the property uninvited. Is that the gist?"

I groan. "I should have found myself an idiot to marry. She would have been so much easier to deal with."

"True," Paige agrees. "But you wouldn't have been as happy."

That strikes me somewhere between the head and the chest. Happy? Is that what I am right now? If I could forget the small problem of Petyr Ivanov and the Babai, then maybe I could consider myself happy.

But I can't.

"Right?" Paige trails her fingers across my cheek.

"Right," I agree. "Right."

She smiles again. "Should we be worried about these guys? The Babai?"

I kiss her temple. "I'll keep you safe, Paige. Trust me."

"I do trust you," she says. "I just don't trust anybody else."

"Now, you're starting to get it."

56

PAIGE

I wake Misha up the next morning with his cock in my mouth.

His hips move before his eyes even open, shallow thrusts seeking out the unexpected pleasure. But then he is wide awake, his hand on the back of my head while he fucks my mouth.

"D-don't..." he groans, fisting my hair in his hand. "Don't fucking stop."

And I don't.

Not until he spills into my mouth, and I've swallowed every drop.

Afterward, I lie on the sofa bed with Misha's head in my lap. I run my fingers through his hair without a single thought in my mind.

I'm only distracted when Misha reaches up and touches my dangling pendant. "You told me once that you and Clara believed this was your amulet of protection." He pauses, then asks, "Why did she give it to you? It sounds like she needed the protection more than you did."

"You know, I've spent so many nights asking that exact same question. But Clara always cared more about me than herself. She was sad, but she hid it for my benefit." I sigh. "Sometimes, I think that maybe she gave me the pendant because she knew it wouldn't make a difference to her. She'd written herself off from the beginning. I just didn't realize it."

"Maybe she didn't realize it, either," he offers gently.

"I wish I could have helped her like she helped me."

I say the words like a prayer. Wherever she is, I hope she can hear me.

"You gave her your friendship. That counts for something."

I shake my head. "That's the thing—it feels so pitiful in comparison to what she gave me. She was a stand-in for every other person in my life. Siblings, parents, other friends. She was everything to me."

He glances at my chest. Only then do I realize that I'm holding onto my pendant for dear life.

"No one can or should be everything to you, Paige. It's too much pressure for any one person."

I nod tearfully. "Do you think that's why—"

"No," he says, stopping me before I give life to that terrifying thought. "She did what she did for her own reasons. She did what she did because of something inside of her. It had nothing to do with anyone else."

I take a deep breath, and as I do, I resign myself to the harsh truth that I can't rage about Misha keeping things from me if I'm doing the exact same thing to him.

"There's something I have to tell you," I confess. He tenses, and I rush to explain. "It's not, like, a DEFCON-1 or anything. But I want you to know." I take a deep breath, forcing out the words. "My, uh… my parents called me last week. They called to ask for more money."

"*More* money?" he asks, not glazing over that point the way I hoped he would. "Is that why the monthly withdrawal has been increased?"

I sit up straight. "You already knew?"

"I assumed you raised the amount you wanted to send them," he says, looking pissed now. "I didn't realize they were extorting you."

"I… I wouldn't call it extortion—"

"They're using you, Paige. That's exactly what it is."

I sigh. My hands fall limp in my lap. "I know that. But they're still my parents. They've lived in that godforsaken trailer park their entire lives, and I'm not about to visit them anytime soon. So sending money, it feels—I don't know… I feel like I should."

"Why? Because they deserve it? I think we both know that they don't."

"Maybe this is not about what they deserve," I ponder. "Maybe this is just about me trying to do what's right." He looks so annoyed that I have to laugh. I pat his cheek. "It's okay, Misha. I don't mind."

"*I do*," he hisses. "Why should they benefit from your hard-earned money when they never appreciated what a prize they had?"

I smile tenderly. "Just as long as you do, I'm okay with that."

He leans up and kisses me passionately on the lips. It's an angry kiss, like he's getting back at them through me and it. I curl my fingers through his hair, feeling my body respond immediately. When we pull apart, I feel so much better on so many different fronts.

"This honesty thing is pretty cool, huh?"

He chuckles. "I wouldn't go that far. But it's certainly less irritating than I thought it would be."

"Speaking of…"

"Here we go," he says, feigning dread. "Strike my last comment."

I playfully hit him on the arm. "It just occurred to me that I don't know what happened to Anthony after he came to the hospital that day. He went silent. I guess I just figured he took the hint and disappeared, but…" I trail off, wondering if I should have brought this topic up at all.

Misha's face is a mystery. "He's still alive, if that's what you're asking."

"I'm not sure if that's comforting or not," I say. "Did you… hurt him?"

"I probably should have. But no, I didn't."

"I mean… I am happy about that. As mad as I am at him for what he did, I still don't want him to suffer. But I'm also a little surprised."

"Why?" he asks. "Because you expected me to behave like the possessive beast I've shown myself to be in the past?"

I suppress a smile. "Your words, not mine."

He sighs. "Anthony came to me after the hospital. He wanted to talk, man to man. He told me that he was going to leave you and us alone. I decided to take him at his word."

"Why?"

"Because I realized that he really did care for you. In his own way."

I'm silent for a few moments, taking that all in. "Wow. Okay then."

"I didn't tell you because—"

"There was a lot going on. I know, I get it. But I'm glad you told me the truth now. You know what this is right here?" I ask, gesturing between the two of us.

"What?"

"Growth!"

He stares at me blankly for a second. Then he bursts out laughing.

I can really feel it this time. Things changing. Shifting beneath our feet and reaching towards a new, fresh light overhead.

Our love is a living thing. And the days ahead are starting to look like summer.

57

MISHA

"This is the seventh Ivanov body that's washed up outside our doors." Savva's gaunt face is thick with unkempt scruff and his eyelids droop in heavy purple bags. It's clear he hasn't been sleeping.

"Seventh on your side of town," I correct. "Igor reported three more bodies in the meatpacking district this morning."

Savva casts nervous glances from me to Konstantin. "These murders didn't happen under my order, boss."

I nod. "I know. They happened under mine."

Savva frowns. "But who carried them out? We're your men—and believe me, I'd be more than willing to slit those bastards' throats one by one if you gave the word—but you didn't order us to flush out the Ivanov scum."

"Because I already dispatched a separate task force to do exactly that," I tell him. "Alert the men that more bodies are likely to wash up in the next few days."

"And if one of them is Petyr Ivanov…?" Savva ventures.

"It won't be," I tell him confidently. "The only door he'll wash up outside of is mine. Thank you, Savva. That will be all."

The lieutenant looks very unsettled, but he gives me a half-hearted nod and leaves my office.

Konstantin sits down in the now-vacated seat. "What's the end goal here, man? You're making the rank-and-file uneasy. They're gonna start making guesses, and eventually, they might actually make the right one. How do you think they'll feel when they know the Babai are wandering around the city with murder on their minds?"

"What they don't know won't hurt them, and this will be over long before they find out." I wave my hand. "The point is that Petyr needs to know he's being hunted. Sooner or later, he'll feel that pressure and make the wrong move. Desperate men always do."

"Fine, but in the meantime, the men are going to want to know what's going on. You saw the look on Savva's face. He's scared shitless."

"For now, they can make their guesses. They'll get an explanation once I've got Petyr in the palm of my hand."

He shakes his head. "I still don't like this. In case you needed a reminder of where I stand."

"You're more scared of the Babai than Paige was," I snort.

Konstantin's brows leap nearly to his hairline. "You told Paige about the Babai? Jesus H., man, were you drunk? High? Concussed?"

"None of the above," I say. "She walked outside while I was talking to them and demanded to know who they were. I decided that she deserved to know."

"Fucking hell, brother." Konstantin runs a hand through his hair. "It's déjà vu all over again. This is exactly what happened with Maksim when he fell in love with Cyrille."

I'd forgotten that part. Or maybe I just blocked it out. I used to take it personally when Maksim chose to share his plans with Cyrille before he shared them with me. Am I doing the same thing to Konstantin?

I might be, and I'm not sure what to say. Because I won't apologize for it. Knowing Konstantin, he wouldn't ask me to anyway.

"What does it feel like?" he asks unexpectedly. "Falling in love, being in love."

I hesitate to choose my words carefully before answering. "I'm not as good at the 'being in love.' That part is new. But the falling… That's appropriately named. Because that's exactly what it feels like. Like you're falling and you have no control."

"So it's terrifying?" Konstantin deciphers.

Usually, I wouldn't admit as much, but there's no denying the truth. "Yeah. Extremely fucking terrifying."

He laughs, and I laugh along with him. It's crazy that we're having this conversation at all. I think we both realize it, because a beat later, both our smiles fade in sync.

"Do you think Petyr knows by now?" he asks quietly. "About your twin heirs?"

"I'm counting on it."

"Fuck," he breathes.

"Yeah," I agree. "Fuck."

58

PAIGE

I'm antsy in the car after a routine check-up with Dr. Mathers the next day. "Thanks for driving me to my appointment." I lean over the console and kiss Misha. He wraps a hand around the back of my neck and holds me there, deepening the kiss until I start to get the squirmy butterflies.

Finally, I break away, breathless. "If you keep that up, I'll never go inside."

His eyes are still closed as he smiles. "Good."

"No, not good! You need to get to work, and I need to eat." I kiss him quickly on the cheek and back out of the car. "I'm starving."

He groans and places his hands on the wheel. "Fine. Go feed those babies of mine. We'll pick up where we left off later."

I stand in the drive and watch him pull away with a huge, goofy smile on my face.

I'm still wearing that smile when I walk into the kitchen and find Nessa standing at the stove, stirring around something thick and sludgy that looks like it requires some serious muscle power.

"Paige, dear!" she greets. "How did the doctor's appointment go?"

I walk to the island and try to keep my nose from wrinkling against the oppressively bitter smell as I hoist myself onto one of the bar stools. "Great! Everything is good with the babies. They're healthy."

She exhales with relief. "How wonderful. I was praying about it all day. Did you find out the sex of the babies?"

I give her a sympathetic smile. "No, sorry. We're still waiting."

"Well, it's your decision." But it's obvious to anyone with eyeballs that she's desperate to find out.

I watch her running around the kitchen with her pink apron, bare face, bare feet, and a string of pearls around her neck. The woman can't help but maintain a touch of class at all times.

I've grown used to Nessa living with us, to her being here when I come home. But I can't help but wonder what it would be like to be this close with my own mother. How wonderful would it be to be able to call her up and share details of my pregnancy with her? How wonderful would it be to watch her get excited with me, to offer unsolicited advice, to share stories from when she was pregnant with me?

For a moment, I try to imagine what that would feel like. But it's like running into a brick wall again and again. It hurts and it's pointless.

There's no way I can imagine Jillian being excited about my pregnancy. I can't imagine Jillian being excited about anything. Certainly nothing that has to do with me.

Suddenly, there's a hand on my shoulder. I jerk upright and my eyes focus on Nessa. "I'm sorry—I startled you."

"No, it's okay. I'm sorry. I was thinking."

"About?"

"About... my mom, actually." I shake my head. "It's stupid. I was just imagining a world where she might care about me and the babies and... Never mind. It was silly."

She leaves her pot of stinking stew and joins me at the kitchen island. "Oh, honey, it's a perfectly natural thing to want your mother around when you're having your first baby. I felt the same way when I was pregnant with Maksim."

"Was your mother around for his birth?"

"No," she says regretfully. "She passed away eight months before he was born. Cancer. She was diagnosed thirteen years earlier. Went into remission three times. The fourth time the cancer came back, she decided not to undergo treatment. She said, 'Some battles aren't meant to be won.'"

"Nessa, I'm so sorry." I place my hand over hers.

She gives me a sad smile. "She didn't know she was going to be a grandmother. When she passed away, even I didn't know I was pregnant. I found out a few weeks after her funeral. But in a strange way, it felt good. Almost like the universe was offering me a lifeline. I had lost my mother, but here was another life that I could devote myself to."

It's such a Nessa thing to say that I smile. She is so devoted to everyone in her life. I wonder if anyone was willing to devote themselves to her in the same way.

"Nessa, can I ask you a personal question?"

She smiles and nods. "Of course."

"Did you ever consider just leaving your husband?" I ask. "I mean, you're an amazing woman. You could have found a man who actually made you happy." She hesitates for a moment, so I add, "Whatever you tell me stays between us. I won't even breathe a word to Misha."

She stirs the sludge in the pot for a while, not saying anything. "I've never told anyone this before," she admits at last. "But since you asked… There was a man once. I was in love with him. Very much in love."

"Don't tell me you were forced to break up with him because you were given to Misha's father."

"Oh, no," she says, her eyes turning fondly back into the past. "I met him years after I married Maksim Senior." I try to control my expression, but I'm not sure I'm doing the best job. She takes one look at my contorted face and laughs. "Didn't expect that, did you?"

"Not even a little bit, if I'm being honest."

Mostly because I would have assumed her husband would have killed her for even looking at another man.

"Everyone assumes I followed all the rules," she says. "But some rules are worth breaking."

"I completely agree. Tell me everything."

Nessa laughs, and for a split second, I see a much younger woman tucked away in the lines of her face. A happier woman, if only she'd been allowed to take a different route through life.

"His name was Anisim. He was a Vor to my husband. It took ten years and three children before I realized that the reason Anisim was rude to me every time we had an interaction was because he was attracted to me. He didn't want Maksim Senior to know." She sinks into the seat next to me, my hand still clasped in hers. "It—the inevitable *it*—happened one night while my husband was on a business trip in Russia. Anisim was tasked with protecting the house while he was gone. We ran into each other in the wine cellar late at night and… Well, one thing led to another."

"Oh my God!" I cry "This is so romantic."

"The beginning certainly was," Nessa says with a little sigh. "Even if the ending wasn't."

"Nessa…"

She pats my hand. "Don't be sad, Paige. I'm certainly not. We had seven years together. And for me, that was a lifetime."

I don't even want to ask; I'm that afraid of the answer. "Seven years? What happened after that?"

"He asked me to run away with him," she explains. "He said he wanted more than the half-life we were living. He wanted to be able to kiss me in public. Hold my hand when we walked down the street. He wanted to marry me. I could have run away with him, and if I'm being honest, there was a split second when I actually considered it. But I would have had to take the children with me or leave them behind. The first was a life sentence that we would never outrun for good. The second was never a real option for me."

"You chose them. Your children."

She smiles and nods. "And I have never regretted it for a moment."

I shake my head, completely in awe of this woman. "I'm not sure that any of your children know how lucky they are. My mother would have sold me to the devil if it meant getting a fraction of what she wanted."

Nessa winces. "Well, I'm more than happy to fill that void for you. If you'll have me."

Nessa has treated me like her own daughter since day one. But hearing her say those words out loud makes my eyes well up with tears. I swipe at my eyes. "I'm pathetic. I'm sorry."

She squeezes my fingers. "Never apologize for letting yourself be vulnerable. It's the best part of being human."

I laugh through my tears. "You're amazing, Nessa. I already think of you as my mother." Sniffling, I ask, "What happened to Anisim?" I'm hoping to God his story didn't end in death. With the Bratva, you never know.

"He retired from the Bratva shortly after I gave him my answer," she admits. "He left the country, went to Russia for a bit. I heard he moved to Chicago about fifteen years ago. After that, I lost track of him. I think it was probably for the best. He has a wife now and a couple of kids. He deserves that life."

"So do you."

"I had it for a time," Nessa says. "And I got to be a mother. That's enough for me."

I shake my head. "I'm not sure if that would be enough for me."

"That's the beauty of life, isn't it?" she says gently. "We all get to decide what's important to us. What's worth fighting for and what we need to let go of."

"Niki and Misha should know this story, Nessa," I tell her.

She smiles and pats my hand. "I'm happy to keep this our little secret."

I nod. "Okay. Our little secret."

She gives my knee a reassuring touch and heads back around to the stove. "I'm making a special porridge that my grandmother used to make in Russia. It's supposed to give you strength for your pregnancy."

"You're making it for me?" Her story distracted me enough that I almost forgot about the smell. But now, it is invading my nostrils, impossible to escape.

"Yes," she says. "How about a taste?"

She brings over a spoon dripping with something thick and lumpy and gray. Because I don't want to make her unhappy, I hold my breath and taste it.

"Well?" she asks, looking at me hopefully.

I give her a sympathetic smile. "Nessa, it tastes... awful."

We make eye contact. And then we burst out laughing.

59

MISHA

It's been more than a week since the dinner party and there has been no word from the Babai. They're picking off the Ivanov trash one by one, which isn't nothing.

But Petyr is still a ghost.

I'm halfway home when my phone rings. I accept the call on the car speaker when I see Konstantin's name on the display.

"Did you just leave the office?" he asks.

"I've had enough for one day. Everyone is pissing me off."

"I figured as much. No other reason you'd leave Orion before five o'clock."

"If you suspected, then why are you calling me?"

"Just an update. We have four more Ivanov bodies," he informs me. "One was in pretty bad shape. The idiot must have put up a fight."

"Still no Petyr?"

"Nope. Maybe this is part of the Babai's process?"

"Or maybe they're not all they're cracked up to be," I say through gritted teeth. "Call me if there's any other information. I'm going to be at home for the rest of the night."

"Got it. Say hi to Paige for me."

Just the mention of her name is enough to calm the anxious energy inside of me. She's the main reason I left the office.

I needed to see her.

But when I walk into our bedroom, she's at her desk and surrounded by paperwork. This is one of those rare times when I wish she would consent to being a kept woman and save the work for me.

I walk up behind her and place my hands on the back of her chair. "Hello, *kiska.*"

She jumps a foot in fright, obviously having missed my entrance. "Misha! You're home early."

"I thought I'd come home and surprise you."

She wraps her arms around my neck and kisses me tenderly on the lips. "It's a great surprise. The only thing is, I have some more work to finish up. Probably about an hour's worth." I groan and she pats my back and laughs. "The crib arrived this morning. Maybe you could set it up while I finish here?"

"If I were more cynical, I'd almost think you were trying to get rid of me," I drawl.

"Just for the next hour," she says with a cheeky little wink. "Pinky promise."

I slap her ass as she turns back to her work. It's frustrating as hell because all I want to do is bend her over that desk and fuck her senseless. But watching her work is a turn-on, too. A catch-22 designed by the devil himself.

It leaves me horny and irritated. Not the best condition to be in after a futile day at the office. I take my irritation into the next room to unleash it on the crib.

Instead of finding the silence I'm craving, though, I walk in on my mother and sister. They're perched at the window seat overlooking the backyard.

"My wayward brother! What a surprise," Niki greets.

"You sound happier to see me than my wife did just now."

Niki snorts with laughter. "She kicked you out while she finishes working, huh? I love it."

"That makes one of us."

She cackles happily. "No other woman has ever refused you. I love that she's prioritizing her work instead of dropping her panties the moment you get home."

"Really, Niki," Mom says, sounding horrified. "Must you be so crass?"

She smiles and lifts her chin. "Apparently, I must."

"Why are you so damn happy?" I ask.

"I moved into my new place yesterday."

I frown and cross my arms over my chest. "I see. It'll need to be inspected. I'll send Konstantin over to set up—"

"No."

I raise my eyebrows. "Did you just say 'no'?"

"N-O. No. It is a gated community, so there's security at the entrance. I'm not about to let you set up bodyguards outside my sanctuary. I want a *normal* life, Misha. I can't have that with shaved goons lurking outside my door at all hours of the night."

"A fucking *gate* isn't going to protect you from Petyr Ivanov, Niki."

But she doesn't back down. "I've already met two of my neighbors and I like them both. They think I'm a nice, normal, all-American girl. I'd like to keep it that way."

"Nik—"

"Stop. I know what you're going to say, but you're wrong. I'm not in any danger," she interrupts. "Petyr is not interested in me. Even if he was, no one knows that I've moved out on my own. As far as the underworld is concerned, I'm still living with Nessa and Cyrille under your protection."

A few months ago, I would have forced the issue. I would have rolled tanks over that flimsy gate and installed my own army between my sister and the outside world.

Paige has forced me to reconsider those methods. Occasionally, I need to loosen the reins. Is this one of those times?

I glance at my mother, who smiles and gives me a slight shrug. It's easy enough to interpret. She's worried, but resigned.

"Alright, fine." I walk over and kneel next to the crib components scattered across the carpet. Someone clearly tried to put this together already and failed.

"Whoa. Did you just concede to me?"

"You're a grown woman, Niki," I say as I start to sort and organize the pieces. "If we were normal, you'd have moved out a long time ago."

She blows out a long breath. "Paige really has changed you."

I flip her the bird, and Nessa scolds us both like she used to when we were teenagers.

Chuckling, I settle in to put together the first of the two cribs. Maybe working with my hands will stave off some of my frustration.

Niki joins me on the floor and grabs the instruction manual. "Thanks, by the way. For letting me have this victory. I needed a W."

I pass her the bag of screws. "I can't picture you in a gated community."

She smirks. "I know. It's not what I'm used to. But I kind of like that. One bed, one bath—what is it, a house for ants, y'know? But the kitchen is nice and I can see the sunset from my bedroom. I'm gonna get a bookshelf in the living room and fill it with trashy romance novels. You'd hate it."

"Jesus," I mutter. "How do people live like that?"

Niki just laughs. "I'm thinking of getting a dog, too."

"Good. Get a Doberman. Make sure he bites."

She rolls her eyes. "I don't need a watchdog. I'm trained in martial arts and Jiu Jitsu, remember? I also know how to use a gun."

"Do you?"

She nods. "Maksim taught me."

That takes me by surprise. I had no idea they'd done that. She never even asked me to train her.

"I'm training Paige to handle a weapon," I confess. "It's... weird."

"Why? She's smart and capable. Why shouldn't she be able to carry?"

"Because she's my wife," I say. "She shouldn't have to carry a gun or learn to defend herself. She shouldn't have to work or earn money. That's my job."

Niki rolls her eyes. "Paige is an independent, twenty-first century woman. She wants to be able to stand on her own two feet. I want the same."

"Women," I sigh under my breath, knowing it'll piss Niki off. She punches my arm harder than I would've expected. "Fuck, *ow*. Maybe those martial arts lessons aren't a total waste."

She shakes her head and starts flipping through the manual. I look over and realize Mother has been watching us this entire time. She's smiling fondly.

"What?" I ask her.

She shrugs. "I was just thinking how nice this is."

I don't need to ask what she means. I spent the entire year after Maksim's death avoiding the family. But since Paige has entered my life, that has changed. I've found a certain level of comfort with them again. Tentative and fragile, but real. Being with them isn't just a constant reminder that Maksim isn't here.

It's nice in its own right.

"All thanks to Paige," Niki says. "She's like the wizard who gave ole' Tin Man his heart."

I want to shoot back a snarky retort, but how can I?

She isn't wrong.

60

PAIGE

I step out of the car and breathe in deep. The fresh air is like a balm to my soul.

Then I turn and see the cabin nestled between the trees like something out of a storybook. "Oh my God. Is it made out of gingerbread, or what? Are you gonna cook me and eat me?"

Misha just smiles. "Eat you, maybe. But not the way you're talking about."

I roll my eyes and whack him in the arm. He surprised me with this impromptu trip only this morning. He said it was to celebrate my first hosting gig as a Bratva wife, but I suspect it was his way of forcing me to quit working. Either way, I agreed.

But I would have agreed a lot more readily if he'd shown me a picture of this cabin.

The roof is conical and thatched, and so quaint it hurts. I half-expect to see storybook animals waiting on the porch to greet us. Little squirrels will make our coffee in the mornings and singing songbirds will braid my hair.

I turn around, tilting my ear towards the trees. "I can hear water."

"There's a waterfall not far from here. If you walk around the back of the cabin, you should be able to spot it from the lookout point."

"Then that's exactly what I'm going to do. Do you want to come?"

He shrugs his shoulders, lifting the bags in either hand. "Let me put the bags in our room first."

I watch him walk across the ground littered with pine needles and through the front door that bears a large, gold knocker set into the center of the wood. I can't stop grinning from ear to ear.

This place is magical.

He reappears on the porch with a stretch, his muscles straining against his shirt. "Okay. Quick walk before dinner."

"Why does it have to be quick?"

"Because the sun will set in less than an hour and you haven't eaten anything since last night."

I loop my arms around his waist and pull him closer. At almost seven months along, my growing stomach has become somewhat of an impediment, but Misha doesn't seem to mind. "I'm only hungry for you right now," I say flirtatiously.

He smirks. "That will have to wait until after dinner."

"Seriously? I know you're not actually turning me down right now."

"You need to eat, Paige. The babies need sustenance. So do you."

I roll my eyes and throw him a sloppy mock salute. "Yes, sir, Drill Sergeant."

Laughing, he takes my hand and we make our way around the cabin.

Moss creeps between the stones of the cobbled pathway that leads down to the lookout point. It's just chilly enough that the air stings my lungs, but it's a refreshing kind of sting. Cleansing. The scent of damp bark and leaves is a nice change from the city.

When we reach the rocky outcropping of the lookout, I point and gasp simultaneously. "I see it!"

Sure enough, there it is. The promised waterfall.

Mountain spring water cascades down a jagged rock face, shimmering in the late afternoon sun like diamonds. It collects with a murmur in a smoothed marble pool at the bottom. Ducks float idly around the perimeter and little sparrows dip in and out for a drink.

"Let's go closer!"

Misha studies the slope. "It's steep."

"Please?" I beg. "I've always wanted to makeout under a waterfall."

His lips twitch into a smile, and I know I've got him.

"Alright," he says, still pretending to be surly and dour. "But carefully. And hold onto me."

By the time we get there, I've worked up a bit of a sweat. The path down was a little more strenuous than it looked from the top—not that I'm about to admit as much to my husband.

The bonus of the exercise is that I'm warm. My body is flushed. Hot, even.

In more ways than one.

Misha didn't let go of me the whole way down, and those displays of possessiveness he does so well have a predictable effect on me. As soon as we're on level ground, I turn to Misha and pull him into a passionate kiss. I slip my tongue into his mouth and we stand there for a while, necking like teenagers.

When I finally pull back, I'm even hotter than before. But the mist coming off the waterfall is cool against my skin, and I want more.

"What are you doing?" Misha growls as I take a step back and pull my sweater over my head. His eyes slip down to my breasts.

"What does it look like?" I wink at him. "Why don't you join me?"

"Paige, we're out in the open."

"There's no one around!" I pull my leggings down.

Goosebumps rise across my legs. It might be a little too cold for this, but I'm fueled by the hungry look in his eyes. Once I'm naked, I turn and dip my toe into the water.

"Jesus!" I hiss, yanking my foot back.

Misha laughs. "I could've told you it would be cold. Not that you would've listened."

I can see that he doesn't think I'm going to do it. So without thinking, I turn and jump straight into the water.

The icy water closes over me like cement, pulling me down. I fight against the tug and resurface with a loud, "Holyfuckingshit!" I find my footing against the soft moss at the bottom and stand. "You're right: it is cold. You'll have to come on in and warm me up."

"You are a saucy little temptress, aren't you?" he teases. "Stubborn, too."

"And sexy. Don't forget sexy."

Laughing again—a sound I will never, ever get tired of—Misha strips down and leaves his clothes in a pile next to mine.

When he jumps in, he doesn't resurface right away. I watch his long body glide under the water towards me until his hands find my waist.

He rises out of the water like a god, water streaming off of his broad chest in a hundred mini-waterfalls. I hook my legs around his waist and latch onto his neck.

"Now, I'm wet in more ways than one," I whisper into his ear.

He laughs. "Paige Orlov has a kink for outdoor sex. Who knew?"

"I have a kink for *you*," I correct. "We just happen to be outdoors."

We kiss, our bodies naturally sliding together until he slips inside of me. Then we make love under the waterfall, our bodies rocking in time with the beat of the current.

When I climax, my screams are lost in the roar of the water.

61

MISHA

Paige is sprawled on the cabin bed, my massive sweater rolled up around her wrists, with a huge bowl of pasta in her lap. Her hair is a matted mess. There's pesto on her teeth.

She has never looked cuter.

That thought is the final nail in the coffin. I have fallen in love with my wife. And there's no going back.

Paige looks over and frowns. "What?"

"You have pesto in your teeth."

"Oh, shoot." She ducks behind her hand to try and clear it away with her tongue. Then she turns to me and grins for my inspection. "Now?"

I start laughing and she groans. She grabs her phone and uses the camera to check her reflection. "Oh, man. That's so extremely attractive."

"It is, actually."

She rolls her eyes. "You don't have to do that anymore. I'm your wife already. No need to lie."

"I'm not lying," I tell her honestly. "You look cute enough to eat."

She sets her pasta to the side and crawls across the bed to me. She presses a kiss to my cheek. "Yeah? Then, while I've got you in the palm of my hand, we should probably talk baby names."

"Sure. You can choose."

She blinks at how quickly I let her win. "Really?"

"Yeah," I say, grinning wickedly. "You can choose which baby is Misha the second and which one is Misha the third."

Gasping in shock and delight, she slaps me in the chest. "Misha!"

"Mm, yes. It has an even nicer ring to it when you say it. And it works for both boys and girls."

She laugh-snorts, a sound that somehow just makes her that much cuter. "You're ridiculous."

I laugh. "I do have one other idea."

"Oh? Hit me."

I take her hand and squeeze it gently. "Do you like the name Clara?"

Paige pauses. No words, not even a breath. Then she gives me a soft, watery smile. "Yeah, I think so. I mean, I know Clara had a lot of issues. It could feel a little morbid naming our daughter after her given the circumstances of her… of what happened to her. But on the other hand, she was such an amazing person. She saved me."

"It would be good to keep her close." I kiss her knuckles. "We can come back to that idea. Just sit with it for now. See how it feels."

"What about boy names?" she presses. "Do you think you'd like to name our son Maksim?"

I hesitate, trying the name on for size. It takes me only a few seconds to make up my mind. "There have already been two Maksims in two generations. I think that's enough."

"Okay." She looks at me and shakes her head. "Sometimes, I can't believe this is really happening."

"Which part?"

"All of it," she says. "You, mostly. I mean, everything with Anthony was a fight. I should count myself lucky I never got pregnant with him. We never would have settled on a name. But things with you are so easy."

"Minus the enemies and living under constant security, right?"

She rolls her eyes. "Yeah, besides that. But even with all of that, I've never felt safer with anyone else in my entire life."

The weight of her faith settles on my shoulders. It's heavier than I expected. Another reminder of everything I stand to lose if things with the Ivanovs don't end the way I hope they will.

She runs her hand over my forehead and down my nose, forcing my gaze to hers. "You're worried about the situation with Petyr, aren't you?"

It's weird to know that she can look at my face and know exactly what I'm thinking. It's not as intrusive as I expect, though. I feel more understood than I do exposed.

"The Babai are picking off his men in droves. That's got to be getting to him, but he still hasn't surfaced."

"Why would he? He knows you're waiting for him."

"That's exactly it—he seems to know where and when I'm waiting for him, too. Every time we get a tip and we blow the place up, there's no Petyr in the ashes. Almost like... almost like he knows too much. Like someone is telling him—but no, no." I shake my head in frustration. "No, there's no way. The only people who know my plans are Konstantin and you."

"And the Babai," Paige suggests.

"The Babai have a code. They'd never betray it. Konstantin would sooner than betray me. And you? I don't let you out of my sight long enough for you to be a rat."

She giggles as I kiss the sensitive spot of her neck for a moment before pushing me away. "I don't know this world nearly as well as you do. If you think you can trust these men, then I won't question it. Because I trust you."

62

MISHA

It's early when I walk out onto the cabin porch. Steam from my coffee swirls into the damp morning air. Mist hangs low over the trees, blotting out the rest of the world.

I could get used to this.

I'm making my way to the porch swing when I see the paper at the foot of the steps. At first, I want to say it's a piece of trash that was caught in the wind, blown here for no particular reason at all. But the white square is pristine and perfectly placed.

Not an accident.

I put my coffee mug down and go down to examine the paper. It's an envelope.

"Fuck."

I tap the envelope on the porch to see if any dust or debris that falls loose. Anything that could signal a threat. I wave my hand near it, wafting air towards me to see if there is any smell.

No dust. No scent. It seems safe, as far as I can tell, so I grab a twig from the ground and break the seal. Immediately, I see a corner of a glossy photograph, and my heart thumps dangerously.

I slide the photo free.

It's immediately obvious what it is. My body knows the truth even before my mind does. My skin flushes; my pulse swoons; sweat breaks out at my temples. It's as if I'm under attack from the inside out. Every cell rebelling, screaming, saying *No, no, no!*

The photograph shows Paige in profile, the swell of her stomach visible against the backdrop of lush green. She's standing next to the pool of water we dove into yesterday. I'm behind her, smiling and oblivious. I look so fucking *happy*, goddammit. Happier than I've ever been in my entire miserable life. I'm only realizing now how foolish that was—because this photograph, this envelope, it can only mean one thing.

Someone was watching us.

I grab my phone and call Konstantin.

I'm furious that, one, I hadn't fucking noticed a thing. And two, this motherfucker, whoever he was, had seen my wife naked. It feels as though he's stolen something precious from me. From us. A peace we fought hard for.

The fury surges through my hands as I wait for the dial tone to catch.

"It's early, bro." When he answers, Konstantin sounds like he just woke up. "Aren't you supposed to be on vacation?"

"Wake the fuck up. We have a problem."

"What happened?" All sleepiness is gone from his voice now. He's wide awake.

"Someone is watching us. Whoever it is took fucking pictures." I have to stop and unclench my jaw. I'll never forgive myself for not noticing someone lurking in the woods. "They put them in an envelope and left them at my front door."

He sucks in a sharp breath. "That's a threat."

"Obviously," I agree. "It's Petyr."

"No way. Petyr is not that stupid."

"Maybe he thinks he can afford to be," I suggest. "It's been months and I still haven't managed to corner him. He obviously thinks he has the upper hand."

"His men are dropping like flies. No way does he think that. Nuh-uh."

"It's him. He's trying to goad me into making a stupid move."

Konstantin hums, considering. "That is perhaps a bit more likely. What are you thinking?"

"First, I need to find the son of a bitch who took these pictures," I snarl. "Then I gut him until he squeals."

"I've got an alternate idea," Konstantin says. "Petyr has a half-brother. I've been keeping an eye on him, just in case Petyr went to him to hide out. It doesn't look like they have much contact, but that could be what Petyr wants me to think."

"Tell me more."

"Kid's name is Alexei Ivanov. He was born to one of the old man's mistresses."

A vague memory resurfaces. A snot-nosed little punk scurrying underfoot at one of the Orlov family dinners, back in the days when Petyr was an ally, not a dead man walking. "That kid is half Petyr's age, isn't he?"

"Mhmm. Twenty-one now. He lives in a shitty studio apartment uptown. I haven't noticed anything suspicious yet, but that doesn't mean the kid doesn't know something. I could talk to him."

"Let's call that plan B," I say. "For right now, get a team up here immediately. I want to comb the woods in case the rat didn't scurry far enough away."

"Your wish is my command. The team will be there in a few hours. I'll come with."

I hang up with Konstantin and examine the envelope again. There are three more pictures inside, all of which are of Paige and me in the waterfall. Two of them were taken while we were fucking. The water and distance hide a lot, but not enough for my liking.

It's a professional camera with a telescoping lens. Someone knew we'd be here, and they came prepared.

When I hear Paige moving inside the cabin, I hide the envelope under the swing cushion and take my coffee back inside.

She's standing by the stove in nothing but my white t-shirt. It swallows her whole, hanging down around her thighs. Something about that scene, the way she looks in my clothes, makes my heart jump to the left.

I swallow it down, walk over, and press a kiss to her neck. "Good morning, princess."

She blushes and squirms under my touch. "Where did you disappear to?"

"I was going to drink my coffee on the porch. But I like the view in here better."

She takes her milk off the fire and twists into my arms. "It was weird waking up to an empty bed. I've gotten used to having you around. Although this place is cute enough that it wasn't *so* bad."

I can't help sighing. "Don't get used to it. We might have to leave tonight."

She whips around to face me, eyes huge and imploring and panicked. My heart leaps again in that sickening, dizzying way it does whenever I let myself think of someone hurting her. "What? Why?"

"Something has come up," I tell her, knowing how vague I'm being and how much she'll hate it. "I'll be busy today. Konstantin is coming up in a few hours."

She grimaces. "You invited your cousin on our romantic getaway?"

"When all this is over, we are going somewhere far away with no interruptions," I tell her, adding another promise to my already-long list. "But I have to see to a few things first."

Paige sighs and crumples forward. "Should I know what they are?"

I'm not inclined to tell her about the pictures until I absolutely have to. Knowing that we were being watched yesterday would creep her out, and she doesn't need the stress. "We've got a lead on Petyr. I have to see it through."

"Okay," she mumbles. "I'll just go for a walk down to the—"

"No!"

She jerks back, startled by my response. "Why not?"

I try my best to keep my voice calm and level. "It would be best if you stayed in the cabin today. Konstantin will be here soon enough. Until then, stay put."

"Misha, what's going on? Why are you so afraid all of the sudden?"

So much for not stressing her out.

I drag a hand through my hair. "There may be eyes on us."

She stiffens instantly, and I despise that I can't protect her from everything. I know we're supposed to be honest with each other, but she was happy one minute ago. Content. Now, she's a ball of nerves.

Fuck honesty. It's highly overrated.

"I don't like when you say vague stuff and go do vague things," she admits in a small voice. "I'm never sure if you're going to come back."

I place my fingertip under her chin and force her teary eyes to mine. "I'm going to do whatever it takes to get back to you, Paige. I swear it."

But even as I say it, I grimace.

It's yet another promise I may not be able to keep.

63

PAIGE

The passing of time takes on a weird quality once Misha leaves, though he only goes only after making me promise three separate times to keep the door locked until Konstantin arrives.

The first hour passes, silent and still. I spend most of it watching the dust floating through the skinny beams of sunshine streaming through the gap in the curtains.

Another hour passes in the bath. The only sound is the *plink* of water dripping into the tub. I want to cry, but I don't.

A knock on the door, the prearranged signal, tells me that Konstantin is here. He doesn't say much as I open up and let him in. Just asks me if I'm packed and where my bags are. Two of his men transport my things from the bedroom to a waiting jeep. Two more stand guard outside with scary-looking rifles, their eyes never resting as they scan the woods again and again.

We're back home at the mansion before dark, but I go straight to bed. The next day passes in similar fashion—too quiet, too still, too depressing.

I call Cyrille at ten-thirty after finally succumbing to tears. Twenty-five minutes later, she shows up with ice cream and a sympathetic shoulder.

"He didn't come home last night?" she asks as soon as she arrives.

I shake my head. Tears are soaking into Cyrille's sleeve, but I can't bring myself to care. There's a void where my husband should be, and the ice cream tastes like wet ashes on my tongue.

"It's some mission." I sniffle, swiping my nose with the cuff of Misha's sweatshirt I stole from his closet. "We had one amazing day at the cabin, but then we had to leave. He barely even explained what or why or where or any of it."

"Did he tell you when he'd be back?"

"No. He didn't tell me anything." I choke back another sob. Fear, frustration, and an overwhelming dose of baby hormones are making it impossible to turn off my tears.

"Okay, well, it sounds like he's just—"

"How in the world did you do this?" I rasp before Cyrille can finish her sentence. "Be a Bratva wife, I mean. It's like, he walks out the door and you know he's going to deal with dangerous people. People who would love nothing more than for him to die. I keep thinking this will end when Petyr is dead. But when I woke up this morning alone, I think it hit me—this is going to be the rest of my life, isn't it?"

Cyrille pats my hand sympathetically. "A good portion of it, yes."

I drop my face in my hands. "I don't know how long I can live like that."

"I know you don't believe it now, but you will adapt. You'll develop a tolerance for these things."

I'm not sure I could ever develop a "tolerance" for losing my husband. When Cyrille's chin dimples, her lower lip shaking, I know she hasn't developed a tolerance for that, either.

"He's the man you chose, Paige," Cyrille tells me when she catches me looking. "This is part of the package."

I close my eyes and feel the tears slip down my cheeks. "I'm not sure I'm strong enough."

"You have to be," she says firmly. "If not for you, then for the babies you're carrying. In the end, they're the ones that will save you. Ilya saved me."

"I can't do this without him, Cyrille."

"That weight in your belly, that sense of dread in your gut—it's the price we pay for loving them. It's worth it, don't you think?"

I try to breathe through the terror surging in my veins, but every inhale is a struggle and every exhale hurts. "Probably. I mean, yes, it is, of course it is. I just can't think straight right now."

"Ice cream usually helps me."

I laugh through the tears. "When I get my appetite back, I'll let you know."

A moment later, the door opens and Nessa walks into my bedroom. She takes one look at me and understands. "Misha isn't back yet?"

Cyrille and I shake our heads in unison.

She's eerily calm as she walks to the edge of my bed and sits down facing the two of us. She pats my outstretched leg. "This is always the worst part. The waiting."

It occurs to me suddenly that I'm looking at two generations of women who have sat at home, miserable and afraid without their husbands just like I am. And just like that, my sadness turns to determination.

"Why should we have to sit here and wait?"

Cyrille arches a brow. "What does that mean? You want to be out there with him?"

"Why not?"

"You're seven months' pregnant with twins, for one thing," Nessa points out wryly.

"And for another," adds Cyrille, "your husband would lose his mind. He could barely stand to teach you how to fire a gun. He's not going to come scoop you up and take you on a raid."

"He wasn't going to fall in love with me, either," I remind them. "But that happened. He can change his mind."

Nessa smiles. It's sympathy, but of a limited variety—the kind that says, *Pretend anything you want; we all know you aren't going anywhere.* "You can stand to be left behind, Paige. You're strong enough for that."

"And if you need support, you have us," Cyrille offers. "Niki, too."

I smile through the tears and slump back down. They're right —I'm not going anywhere. But with them here, my hands holding each of theirs, I feel like maybe I can see a sliver of light at the end of this dark tunnel.

I lived most of my life as an orphan. I never thought I'd have a real family, a support system. But they're here. When I need them most, they're right here at my side.

"I couldn't do this without you guys," I say softly.

"Of course you could," Cyrille says. "Luckily, you don't have to."

64

MISHA

Alexei Ivanov walks into his apartment and drops his keys into a glass bowl. He hangs something from a hook, drops something else on the floor, curses under his breath in Russian. It's business as usual as far as he is concerned.

That's only because he hasn't seen me sitting on his sofa yet.

He pads down the short entryway and flips the light switch. The lights are on for a few seconds before he turns and catches sight of me.

For a second, he freezes up. He's stunned. Speechless. Not computing that his life is about to change forever.

Then his brain catches up, and he jolts back, smacking into the wall. "Wh-who the f-fuck are you?"

I regard him coolly. "I think you know exactly who I am."

He gives me one lookover and lunges for the front door. But the moment it's open, he's forced back inside by Konstantin brandishing a gun.

"Sit down and talk to me, Alexei. Or, if you prefer, you can take your chances with my friend and his gun." I shrug. "It's your choice."

He shuts the door and turns around slowly. Sweat is already beading on his forehead. He keeps glancing towards a cabinet on the side of the room.

"I wouldn't bother," I tell him. "I've removed the gun you hid in there. The one in your bedroom, too. You should update your hiding spots."

"What the f-fuck do y-you want from me?" he stutters.

"Do you know who I am?"

He shudders and his chin falls to his chest. "Don Misha Orlov."

"Smart boy. And how did I manage to find you?"

He hesitates. "I… I don't know. I don't know what you want with me, either. I have nothing to do with my brother."

I click my tongue against my teeth. "Don't lie to me, Alexei. I'm not inclined to be generous under the best of circumstances, and this is certainly not that."

He swallows hard. "Listen—"

"Do you know a man named Simon Maher?"

"N-no!" he says, sealing his fate with a single word. "No, I don't."

"Funny. Because he knows you." I pull out the white envelope that was left on my front porch and dangle it in front of him. "In fact, he told me you were the one who hired him to follow my wife and me and take those pictures."

Alexei stares cross-eyed at the envelope like he might be able to make it disappear if he focuses hard enough. "He… he was lying."

"No, he wasn't. I'm good at reading liars. It's why I know you're one right now. Also, I highly doubt he'd have the presence of mind to lie with a knife in his kneecap."

He gawks up at me, as if just now coming to the understanding that I'm two heads taller than he is, and that even if I didn't have a gun and a spare, that he would stand no chance of seeing tomorrow's sunrise.

I feel a tiny spindle of pity for this pitiful little kid. Konstantin told me he was only twenty-one, but he looks even younger than that. His facial hair is patchy, and he doesn't seem to know how to hold his long limbs still.

"I… I…"

"The next words out of your mouth better be useful to me."

"Okay!" he practically shouts, a trickle of sweat dripping down the side of his face. "Fine. I know Simon Maher. I hired him."

"Why?"

"Because I was told to."

I narrow my eyes. "By your brother."

"He's my half-brother." Alexei is eager to make that clarification. "One of his men showed up and made the demand. Petyr couldn't even ask me to do it himself."

That's noteworthy. The fucker is actually scared shitless of moving out in the open. Perhaps I've been giving him too much credit.

"We hadn't even talked in months before then. And we haven't talked since."

"So why did you do it?"

"Because you can't say no to Petyr," Alexei murmurs. "He would have killed me if I tried, just for knowing what he wanted done. That's how it works with him. Either your hands are just as dirty as his, or you're a loose end."

I believe him. There is no part of me that doubts his story.

It's why I decide to let him live.

Killing a man is one thing. Especially a guilty man. But Alexei Ivanov is just a scared kid, too stupid to know he should run away and never look back.

So I holster my gun. As I head to the door, Alexei jumps out of the way, keeping a safe distance between us, like he's expecting me to turn around and finish him at any moment.

I stop at the threshold. "Your brother killed mine. Some would call it poetic justice if I were to kill you right now."

His eyes bug out with fear.

"But those people would be wrong," I continue. "Poetic justice would be killing someone that Petyr actually cares for. And he clearly doesn't give a shit about you."

He gulps, as if he isn't quite sure whether he should be relieved or offended.

"Take it from a man who loved his brother: stay away from Petyr," I warn. "Get out of this cursed city and drop off his radar for good. Start your life over somewhere else, out of his shadow and his hold. You hear me?"

The kid nods, but he's still more worried about being shot in the head than anything I'm saying. Hopefully, he'll process my wisdom later. If not, he'll die. Either way, it's no longer my problem.

Konstantin is waiting for me by the stairs. He's leaning against the railing, his legs crossed at the ankle. "Is the kid dead?"

"I spared him."

Konstantin smirks. "You're getting soft."

"He's a stupid boy. Still a child. I'm not going to hold him accountable for the sins of his brother. I may be a don, but I'm no monster."

"Wow."

"What?"

"Nothing," he says, shaking his head. "It's just that you spoke and all I heard was Maksim."

For the first time in a long time, the comparison doesn't sting. I take it in stride. If the best I can do is emulate my brother…

I'm okay with that.

65

PAIGE

"I have something to tell you!" Cyrille drops down into the lawn chair next to mine, scaring the bejeezus out of me.

I shield my eyes from the sun. I've been staring blankly at the same page of my book for hours while I roast in the heat and wait for Misha to call or text or come home to me. It's been two days and still no sign of it, though.

"I didn't know you were coming by today."

"Sorry, I should have texted." She dismisses the words with a wave as soon as she says them. "But I have something to tell you."

"Yeah, you said that." I chuckle, but a knot of anxiety is forming in my stomach. If something has her this worked up, I'm willing to bet it's big. "Is everything okay?"

"I kissed another man."

I stare at her open-mouthed, trying to process.

She winces and wraps her arms around her knees. "Please say something."

"Um, well… congrats on the sex, first of all," I stammer awkwardly. I shake my head and smile. "I'm sorry. You caught me off-guard, that's all. I was expecting something diff—I mean, this is good. This is good, Cy! Who's the lucky man?"

She shakes her head. "Don't say it like that."

"Like what?"

"Like you're excited for me."

I frown. "Okay. I was, but should I not be? Am I missing something?"

Cyrille glances at the two glasses on the table between our chairs and suddenly goes ghost-white. "Oh my God. Were you out here with Nessa? Where is she? Can she hear us?"

I reach over and touch her bouncing knee. "Relax. Nessa has a meeting with one of her charity boards this morning. She's not even here. Both glasses are mine; I'm just thirsty and I couldn't decide if I wanted tea or lemonade. Back to the point: why are you so jumpy?"

"Didn't you just hear me?" Cyrille bleats. "I kissed another man! I don't want my mother-in-law to know that."

"Cyrille, honey, you do realize this isn't cheating, right?"

"Then why does it feel so much like it?" She drops her face into her hands. "I feel so guilty."

I got the glass of lemonade for myself. It's the only thing that settles my stomach these days. But Cyrille needs it more than me.

"Here." I press the glass into her hand. "Take a drink."

She takes a reluctant sip and wrinkles her nose. "Paige, this is not a problem lemonade can fix. I need hard liquor."

"This isn't a problem, babe. It's been more than seven months. You're allowed to move on."

She bites her lip. "That's the thing—I'm not moving on, really. I don't even know if I like this guy. Not yet. It's more… physical."

"Well. That's, uh… certainly something."

"Oh God," she gasps again, dropping her face back into her hands.

I reach out and grab her wrists to make her look at me. "You need to stop. This is not a bad thing."

"It's Pavel. His name is Pavel."

I stop short. "Why does that name sound familiar?"

"Because he's one of Misha's Vors." She swallows hard. "He can't know about this, Paige. You can't tell him anything."

"Why? He's not going to care if you—"

"Please!"

I see the desperation on her face and sigh. "Alright. If you'd rather he not know, then I won't say a word."

"Thank you."

"But you still have to tell *me* everything. How did this happen? How'd it start?"

She slumps back in the lounge chair. "He joined the Bratva only a year or so before Maksim died, and Misha kept him on. We'd run into each other sporadically, but we really started talking the night of your first party."

"So *that's* where you were all night! I assumed that you were just avoiding people, but you were with him."

Cyrille nods miserably, but I don't miss the subtle tremor of excitement floating beneath her fear. "It happened by accident. I was taking a breather because I really did want to avoid a few people. He happened to walk into the same room and… I don't know. Everything was different. I wasn't the don's wife and he wasn't the Vor who worked for him. We were just… normal people." She glances at me through her eyelashes. "One thing led to another and… we kissed."

"Was it a good kiss?"

She sighs longingly. "It was a very, very good kiss."

I clap my hands together. "Then this is a good thing, Cyrille."

She looks like she's still not sure, though. "I thought it was just a fling. I thought it would play itself out, and I could go back to my life."

"But…?"

"He seems interested in turning it into something more," she admits. "He's been calling me for weeks, but I haven't picked up. Until today, he called again, and I wasn't looking, so I answered, and then I heard his voice and realized what I'd done and I just *froze,* and then he asked me that question—"

"What question?" I practically scream.

"He… he asked if I want to go to dinner with him."

I'm about ready to jump out of my chair now. I have to force myself to be patient and comforting. "And do you want to go? Is that something you're interested in trying?"

"I'm not sure I'm ready to date just yet. That's why I'm so hesitant about this whole thing. I was happy to just have a fling. But a relationship? I'm not sure."

"If you're feeling guilty, then I'm sorry about that. But that's not a good enough reason to turn this guy down, is it?"

"It's not just the guilt," she explains. "I'm still a widow. I still think about Maksim every single day. Is it fair to get involved with anyone in that state?"

"Okay, I see your point. But—"

"Selfishly, I want to see Pavel again," she blurts. "I'm just not sure I can give him what he wants."

I cup her hand between mine. "Listen to me: for the moment, he just wants to have dinner with you. I think you may be overthinking this, Cyrille. He's asking you to dinner, not to marry him. Take things one date at a time."

She considers that for a moment, then sighs and nods. "Yeah. You're probably right." She fidgets with her bracelets before looking up at me again and smiling shyly. "He's really cute. Blonde hair, really blue eyes, the kind of jaw that makes you want to take a bite out of him. Wears the hell out of a suit."

I laugh. "Now, I remember. Has the one dimple when he smiles. Definitely cute."

"Bingo. And he seems genuinely interested in me and my life," she adds. "He opened up first, though. He told me about his parents, his brother, all this shit from his childhood. I guess it made me open up a little about my life in return. Ilya, Misha… you."

"Me?"

"I just told him about you. About how you're such a huge part of our lives now. I can't imagine not having you as a sister-in-law."

"Aw, Cyrille, stop. You're gonna make me cry now."

She gives me another meek smile. "Thanks for listening. I wouldn't have been comfortable going to Niki or Nessa. I mean, I love them but—"

"I get it; don't worry. Your secret's safe with me. I won't say a thing until you're ready to share it with the rest of the family."

"Thanks, Paige."

"Anytime. I just want you to be happy, Cyrille. We all do."

"I know, and I—" She stops short when someone comes around the corner. Her shoulders tense, but it's only Noel.

"Sorry to disturb you, ma'am," he says, "but this envelope just came for you."

Frowning, I check the return address.

Corden Park.

My jaw falls open. "Oh my God."

"Everything okay?" Cyrille asks, brows furrowed with concern.

"I… Yes. Sorry. It's just—It's a letter from my parents." I weigh the envelope in the flat of my hand. "It feels like there's more than just a letter in here, actually."

"Why do you seem so shocked?"

"If you knew my parents, you would be, too. They're not the letter-writing type. Not the texting or calling type, either, actually. In fact, they're the type to forget I exist unless they want something from me."

My stomach twists with nerves as I tear the seal open, bracing for whatever they've written. But it's not a letter inside.

It's a set of pictures.

Pictures of the trailer I grew up in—the trailer my parents still live in.

Except it's been burnt to the ground. All that remains is the smoldering carcass.

I throw the pictures down like I might be able to distance myself from the sight. Like throwing them might make it no longer true.

Cyrille grabs my arm. "Honey, Paige, what's going on?"

"My parents," I gasp, fighting to suck in every new breath. "I… I think they're dead."

66

MISHA

When I return at last to the mansion, Paige is in the garden, sobbing into Cyrille's lap.

Cyrille sees me as I approach and points wordlessly to the envelope in the chair next to hers. As soon as I see the familiar white envelope, I stiffen.

With frozen fingers, I slide the photographs of the charred trailer out of the envelope and flip through them.

Fucking hell.

I toss the photos back into the chair and drop to one knee in front of my distraught wife. "Paige, baby, it's me."

She rocks back and forth, tears and mascara smeared across her cheeks, eyes open but totally unseeing. "They're dead, Misha. They're dead. And it's my fault."

"We don't know anything yet."

"Look at the trailer," she hisses through her sobs. "Look at it!"

I hoist her into my arms. "Thanks, Cyrille. I'll take it from here."

I carry my wife upstairs and into our bedroom. She mumbles something into my chest, but I can't understand anything she's saying. I place her on our bed and peel off her sandals.

"Where were you?" she demands. "You just left the cabin without a word, without anything. I tried calling you. You didn't pick up. Neither did Konstantin."

"We were in the field. We couldn't pick up."

"Okay, great. So that's just how it's gonna go? I won't have any information about where you are or what you're doing until your enemies decide to send me pictures of your dead body?" she demands. "Is that how this works?"

A few months ago, I would have snapped back at her. But the instinct to fight is overpowered by the instinct to take care of her.

"I don't intend to die anytime soon."

"Funny—my parents probably would have said the same thing. And look at them!" Knocking my hands aside, she jumps off the bed and runs into the bathroom.

I want to follow her, but she locks it from within. I'm not sure breaking down the door is going to endear her to me.

Muttering angrily, I storm downstairs. I don't know why I'm surprised to see Konstantin in the entryway, but there he is.

"Cyrille showed me the pictures," he explains. "Is she okay up there?"

"She's in shock. Petyr is clearly getting desperate, going after her parents."

"Maybe he assumed they were close."

"Shows how little research he does. If he was that sloppy with the idea, maybe he was sloppy with the execution, too."

"You think they're alive?" Konstantin asks.

"I saw a burned trailer, but I didn't see bodies. If he knew he'd kill them, he wouldn't have skimped on the close-ups."

Konstantin nods in agreement. "I'll get someone to check out the situation over there."

"If you find those two idiots, get them to a safehouse somewhere and make sure they're comfortable. They don't deserve it, but do it anyway."

My cousin nods again and hurries off to get started.

67

PAIGE

My tears are hot and angry. But it's not Misha I'm angry at—it's myself.

Why? Because one intrusive, repetitive thought won't leave me alone. It keeps buzzing in my mind like a mosquito. A question: am I upset because they're dead—or because they're dead and I never got the chance to tell them how much they broke my heart? To ask them if they even cared to try fixing it?

Every time that thought circles back around, I cringe away from it. It's selfish and cruel and wrong. What kind of horrible person has *that* reaction to finding out she's an orphan?

It's even more embarrassing that Misha saw it. That he witnessed a side of me I wish didn't exist.

When he walks back into the bedroom, I'm on the bed. I've been sitting here in abject misery for half an hour. I have a hard time meeting his eyes.

He sits down next to me. "Hey."

"Hi."

"How are you?"

"I mean... I just found out my parents are dead," I say. "So, not great."

He shakes his head. "Your parents are not dead."

I turn to him, blinking. "What?"

"I had my men travel to Corden Park. Garrett and Jillian Masters are both alive. They've been moved temporarily to a safehouse not far from there."

I stare at him in shock. "You're serious."

He nods. "The trailer is a lost cause. There's nothing there to salvage. But they weren't home when the fire started. They're okay, Paige. If you want to speak to them, I can call my guys and patch you through."

I look up at him. "I'm so sorry, Misha. I was a bitch to you. You didn't deserve that."

He kneels down in front of me and palms both of my thighs with his huge hands. "You don't ever have to apologize about your worst reactions, Paige. The whole point of doing this together is that we can carry each other through the hardest times. Maybe that means that, every once in a while, one of us will be a punching bag for the other. That's okay." He strokes my knee and smiles. "I used to think that it was the worst thing in the world, having you really see me. I was convinced you'd hate me the moment you saw who I really was. And somehow, you're still here."

"Because I love you."

"As I love you," he says simply.

He says it so easily, as if it's a simple, obvious fact rather than what it really is—a miracle.

Tears stream down my cheeks. I throw myself into his arms and wrap my arms around his neck. He holds me close and kisses my temple again and again.

"So." He shifts me onto his lap, his fingers stroking my arm. "About your parents... do you want to see or speak to them before I move them?"

"Move them?"

"They're a target now that Petyr has set his sights on them. The plan is to move them to Australia for the foreseeable future. I've already arranged to set them up in a cottage in Dubbo."

"Is that a real place?"

He chuckles. "It's about five hours outside of Sydney."

"And they've agreed to this?"

"My men went over the plan with them. They jumped on board pretty quickly when they realized they'd be getting a free two-bedroom house and a monthly stipend."

I gawk at him in awe. "You don't have to do all of that for them. Or any of it, really."

"I know that. But they are your parents. Even if they're wastes of breath, they're responsible for your existence. So, for that fact alone, I want them taken care of. That, and the fact that *you* would want them taken care of."

I touch his hair, almost just to confirm that he's real and this isn't some twisted dream. "You're amazing, Misha. But... I think it's enough to know that they're alive. It's enough to know they're taken care of. They don't want to hear from me, anyway, not really. And I don't want to shatter my peace of mind for a conversation that will never go the way I want it to."

He nods and kisses my shoulder as he rises. "They'll be on a plane this evening. You won't have to worry about a thing. You'll never have to worry about a thing, Paige Orlov. I'm here for you."

68

PAIGE

"Misha, it's really not a big deal." He's snarling so heavily on the phone I'm not even sure if he can hear me. "I can go to the doctor's appointment on my own."

"No," he growls. "I can still make it. We'll just have to meet at the hospital."

"It's just one appointment. I can handle it myself."

"I don't want you going alone."

I roll my eyes. "When am I ever alone? There's always four burly men shadowing my every step."

"I'm not talking about protection. I want someone there for emotional support."

"Oh, then I can use Boris. He's hot."

"Remind me to fire him when I get home," he mutters. "Or kill him."

"I'm only joking, you beast," I laugh. "Cy is with me. She can be my moral support."

She waves at me, demanding the phone, so I pass it over to her. "You seriously need to stop suffocating the girl," Cyrille snaps. "It's a routine check-up, not open heart surgery. In any case, I will be with her." She nods and agrees with whatever Misha is saying. "Yes, I know. No, I won't let her out of my sight. Yes. Yes. No. Okay. Bye, you overprotective weirdo."

She hands my phone back to me with a smirk. She's in a good mood today.

"The two of you are nauseatingly cute," she remarks. "Like, I'm actually feeling a little queasy now."

"Speaking of nauseatingly cute, how is Pavel doing?"

She blushes but tries to hide it. "He's fine. We're actually meeting for dinner after your appointment. We're keeping things casual."

"But you're breaking bread together now. That's a step up from casual sex. And it's only been a few weeks. Moving fast!"

Her eyes dart around the living room in panic. "Shh! Don't say those things so loud."

"Nessa is up in her room. And you need to give her more credit. She loves you. No one in this family expects you to stay single forever."

She sighs. "I know, it's just… I still feel guilty."

"Well, don't," I tell her firmly. "You deserve to feel special. You deserve a man who wants to take you out to dinner."

She bites her bottom lip. "I really didn't expect that from him. I mean, it feels so public."

"But you're comfortable around him?"

"Yes, in some ways. No, in others. I'm so... *aware* of myself around him. It's like I've forgotten how to date."

"Fair enough. You haven't been in the dating game for over a decade."

"That makes me sound old," she groans.

"You just need to get out of your head a little. Focus on Pavel and the conversation."

"I think that's what I like about him the most," she admits hesitantly. "He actually seems interested in talking. In getting to know me."

"That's a great sign!"

She gives me a half-hearted nod. "I suppose."

I wrap my arm around her and lead her to the front door. "Trust me, Cyrille: this is a good thing. Tell me more. What kinds of things do you two talk about?"

"The family, mostly. You and Niki and Nessa. I talk a lot about Ilya, of course. I try not to, but sometimes, I slip up and end up being that annoying mom who can't stop talking about her kid."

I chuckle. "Well, it clearly hasn't scared him off so far."

We get in the car and drive to my appointment. As we pull into the hospital parking lot, Cyrille looks around. "I told Pavel to park in the rear lot. I'll ride with him to the restaurant once Misha is here."

"Okay." Hopefully, she'll be discreet. Misha doesn't know about Pavel, and he might not be too thrilled about his sister-in-law dating a Vor.

As much as I love my husband, he still believes in a few archaic rules that were programmed into him since birth. And even if he wasn't so rigid at times, he's not exactly the most subtle of creatures. Cyrille is still in the fledgling state of her relationship with Pavel, so there's no need to tell anyone until it becomes more serious. *If* it becomes more serious.

She escorts me inside and follows me back into the examination room. Usually, Dr. Mathers is waiting for me at the door, but she's nowhere to be seen today.

"She's not normally late," Cyrille observes.

"Neither is Misha. Must be something in the air."

Cyrille smirks. "He's more anal than Maksim was, and that's saying something."

"It's cute, though."

She takes my hand. "I love how far the two of you have come. It gives me hope that maybe there's another love story out there for me."

"A love story by the name of 'Pavel,' perhaps?"

She giggles. "Honestly, I don't know. Maybe. I see myself potentially having feelings for Pavel in the future," she says. "But for now? I don't know. I think—"

Before she can finish her sentence, the door flies open and Misha storms in. "Did I miss anything?" he booms.

I smile and twine my fingers through his. "Nothing at all. Dr. Mathers isn't even here yet."

"That's my cue," announces Cyrille. "I'm gonna make myself scarce and leave you two lovebirds to it." She leans in and gives me a peck on the cheek, then does the same with Misha. "Let me know how it goes."

Misha takes in Cyrille's all-white silk ensemble. "Do you have a meeting after this? You look nice."

"Dinner plans, actually. With a friend. I'll see you guys later." She blows us a kiss and steps out.

"She seems to be in a better place lately." Misha glances at me shrewdly. "Something new in her life that I should know about?"

Damn, the man is obnoxiously perceptive. "Um... no?"

"You're a terrible liar."

"You're being nosy. Whatever is going on in Cyrille's life is her business."

"And yours, apparently."

"She confided in me."

His eyes widen. "So there *is* something going on in Cyrille's life."

I groan. "I'm pregnant. Stop stressing me out."

"You can't always use that as an excuse."

"I'll only use it until these kids pop out. Then I'm gonna use the whole 'new motherhood' thing until they're five. After that, it's the heartbreak of them not being my little babies anymore. Then they'll be teens, so that's stressful, too, then they'll go to college and..."

He's still chuckling and I'm still talking when Dr. Mathers walks into the room, looking uncharacteristically flustered. "I'm so sorry. It's been a hell of a morning. I had three deliveries, and one ended up being a complicated C-section. It took longer than expected."

"Are the mother and baby okay?" I ask.

She smiles triumphantly. "Of course. They don't call me the best for nothing. Now, let's get this show on the road, shall we? You guys must be waiting to see those little munchkins of yours."

"Yes!" I squeeze Misha's hand.

Dr. Mathers lifts up my blouse and squeezes the gel onto my rounded stomach. She probes at my stomach. Instantly, I see two little forms wiggling and shifting on the screen.

"Aw, look at them in there together!" Dr. Mathers points to the screen. "It's like they're holding hands."

"Oh my God," I gasp. "I see them!"

Dr. Mathers laughs. "It looks like your little girl has a tight hold of her brother."

It takes a second for the words to process. For me to understand what Dr. Mathers just said. Then my jaw hangs open. "What did you say?"

It takes her a moment longer. Then she slaps a hand over her mouth. "Oh my God! You didn't want to find out the genders, did you? I'm so sorry! I really should have rescheduled. I'm exhausted."

I can't even tell her it's okay because I'm distracted by the look on my husband's face. He is shocked, but smiling.

"A boy and a girl," he whispers in awe. "We're having one of each. We're having a son and a daughter."

Misha presses a kiss to my forehead and then catches my mouth. He sucks on my lower lip and works his gratitude into every stroke of his tongue and press of his lips.

We kiss for so long that I forget anyone else is in the room. When we finally part, Dr. Mathers still looks mortified for her slip-up.

"I'm so, so sorry," she says again.

"I'm not," I tell her firmly. "That was amazing news. I'm glad we know."

She gives me a grateful smile. "That's good to hear."

"Simone, would you mind giving us a moment?" Misha asks.

"Of course!" She looks relieved to be excused as she slips out of the room, leaving Misha and I alone together.

"A boy and a girl," I say out loud. "Misha, we're so lucky. We're complete now."

He lifts my hand to his lips. "I expected it to be twin boys. Nikita was the first girl in the family in two generations."

"You're going to be a father to a daughter," I say. "How do you feel about that?"

"Terrified."

I chuckle. "I didn't think anything terrified you."

"Normally, no. But this is a whole different beast." His eyes soften. I can see that this information is already changing him. "This is going to be quite the adventure."

"We can do this, Misha," I tell him. "It's the four of us against the world now."

He smiles. "The world better watch out."

69

MISHA

Paige ditches her jeans and top in favor of one of my shirts the moment we get home. Yesterday, she complained about none of her clothes fitting and how she was jury-rigging the button of her pants with a hair tie to create extra space. But today, there are stars in her eyes as she peels herself out of her too-tight clothes with a sigh of relief.

I'm waiting for her on the bed, but instead of sitting next to me, Paige straddles my lap. I curl my hands around her backside, hauling her against me.

"I've thought about it," she announces, "and I think our little girl deserves a name as unique as she is. Clara can be her middle name."

"Great," I drawl. "So we have two middle names, but no first names. Wonderful progress we're making."

She laughs. "We have time." She links her fingers through mine and we stare at one another, letting each process in our own way. "You're going to be an amazing father, Misha."

"How do you know?"

"Because you love fiercely and you're protective to the point of annoyance. Family is everything to you. Underneath all that strength and steel, you're just a big softie."

I growl and take a playful bite of her jaw. "No part of me is soft right now. Feel free to check for yourself."

She laughs and drags my face up for a kiss. What starts off tender quickly turns heated. Paige yanks her t-shirt over her head a mere sixty seconds after she put it on in the first place. I consider teasing her about how quickly her clothes go on and off these days, but then she rolls her hips against my already pulsing erection and I forget all about those jokes.

Before I explode in my pants, I roll her onto the mattress and hover over her.

I can't press myself against her anymore these days; her stomach is in the way. Instead, I turn her on her side and shift behind her.

She grabs my hand and drags it over her hip, then lower. I drag my finger through her wetness, teasing her until she's trembling.

"Misha," she gasps. "Fuck me. Please... just fuck me."

She breaks every rule I've ever given her and she does it with a taunting smirk—but how can I ignore a demand like that?

Short answer is, I can't.

So I kick my pants down my thighs, press my cock to her aching center, and dive into her.

She takes me in entirely, her body stretching to welcome me. Paige yelps, but quickly grinds back against me, working me in and out of her.

It's a simple and slow coming together, but I've never experienced this level of passion. There's more to it than just our bodies meeting. There's soul in it. Energies mingling that I didn't know existed.

Paige curls her hand behind her to hook it around my neck. She strokes my hair as I stroke into her, filling her again and against. My hands find her nipples and her clit. I explore every inch of her body, inside and out, until she is shaking and panting.

"Fuck," I grit out, struggling to stave off my orgasm long enough for her to finish first.

"Right there, Misha. Right—right—I'm... Oh, God, I'm coming."

She clenches around me, and I spill into her.

We finish together, our breath mingling as our bodies peak in a fiery explosion and then come floating down from the high.

Paige sighs deeply, and I kiss a trail down her spine. When I slide out of her, she twists around, beaming, and picks up the conversation right where we left off. "I can't wait to tell everyone. They're going to be so excited."

"About this?" I tease, stroking my finger through the sheen of sweat on her chest.

She elbows my arm. "About the babies! Nessa is going to be over the moon."

I groan. "She's going to go so overboard. Our house will explode with pink and blue baby clothes."

Paige laughs. "I don't mind so much. It's lovely to have someone be that excited for you. I never got that level of excitement from my parents."

"Well, you've got it now in spades."

"I know. I'm the luckiest girl in the world." She kisses me again and then pulls away. "You realize your phone has been going off, like, this entire time, right?"

Frowning, I disentangle myself from Paige and reach for my phone. There are missed calls from Konstantin and a number I don't recognize. "Sorry, but I have to—"

"Go on," she says. "I'm going to shower."

"Is that an invitation?"

She laughs and sashays into the bathroom, knowing damn well I'm watching every shimmy and switch of her hips. Then, regretfully, I call Konstantin back.

"Where have you been?" he demands the moment he answers.

"I had to take Paige for a check-up. What's going on?"

"We just got a lead about Petyr's whereabouts."

I sit up and immediately reach for my jeans. "No fucking way."

"The Babai were trying to contact you. When they couldn't, they contacted me. I don't even fucking know how they found my number, it's unlisted and—"

"Not the time for this, Konstantin."

"Right. Anyway, I met them in Little Russia. We're hot on his trail."

"Right now?"

"Literally as I speak," Konstantin confirms. "He's been hiding out with an immigrant family in an apartment complex in the heart of Little Russia. It's nothing like his usual digs. No wonder he escaped our notice all these months."

"Who are you with?"

"The Wolf," he tells me. "The Tiger and The Bear are approaching from different directions. We want to try and corner him. Fucker is on the nineteenth floor of this shithole. Christ, though, the place is depressing. At least they put a shitty little balcony on all the units so it's easy to jump when you've had enough."

"Are you going in now?"

"I'm on the seventeenth floor. But—goddammit, I can't breathe. Shitbox elevator got stuck halfway up. We had to pry the bastard open and take the stairs like peasants."

His panting gets more labored to the point where I can only make out every third or fourth word, but I can't make myself get off the phone.

I should be there with Konstantin.

This is my fight.

So why is my first thought that I'm mostly glad I didn't miss that moment in the doctor's office with Paige?

"Are you armed?"

"To the motherfuckin' teeth. This isn't my first rodeo, cuz. Up on the nineteenth now. Closing in."

I hear a muffled voice, deep and confident and spooky enough to make the hair stand up on the back of my neck. It has to be The Wolf.

"We're going in," I hear Konstantin say, before there's a crash that gets lost in the static. He must be kicking the door in.

I wait with bated breath, waiting for the sound of a gunshot, a scream, fucking *something*.

There's nothing.

Nothing.

Then: "Fuck!"

"What?" I demand. "What happened?"

"He's… goddammit, he's gone."

My hand tightens around the phone. "What do you mean, 'He's gone'?"

"The kettle is still on the fucking stove. But it looks like he disappeared out the back window minutes before we got here. Shimmied down the fire escape and ducked The Tiger and The Bear somehow."

"He knew you were coming," I growl.

Konstantin curses again. I hear something bang on the other end of the line. He must be turning the apartment upside down. "Sure as shit looks like it. But how?"

"You know how," I snarl.

I can practically hear his grimace as he comes to the same conclusion I have. "He had to have been warned. Which means…"

Anger boils in my veins. "We have a fucking rat."

70

PAIGE

When I come out of the shower, Misha is frowning and surly. He tells me he has somewhere to go for work and that he won't elaborate. Then he grabs his keys and disappears.

He's in a mood for the two days that follow. Whenever I see him, he's turned inward. Quiet. Brooding. He's still loving, of course, still wanting to touch me every chance he gets, but there's this lingering melancholy to his aura that puts a frown on my face.

He's holed up in his office with Konstantin overseeing more Bratva business, so I go down to the kitchen for a snack. It's dark. How strange. Jace always leaves the lights on until he knows we're in bed for the night. I'm reaching for the switch when a burst of noise scares the bejeezus out of me.

"SURPRISE!"

The sudden shouts have me leaping out of my skin. I stumble back and barely manage to catch myself on the kitchen doorway before I tumble ass over teakettle.

Cyrille lunges over and grabs my arm, steadying me. "Don't scare a pregnant woman who is already fairly clumsy. Noted!"

"What in the—" I peek into the dining room and see a banner hanging across the open French doors that says **CONGRATULATIONS, MAMA** in bright neon colors.

Then I see Nessa, Nikita, Rowan, and Ilya standing around, smiling at me.

"What is this?"

"This is your baby shower," Rowan announces. "We got you good, didn't we?"

I press a hand to my racing heart. "If scaring me to death is getting me good, then no one has ever done it better."

Nessa comes over and loops her arm around my shoulders. "Sorry we frightened you, darling. But trust me, the presents will be worth it."

"Presents? No, no, no. You guys didn't have to do that," I protest. "You've already done so much."

Nessa waves me away. "Nonsense. Every new mother deserves a proper baby shower."

She steers me towards the humongous pile of wrapped gifts taking up two entire corners of the sitting room. It looks like Santa Claus crashed his sleigh right here in the house. "This is… good Lord, this is insane."

"Quit your bitching and let us pamper you for a change," Nikita says impatiently. "Enjoy yourself. Let's party!"

I sigh and relent. They really have gone all out. The table is covered in delicious pastries, and the thought of biting into a gooey chocolate croissant is enough to make me go cross-eyed with delight right now.

"These gifts are for the babies," Cyrille says, pointing to the first massive pile. Then she pivots to the second pile. "And these are for you."

"Gifts for the baby *are* gifts for me," I argue.

I'm quickly overruled and presents are thrust at me from every direction. By the second one I unwrap, I'm completely overwhelmed.

I'm staring at the nicest stroller money can buy. I know that because I joked with Misha about adding it to our nonexistent registry, "just in case any billionaires decide to gift us something." I stroke the leather handle tenderly. "This is too much!"

Nessa raises her hand. "That one is from their grandmother."

Misha was right: his mother has gone completely overboard. But I have to fight back tears of gratitude as I continue opening present after present.

When I grab Rowan's gifts, she gives me a nervous smile. "It's not much, not like the others. But I hope you like it."

"Whatever it is, I'm sure I'll love it." I tear into the box and pull out two knitted baby blankets. One in a soft shade of blue, the second in a pastel yellow. "Oh my God, Rowan! They're beautiful. Where did you get these?"

She blushes. "I, uh…" She says something I don't catch.

"Come again?"

"I said, I knitted them myself."

I look at her in shock. "Seriously?"

"I like to knit. My grandmother taught me. As soon as I found out you were having twins, I got to work."

I walk over and squeeze her half to death in a hug. "Thank you, Ro. These are—they're perfect. You're perfect."

We're still hugging when Misha and Konstantin join the party. Rowan shifts away from me as Konstantin arrives, lowering her head. She won't even look at him.

Konstantin throws her a cool, casual nod and then kisses me on the cheek. "The box in the red wrapping paper is mine."

"You got me a gift, too?"

"Duh. Go ahead," he prompts. "Open it."

I tear apart the red wrapping paper and find a fancy baby monitor inside. It's insanely complex, all decked out with a bunch of gadgets I can't even name. I'm pretty sure this thing could launch spaceships.

"It's been vetted by your husband and the security team," Konstantin tells me. "It's the best one on the market. Doesn't matter where in the house you are; these things will pick up every single sound. Your little buggers won't even be able to blink without you knowing it."

I hug him tight. "Konstantin, you're the best."

"Again—duh."

When everyone is eating and mingling, I walk over to where Misha is standing by the French doors. He has a glass of champagne in his hand, but he has barely touched it.

"You okay?" I ask.

He tries out an unconvincing smile. "Fine."

"You've been distracted the last few days."

"I'm just preoccupied with… resolving things."

I smooth my hand down his arm. "You don't have any control over that, my love."

His eyes darken. "That's exactly what is worrying me."

"I get it. I really do. But it's our baby shower. Let's just try and enjoy it, yeah?"

He hides his worry behind a smile and kisses my forehead gently. "I haven't given you my gift yet."

"Oh my God! Not you, too!"

He laughs softly at my reaction and reaches into his pocket. "That is not how most women react to getting a gift."

"Well, I'm not most women."

"Don't I know it."

I smack him on the arm, but he ignores me and produces a little black box in the palm of his hand.

"Jewelry?"

"Open it and see."

I flip open the lid, but instead of diamonds, I see a shiny black key.

"Misha," I breathe. "Is that…?"

He smiles. "That is the key to your brand new Rolls Royce Phantom."

"Misha!"

"You needed a new car," he says, as though the decision is purely practical and completely unemotional. "And this one is fitted with every safety measure known to man, including being one hundred percent bulletproof."

"Don't you think that's a little... much?"

"Not for my wife. If you want your independence, my love, this car is the only way you are driving anywhere without me."

I pout, just a little. "You sure know how to take the fun out of my independence."

"Most people would say this car is fun. And I'm just trying to keep you safe."

"I know. Which is why it's so hard to be mad at you."

I stretch onto my toes to kiss him, and Misha loops an arm around my lower back and dips me low. We kiss until someone aggressively clears their throat.

"This is a shower for the babies you already have, not a venue to start making more, you horny little rabbits," Nikita scolds.

Nessa chastises Niki for being crude, and then Nessa, Niki, and Misha slip into the kinds of memories and reveries that only a loving family can have.

I leave them to it as I creep away to find Rowan. I find her talking to Konstantin in a dark, quiet corner, so with a sly smile, I change course and head to the porch instead.

"Having fun?" Cyrille asks when I find her out there.

I sit on the swing next to her. "You guys have gone above and beyond. I can't believe how lucky I am."

"You deserve it."

I inch a little closer so that we're less likely to be overheard. "How's Pavel?"

She suppresses a smile. "He's on the job today, but we're meeting tonight for dinner."

"Another dinner?" I wag my brows. "That's a good sign."

"He is definitely hitting the gas, but I'm not sure I want things going that fast. I have Ilya to think about."

"So tell him that."

"I have," she says. "He insists that he wants to take things slow himself, but then he keeps asking me out to dinner and parties and this and that. He asks me all these deeply personal questions. He seems interested in hearing about my day, my life. When I told him about your baby shower, he spent half an hour asking me about what we had planned."

"Wow. He really is interested in you."

She nods. "It freaks me out a little."

"The man has good taste."

She laughs self-consciously. "Sometimes, I think I should just end it. But selfishly, I'm having too much fun to seriously consider it."

"Then don't. You've told him where you stand. If he doesn't listen and gets his heart broken, that's on him."

She considers that for a moment. "Maybe you're right."

"As Konstantin would say: duh." I pat her knee. "You deserve to be happy, Cy. And if Pavel's able to see how amazing you are, then maybe he deserves the right to be in your life."

She gives me a grateful smile before her eyes veer into the sitting room. "Rowan and Konstantin seem to be getting along famously."

"Yeah. Interesting, isn't it?"

She grins. "Interesting, indeed."

71

PAIGE

My phone buzzes again. I know who it's going to be before I even check.

MISHA: *Why are you still at the office? You should be at home. Resting.*

PAIGE: *I'm pregnant, not broken. I can work. And I've got security here. Are you telling me you're at home right now?*

MISHA: *I'm chasing a lead.*

PAIGE: *And I'm chasing facts on paper. How about we support each other?*

MISHA: *I'd be happy to. After I feed Petyr to the sharks and those babies are delivered safely, I'll support you from the back, from the bottom, from your knees... As much support as you need.*

PAIGE: *You're sexy when you're scolding me.*

MISHA: *Distracting me is not going to work.*

PAIGE: *How about bargaining? Will that work?*

MISHA: *You have half an hour before I send Konstantin to get you.*

PAIGE: *Did I mention I bought new lingerie yesterday?*

MISHA: *Are you trying to bribe me, Mrs. Orlov?*

PAIGE: *It's not a bribe, it's a compromise.*

MISHA: *One hour. No arguments.*

PAIGE: *Sold. See you at home, handsome. Love you.*

We've said "I love you" before, but I still get butterflies in my stomach watching those three little dots appear. Then his text comes in.

MISHA: *Love you too.*

Swoon. I just bargained for another hour at the office, but now, it's going to be impossible to concentrate on anything except my husband.

After fifteen minutes of fantasizing, I'm finally getting back into the groove of things when I hear a knock on my door. I let my assistant head home early, so it's probably someone from my security team.

"Gorvic?" I call. "You can come in."

The door opens, but the man who walks into my office is definitely not Gorvic. He's familiar, though, sickeningly familiar—because even though I've only ever seen him twice face-to-face, he's haunted my shadows for the last eight months.

Petyr Ivanov.

I gasp, unable to stop myself. Petyr chuckles at my reaction and takes the seat opposite me. "The last time we met, you were Misha's secretary. Now, look at you. Bigger office, bigger belly… Smarter women than you have tried and failed to tie down Misha Orlov. Well done. Hats off to you indeed."

I swallow back my shock and try to think. My phone is on the desk a foot away from my hand, but there's no way I can reach for it without him seeing.

"How did you get in here?" I ask through a dry mouth.

"The front door, as a matter of fact. Security is quite lax around here. You should really talk to your husband about that."

He's talking a big game, but I've heard enough about how he operates to guess that he didn't come alone, and that he probably left a trail of blood in his wake on the way in. My palms start to sweat. This man has tried to kill me multiple times in the past. Now, here he is, nothing between us but a desk.

The desk…

I remember all at once that this desk has been fitted out with a panic button. When Misha told me about it, I barely paid attention. I thought he was overreacting, as per usual.

If I survive this, I'll have to tell him later that he was right.

"What do you want from me, Petyr?"

"Just a conversation."

"You can't have conversations with a corpse," I spit back. "Which is what I very nearly was after your last attempt on my life."

"I hope you know that wasn't personal," he says, sounding surprisingly sincere. "I had to respond to Misha in kind."

"By killing me and my children?"

His eyes slide down to my stomach. "By doing what was necessary. Speaking of which, congratulations on the twin bundles of joy. How amazing to produce two heirs at the same time. Misha certainly won the lottery when he plucked you out of that trailer park."

I stiffen and lean back against my chair, casually sliding one hand off the table. "Do you think you're insulting me? I know where I came from, Petyr. But character matters far more than circumstances. Misha knows that, too."

"You puzzle me, Paige. I can't figure out if you're truly a bleeding heart or just a very adept manipulator."

"I'm sure sincerity is alien to you, but I assure you, I'm here for all the right reasons."

"And what reasons are those?"

"That I love my husband. Simple as that."

"Love." He wrinkles his nose. "Did Misha really fall into that trap? The same one Maksim fell for?"

"You and Maksim were friends once," I say, leaning forward. "When did that change?"

While Petyr seems taken aback by how much I know about him, I slip my fingertip slowly under the table and catch the small panic button. I press it slowly so it doesn't click and give me away, then let my hand fall back in my lap.

Petyr composes himself and blinks away his surprise. "Nothing changed. We were never friends. We were always rivals, pitted against one another from birth."

"Bullshit. You chose to make it a competition when it didn't need to be," I say. I'm taking a shot in the dark here—I have no idea what motivated Petyr to make the choices he made. I just need to keep him talking. "You chose to make an enemy out of an ally."

"An ally?" he says, glowering at me. "Maksim was never an ally. He liked to keep me under foot. He threw me scraps when he was done eating and then expected a groveling thanks in return. I wasn't interested in being second-best; I wanted to be top dog."

"And how has that worked out for you?"

I've crossed the line into goading now. I'm not so sure that's the right decision, considering I'm trapped alone with a trigger-happy maniac who's thirsty for revenge.

"I've lost a lot of men recently, thanks to your husband. Tell me, Paige, if you know Misha so well, do you know the body count?"

"No, I don't," I tell him. "And I don't care to. If Misha decided to go after your men, there must have been a good reason. You are the one responsible for their deaths."

"What beautiful justification. Do you sleep well at night?"

"I'm not justifying anything," I say. "I'm—"

His phone pings, and he checks the text. As he does, his mouth puckers in disapproval. "And here I thought we were getting along so well, Paige. When did you call in the reinforcements?"

My heart is thundering, but I try to project outwards calm. "I have my ways."

He clicks his tongue. "A panic button, no? Where is it? I should have known Misha would be prepared like that."

"You have maybe five seconds before Misha and his team are up here."

"Wrong," he says with a self-satisfied smirk. "I have sixty seconds, which is more than enough time for me to take my leave. Give Misha my regards. You and I will see each other again soon."

He walks straight to the door. When he opens it, there's no one waiting outside. I'd expected Petyr to have shown up with an entourage, but it looks to me like he's working alone.

Except for the text. Who sent that? None of this makes sense.

He shoots me a wink over his shoulder and then the door slams.

By the time I regain control of my legs and stand up to follow him, the door bursts open again. I scream and fall back just as Misha hauls me against his sturdy chest. "Are you okay? Where is he?"

"He just left! You—"

"Fan out!" Misha roars. "He should still be in the building. Get the motherfucker before he gets away!"

The men in the hallway scatter in every direction. Misha is obviously itching to join the hunt, but he's still worried about me. His hands outline my face. "Are you okay? Did he hurt you?"

"No," I assure him. "I'm fine."

"How the fuck did he get past security?" Misha asks, mostly to himself. "How the fuck did he get all the way up here? Heads are gonna roll for this."

I grab his hands. "Misha, calm down. Just breathe."

His expression is murderous. Even when he blows out a breath, it doesn't seem to make a difference.

"You can go, you know?" I tell him. "I'm okay."

"I'm not leaving you for another fucking second," he says. "Collect your things. You're done working from the office. From now on, you're staying at home. I'm not letting you out of my sight."

72

MISHA

It's almost 2:30 in the morning when I slip upstairs from my home office to the bedroom, but Paige is up and waiting for me.

She's wearing one of my sweaters and sitting by the window in a beam of melted moonlight. Her legs are drawn up underneath her, and she looks so young with her hair flowing down her shoulders in wild waves.

The moment I walk through the door, she turns to me. "Did they find him?"

I sigh and shake my head. "His trail went cold. He slipped through our fingers. Again."

"How is that possible?"

I've asked myself that same question too many times to count in the last couple hours. And every time, I arrive at the same unforgivable conclusion.

"There's only one way it's possible: I have a mole."

"Someone on the inside is a traitor?" Her brow knits together, and I know she's thinking the same thing I am. *How could someone I trust do this to me?*

I cross the distance and tuck a loose lock of hair behind her ear. "You should be sleeping. I don't want you worrying about any of this. I'm sorry you had to endure what you did today."

"I'm not concerned about myself. I'm worried about… well…"

Her eyes dart to mine, and I see something I didn't before: Paige isn't just worried about me. She's keeping something from me.

"Paige," I growl, "what's going on?"

She exhales sharply. "I have a… a feeling. Maybe it's nothing, I don't know. But it's keeping me awake. It took me hours to fall asleep in the first place, and then I woke up and couldn't get back to sleep. This thought just keeps tickling the back of my mind."

"Paige, you're saying a lot of words without actually saying anything."

She chews on her bottom lip. "I'm supposed to be keeping this a secret."

"We're married. We don't keep secrets from one another anymore."

"I know, but this was an innocent secret. At least, I thought it was. But maybe…"

"Paige," I say impatiently. "Spill."

"You said there might be a mole. Well, I have my suspicions about who it might be."

Of all the things I expected her to say, that never crossed my mind. "Who?"

She takes a deep breath. Her shoulders sag when she exhales. "Cyrille."

"Excuse me?"

"Oh God! No!" She shakes her head. "I didn't mean Cyrille is the mole. I meant that the man she is involved with might be."

I relax, but only slightly. "She's involved with someone?"

"It's new," Paige says tentatively. "Again, I have no proof of anything. This is just a gut feeling, which is why I feel like a backstabbing little bitch for telling you about—"

"Paige."

"Right." She shakes her head. "I'm sorry."

"Who is the man she's involved with?"

Paige winces. "Pavel."

I stand up. "Pavel? As in the Pavel who works for me?"

"Yes, which is exactly why Cyrille felt like she couldn't tell you. She seemed to think that you would object to her dating someone so far below her."

"And she was right. She's the widow of a don," I snap. "She deserves better than some petty fucking—Pavel, Jesus. I can't believe this."

"Like I said, it's new. But something doesn't feel right about it."

I shake my head, trying to focus on what's actually important. "What makes you think he could be the mole?"

"He seems intensely interested in the family. He asks her about me and you, about our relationships. Cy and I both just assumed he wanted to get to know her. But what if it's more than that?"

I stroke my chin, deep in thought. "You might be onto something here, Paige."

She grabs my arm. "But you have to be sure before you confront him, Misha. You can't just accuse him without proof."

"If he really is the mole, then he's going to give himself away." I turn towards the door.

"Where are you going?"

"To see if this lead pans out."

"It's the middle of the night!"

I spin back around and kiss her softly on the lips. I can't wait to taste her when the threat of imminent retaliation isn't hanging over our heads. How much sweeter will her kisses be then?

"I'll be back. Lock the door behind me."

73

MISHA

Pavel has been around long enough to know that Cyrille is off-limits. Maksim may be dead, but she is still a Bratva wife, and he is still nothing but a grunt in the army I command.

Or at least, he was.

After tonight, he'll be nothing but a stain on the ground and a distant memory.

"They're coming," Konstantin says, standing aside to allow the three enforcers to pass into the room. Pavel walks in first, followed by two other soldiers, Stanislav and Augustin.

"*Pakhan.*" Stanislav bows to me, but he's bouncing on the balls of his feet, all geared up for the hunt. "What's the order?"

"We know where Petyr is," I inform the men. "We managed to zero in on his location five blocks east of Orion. He still has no idea we've got eyes on him, which means we have to move fast. It doesn't look like he's likely to stick around long."

"So we'll strike now," Pavel says from behind a perfect mask of sincerity.

I nod. "Before you go, you should know that we've received a tip. We have an informant in the ranks."

Stanislav and Augustin frown, outraged at the mere suggestion. Pavel, on the other hand, doesn't so much as blink.

"No one would be foolish enough to go against you," he suggests.

"What some men call foolish, others call brave," I say. "Either way, until I weed out the rat, I'm taking precautions. Hand over your phones."

All three produce their phones instantly. Pavel hands his over without any visible hesitation.

"Petyr should be hiding somewhere in the middle of Ranger's Park. I need the three of you to split up and close in on him from different directions. That way, there will be nowhere for him to escape. Now, go."

The three of them file out. When they're gone, Konstantin walks over to me. "How much of a head start should we give them?"

I check my watch. "Two more minutes. If he's going to go save Petyr's ass, he's probably halfway to Ranger's Park already."

Konstantin and I step out, swapping the car for two blacked-out Harley Davidsons. We tear through the streets, weaving in and out of the sparse traffic on the road until we reach Ranger's Park. The day is overcast, the clouds hanging low. The world feels smaller.

My cousin and I park the bikes and head into the park. As we're walking in, Augustin texts.

AUGUSTIN: *He just picked up a burner phone, boss. Looks like he's trying to send a warning.*

MISHA: *Stop him. Now.*

A few seconds later, Augustin sends me another text with his location. They're about three minutes from where Konstantin and I are standing, over on the southeastern edge of the park. We follow the route my phone maps out for us until we find them.

When I round the corner, Augustin is sitting on Pavel's chest like a proud hunting dog.

Stanislav appears just after Konstantin and I arrive. The three of us converge around Pavel, who is spluttering on the ground, eyes wide and ringed red with panic.

"It's not me!" he gasps. "I'm not the fucking mole!"

"What's the burner phone for then, motherfucker?" Konstantin asks, plucking the phone off the ground. "Who were you trying to call?"

Pavel blinks up at me for a second, realizations washing over him one by one. "You never had Petyr…"

"No, I didn't. But now, we have you." I screw the silencer onto my gun's barrel and raise it to his face.

He cringes, tears gathering in his blue eyes. Those baby blues were probably responsible for turning many heads, including my sister-in-law's. But that's all about to end.

"Please…" he whispers without any real hope in the begging.

"Was it worth it?" I ask. "Betraying your *pakhan* for that spindly little motherfucker?"

"He made me a better offer," he admits.

"And look how that worked out for you."

I don't allow him any last words—I just shoot him in the forehead. His body jerks once and then goes still.

I motion to Augustin and Stanislav. "Deliver the body to Ivanov headquarters. Don't bother wrapping it up. I want Petyr to see what he's done."

74

PAIGE

Misha is sleeping soundly when I wake up the next morning. I desperately want to know what happened last night, but I don't have the heart to wake him. So instead, I watch him for a little while. I wait.

Then, when I start to feel like a shameless creep and he shows no signs of stirring, I kiss his brow and go to the bathroom for a soak.

I'm just sliding into the water when the door opens. Misha glides in, bleary-eyed and stooped. He sees me and, without breaking stride, sheds his clothes on his way over before joining me in the tub. I settle between his legs as steam rises from the water.

It's nice in here. Quiet and calm and warm. The only problem is that I can't block out the question burning inside of me.

"Misha, what happened last night?"

He sighs. "You were right."

I wince. It's exactly what I was hoping he wouldn't say. My heart cracks in two, oozing with pain on Cyrille's behalf. She deserves so much better than this. "I so wanted to be wrong. Does Cyrille know?"

"Not yet. I'm going to go tell her today."

I twist around to face him. "I want to come with you."

"I'm not sure if—"

"It wasn't a question," I snap. "I'm coming with you. Final answer."

He sighs, but the gentle weight of his hand on my thigh as he eases back lets me know I've won.

I lean into him and loll my head against his chest. "Why did he have to set his sights on her?"

"Because he saw that she was lonely and vulnerable. And he took advantage of that. That's what evil men do."

∼

Ilya has already gone off to school by the time Misha and I arrive at Cyrille's. Her butler leads us to the breakfast nook where my sister-in-law is sitting at the table in a floaty periwinkle blue robe, sipping a cup of coffee.

She grins when she sees us both. "Well, this is a surprise!"

"We're sorry to barge in unannounced," I say.

"Nonsense. Family doesn't need an invitation." She looks between the two of us. The smile slowly fades from her face. "Oh, boy… This isn't a fun visit, is it?" Her gaze flickers from Misha to me. "Did you tell him?"

"Cyrille, I'm sorry but—"

She shoves her chair back violently as she gets to her feet. "I trusted you to keep this a secret. I would have told everyone when I was ready."

"She had good reason to tell me, Cyrille," Misha interrupts.

"Which is what?" Cyrille snaps.

I hate that she's looking at me like that. Like she doesn't really know me at all. I take a step forward, desperate to make her understand. "Petyr came to Orion yesterday. He cornered me in my office."

She is horror-struck. "He *what?*"

Even in the midst of her anger, she's worried about me.

"It's okay," I amend quickly. "I hit the panic button and he disappeared just before Misha arrived."

"You mean he got away?" Cyrille asks.

"Just barely," I say. "He received a message while he was there. Someone told him I hit the panic button. It was clear that someone was tipping him off. Someone... on the inside."

Cyrille stares at me for a moment as she starts putting the pieces together. "Wait... You think that *Pavel* was the one tipping him off?"

"We cornered him last night and he confirmed it himself," Misha explains. "He's been working with Petyr this whole time. This is how it had to be."

Cyrille's face drops. She looks so incredibly fragile for a moment that I feel the need to grab hold of her just to keep her from crumbling.

"Cy, I'm so sorry…"

She lifts her eyes to mine. For a moment, she looks like a cornered animal. I think she's going to lash out at me. Then I realize the anger I'm seeing is aimed at herself.

"I can't believe what a fool I've been," she spits.

"No! This isn't your fault."

"I gave him information, Paige!" She chokes on her own words. "I told him things that he would never have known if it weren't for me."

"You didn't know. How could you possibly have known?"

"Jesus!" she cries, talking over me. "Of course that was why he was so interested in getting to know me. He was grooming me. He was manipulating me. He was fucking *laughing* at me."

"He was an asshole," I say bluntly. "And now, he's dead."

She looks at me. Then past me, to Misha. "He's… dead? You're sure?"

Misha nods. "I pulled the trigger myself."

"Good." Her sneer is vicious and violent, and when I see that, it's easy to understand how she could've been a Bratva queen. So cold. So imperious. Even I'm frightened of her.

I take her hand. "I know it wasn't love, but betrayal hurts, no matter what."

Her sneer doesn't change. "Not as much as death."

75

MISHA

I've been working for hours and my eyes feel like burnt-out coals in their sockets. After the debacle at Cyrille's, I took Paige back home and went to Orion. I was hoping work would take the sting out of the grief sitting heavy on my chest.

Watching Cyrille process as her lone flicker of hope for love after Maksim was snuffed out... It was a difficult thing to witness. Her words and her icy rage are still ringing in my head, echoing endlessly.

All I could think about was, *I can't let this happen to Paige.*

This war has taken too much from my family. Losing Maksim tore a hole in my chest that will never heal. But losing Paige? Losing our children? It would take something from me, something essential that I'd never get back.

I can't let that happen.

Sighing, I shove back from my desk and crack my neck. My nose is tingling, and for a moment, I think I'm hallucinating again. Going back to the smell of gunpowder that accompanied the sound of my brother's lifeless body hitting the floor.

Then I realize I'm not imagining the smell.

It's real.

I lurch up and cross the room to my door. When I open it up, the air is thick. There's a haze hanging in the hallway. Smoke, yes, but underneath it is an acrid chemical stench that makes me shiver.

"Hello?" I yell down the hall.

My assistant went home hours ago. Most of the building is gone. Apart from security and the cleaning crew, I'm the only one still working.

I take a few more tentative steps before I finally recognize the chemical odor: kerosene.

Just then, the fire alarms go off. I cover my ears against the blaring siren and continue down the hall. With every step, heat envelops me.

The fire is close.

I rush through the thick smog towards the elevators, but they're dark and lifeless, caught between floors in a way that strikes me as unsettling.

My heartbeat picks up speed.

I whip around and run towards the main lobby on this floor. Luka is on security duty on this floor tonight. He ought to be stationed just around the corner.

"Luka!" I call, but he doesn't answer.

Then I round the corner and see why. Luka is sprawled across the floor, face down. When I turn him over, I see his throat has been slit from ear to ear. A permanent bloody grin etched into his neck.

"Fuck." Twenty years of loyal service and this is how it ends for him.

I press a hand to his chest, saying a silent goodbye. Then I rip off the bottom of his shirt and turn it into a bandana for my face. I tie the shredded ends at the back of my head and stay low as I move towards the fire escape.

But the moment I pull the door open, plumes of smoke and heat billow into my face and force me to retreat.

I run back to my office and grab my phone. It's buzzing on my desk, and when I pick it up, Konstantin's voice crackles through.

"Jesus Christ. Don't tell me you're still in there."

"Sorry to disappoint." I cough. "Where are you?"

"Standing outside. The fire department just arrived. The fire is—shit, brother, it looks really bad from out here. Where are you?"

I can hear people talking and officers yelling commands. I ignore his question. I have another one that matters more.

"Where's Paige?"

"She's at the mansion. She's safe," Konstantin assures me.

"Make sure she doesn't know a thing."

It's getting hotter and hotter with each passing second. I cough into my elbow and drop to the floor, trying to escape the foul smoke. "How did the motherfucker even manage this?"

"I honestly don't know," Konstantin admits. His voice is drenched with panic. "It's like he's got a fucking ghost on his side."

That strikes a nerve. A puzzle piece clicking into place.

Konstantin might be onto something.

"The fire chief just got here," he tells me. "They estimate that the fire should be out in an hour."

Neither one of us says anything for a second. We don't need to. We both know I'll be burned to a crisp long before then.

"Brother—"

"Listen to me," I interrupt. "You know what I'd want. My will is in the safe in the cellar. Half the combination is with Niki, and the other half is with my mother."

"You're going to—"

"If I don't make it out, finish that motherfucker," I growl furiously. Glass panes shatter just outside my office. The heat is claiming its victims, one by one.

First, my men.

Then, my property.

It'll come for me last of all.

"You're going to make it out!" Konstantin roars. "I'm going to be here when you get out and—"

I hang up while Konstantin is still talking. He calls back instantly, but I drop it to the floor and let it ring. The air burns. My lungs ache.

I stand up and walk out of my office, feeling a strange sense of calm overtake me. Is this what it feels like to stare death in the face? Is this how Maksim felt when that bullet hurtled toward him, the one I should've seen coming?

Honestly, it's not as bad as I might've expected.

I walk down the hallway, but I don't bother hurrying anymore. You can't outrun Death when he has finally come for you. I won't beg for his mercy, either.

I'd much rather meet the Reaper upright and proud.

Then I spot Paige's office door through the plumes of oppressive smoke. My heart leaps again, that two-inches-to-the-left feeling I've come to associate with my wife. At least I had the pleasure of knowing her before I died. I got to experience love and feeling whole. I got to see how it is to taste champagne off her lips. Even if it was only for a brief time.

I walk into her office, lost in thought. The smoke has seeped in, staining everything. A white coat of hers slung across the back of her chair is blackened with the stuff. It's a sad sight, for reasons I can't explain. I'm fixating on details. If I die here, this will be the stuff I never enjoy again. I wish I could lock it all away somewhere safe, so that even after I'm gone, it will be untouched and—

Something occurs to me. I stop and look around the room.

And I see what I'm looking for. I call it sheer dumb luck. Paige would probably call it a miracle.

Maybe Death won't take me yet after all.

76

MISHA

An hour and twenty-three minutes later, I walk out of Orion. I'm soot-stained and sweaty. My lungs burn and every inhale is hell.

But I'm alive.

Konstantin is standing next to Nikita and Cyrille, who are both huddled over my mother. She is seated on a curb, shaking with sobs.

My cousin is the first to look up. He is distracted and misty-eyed, glossing over me amidst the chaos of firefighters scurrying back and forth, rubberneckers gawking from behind the barriers, so he misses me on his first pass.

Then he does a double take.

When he realizes what he's seeing, his jaw drops. "Misha!" he all but screams.

Cyrille and Niki jerk away from Mom, spinning around, searching for me in a desperate kind of hope I've never seen before.

Then all sets of eyes converge on me and they come rushing over to swaddle me with their embraces.

"Brother!" Konstantin gasps. "Brother…"

We break apart and Niki takes his place. She buries her face in my chest and sobs. I rope Cyrille in, too.

My mother is the only one still sitting, staring over at me with wide eyes. She can't believe what she's seeing.

I walk over and lower myself down so that we're at eye level. Then I put my hand on her arm. "It'll take more than a fire to kill me."

Tears pour down her cheeks. She yanks me towards her, squeezing a fresh round of coughs out of my throat. "My boy," she whispers into my neck. "I thought you were with your brother."

"I will be one day, but not yet."

Konstantin, Niki, and Cyrille converge around the two of us. "How the fuck did you survive that?" my cousin asks in amazement.

"The panic room," I tell them simply. "I had it installed in Paige's office months ago. I wanted to make sure she was safe if he ever happened to drop a bomb on us. Turned out to be my salvation, not hers. I hunkered down in there until I heard voices. One of the firefighters nearly had a conniption when I walked out of that room."

Konstantin claps me hard on the back. He's beaming from ear to ear and his relief is palpable. "Motherfucker," he says again and again. "You crazy motherfucker."

"Looks like you won't have to take over for me," I chuckle.

"Thank God for that."

I turn to the women in my family. "None of you are supposed to be here."

"We don't take orders from you, Misha," Niki says, her eyes narrowed. "Pakhan or not."

"No wonder Paige fits in so well with you. She doesn't know about this, does she?"

"No, not yet," Cyrille says guiltily.

"Let's get back to the mansion right now. And someone get me a phone. I left mine inside."

Konstantin hands me his phone. I'm about to dial Paige's number when her name pops up on the screen first.

"Fuck." I answer the call. "Paige!"

There's a moment of stunned silence before her voice rasps through the line. "Misha?"

"It's okay," I tell her. "I'm fine. Everything here is okay, so don't worry about—"

"Misha, I think… I think someone's in the house," she whispers. "I hit the panic button a few times, but security hasn't shown up. The power went out a few minutes ago. Misha, I'm scared."

For as hot as I was a minute ago, my veins are ice now. Dread pools inside of me.

The fire wasn't meant to kill me; it was just a distraction.

Petyr had his sights set on Paige this whole time.

77

PAIGE
FORTY MINUTES EARLIER

I'm three episodes into some reality television show about couples trapped in submarines together when I hear a thud from somewhere upstairs.

I jolt, my body on high alert at even the most subtle of noises. "It's probably just Rada," I whisper to myself.

The theater has no windows. The walls are black and so is the furniture. The black leather sofas seem to absorb all the light in the room. I'm suddenly very aware of the fact that I'm alone.

"Don't be silly."

I push away my doubts and turn up the volume. It's hard to feel threatened when you're watching ridiculous reality TV. And it doesn't get much more ridiculous than this couple trying to make a lasagna on a single hot plate while they're twenty thousand leagues under the sea.

Then the power goes out.

The room is plunged into darkness, and I slip out of my seat onto my knees. My heart is hammering. I look over my shoulder and see nothing but endless black.

There's only one door in and out of here. I would definitely have seen it open.

"Calm down, Paige," I tell myself. "Your imagination is running wild, that's all."

But my instincts are saying something different.

Being with Misha has taught me to listen to myself. To trust myself. And right now, my body is telling me that something is terribly wrong.

I stumble towards the wall and run my hand along it until I feel the panic button. Misha had them installed in most of the rooms, though they're tucked away in discrete places. Each one is supposed to be a direct line to the security shack out front. But I press it and nothing happens.

I press the button three more times. Still, nothing.

There's another thud from upstairs. Then a sharp kind of clicking sound. I grab my phone and call Misha. But he doesn't answer. There isn't even a dial tone.

Panic grips my chest. I feel claustrophobia tapping on my shoulder, reminding me I'm in a windowless room. I'm alone.

The dark presses in on me like the walls of a coffin.

I'm about to reach for the doorknob when I realize that one hand is clutching my phone and the other is clutching my pendant.

Champagne Wrath

I grit my teeth, let go of my necklace, and push the door open.

It's just as dark out in the hallway. The windows are open, but the sun is going down. I'm still looking at the window straight ahead when something moves past it.

I bite down a scream and duck into the nearest room.

The grand piano is off to my right, so I crawl underneath it and call Misha again.

Nothing. The dead silence makes me shiver.

In my stomach, the babies are kicking like crazy. I wonder if they can feel my panic. My heart is pounding. Maybe it woke them up. I run a hand over my swollen belly and take a deep breath.

"It's okay. It's okay, I've got you."

My fingers are trembling as I search for Konstantin's contact. I press dial, muttering the entire time. "Please pick up. Please, please, please, please, ple—"

"Paige."

It's not the voice I expected, but it's the only one I want to hear right now.

"Misha!" I rasp, beyond grateful for this miracle. He's saying something, but I can't understand him. "Misha, I think... I think someone's in the house."

"Stay on the phone with me. I'm on the way, okay?"

"It's really dark, Misha. I can't—I don't know where to go."

"Go down to the cellar and seal the door."

The last thing I want to do is crawl out from under this piano, but I also don't want to be caught underneath it if someone walks in.

So I follow his instructions and inch my way out. I find the wall and follow it, edging out of the room on silent feet.

Then I trip over something large on the floor.

I barely manage to catch myself. It takes a moment for my eyes to adjust, but when they do, I look down at what I tripped over.

Oh my God. Oh my God. Oh my God.

"It's Augustin," I sob. "I just stumbled over him… h-he's dead. Oh my God… someone has slit his throat."

"Paige, listen to me—"

"Misha, I think—"

Then my eyes flicker to a spot of deeper darkness in the corner.

I scream.

Then the darkness lunges for me.

78

MISHA

The sound of her scream slices straight to my core. Like my whole world tearing itself apart at the seams. Death is here—but it isn't coming for me after all.

It's coming for my wife.

"Drive!" I yell at Konstantin. "Now!"

He careens into the courtyard of the mansion, which is littered with the burning bodies of a dozen of my security patrolmen, each of them weeping blood from jagged wounds in their throats.

But I know without even having to look that it's too late.

Death is already here.

79

PAIGE

I stumble backwards and trip over Augustin's body. I hit the ground hard. Pain blooms in my hip and my head thwacks against the floor.

When I blink back to reality, I see that I'm staring right at Augustin's corpse. His brown eyes, glassy and disinterested, gaze at nothing and everything at the same time.

A sob wrestles free of my throat, but before it can even finish, I'm being yanked onto my feet like a ragdoll.

I smell the man first. He smells like kerosene and gunpowder. I've spent enough hours in the warehouse with Misha, shooting at lifeless targets, to know that smell—and strangely enough, it's comforting. It reminds me of how it feels to be held close in Misha's arms, to be taught by him, guarded by him, loved by him.

Then I look into the man's eyes, and I understand that that sense of safety is exactly what he's come here to destroy.

I've seen him once before, though it was a dark night and he was just one of three of the phantoms lurking there in my home where they didn't belong.

The Babai.

This one, one-third of that repulsive trio, has blue eyes. An unearthly blue, uncanny and unsettling. His face is mottled with a thousand tiny little scars like paper cuts.

My instinct is to cringe away, but he holds me close with an iron grip. "P-please," I manage to stammer out. "I'm pregnant."

"There's no point begging," another voice interrupts just as its owner appears from around the corner. "He's not the kind of man who can be moved by tits or tears."

This man, I'm a little more familiar with. Petyr Ivanov leans against the wall and smirks at me. "Come, Tiger," he says to the man holding me. "We've overstayed our welcome here."

The Tiger, who still hasn't spoken, nods mutely and starts carrying me down the hall. It's like being swept away by an avalanche. There's no chance of fighting back.

We move through the house and out into the backyard. The path we're walking is lined with bodies. At the sight of them, another sob tears out of me.

Mario and Danica are lying side by side. Their eyes are milky, their clothes clotted with blood. I want to stop and scream and cry next to them, but we just keep moving inexorably away from everyone.

I see Jace. I see Noel. I see more of the people who've loved and cared for me since I came to this house.

All of them are dead.

There's a car sitting just beyond the fence with its engine running. The Tiger grunts as he opens the back door and hurls me in. He follows, and, as I open my mouth to scream, slaps a thick piece of duct tape over my mouth. He binds my hands together with zip ties, too, then pushes me low into the gap between seats.

The other doors slam as Petyr gets in behind the wheel and we pull away with screeching tires. I try to keep track of the turns. Right, left, left, right. But we drive for a long time. Long enough that I start cramping in the middle of the journey and lose all the feeling in my legs.

By the time the car comes to a stop, I'm numb from the neck down. I don't think I could move if I wanted to, but no one asks me to, anyway. The Tiger just grabs hold of my legs and hauls me out of the car feet-first. Then he hoists me back into his arms.

We emerge into a small, dark space. A garage, I think. But by the time I'm able to compute what I'm seeing, a door opens and dingy light blinds me from within.

The air in here is musty and damp. Paint is peeling from the walls. Mouse droppings litter the counters and black mold dots the drop ceiling.

The Tiger carries me from empty room to empty room, revealing a sprawling, crumbling mansion. Broken banisters, cracked paneling, fungi in every corner. In the hallway, I notice bullet holes in the wall and rusty red stains splattered across the wallpaper like an abstract painting.

I bite back a whimper and look away.

Finally, he carries me into what must have once been a formal living room. The fireplace is overgrown with vines and a doorless doorway yawns open like a dark mouth. The yard beyond the windows is densely weeded, with looming hedges blotting out the night sky.

In the middle of the space is a rickety wooden chair.

The Tiger stands me next to it. I tremble on shaky legs, but I force myself to stay upright as Petyr walks into the room after us.

"Take off her bindings," he orders. His eyes are bloodshot and his cheeks are gaunt. He looks like a man who's been drained of life.

The Tiger slices off my zip ties, then rips the tape from my lips. I barely register the pain of either thing.

I glance up at the beefy man with scars on his face. "I know who you are. What you're doing here is wrong. You have a code you stick to. A code you're *supposed* to stick to."

A vein in his forehead is bulging. He says nothing.

"Misha paid you for help," I continue. "You're breaking your word. You have no honor."

"That's enough out of you," Petyr snaps. "I made the man a better offer. It's as simple as that."

I keep my eyes locked on The Tiger. "So you're just a common mercenary, then? A man without principles or ethics. Someone who can be bought. A whore."

I'm so focused on The Tiger that I don't even see Petyr coming. His hand cracks across my face, and I cry out at the unexpected pain.

I'm not at all surprised that Petyr is capable of hitting a woman.

I *am* surprised by The Tiger's reaction to it.

The assassin steps in front of me, putting himself between me and Petyr, and utters his first words of the evening. "You will not do that again."

Petyr looks just as floored as I feel. "Excuse me?"

He points at my stomach. "She is a woman. A pregnant woman. You will not do that again."

I think hauling me out of my home unwillingly, taping my mouth and hands, and shoving me into a car is already crossing the line insofar as violence goes. But as long as he's willing to stop Petyr from hurting me and my children, I'll stay quiet.

Petyr laughs cruelly as The Tiger glowers. "You've already broken one cardinal rule. What's one more? Your job is done here. Just stand back and let me do mine."

"You paid me for the death of Misha Orlov," The Tiger hisses. "Not for the death of his pregnant wife."

Petyr's eyes narrow. "I've already told you what you stand to gain—freedom from the oath you swore and more money than you can spend in a lifetime. But for that to happen, I need this bitch as collateral."

"The man is dead," The Tiger intones. "You no longer need collateral."

The man is dead? He seems so sure, but I spoke to Misha only seconds before the two of them grabbed me. They couldn't have killed him in that time frame.

Could they?

Could they?

No. I don't believe it. If Misha was dead, I would feel it.

"The man may be dead," Petyr retorts, "but his legacy still remains. His wealth, his property, his people. If I hope to gain back everything I've lost, I'll need *her* to bargain with the bastard cousin."

A bubble of laughter escapes my lips. I should probably stay silent, but I can't help myself. Both Petyr and The Tiger turn to me.

"Is something funny?" Petyr growls.

I laugh a little bit more, just to piss him off. "Konstantin will never give you the Bratva. You can kiss that dream goodbye."

He shakes his head. "You forget, princess: I know this family. I know Konstantin Orlov better than he knows himself. *Vse dlya sem'i.* 'Everything for the family.' Konstantin will give me whatever I ask if it means he can save you and those little whelps in your stomach. Your husband may have burned down my home; he may have killed half my men; he may have stolen all my wealth. But I'll replace it all with his." He looks at The Tiger. "Only after I get what I want do you get your money. All of that hinges on her. So drop the chivalry and help the man who is trying to help you."

Petyr has no idea that his plan actually hinges on Misha being dead.

And I know in the marrow of my bones that he is very much alive.

"The two of you make quite the pathetic pair," I remark.

"Shut your fucking mouth, you little c—"

"Enough!" The Tiger roars.

The two of them stare at each other with open contempt. I lean forward, interrupting their standoff. "It's a great plan, Petyr. But there's only one little problem. Well, not so little, actually. In fact, rather big."

"What the fuck are you talking about?" he spits.

"Misha isn't dead."

Petyr and The Tiger exchange a glance. "Bullshit," Petyr pronounces flatly. "You're lying."

I stand my ground. "Look me in the eyes and tell me it's not the truth."

He stares at me for a long time, unblinking. But he sees it. I recognize the moment he does. His jaw twitches and his teeth grind as his little plan goes up in smoke.

Snarling, Petyr grabs his phone and turns to The Tiger. "Go see if the bitch is right. If you don't deliver what you promised me, I'll have your head on a spike—right next to hers."

The Tiger barely looks at me as he storms out of the decrepit house.

"Listen to me," Petyr says, pacing the floor as he talks on the phone. "Things didn't go according to plan. I need reinforcements." He glances at me for a moment and grins wickedly. "Yes, yes… Bring him, too."

80

MISHA

The bodies of my staff are laid out in front of me. I want to mourn them, but there will be time for sadness later.

Now, there is only rage.

Konstantin steps through the patio doors, talking softly. Then I see why. A small, trembling woman is with him.

"Rada!" I call out, relieved that at least one person made it out alive. "Are you okay?"

She tries to nod, but she doesn't have the energy for the lie. It's obvious she's not. "I-I-I'm sorry, s-sir. I was in the nursery when the l-lights went out. I was going to find Mrs. Paige, but I looked out the window and… and I s-saw a man." Her eyes are glazed with the memory. "Big man. I saw him kill… He killed Mario."

She breaks down into sobs before she can say anything else. I gesture at Konstantin, and he ushers her away with whispered words of comfort.

I can't be in this room littered with innocent bodies for another second. I walk into the back gardens—just as two men appear from the shadows.

I see them before my men do—the twin Babai, marching shoulder to shoulder towards me. Someone yells and my soldiers turn their weapons on the intruders.

"Stand down!" I yell. "Collect the bodies and prepare them to be returned to their families. Be ready to move out in ten minutes."

My men reluctantly pivot to the task I've assigned, leaving me alone with The Bear and The Wolf. I'm thinking about what Konstantin said as I sat in the burning husk of my company. *It's like he's got a fucking ghost on his side.*

I don't know how I didn't see it before. I've been scrambling, checking everywhere for leaks—and the answer was so obvious from the start. The two of them showing up here without their third is proof.

"Your brother has betrayed you," I tell them.

They nod in grim understanding. "He will pay for it," The Bear growls. "Broken blood oaths cannot be forgiven."

The Wolf sighs. "He broke the oath, but—"

"There is no excuse for what he has done," The Bear snarls. "He is a traitor to our brotherhood. He is—"

The only warning of another man's approach is the single snap of a twig.

We all whirl as one, weapons drawn, a group of stone-cold killers ready to unleash hellfire on whoever dares venture too close.

But even I am taken by surprise when I see who it is. The one man we are all most eager to kill.

The Tiger bows his head as he steps into the open. His scarred face is twisted in regret. "The Bear is right," he says. "There is no excuse for my sins."

I clench my fists. I hate Petyr and he will pay for what he has done, but I never expected better of him. But The Tiger? I trusted him. He broke an oath and betrayed me. I don't have forgiveness enough for that.

Neither does The Bear.

A low growl rumbles deep in his chest. "You are a disgrace to the Babai and a shame to your brothers."

The Tiger stands his ground. His eyes are downcast and his body is slumped, but I'm not willing to take his submission at face value. He's lied before. I won't give him the chance to do it again.

The Wolf and The Bear close in on him from either side. They're so perfectly synchronized, so rehearsed—but there's no circumstance under which they could have prepared for this.

I step forward. "Are you here to fight? Or die?"

His eyes flicker to his brothers. "I'm prepared to die here today. And I will take my dishonor with me."

The Bear pulls out a sleek silver knife from a hidden sheath. It glints under the moonlight, betraying how deadly the blade is. "If only it were that simple. Your dishonor taints us all. You know the rules as well as I do. You know the punishment for betrayal."

The Tiger looks resigned to his fate. "Death by a thousand cuts."

"And I shall make each one hurt," he snarls. "You will stay alive until the last of them."

The Bear's jaw quivers as he vibrates with rage and grief. He's not going to take any pleasure out of killing his brother. He has to do this because the rules demand it.

I almost empathize with him.

I know a thing or two about being a slave to the rulebook.

The Wolf turns his head from his two brothers in disgust. "I want no part in this bloodletting. Pakhan Orlov—I will accompany you to see that our purpose is served in full."

I nod in acceptance. As I do, my phone pings. I check the message and see the address I've been sent. I recognize it, and it's ironic enough to make me laugh, but I'm numb to shock at this point. The only thing I feel is the urge to march onward, to keep moving until I find my wife.

So I pocket my phone and leave these ancient ghouls to their rituals.

As The Wolf and I walk out of the garden, I hear The Bear make his first cut. The night swallows up The Tiger's moan, waiting hungrily for nine hundred and ninety-nine more.

My men are waiting for me at the entrance of the mansion. Every one of them glances curiously at the silent Wolf by my side, but no one questions his presence with us.

I get into the lead car with Konstantin and The Wolf.

"You know where he's keeping her?" Konstantin asks.

"The same place where it all started," I tell him. "The house where Maksim died."

81

PAIGE

Petyr leads me to a room upstairs. Strangely enough, The Tiger's presence was a comfort. Now that I'm alone with Petyr, I don't know what will happen next.

He pushes through a rotten wooden door to reveal a room with nothing but a moth-eaten mattress shoved in the corner.

"Don't turn your nose up at my accommodations," Petyr sneers when he sees my face. "This is what your husband's home will look like once I'm through with him."

"You really think the Tiger can kill Misha? He's tried once already and failed."

"Tut tut, princess. 'If at first you don't succeed...'" His voice is sing-song, eerily light for the current mood.

He forces me onto the bed. It smells like mold and urine. I sit on the very edge, trying to touch as little of it as possible.

Petyr scowls down at my stomach, pure disdain written in every tired line of his face. "You're close to popping, aren't you? When is the big day?"

"None of your business."

He smirks. "Once those babies are born, it will be."

"These babies aren't going to be born anywhere near you," I spit. "You'll be dead. Misha is going to kill you for this."

He laughs manically. "Misha may be alive, but as long as I have you, he is powerless. He made the foolish mistake of falling in love with you. It makes him weak."

"Only a fool sees love as a weakness."

"If you were smart, you'd see that the only path forward for you and your *love* is to negotiate for me. It's the only path forward for your children, too."

I place a hand on my stomach, instinctively wanting to protect them from the pure evil standing in front of me.

He laughs and turns to leave. "I'll give you some time to think about your options."

When he disappears, the door locks from the outside.

Immediately, I stand up and rush towards the windows, but they're all sealed. There's a connecting bathroom, but those windows have been sealed, too. Even if they weren't, I'd have a hard time escaping through them. Assuming I somehow squeezed my eight months' pregnant belly through the tiny gap, there's no ledge and nothing at all to climb down. There's just a sheer fall to the ground below. It would be dangerous but perhaps survivable—if I wasn't pregnant. But as it is, it would be a death sentence for either me or my babies. Maybe both.

I'm still staring out the window, contemplating my options, when I hear the rusted gates of this crumbling mansion squeal open.

Petyr's reinforcements have arrived.

So I do the only thing I can do: I huddle in a corner, close my eyes, and clutch my pendant.

And I pray for a miracle.

82

PAIGE

When I peel my eyelids open, the world outside is still dark.

I make my way to the window and see that Petyr's men have spread out across the property. They're guarding all of the entrances and exits, snuffing out any hope I might still have of escape.

The lock to my door clicks open, and I spin around. On instinct, I search for a weapon, something I can swing or defend myself with—but the room is empty. So I brace myself against the window and wait for Petyr to appear.

But the man who appears in the doorway isn't Petyr.

"Anthony!" I screech.

My ex-husband pushes the door closed and places a finger over his lips. "Are you trying to get us both killed?"

I clap a hand over my mouth and try to process what I'm seeing. "What—Why—How are you even here? Oh my God, are you… Are you still working for Petyr?"

"No," he says quickly, his voice low. "I mean, I was. But that is done now."

"Then why are you here right now? *How* are you here right now?"

"I was in deep shit with your... your *husband*." He says the word grudgingly. "He offered me a way to redeem myself."

"Wait—Misha knows you're here?"

"Yes. And he knows you're here, too. He's on his way." Anthony doesn't give me time to process any of that before he pulls out a gun and hands it to me. "Hide this somewhere. Misha told me you know how to use one now. We've got a small window of time. I need to get you out before all hell breaks loose."

I check to make sure the safety is on before I slide it into the waistband of my maternity pants. "Is it a good idea to leave right now? The place is crawling with Petyr's men."

A layer of sweat coats Anthony's brow, though it's a cool night. He's even more nervous than he's letting on. "Petyr is going to walk in here with a bomb that he's going to strap to your chest, Paige," he says in a somber whisper. "Do you want to stick around for that?"

Well, that settles that. "You're right. Let's go."

Anthony stops at the door and checks to make sure the coast is clear. He holds up his hand, indicating that we need to wait. The couple seconds of pause gives me a second to focus on the fact that Anthony is here. *My ex-husband is here.* And he's putting his life on the line for me. I wouldn't have believed it was possible an hour ago. Part of me still doesn't.

"You said Misha offered you a way to redeem yourself," I whisper. "What exactly did the two of you discuss?"

"I made a lot of mistakes, Paige. I fucked up big time getting involved with Petyr. By the time I realized just how bad, it was too late. So I left to protect you—"

"You left with all the money, Anthony," I can't help but hiss.

"Okay, so I wasn't a total martyr," he admits. "The thing is, I knew you'd find a way to survive. But without money, I just wasn't sure I would. That's a pathetic excuse, I know, but it's the truth."

I sigh. "I suppose I can appreciate that."

Anthony checks the passageway again and then nods to me. "Okay, I think we're in the clear. Stay close to me and use the gun if you have to."

He exits the room first. I follow after him, taking his instructions to heart. I haven't actually shot a real person before, and the realization that I might have to is terrifying. Lifeless dummies are one thing; human beings are another.

Every time he thinks he hears something, Anthony puts his hand out to stop me. The second time he does, I knock into his elbow. I'm about to tell him to give me a little more warning, but before I can get the words out, I hear the screech of tires.

"Misha," I whisper.

His name is drowned out in a torrent of explosions and gunshots.

My husband is charging in, guns blazing. *Literally*.

"Quickly!" Anthony hisses.

We turn the corner just as a door flings open to the right. Before either one of us can back out of the hallway, Petyr steps in front of us.

His face twists in a vicious snarl. "Going somewhere?"

83

MISHA

"I have no interest in prisoners!" I roar at my men. "Bring me bodies, not captives!"

A war cry ripples through the army at my back. We tear through the gates of Petyr's last stronghold.

As the gates rip apart, Petyr's men scatter like headless chickens. We've been picking them off one by one for weeks, so they understand how this is going to play out. They know there's no way they can win this.

They know we've come to kill.

The smarter men abandon ship almost immediately. Only a stubborn few stand their ground.

I can respect their loyalty, but it's not going to win them anything except a quick death. I dodge a barrage of bullets before jumping out of the car and returning fire.

A handful of Ivanov men crumple to the ground. I look behind me and see The Wolf roving amongst Petyr's men. He has long blades in each hand, wielding them with ease. They glitter in the moonlight as he whirls them through the air. He's a blur of death, too fast to follow. The only reason I know his knives are finding their targets is because of the trail of bodies behind him.

Suddenly, Konstantin roars my name.

I duck down as my cousin shoots past me, blowing away one of Petyr's soldiers who was coming at us from the shadows.

"I got your back," he says, pointing to the house. "Go get her!"

I thank him with a nod and run into the dilapidated building. I'm almost at the staircase when I hear her scream.

Paige.

I tear up the stairs, a new kind of determination crackling inside of me. I'm burning up with it from head to toe.

One man appears at the top of the staircase. I shoot him, and he falls back into a second. As he tries to throw off his friend, I shoot him, too. They tumble down the stairs in a tangle of limbs.

A third man meets me at the top of the landing. After a brief tussle, I hurl him over the railing. His wail is cut short the moment he meets the marble floor at the bottom.

I move down the hall, reloading my guns as I go. Then I turn the final corner, and I see her.

Paige is crying and fighting, giving her all to avoid whatever Petyr is holding in her direction.

Anthony was supposed to shepherd her away from danger, but he's wrestling with another Ivanov soldier and losing badly.

Then Petyr shifts slightly, and I see what's in his hands. It's a vest… covered in wires.

Fury courses through my veins when I realize in an instant what that motherfucker is trying to do. He's going to strap my wife with a bomb and then force me to choose: Paige's life or my Bratva.

"PETYR!" My voice echoes down the hall like thunder.

The scene freezes. For a fraction of a second, everything is still. Paige looks at me, her face shining with fear and relief and love.

Then she turns her eyes back to Petyr—and withdraws a gun from the waistband of her pants.

She moves quickly.

She doesn't hesitate.

But it's still not fast enough.

Petyr spots the weapon and throws himself on her. I rush forward, but before I can get there, Anthony throws off his assailant and lunges for Petyr. The soldier tries to stop him, but I put a quick bullet in the back of his head.

It gives Anthony a chance to rip Petyr away from Paige.

I vault over the body of the dead guard and land on my knee, muzzle pointed at Petyr before squeezing the trigger.

But he ducks. My bullet whizzes past his head and imbeds harmlessly in the wall behind him.

"Stay down!" I yell.

Petyr knows he is cornered, though. And desperate rats are the most dangerous. "You can kill me, bastard," he howls. "But not before I kill your bitch!"

He raises his weapon and aims at my wife. A cry wrenches from my throat.

But my cry is drowned out by Paige's. "Anthony, no!"

BOOM. The gun erupts.

Her words don't stop him. Her ex-husband, the man whose sins brought her to me, throws himself between my wife and Petyr's gun, just in time to intercept the bullet. I hear the awful, gut-wrenching sound of blood meeting flesh.

When he hits the floor, blood spurts out of him with the same intensity that Maksim's did.

One thing is beyond doubt: he's going to die.

Paige drops to her knees next to his crumpled body. She's forgotten all about Petyr, who is now pointing his gun at her.

But I haven't forgotten.

I send a bullet right into the hand that's holding the gun. He bellows with pain and the weapon clatters to the floor.

It's too late for him to grab for his gun, so he runs. I fire off two bullets, but he manages to dodge them both.

"Fuck!" I yell.

Then I hear another gunshot.

Petyr crumples to the floor, taken down by the bullet to his thigh. I glance back and see Paige still lying on the floor… with her smoking gun raised.

Her eyes meet mine for a moment. She grins. It's weak and heartbroken and heartbreaking, and her voice is all those things, too, as she says to me, "Good thing you taught me how to aim."

84

MISHA

I stand over Petyr, looking down at his bleeding, broken body. There are tears in his eyes, but his mouth is set in a relentless line. Even at the end, he won't admit defeat.

"I've thought about this moment a lot over the last two years," I tell him.

He coughs and blood dribbles down his chin. "Killing me won't bring him back," he rasps.

I nod. "You're right. But it's something."

He's trying to edge away from me. A streak of smeared blood follows him like a snail's trail. But there's nowhere to escape to now. More blood splatters on the ground from his fluttering lips as he tries and fails to talk.

"You brought this upon yourself, you know," I growl. "We were allies, Petyr. Until you thought you deserved what was Maksim's. And you know what's funny? I never wanted what he had, but it was given to me anyway. A wife, a crown, a Bratva

—nothing I ever asked for. It's a fucked-up world we live in. We get what we don't want; and what we want, we don't get. There are lessons in there, though. I've learned mine. You refused to do the same. So consider this a mercy. From Maksim to me."

I put my gun away and pull out my knife. He's sucking in air, greedy for just one more second of life.

I had all sorts of grand plans about how to kill Petyr. For so many nights, I've dreamed of all the different ways I would make him suffer before he went.

But in the dim light of this moldy hallway, in the same home that saw my brother's last breaths, I realize that the fire that's lived inside me since Maksim's death is nothing but an ember now. My thirst for revenge is gone.

All I want is peace. A little slice of quiet where I can sit with Paige and talk about our future. I want a nursery with two cribs and the sounds of our babies laughing. I want a glass of champagne and a starlit night on a balcony overlooking the city.

Everything else is unimportant.

I press the knife to his throat. "Enjoy hell, Petyr."

Then I slash the blade across his neck.

The life pours out of him. He sputters and gasps, gurgling and choking on his own blood as he struggles to breathe.

Then... he stops. He just stops. So much endless chase, and it's all over in a second. It almost feels anticlimactic.

I turn away from him and walk back to Paige.

She's sitting on the floor with Anthony's head in her lap. She looks up at me, a tear rolling down her cheek. "He's dead, Misha. He died for me."

I kneel down in front of her. "He had a hero's death. It's what men of the Bratva dream of."

She chuckles humorlessly. "I think he'd have taken a dishonorable life over a hero's death any day."

"He earned his honor when it mattered most. He's not half the fool I thought he was."

Her big, beautiful eyes are swimming with tears. She blinks them all down and focuses on me.

I take her hand. "He made a choice, Paige. He was a grown man who made a choice. His death is not your fault. Do you hear me? None of this is."

She nods half-heartedly. Then she sucks in a sharp breath.

I look around for any sign of danger. "What's wrong?"

She places a hand on her stomach, blowing out a slow, even breath. "I… I just had a pain. It felt like a contraction."

No. It's early. Too damn early. Her due date is not for another five weeks.

"It's the stress," I tell her. "Let's get you to the hospital and have Simone check you out."

I shift Anthony off her and help her to her feet. Looping her arm over my shoulder, we stagger down the hallway. We're halfway down the stairs when she gasps again. This time, I know why.

There's a small puddle of water between her feet.

"Oh my God. Misha… Did my water just break?"

Fuck this three-legged race bullshit. We no longer have time to spare. I scoop her into my arms and hustle out of this godforsaken house.

"Konstantin!" I call as I burst through the front doors.

The Wolf appears first. He is covered in the blood of other men. My cousin comes a moment later from around the corner.

"I need a car," I tell him. "Paige is in labor."

His eyes bug out. "But it's too early!"

"Tell that to the babies." I move past him hurriedly and tuck Paige in the back of one of the cars. When I race around to the driver's side, Konstantin pushes me back toward the passenger seat. "I'll drive."

I call Simone on the way to the hospital and instruct her to be ready. When we get close, I glance back at Paige. She's spread out on the backseat with her legs bent in front of her. She's breathing through her contractions, which seem to be coming faster and faster.

"Oh God, Misha. I'm not ready. The babies are not ready. It's too early."

"They're going to be just fine. Everything is going to be just fine."

I did not just save her from Petyr to lose her now.

∼

Simone is standing by the door when we arrive. "Hey, Paige. Missed me so much you decided to have the babies early just to see me again?"

Paige laughs, but it comes out as a groan. Simone abandons some of her easygoing attitude and points to an examination room. "Let's check you out."

A team of nurses gets Paige into a hospital bed and strips her down. Simone moves between her legs, feeling for something.

"Exquisite timing," she says, withdrawing her hand and pulling off a glove. "It looks like you made it right on time."

Paige turns pale. "Wait—you mean they're coming right now? Like, right now?"

Simone nods. "Yes. But don't you worry about a thing. These babies are a good size. They'll be small but tough. Just like their mama."

I can see the panic on Paige's face, and it unravels me. I'm useless here, so fucking useless. All I can do is pace up and down the ward with my hands knotted into fists, clenching my dog tags like they'll bring miracles the way Paige's pendant does for her.

I watch a nurse set up a tray of tools for Simone. "What the fuck are those for?" They look like torture devices. I should know.

Simone lays a hand on my arm. "Misha, you need to calm down."

A nurse points to a recliner next to the bed. "There's a chair in the corner for fathers when they need to—"

"Stop telling me what I need. I don't need a fucking thing," I snap. "Here's what I *want*. My wife wants drugs. She doesn't want to be in any pain. I don't want her to be in any pain."

Simone arches an eyebrow. "It's childbirth, Misha. It's going to hurt."

"She needs some ice chips or something." I point at one of the younger nurses. "You! Go get some ice chips."

Paige groans through a contraction. "M-Misha… I don't want fucking… ice chips." She moans again and I nearly punch through their perfectly sterile wall.

"Where the *fuck* are the drugs?" I demand loudly.

Simone steps in front of me. She's an entire head shorter than me, but she holds herself like someone miles taller. "It's too late for an epidural now. The babies are coming. Paige is going to have to do this without the drugs."

"That is fucking unacceptable. She doesn't want—"

"Misha!"

It's the only voice that has the power to stop me in my tracks. I turn to my wife, and she waves me over. The moment I'm close enough, she takes my hand and kisses it.

"Misha," she says again, "I know the Bratva is your life. But right now I don't need you to be the don. I need you to be my husband."

All at once, the weight on my shoulder falls away. This situation is not mine to control. What happens here is up to Paige and Simone and the universe—the last of whom really owes me a blessing or two.

I take a deep breath and lean down to kiss her forehead. "I'm here with you, *kiska*."

She closes her eyes and breathes through another contraction. "Tell me something nice. Something you've never told me before."

I hold her hand and wrack my brain for something to say. I've told her she's beautiful, she's sexy, she's wise, and she's brave. I've told her I love her, and I do. I've told her I'll fight for her, and I have. After all that, what else is there to say?

Then it occurs to me.

I lean down and whisper in my wife's ear, "Maksim would have loved you."

It's the highest compliment I can give.

85

PAIGE

I'm a few minutes into motherhood and I already feel overwhelmed. How can you mother children when you yourself have never been mothered?

Then I heard them cry.

And all that worry vanished at once.

I can do this. I'll make mistakes. I'll screw up. I'll be scared and unsure, but I'll always be there for them. Always.

So now, it's easy to lie back in my hospital bed and watch Misha. He's standing by the window, our son slung across his right arm, our daughter tucked in his left. His eyes veer back and forth between the two of them, irises shining like they're lit from within.

When he turns and catches me watching, he comes over. He hands me our baby boy, swaddled in blue, and sits down in the armchair next to my hospital bed. Our girl's tiny pink fingers splay across his chest. Small as that hand is, I can see the possessiveness in it already. I sense more of the same in her father's eyes. It'll take the Jaws of Life to separate those two.

"Ava Orlov," I murmur. "I like saying it."

"Ava and Anton. My children. Our children." Misha grins. This grin is unlike anything else I've ever seen from him. It's warm and soft and contemplative. Most of all, it's at ease.

His grief has melted away.

I glance down at my son. After his initial introduction to the world, he hasn't made a peep. One cry, which quieted down the moment he was put at my breast.

I kiss his little brow and he wriggles his nose. His eyes blink open a fraction and he yawns lazily.

"He's got your eyes," I say with a smile. "I was hoping for that. He's going to look just like you."

"And Ava is going to look just like you," Misha says, bending over to press his lips to mine. "Lucky girl."

The door opens and one of the nurses walks in. "Sorry to interrupt, but your family is waiting outside to see the babies."

Misha looks at me and scowls. "Do we have to?"

"Don't be sour." I smile up at him. "Time to let them in."

"Alright," he grumbles. "Can't delay the inevitable. Go on then—send the jackals in."

As soon as the doors part, they descend on us in hushed cheers and bright smiles. Nessa leads the group. She has tears in her eyes before she's even seen them.

She strides forward and gazes down at her granddaughter in awe. "Look at her. Give her to me, Misha… Oh my, she's a beauty."

Nikita carefully plucks Anton out of my arms. "So is he. Look at those eyes!"

Cyrille peers over Niki's shoulder and Ilya rises up on his tiptoes to get a better look at his cousins. Konstantin stands in the center of it all, carrying a huge bouquet of flowers and an armada of translucent, pink and blue balloons with confetti floating around on the inside.

"How did I get stuck with being the delivery boy?" he asks grumpily.

"Suits your skill set," Misha retorts.

Konstantin fires him a middle finger with a roguish grin. "I can't believe it," he sighs. "Misha has babies. Miracles never cease."

Nessa echoes the same sentiment. "My baby has babies. Miracles never cease, indeed."

A slow, soft smile spreads across my face. They're not wrong. When I lost Clara, I stopped believing in miracles. I kept a junkyard necklace tied around my neck for so many years out of nothing but sheer stubbornness, not because I still believed in wonderful things happening.

But then, out of nowhere, miracles started cropping up again. Now, I'm swimming in them.

I have a husband.

A family.

A future.

I have *hope*.

And when I look through the windows, the starlight is the color of champagne.

EPILOGUE: MISHA
ONE YEAR LATER

I'm sitting on Maksim's bench in the gardens, watching as the twins crawl around the grass. Ava is already pulling herself up, trying to walk. Anton is content to crawl around. Sometimes, he does away with crawling altogether and rolls like a pillbug.

They couldn't be more different. I love that about them. It still amazes me how anyone could look at a child and see raw clay to be shaped and molded by the adults around them.

I look at my boy and my girl and I see flowers waiting to bloom.

I hear shuffling footsteps from the path and turn to see Ilya. It's still a shock to see how much he has grown in the last year. The boy is at my shoulder now and he's only eleven. He's going to be taller than Maksim was. Hell, he might be taller than me, too.

He jumps onto the grass. "Aunt Paige is looking for you. She says everything is ready."

"Aunt Paige can wait for a second." I pat the empty seat next to me. "Sit down." He sits, and I drape my arm over the back of the bench. "Thanks for helping out today."

"It's cool. I like hanging out with the family."

"So do I."

Not so long ago, I couldn't stand being around my family. I loved them all so much, but it hurt. I sure as hell didn't come hang out in this corner of the garden. Everything about them just made me think of Maksim.

Now, that isn't a bad thing.

"Your father loved this part of the garden," I tell Ilya. "He liked to meditate here."

"Papa meditated?"

"He took it up after meeting your mother. He was all fire, all the time. She made him calm down."

Ilya grins. "Mama says the same thing about you and Aunt Paige."

"I can't exactly argue with that." I pat his back. "How are things? Is school okay?"

"Yeah, school is fine. Boring, but fine."

"I heard you met Dima."

"Yeah," he mumbles. "I did. He's fine, too."

I lean in, voice low. "You know your mother will always love your dad, right? That's not going to change just because she met someone new."

Ilya gives me a reluctant nod. I can tell by the angle of his jaw that he's trying not to cry. "I know. I just... I still miss him. A lot."

My heart aches. I want nothing more than to take that pain away from Ilya. Ava must feel it, too, because she totters over and pats Ilya on the leg, her chubby fist pulling at his pants.

I take her by the waist and lift her onto my lap. "I miss him, too. Every single day."

"Sometimes, it feels like everyone has forgotten him," Ilya admits.

"None of us have forgotten your father. He's a part of every aspect of our lives. And the best thing we can do to remember him is to live well. Do you think your father would want you to be sad all the time?"

"Probably not."

"Exactly. He'd want you to live. He'd want you to remember him, but he wouldn't want you to fall apart with grief. We have to live the way he did—boldly and without regret."

Ilya considers that for a moment. Then his gaze slips to Anton, who's decided it's a good idea to rip out handfuls of grass and stick it in his mouth.

Laughing, Ilya walks over and dusts the grass out of his hand. "I wish he could have seen them. He'd like these little gremlins."

"So do I, Ilya. So do I." I swipe at my misty eyes and get to my feet, hoisting Ava on my hip. "Let's go. Everyone will be waiting."

Two long tables are set up in the middle of the patio, lace tablecloths fluttering in the wind. Both are littered with pastries and cakes, pitchers of lemonade, finger sandwiches and more. Our new chef, Vitaly, went to great lengths to make this a memorable first birthday for the twins.

It's still strange to see new faces in my kitchens and hallways. I feel the weight of the people they replaced. We still see Rada every Christmas, when she comes to town from her new job. The others' families receive yearly stipends. Paige and I do what we can to honor their sacrifices.

My mother is at the head of the table, trying to light the candles on the two birthday cakes she'd insisted on baking for the twins, though the wind keeps snuffing them out.

"There you guys are!" Paige is holding a disposable camera. Rowan is right beside her, carrying a bottle of champagne in each hand.

"Mama!" Ava cries, though she makes no attempt to reach for Paige. Her brother, on the other hand, practically jumps from Ilya's arms into Paige's. He's a mama's boy to the core.

She laughs and kisses his brown hair. It's lighter than mine, but our eyes are almost identical. It's uncanny. "Are you ready for cake, Ant?"

He nods excitedly and licks his plump lips.

I'm doing the same, albeit for very different reasons. My wife is wearing a simple white dress that hugs her curves. Her body has changed after having children—but in all of the right ways. She sees stretch marks and scars—I see reminders of what she's done to bring our family into the world.

"Can you take our picture?"

Epilogue: Misha

I sling my arm around Paige's shoulders, and we both smile while the twins squirm in our grasp. The moment the picture is taken, Cyrille rushes forward to take Ava off my hands. My mother does the same with Anton.

People say it takes a village, but some days I'd prefer a smaller village.

The perks are that Paige and I get quite a bit of alone time.

We watch our misfit band of friends and family in silence for a moment. Mother and Cyrille, both doting over the babies. Rowan and Konstantin chatting in the shade up by the house. Niki posing for the camera while Ilya snaps a picture of her. And then another. And another.

But that's nothing new. What *is* new are the two dour men standing a few feet away from the rest of the group. They came to pay their respects, and Paige insisted that they stay for a piece of cake.

It didn't shock me that Paige asked them to stay. But it shocked me when they accepted. It's weird to socialize with men whose names you don't even know. You treat someone like the star of a ghost story long enough, and you almost start to believe in the fantasy.

But the Babai are only human. Just like the rest of us.

Paige turns to me, wrapping her arms around my body. I lean down and kiss her long and slow. Usually, Niki would yell for us to get a room, but whenever the twins are around, they're the star attraction.

"This is exactly what I wanted for their first birthday," Paige says with a contented sigh. "It's a beautiful day and everyone I love is here to celebrate."

"I'm glad you got what you wanted."

She smirks. "You would have been happy doing nothing at all." She pinches me playfully, then loops her arm around my waist. "I know they won't remember this. But we will. And now, we have pictures to show them when they're older."

I kiss her forehead. "If you're happy, I'm happy. Although, why you asked those two to stay, I have no idea."

She glances back at the Babai and shrugs. "I like them. Both of them. I know they're a bit odd. But we all are."

"Speak for yourself."

She pinches me again and giggles. "You know, the taller one isn't bad-looking."

I spin her around so that her back is to him. "Keep talking like that, and I'll be forced to go over there and mess up his face."

"But he's Babai," she says with teasing false reverence. She's never been able to understand the legend of the Babai. I suppose it's just something you have to grow up with. "He could totally take you."

I snort in her face. "And I'm Misha fucking Orlov. He doesn't stand a chance. But if you need me to prove it…"

I start marching toward him with a fierce scowl. Paige pulls me to a standstill and kisses me through her laughter. "I only mention it because I was thinking… you know, maybe him and Nikita could…"

"No. Absolutely not."

Epilogue: Misha

She rolls her eyes. "It's not really your call, Oh Great One. Niki is her own woman. She's smart enough to make her own decisions."

"Exactly. She doesn't need you to play matchmaker."

"But I'm a good matchmaker! Just look at Rowan and Konstantin over there. The two of them haven't stopped talking since she got here."

I shake my head. "Just stay out of it, Paige."

She grins at me, and I know she's not about to listen. It's one of the most infuriating, amazing things about her.

"This is your fault, you know." She smooths a hand down my chest, her finger drawing circles.

"Explain."

"Because of you, I'm happy. Deliriously, wholly, wonderfully happy," she tells me. "And I want to make sure that everyone I love feels the kind of happiness I feel."

"So I need to make you less happy?"

"Or you need to make me *so* happy that I'm too busy to play matchmaker."

I look at her through hooded eyes. "Sounds like you have a very specific idea on how I might accomplish that. Care to share?"

She gives me a shy smile. "I want another baby."

"Another one?" I look over at the two we already have, both of whom are currently trying to eat butterflies. "I mean... we've got two."

"I know, but if this year has taught me anything, it's that I love being a mother. Don't you love being a dad?"

"Of course I do." She pouts and I brush my thumb over her lower lip. "But I love you. More than anything in the world. If you want another baby, then you'll get another baby. No matter how many times we have to try."

A blush spreads over her cheeks. "That's the spirit, Mr. Orlov."

I groan. "Maybe we should get started right now."

She laughs and flounces back to the party. Over her shoulder, she calls, "You better give me a glass of champagne before you start talking like that."

EXTENDED EPILOGUE: PAIGE
FIVE YEARS LATER

Check out the exclusive Extended Epilogue to CHAMPAGNE WRATH! Five years into the future, see the Orlov twins growing up, Cyrille and Nikita finding fresh love, and life taking on new challenges for Misha and Paige!

CLICK HERE TO DOWNLOAD

Printed in Great Britain
by Amazon